BORDERLANDS

An Anthology of Imaginative Fiction

edited by

Elizabeth E. Monteleone
Thomas F. Monteleone

Cover Illustration: Dave McKean
Cover Design: Michelle Prahler

BORDERLANDS PRESS
Baltimore © 1994

Borderlands Press P.O. Box 146 Brooklandville, MD 21022
800-528-3310

Acknowledgments

Whenever an anthology is assembled, there is always plenty of work to go around. In the case of this book, the editors would like to thank the following people for their respective contributions:

Richard Chizmar and Kara Tipton of *Cemetery Dance* magazine for the full-page ad.

Marie E. Monteleone for numbering and slipcasing the entire edition.

Damon A. Monteleone for discovering the magic mouse of Irie, mon.

Dr. Julio C. Novoa for proofreading.

Isabel Barrero-Novoa for plenty of bowls of *sopa de grasa*.

The hundreds (and maybe thousands) of writers who continue to defile our mailbox with unnatural acts and unspeakable practices — all neatly enclosed in their manila envelopes.

And, finally, Blockbuster Video for all those tapes and games that kept Olivia and Brandon occupied long enough for us to get this project done.

CONTENTS

A Wind from the South	Dennis Etchison	1-11
House of Cool Air	William F. Wu	12-32
Morning Terrors	Peter Crowther	33-47
Circle of Lias	Lawrence C. Connolly	48-72
Misadventures in the Skin Trade	Don D'Ammassa	73-82
Watching the Soldiers	Dirk Strasser	83-97
The Ocean and All Its Devices	William Browning Spencer	98-123
One in the A.M.	Rachel Drummond	124-128
A Side of the Sea	Ramsey Campbell	129-140
Painted Faces	Gerard Daniel Houarner	141-161
Monotone	Lawrence Greenberg	162-170
Dead Leaves	James C. Dobbs	171-205
From the Mouths of Babes	Bentley Little	206-216
The Long Holiday	William Ellis	217-224
The Late Mr. Havel's Apartment	David Herter	225-236
Union Dues	Gary A. Braunbeck	237-263
Earshot	Glenn Isaacson	264-267
Fee	Peter Straub	268-337

This is for
Analia Barboza.
Just a little reminder that
anything is possible.

A WIND FROM THE SOUTH

Dennis Etchison

It is the exceptional writer who can create and sustain a career by writing short fiction almost exclusively. Most of us eventually turn to the novel because it provides the income necessary to earn a living by writing and reaches the widest possible audience. There have only been a handful of writers who've made their reputations and their money primarily by the short story. Lovecraft, Bradbury, and Ellison are probably the major practitioners, but native Californian Dennis Etchison also deserves mention in that elite group. His stories are subtle yet seething with dark energy. His prose is clean, crisp, and always literate. "A Wind from the South" is a perfect example of what makes his fiction special. It is an excerpt from his new novel California Gothic. *The story is his first appearance in* Borderlands; *we hope he plans a few encores.*

As Evie ran through the house, the morning light followed her. There was a white burst in each window, as if her passing had triggered a row of flashbulbs outside. Near the bedroom, she thought she saw a tall, dark outline squeeze from one pane to the next, pacing her, but the glass was so old that it flowed with distortion and she was unsure whether anyone was really there. It was not until she had peeled off her top and shorts and was about to step into the shower that the doorbell rang.

"Eddie, could you...?"

But of course he couldn't. Her son had already gone on his way to meet his friends and then to the mall.

"Dan?" she called, hoping that her husband would hear.

She stood with one hand on the hot water faucet and the other on the edge of the shower curtain and waited. But Dan was still in the backyard. Too far away.

The bell rang again.

She reached for her robe. It was not on the back of the door. That's right, she thought, I put it in the laundry basket to be washed.

There was no time to get dressed. Should she ignore the bell? No, it might be United Parcel with a shipment intended for the store; then she or Dan would have to make a special trip just to pick it up.

She found his terrycloth robe in a heap at the end of the bed, where he had left it.

"Coming!" she shouted, tying the robe closed, and padded through to the living room.

She went first to the front window and peeked around the curtain. She could see only half of the porch, but it appeared to be empty, except for a long shadow cast by the overhang. Then something skittered across the lawn. She turned her head quickly, following a small pile of leaves that blew past on the sidewalk. Farther down the street, the mail truck rounded the corner, and a compact car idled under the stop sign. The car looked familiar.

Was it Dan's? That meant he had already left, without saying goodbye.

She let the curtain fall and opened the door.

"Yes?"

A young woman stood there in profile, as though about to give up and move on. Beyond her, the lawn crackled with oak leaves. A wind had come up, as if from nowhere.

"I'm sorry to bother you," she said uncertainly, "but…"

Evie had never seen her before. At least there was no sample case in her hand; with any luck, she was not selling anything. That was a relief.

"It's all right," said Evie, relaxing slightly. "What can I…?"

"Well, you see…" She was hardly more than a girl, in her late teens or early twenties at most, though with the noonday sunlight behind her it was hard to be sure. Her hair was short and plain and she wore a loose, knee-length cotton dress several sizes too large and no belt, as if to conceal her figure. "What street is this?" she asked finally.

"Stewart Way."

"Oh. I was afraid I took a wrong turn."

Did that mean she had or hadn't?

"What address are you looking for?"

She had no reason to hide her body. From what Evie could see of her, long wiry arms, no stomach and short-toed pink feet, she was a perfect size four.

"I don't know. The school."

"Greenworth Elementary?" Was she walking? Barefoot? "You're almost there. Take a left at the corner and then another left. You can't miss it."

"Thanks."

She made no move to leave, but lingered as though she had not yet said what was on her mind. Was she really going to the school? Maybe even a size two, thought Evie. I used to be that thin, once.

"Is there anything else?" Where was her watch? She

had taken it off in the bathroom. "Because I'm kind of late. I was supposed to meet someone at 12:30. For lunch." She gave the younger woman — girl? — a friendly but dismissive smile and started to shut the door.

"Is it far?"

"Just around the corner."

"I mean, where you're having lunch."

"What?" Evie wondered what business it was of hers. "Not really. Just over the hill."

"That's good." The girl looked at her wristwatch. "It's only 11:15."

"Is that all?" said Evie, surprised. "I thought it was at least twelve."

The girl continued to stand there, the yellow-white light behind her, as the oak trees across the street shook down more leaves. Evie heard a scrabbling on the roof, twigs or tiny claws. The kitten? She felt a rush of radiant heat from the porch, moving the hair over her forehead, brushing the nap of her robe. Dan's robe. She retied it more securely.

"Do you think…?"

"What?" asked Evie.

"Could I please have a drink of water? The wind, it's so hot."

"It's a Santa Ana."

"A what?"

"It always comes this time of year."

"Why?"

She was not from around here. "I'm not sure. But it's a warm wind from the south — Mexico, I think. Below the border, anyway." As the trees rustled and waved, Evie opened the door wider. "You don't have to stand out there. Come in."

As she closed the door, the whispering chorus of leaves was silenced. Evie felt better; it had made her uneasy. Then she heard a ceiling beam creak, hammering into place over them. There was a faint scurrying from the fireplace as the wind rearranged the ashes in the grating. It had found a way to get into the house. She would have to tell Dan to close the flue.

"I'll get your water."

She started for the kitchen, then glanced back. The girl was standing awkwardly by the sofa. Was she looking for a place to sit? Evie paused to remove the morning newspaper from the cushions.

"My name's Eve, by the way. Eve Markham."

"I know."

She was dark, probably Hispanic, Evie noticed. Or was it only a deep tan? "How?"

"From the mailbox."

The odd moment passed as easily as a skipped heartbeat. She expected the girl to offer her own name in return. She waited.

"Oh," Evie said after a few seconds. "Well, hi."

"Hi."

She went to the kitchen, took down one of the tall glasses, filled it quickly and returned.

"I didn't ask if you wanted ice."

"What? Oh, no. This is fine." The girl took a sip, that was all, and set the glass on the table in front of her.

She was seated comfortably on the sofa and the hastily piled newspapers were nowhere to be seen. Had she moved them? Where? Evie wondered if she might be a housekeeper, looking for a job. But that made no sense. Why this house? Evie put it out of her mind.

"Do you live in the neighborhood?" Evie asked, sitting down in the easy chair.

"I'll be moving in soon. As soon as I find the right place."

Evie heard a car pass through the intersection at the corner, going away. She lowered her eyes while she tried to think of something else to say and saw her knees poking out under the robe, as though it were not Dan's but her own short one instead. She covered her legs and noted the veins on the backs of her hands. They made her look older, middle-aged. She was aware of the blood pulsing in her wrists, which were glistening. She touched her face, her neck. Her skin felt hot. It must have been the wind. Now she needed that shower more than ever. Why was there no clock in the living room?

"You have a child at the elementary school?" she asked.

"Not yet. I wanted to see the other children first. Is that when they have their lunch, at noon?"

It had been so long — a year? no, more — since her own son had gone there that Evie could hardly remember. The school was close enough that Eddie had come home for lunch most days, even when she and Dan were at work.

"I think so. But there aren't any classes today, only the playgroup."

The girl took another small sip of her water. Was there something wrong with it? Sorry I don't have bottled, Evie thought.

"You'll have to excuse me," she said, "but I really should…"

There was a wrenching sound from the backyard as something fell with a terrible crash.

She hurried through the long house to the back porch.

The yard looked different somehow; at first she could not be sure why. For one thing, there was more sky showing than there should have been. Then she realized that one of the trees Dan had planted between the house and the garage had fallen over. No, not fallen but broken, the top half lying in a pile of dry, misshapen branches and withered, unborn fruit, near the two dwarf palms. The trunk was split sharply and the bark stripped back to expose the soft white center, like a ragged piece of chicken meat that has been peeled away from the bone.

The girl was right behind her.

"The tree," said Evie. "I can't believe it. At least it didn't hit the house."

"Was it the wind?"

"Yes, I suppose so." What else?

"I'm sorry."

"That's all right. It's not your fault! He should have watered it more."

"Who?"

"Dan. My husband."

"I didn't see his name on the mailbox."

It was there. *Dan & Eve Markham*. She remembered the day he placed the adhesive letters on the box at the curb. He had done that, hadn't he? Unless they had peeled off.

She considered the broken tree and felt a pang of sadness. They had neglected the backyard for so long. Once there had been a garden, lush and vibrant. How many years ago? With all the dead plants, and now this, it looked more like a cemetery overrun with weeds. But there was nothing to do about it now.

"Dan won't be very happy, when he gets home."

"What does your husband do?" asked the girl, as they walked back to the living room.

"He has a bookstore — we do. New and used. *Minor Arcana*, on Main and Second."

"Is that where he is now?"

"I hope not. This is his day off." Mine, too, she thought. At least it was supposed to be.

Still, it was good that she was not alone. If she had not answered the doorbell, she would have been in the shower when it happened. She imagined herself running through the house at the sound of the crash, dripping water...

"I'm glad you were here," Evie said.

"So am I."

"Do you want more water?"

"He must be very smart, your husband."

Evie laughed, releasing the tension. "He's the most intelligent man I ever met. That's why I married him. Or one of the reasons."

"Did he get his degree?"

"Well, not quite. He spent years at college, but he never graduated. He only took the classes he liked." It seemed a peculiar question. "What about your husband?"

"He has his own business. And he's very smart, too. We're going to have a nice house, with lots of windows, just like this one. As soon as we get settled."

Evie leaned back in the chair and took a better look at the younger woman. Actually, she might not have been so young after all; it was hard to tell. Her hair was unstylish, as if she had cut it herself and was now waiting to see how it would grow out. The windows were behind the sofa so that her features were backlighted, neutral, but Evie was sure that she wore no makeup. Her legs were strong and well-shaped, with small ankles. And there was the wristwatch, a man's Swiss Army model, above her left arm. But no ring.

She met dozens of people every day, many absolute strangers who came into the store in search of a book. Some of them did not know the name of the author or the title, or even what exactly they were looking for. Evie knew how to talk to them, to put them at their ease and make them feel comfortable, to draw them out and learn what they were really after. Sometimes they did not want anything but conversation. In that case, she still tried to satisfy them before sending them on their way, so that they would come back. Now, however, she was not in the shop, and this was not a customer. What the young woman wanted was unclear. Evie felt at a disadvantage. This one knew the power of silence. It was a way of maintaining the upper hand. But for what purpose?

"So you have children of your own?" Of course she

does, Evie thought. She hadn't said so, not exactly, but why else would she be interested in the school?

"Do you?"

"One son," said Evie. "His name's Edward. He just turned thirteen."

She decided to leave it at that. Her natural impulse would have been to tell the woman all about Eddie, as much as she could stand to hear, his brilliance and precocity. But now for some reason she felt instinctively protective. She was relieved that he was not here.

"Is he at school?"

"Not today. It's Saturday. Remember?"

"Then where?"

Evie was conscious of a chill in the air. She fingered the edge of the robe, pulling it closed at her throat.

"With a friend." Yes, the Oshidari boy, over on Bradfield. That was right, wasn't it?

"Is your husband coming back?"

"Of course he is. Why wouldn't he?"

"I'd like to…meet him."

Evie stood. "Excuse me. I have to get ready now."

"Are you sure?"

What did *that* mean? "I'm afraid so. It's late."

"Is it?"

Danny, she thought, where are you? "What does that watch of yours say?"

The woman looked at her wrist. She tapped the crystal. "It stopped."

"When?"

"I don't know."

Evie went to the bedroom doorway and peered in at the clock on the nightstand.

"It's 12:30!" she said.

"You should have a watch."

"I do," Evie snapped. "I took it off for my shower, and then you rang the bell."

"You need a clock in the living room. I'm going to have one, in my new house."

Evie pulled the front door wide. "I'm sure you will," she said. "Goodbye."

In the bedroom, she glanced around for some sign of her husband's clothes, even his socks by the bed, but they were not there. They were with the laundry, waiting to be washed. Weren't they? She had the urge to go to the back porch, where the washer and dryer were, just to be sure. There was no time. But if she did, she could look in at her son's room on the way. Why? To see that his clothes, his possessions, were still there? She scanned the empty bedroom, frantic. Where were her son's childhood drawings? She had taped them to the wall years ago, hadn't she? *Hadn't she?*

She felt fear then, rising up through her body, going for her throat. Her hands clenched into fists, her fingers so small, her knuckles white as bones ready to pop through the skin. Where was her ring? Had she taken it off in the bathroom?

She struggled to form a name on her lips. Dan, she thought. That was it. And the name of her son. Edward.

Where were they?

A warm wind filled the room, flushing her cheeks.

The front door, she realized. She had left it open.

She went back to the living room.

There was the woman, in the doorway. She was standing in profile again, the hot wind blowing past her into the house, catching her dress so that it billowed out from her body. Now, the dress inflated with air, she appeared to be much heavier, by twenty or thirty pounds at least. The heat blurred, creating a mirage between Evie and the door, so that the woman's legs seemed suddenly thick, grown strong enough to carry the added weight, her ankles swollen and bloated.

"What do you want from me?" Evie said, reeling.

The hot wind subsided, moving on, and something left the house. The woman's dress deflated, hanging once more in loose folds. But, as Evie watched, she saw with perfect clarity that the woman was no longer slender. The front of the dress remained distended like a balloon, straining to cover a round, unmistakably swollen belly, where before it had been absolutely flat and empty.

"Nothing," said the other woman, and twisted the gold ring on her left hand. Then she turned to leave at last, smiling as if she had a secret, something too new and too personal, too private to share with anyone, least of all a stranger, just yet.

House of Cool Air

William F. Wu

Some stories hit us with such force the impact of their originality and uniqueness of vision tells us instantly that something special has been offered to us. Bill Wu has been one of those terribly underrated writers who has labored for a long time in the science fiction genre. The following story marks one of his first forays into dark fantasy and it is an impressive one. To say it's a tour de force of psychological horror and disturbing surrealism does not begin to describe what a wonderful piece of writing you are about to experience.

He shifted uncomfortably on the rounded top of the thick wooden post. His bony bare feet almost covered it completely as he squatted on it, carefully keeping his balance. When his legs began to hurt from that position, he would sit down on the top of the post and let his legs dangle down the sides, but that was more uncomfortable. The top of the smoothly polished, dark brown post was a hard seat for someone who was not allowed clothes at home.

Across the big bedroom, the girls were experimenting with a makeup kit and brushing their hair in different ways. They stroked little brushes on brightly colored palettes and then brushed the colors on their faces.

"Here," said Lena, who was thirteen. She wore a plaid outfit she called a jumper that was mostly red and yellow. As she spoke, she gave a blue hairbrush to June, who was twelve. Both of them had dark, shiny brown hair. "You might like this one."

"Yeah?" June looked at herself in the mirror over the wide dresser. The dark brown dresser was the same color as their hair and had elaborate, curliqued brass drawer handles that were almost as shiny as the mirror itself. "I want to look like you. How do I do it?"

"I'll show you."

The blonde, Mitten, was eleven, the same as he was. She was the baby of the three sisters and the prettiest, who looked almost exactly like a young version of their mother.

He turned to look outside the one big window in the room. The post was so high over the rich stone blue carpet that he could see a long way down. This room was on the third floor of the mansion and today it overlooked an expanse of fine green lawn bounded on all sides by tall trees and heavy undergrowth. The bushes and trees were full of lush, dark green leaves that swayed in the hot, humid summer sunlight.

"I want to try the blue hairband," said Mitten, sorting through a pile of plastic hairbands, brushes, combs, and little colored bottles.

"Go ahead," said Lena, watching June try to look like her.

The only sound besides those of the girls was the quiet hum of air conditioning. He was always cold in the house, just as he was always nude in the house. It came from being skinny, he decided, hugging the ribs that he could feel on his sides. He wasn't tall for eleven, but, proportionally, he had long arms and legs. His thin toes and fingers were especially cold, and so was his grip, as they called it.

In the summer, the air conditioning was always strong. At other times of the year, the cold came in from outside. Of course, there was no school now, during summer, so he didn't do anything all day.

"Do I look like you now?" June asked hopefully, looking at Lena with her eyes wide.

"That's very close." As Lena reassured her and fussed with her hair, he could just see himself, partly behind Mitten. He was darker than they were and his black hair contrasted sharply against Mitten's blond waves. No one had ever explained why he was in this family.

The shiny brass doorknob clicked as it turned from the outside. Then suddenly the door was thrown open. It banged against the wall stop, but Charlotte, the girls' mother, kept it from bouncing back with one arm as she marched into the room.

"Who left that mess in the hall bathroom?" She glared at the three sisters.

He sat very still, every muscle tense. Charlotte had very shiny, wavy blond hair and light blue eyes. Her features were always pretty, no matter what her mood. Today she wore a casual white dress with blue vertical pinstripes. It had a widely scooped, very low-cut front with white lace around the edge. Her large, rounded softness nearly bulged all the way out of it. Around her slender waist, the dress was still snug. Below its knee-length hem, her legs were firm and shapely. He always enjoyed looking at her, but he was deeply afraid of her. His gaze went to her knees and stayed there.

All three girls stood in a line with their hands clasped in front of them, the way they had been taught.

"I did," Mitt said primly. "I forgot to clean it up."

"All right." Charlotte looked down at her a moment and sighed. Then she caught his eye and nodded. When he was squatting on the post and she was standing, his head was at the same level as hers.

Obediently, he dropped to the carpet and stood in front of her with his feet apart. His thin toes anxiously curled, clutching at the deep carpet. Her perfume was light and tangy. Mitt came to stand next to her mother. Charlotte put her hands under his arms and suddenly slammed her knee up into what the girls called his marbles, making her blue and white skirt bounce on her thigh.

Pain shot down to his knees and up through his abdomen, as it always did. He went limp, but she caught his weight under his arms, then shifted him out of the way. She held him up from the side and he saw Mitt step in front of him. Mitt also jerked her slender, bony knee up between his legs. Pain raced through him again and he felt Charlotte ease him to the floor, where he lay curled on the carpet, gasping.

"Now you see what you've done to him?" Charlotte said sternly. "Go clean up the hall bathroom or I'll make you do it again." She strode out of the room but left the door open. Mitt hurried out after her.

As he lay motionless at the base of the post, he heard one of the other girls close the door.

"I'm glad she wasn't mad at me," said June.

"We didn't do it," said Lena. "Here. You can try some of my makeup if you want."

He remained where he was about as long as usual. After awhile, he heard Mitt come back in and resume playing with her sisters. When he could, he climbed back onto the post and sat with his legs dangling. His marbles and his knees still hurt. He watched the girls, hoping they wouldn't make another mess.

They didn't. Later they went down to dinner and Mitt brought up his plate. To eat on the post, he had to grip it with his legs and hold one hand under his plate with two fingers hooked around the handle of his mug. He was used to it, but he still had to be careful.

The girls were out of the room most of the evening, apparently downstairs. While they were gone, he hopped down from the post and climbed up to his bed. That was allowed.

Lena and June, being the elder two, slept in a set of bunk beds along one wall. The beds were made of dark, polished wood similar to that of the dresser. As the eldest, Lena had claimed the top one. Mitt slept in a canopied bed against the opposite wall, under the big window. A wide closet filled one of the walls between them. All three girls had identical white sheets with bluebirds flying on them and matching blue blankets and quilted bedspreads with little blue and white checks.

A horizontal cabinet stretched over the closet, with its own doors. His pallet was up there, and a couple of shelves held the clothes that he wore out of the house and to school. To reach it, he climbed up a ladder that had been secured to the wall on one side of the closet doors. It was a metal ladder and the rungs were always cold.

Once he was up on the white sheet of his pallet, he lay in a position where he could look down through the window and see the green lawn. The yellowish rays of late sunlight angled across it, throwing long shadows of trees and bushes. No one was there.

He would be glad when fall came, because he liked school. After awhile, he fumbled through a small stack of books by the edge of his bed. He picked a short one about a stuffed rabbit that he liked and read it again. After he had finished the book, he knew bedtime was coming soon. As usual, he used the bathroom that opened off the bedroom; they all shared it. By the time the girls came in, he was back in bed, under the covers.

Also as usual, he switched his lamp off so they wouldn't see him too easily. Lena turned on the wall switch by the door, which controlled all three bedside lamps for the girls. In the three pools of light they gave off, he watched them undress, as he did every night.

Lena flipped her shiny dark hair out of the way and took off her white blouse. She wore a white bra under it, much smaller than her mother's. After unhooking it and tossing it into the laundry hamper, she idly rubbed the red welts it had left for a moment. Then she pulled down her skirt, stepped out of it, and went to her dresser in her white underpants for a nightgown.

Some nights they were talkative and giggly. Other nights they argued or maybe Lena and June would tease Mitt about something. Tonight, though, they were quiet and seemed tired.

June looked a lot like Lena. She had a bra but only wore it on special occasions or with certain clothes. It was smaller than Lena's. When Lena had taken a lavender nightgown out of her drawer, June went to get hers that matched it.

He was most interested in Mitt tonight. Her facial features made her look so much like her mother that he expected she would someday be almost like a twin to her. Also, with her blond hair, she stood out from her older sisters. Most of all, though, she was his age today and just as skinny and bony as he was. Sometimes he wondered what she thought about different things, but he never asked. Now she undressed to her white underpants, as her sisters had, but she put on green cotton pajamas instead of a nightgown.

He was relieved when they had all slid into bed and
Lena turned off the lights. Of course, they hardly ever
paid any deliberate attention to him. Still, watching was
allowed, but a stiff grip was grounds for slamming him.
He had one every night at this time.

He drifted off to sleep as they did.

Hours later a loud, distant thud woke him up in
darkness. He had a vague feeling that the house had just
vibrated, even all the way up in this room. The girls stirred
slightly in their beds.

A faint noise outside got his attention. It happened again
and sounded like a shout. He had never heard anything
like that before outside the house at night.

Curious, he sat up and moved so that he could see out
the window. Lights on the outside of the mansion lit up
the grounds. A girl he had never seen before was running
nude across the grass in the summer night. He rose up on
his knees, fascinated. As she ran, her short, limp black
hair bounced on her head. She was skinny, like him, and
looked like she might be his age.

In a moment she was gone, but four more figures ran
through the shadows from the house after her. They
changed direction to cut her off, away from the lights,
but he thought that a man was running in the lead,
followed by three boys, all of them wearing clothes. He
wasn't sure. Then they, too, were out of sight.

He sat watching for a long time, hoping someone would
come back into view. No one did, however, and he heard
no more sounds in the house either. The girls had not
moved again in their beds. Finally, too sleepy to stay up,
he lay back down reluctantly and was asleep again almost
right away.

The next morning, he was awakened by Lena's alarm.
As he did every morning, he waited for his grip to

unstiffen while the girls got up and used the bathroom. As they came out, he also watched the clothes they put on carefully and looked at his own body for a clue to the day. This morning he felt short, and he sat up as soon as they were occupied with dressing. He estimated that his body was six years old today.

The girls, of course, were a day older than they had been yesterday. That was true every morning. He didn't understand why their ages didn't vary like his, but he was used to it. Then he wondered if he would be in kindergarten or first grade. First grade was more interesting, but so far he had tried everything up to and including the seventh grade, one day or another. The room was chilly. As the girls put on warm, casual playclothes, he moved down his pallet to look out the window. Most of the leaves on the trees were orange and yellow, but many were red, which was his favorite. He guessed that Halloween was near.

The air would be brisk and crisp. He went to school in autumn, of course, but today must be a Saturday, judging from the girls' clothes. When they went downstairs for breakfast, he used the bathroom.

Before Mitt came up with his breakfast, he had taken his bath and was on top of the post. Getting to the top was harder when he was only six, but he had managed, jumping as high as he could and grabbing the top surface with his hands. Then he had pulled himself up, using his feet for what little traction he could get.

Mitt left him his breakfast. As he ate, he guessed that this would be one of those Saturdays when the girls were occupied elsewhere most of the day. Days like that were always empty and boring.

He was never actually given permission to leave the room on such days, but the door was never locked.

Lena came for his dishes. After she had gone, he listened carefully to her footsteps going down the hall and then descending the carpeted stairs. Beyond them, he couldn't hear her.

Even then, he did not move from the post for a long time. The room was chilly and he sat huddled on the post to keep warm, his hands rubbing the ribs on his sides. Finally, he heard laughing voices outside and looked out the window. The girls were dressed in their padded red jackets and white knit stocking caps and matching gloves. They ran through piles of dry, brown leaves, kicking them in all directions. Then they began jumping in them and throwing handfuls of leaves all over each other.

He decided to risk leaving the room today. Carefully, he jumped down to the floor, falling with a light thump and rolling on the carpet when he landed. He froze at the noise, his heart pounding, waiting to see if anyone came to check on him. If someone thought he had simply fallen, he would not be punished.

No one came. When he was only six, his weight was negligible. Maybe no one was inside the house.

He got up and walked to the door, conscious of the soft carpet under his bare feet at every step. Still no sounds came from anywhere in the house. He reached up and took the slick, shiny gold doorknob in his hand and slowly turned it. When he heard it click, he pulled the door open and peeked outside.

No one was in the hall. The walls were white and spotlessly clean. High above him, paintings and photographs hung on the walls, but he couldn't see them very well when he was six. The frames looked thick and heavy. Slowly, quivering with tension, he slipped out into the hall and carefully pulled the door shut with a quiet click.

Now, outside his room, he truly felt naked. He did not dare get dressed, because he might need to run back here and get up on the post in a hurry. He would have to explore as he was.

On his way to school or rare trips to the doctor, he turned right and went down the hall to the main stairs. The stairs began as an extension of the hall but then turned at a landing, where a massive dark wooden banister began. It led down to the big living room. He had glimpsed a formal dining room near it, though he had never been inside that room. Still, that direction held few surprises.

Instead he turned left, where the hall led to more doorways. The doors were made of wood and were white, like the walls. They had decorative shaping, though: each door had four rectangular panels indented slightly on its surface. The door knobs were gold in color and smooth to the touch. Every door was exactly the same on the outside.

On the other explorations he had made in this direction, he had seen many doors and even peeked inside some of the rooms. Most were bedrooms, fully furnished and cleanly kept, but without any regular residents. Each room had a different color. One had a dark blue rug, blue and white curtains, and a pale blue quilt on the bed. Another room had green decorations and a third was pink. After awhile, he had quit looking into them.

He had also seen hallways branching away, but he had never had time to follow them.

Today he wondered what had happened to the mysterious girl he had seen outside during the night. If she lived here, he wanted to find her. He had no memory of her or even of any sign of other kids but the three girls who shared his room. Of course, he hadn't made very many trips through the house, and most of his memories of them were blurry and confused.

The hall was chilly. He shivered and walked with his arms wrapped around his skinny torso. His toes were very cold but the carpet was just a tiny bit warm under his feet. Being only six years old today, he was smaller than he would have liked and that made him even more timid than usual.

Even so, he was glad when he reached the first corner. Another hall branched to the right. He crept to the corner and slowly peeked around it.

This hall, though also white, was shorter and no one was in it either. It ended in a doorway with one of those white doors, but the door was standing open. Another hallway continued beyond it. On the right side of this hall, a line of tall windows let in sunlight. Thick, floor-length white drapes had been drawn over them on his last trip here. This time the drapes were open. Now he walked forward cautiously and looked out the nearest window.

It opened onto a courtyard far below. He had never really known what the layout of the house was; in fact, it seemed to change from time to time, though his own room was always the same. Now he could see that it was a massive rectangle with a courtyard in the center. No one was there, but he could see cast-iron furniture with green cushions situated on a pavement of flat, gray stones. The leaves of several trees were just turning to orange and yellow, but the smaller bushes were still green.

"There he is," Lena said triumphantly, behind him.

He flinched, but firm fingers and a thumb caught his arm from behind and spun him around. Lena's hand went all the way around his thin arm as she looked down at him. All three girls were standing over him, their faces still flushed with the cold autumn air outside. They were still bundled in sweaters and heavy socks and shoes.

Suddenly he felt even more naked than usual. Lena's fingers were icy. His whole body seemed to go cold. Since he was only around six years old today, they seemed even bigger than they had yesterday.

"Do we do it here?" Mitt asked.

"Mom isn't home," said Lena, uncertainly. "Um, let's go back to our room first." She reached down to clutch his grip tightly in her cold fist and pulled him back down the hall by it.

The walk back seemed ridiculously short. On his exploration to this hall, knowing that he was breaking the rules and in danger of getting caught, he had felt he was venturing a long way. Now he felt foolish, seeing how little distance he had actually covered.

Back in the room, June closed the door with finality. "I want to do it," she said. "Since none of us did anything, we get to choose, don't we?"

"Mom usually decides who does it when he's the one being punished," said Mitt. "Maybe we should wait for her."

"When we're being punished, she always says punishment should be immediate," said Lena. "Since I'm the oldest, I'll do it."

"I want to," Mitt wailed.

"Stop being a baby," said June. "I spoke up first, Lena. Let me, come on."

Ignoring them, Lena pulled him around until his back was against the post. Then, as he expected, she got both her hands under his arms in the usual position and separated his feet with one cold, hard shoe. She slammed her knee up against his marbles and let go of him.

As always, he collapsed to the carpet, stunned from the pain. Still, he fumbled for the base of the pole, remembering that June and Mitt wanted to slam him, too. Just as he managed to rise into a kneeling position, leaning on the pole, June grabbed his shoulders from behind and pulled him away from it.

He fell onto his back. June stepped between his legs and kicked him with the blunt front of one chilly white sneaker. Pain flooding his abdomen paralyzed him for a moment.

"I want my turn," Mitt whined.

June stepped over him. With effort, he rolled to one

side and pushed himself up, fighting for breath. He was not surprised, however, when Mitt got her hands under his arms, too, and hoisted him to his feet.

He was still standing hunched forward, unable to get his balance, as she slammed her bony knee into his marbles, too. This time, though, she caught him when he fell and gently turned him around to lean on the post. He clung to it, staring at a blur of bedspread without seeing it, as the girls left the room.

When the door had closed again, he sank to the carpet and lay there without moving for a long time. Finally, when he could move again, he slowly sat up. Much more time passed before he could climb to the top of the post again, but when he could do so, he did. Then he stayed there the rest of the afternoon.

He was sitting there when the girls came in shortly before dinner time. They had taken off their jackets and gloves downstairs, but their cheeks and hands were ruddy from more long hours out in the autumn air. They ignored him, arguing among themselves about some game they had been playing outside with the neighbors. He sat as he normally did, watching as they bustled in and out of the room, talking to each other.

When Charlotte arrived home, she called hello to the girls from just inside the front door and then came right up to their room, carrying a wooden coat hanger she had taken from a closet on the way. She was all dressed up in makeup, gold earrings and necklaces, a fancy white blouse, and a gray suit. As she leaned on the doorknob with one hand, she slipped off her high-heeled gray shoes with the other.

"Did you girls have a good day?" Charlotte asked pleasantly. She put her shoes down and unfastened her gray suit jacket. "Don't mind me. I have to get in the shower right away."

Her sheer white blouse had been buttoned tight over

her bulging breasts. He watched uncomfortably as her motion to get out of the jacket strained open the blouse in little arcs between each button, showing him the smooth skin of her abdomen and the white lace pattern of her bra cups.

"Sure, Mom," said June.

"Only, he got out," said Mitt.

"Oh?" Charlotte hung her jacket carefully on the hanger and hooked it over the doorknob. Then she fumbled with the button fastening her skirt. "Where did you find him?"

"Just around the corner up there." Lena pointed vaguely.

"And?"

"We brought him back here. All three of us took turns."

"*My*." Charlotte nodded her approval. "I'm sure he learned his lesson." She smiled at him as she wriggled her skirt down, revealing a white half slip. "All three of you. *My*."

He looked away when she caught his eye, but glanced back to her when she broke contact and leaned forward to step out of her skirt. His leaving the room was very serious and he was afraid she might order one of them to slam him again, but she wasn't saying anything else yet. He watched her hang the skirt with great care from hooks on the horizontal bar of the coat hanger, his heart pounding with a mixture of fear and anticipation.

While the girls chattered on about their day, Charlotte took her earrings off one by one and laid them on top of the dresser. Then she did the same with her necklaces. After that she listened to the girls absently as she unbuttoned her blouse.

He couldn't look away as her hands moved downward. The tight fabric of the blouse loosened and then she flipped the sides back, showing her smooth shoulders striped with the white bra straps. The bra was underwired to support her huge, soft, pale breasts. He looked at the long line of cleavage between them, then at the bra again.

The straps were taut until she reached behind her back and made a quick motion. The bra lost its tension and she eased it off, nodding at something June had said.

He had seen her bare breasts several times, but not often. Her nipples caught his gaze. Pink welts from the bra marked her breasts and her shoulders and her sides. She rubbed the marks with both hands, then leaned down to remove her slip.

June sat down on the bed, talking about the neighbor kids.

His grip was stiffening. He wondered how long it would be before one of them noticed him. They were certain to see him sooner or later. He couldn't hide.

Mitt, whining a little, complained about their game with the neighbors again. Her mother was sympathetic. June argued. Lena went to use the bathroom.

Charlotte paused, listening to June and Mitt. She stood in front of them in only her white underpants, darkened in the front by her triangle of pubic hair. A few stray tufts of it peeked out from the elastic around her thighs.

He looked at her precisely coifed hairstyle and the still perfect makeup on her pretty face. Then his gaze moved down to her breasts again and past them to her stomach. Below her underpants, her thighs were fleshy but shapely and her calves were trim. Her feet were small and her toenails bright red.

Charlotte, still listening to Mitt, slipped the fingers of one hand under the elastic waistband and slid the underpants down as she bent forward. At the same time, she lifted first one leg and then the other to step out of them. She tossed them on top of the slip on the bed and scratched the red line across her waist idly with long fingernails.

He stared at her pubic hair in fascination. This was only the second or third time he had seen her completely nude. His face felt hot and he was covered with sweat.

The bathroom door opened and Lena started out. She saw him, though, and pointed accusingly. "Mom! Look!"

He covered his hard, stiff grip with his hands, but of course he was too late.

"Oh, really." Charlotte sighed and rolled her eyes in exasperation. She shifted slightly to face him, putting her fists on her hips. Her breasts swayed and jiggled with the movement. "All right. Who's turn is it?"

"I want to," June said eagerly, jumping up and down.

Charlotte nodded to him. He jumped all the way down to the floor and caught his balance with one hand on the carpet. Then he stood up, giving Charlotte one more glance. Her pubic hair was just a shade darker than the hair on her head. She stood patiently.

June smiled happily, put her hands on his shoulders, and slammed her knee up into his marbles. He collapsed again in extreme pain, this time falling to the carpet on one shoulder. His grip softened right away.

While he lay on the carpet, now chilly with the sweat that had accumulated all over his body, he heard Charlotte gather up her clothes and leave the room.

That night, in bed, his marbles hurt sharply and his knees and lower abdomen throbbed with a dull ache. He lay awake long after the girls were asleep.

After awhile, he sat up and moved to the middle of the bed so he could see out the window. Dry autumn leaves from the mussed piles drifted slowly in the wind over the dying grass, some of it still green and some brown. No one was out there.

He lay down again. Now, as his lower body still throbbed with the multiple slammings, he wondered what he would do. He did not want to go exploring tomorrow. Charlotte or the girls almost always found him. He had only sneaked out and back undetected a couple of times. They always led him back by his marbles or his grip but usually only one of the girls punished him, under

Charlotte's supervision. Today had been different because she had been out.

In the darkness, the faint light coming in through the window threw shadows on the walls and ceiling of his cubicle. Some were from the stark, empty branches of trees while others, in straight, perpendicular lines, were cast from the window and its casing. He gazed at them absently.

Maybe he would try exploring at night some time. He had never thought of that before. Not tonight, though.

He still wanted to see the mysterious girl. Maybe she could be a friend. He didn't have any.

Finally, despite the pain, his eyes closed and he drifted into an uncomfortable doze.

A noise downstairs woke him up from his fitful sleep. He didn't know what that noise was, but he recognized the next one. It was a swinging door that led from the kitchen to the foyer just inside the front door. It made a distinctive squeak when it was opened and closed. First he had heard it open; a few seconds later, he heard it close.

He sat up quickly, his heart beating fast. It might be that girl he had seen and this might be his only chance to meet her. He threw off the covers and climbed down the ladder, taking care to be quiet.

It was still dark outside, but he had no idea how long he had been sleeping. His feet were quiet on the carpet as he passed the sleeping girls. The real danger was the door.

He put his hand on the cold doorknob and realized that he was older today. From his height, he judged he was about thirteen. He held his breath, looking at the shadowed bunk beds for signs of movement, and slowly turned the handle.

It squeaked slightly. He stopped. The girls did not respond. He turned it more. Then he pulled gently.

The hinges also squeaked, but the sound was faint. The

girls were sleeping deeply. He slipped out into the hall and carefully positioned the door so that it was just barely ajar.

The hall was dark, but a hint of light came from the end that led to the main staircase. He walked quickly toward it, knowing that he would make no noise on the carpet here. As he started down the carpeted staircase, he looked over the banister down into the foyer, but saw no one.

The light came from the kitchen, leaking under and around the door that made the scraping noise. He remembered Charlotte once mentioning that the kitchen light was always left on at night. Against it, the dark polished banister was a long, massive shape that sent weird, exaggerated shadows to the opposite wall as he descended the stairs, searching the darkness below.

Finally the banister ended in a great post, bigger than the one he sat on, with four sharp corners on the sides and a top carved into a smooth globe. As his bare feet felt the cold, slick hardwood floor of the foyer under them, he stepped around the post and froze. The girl was right in front of him, hiding motionless on the other side of the post, staring at him.

He stared back. She was skinny, like him, maybe his age or just a little younger. Her hair was the same flat black and she was naked, as he was. He couldn't see her very well in the shadows, but she had the body of a child just starting to develop.

She seemed to be appraising him the same way. With a jolt of surprise, he realized that she looked enough like him to be his sister. Then, as they watched each other, she slowly began to circle around him to his right.

When he turned, he realized that she was moving toward the big front door. His feet were cold now, as were his grip and his marbles. He didn't know what to say, so he didn't say anything. In a kind of frozen wonder, he watched her snap open the main lock with a loud click, put two small hands on the doorknob, and pull it open.

The sound of the lock and of the door opening seemed to roar through the house. He could see her more clearly now in the light from the porch; she had hints of breasts and long, thin arms and legs. Her hips were no wider than her waist. Now she unlatched and opened the outer door made of decorative cast-iron and some kind of clear safety glass. She stepped out onto the porch with her bare feet, still looking at him, and waited.

Frigid air swirled into the house from behind her. He looked past her and saw that the ground today was covered in a thick layer of snow. It was no longer coming down, and bright moonlight shimmered across the white landscape. The wind was blowing hard and very cold.

A door was thrown open upstairs and then slammed shut. Two pairs of feet came pounding in a fast, deliberate stride. Someone had heard the front door open.

He looked up into the shadowed hall, on reflex, and then back at the girl. Her eyes were wide and quick with fright, too, but she didn't come back inside. Instead, she stepped backward on the porch, holding the door open for him.

His gaze moved from her face to the open space that beckoned, then beyond to the frozen night outside. He wanted to go. Yet he didn't move. All he did was stare and hear the thudding footsteps upstairs coming closer.

Frantically, the girl stamped her foot. He waited for her to give up and go, leaving him behind. His feet would not move.

Suddenly she darted inside, ran up to him, and reached down. She grabbed his grip and pulled him to the door. He followed obediently, as he always had before. Suddenly they were outside and the shock of freezing wind seem to wake him up.

She let go of him and they both ran, the cold snow under

his feet seeming to burn as they did so. The frigid wind brought tears to his eyes and seemed to chill his body from his skin right through his insides. Ahead of him, the night was dark, broken only by yellowish lights from some of the houses and the reflection off the powdery crystals on the blanket of snow.

He had no idea where he was going.

The girl was running to his left and just ahead of him, so he stayed with her. His head was pounding in pain with the cold. Then he heard the shouts behind them. She turned, slowing, to look back over her shoulder, her black hair blowing across her face. Her eyes widened with fear.

He looked back, too.

Charlotte and a strange man were running after them from the front door, and gaining easily on their longer legs. She had thrown on a long, heavy, light blue robe and some kind of black snow boots. Her golden hair still glistened beautifully as she ran toward them through slivers of light. The man with her, who wore only a pair of blue jeans and shoes, was solidly built and tall, but had little muscle definition.

The girl turned suddenly and angled toward trees to her left. The man changed direction to cut her off. Her short, skinny legs flashed across the snow and her feet kicked up tufts of powder after her.

Meanwhile, he could hear Charlotte running right behind him as he turned to stay with the girl. Charlotte's breath wheezed in his ears. He was so cold now that he wondered if his marbles would even hurt when she slammed him.

Suddenly the girl turned in front of him, stumbling. He bumped into her, struggling to keep his balance on nearly numb feet, coming to a halt. The man had grabbed her upper arm and had yanked her around in front of him.

While the man nearly lifted her off her feet and she flailed wordlessly to get free, he quickly darted under the man's arm so that he was in close to the man's blue jeans. If there was any one way he could fight, this was it. He went up on the toes of his left foot, at the same time jamming his thin right knee as high as he could between the man's legs. The man made a sharp, gruff sound in his throat and fell forward, releasing the girl.

He avoided the man by dodging away to one side. The man dropped face first against Charlotte's legs, making her stumble. The girl now pushed Charlotte face down across the man and they both tumbled into the snow. The skirt of the light blue robe skewed open and Charlotte's long legs sprawled across the white powder.

For a moment, he stood over Charlotte and the man, breathing the cold, harsh air as he looked down at them. His whole body quivered with uncontrollable shivering; his teeth were clenched against chattering. Then he looked up into the face of the girl. She met his eyes for a moment.

Behind them the house stood firm and tall and warm in its own haze of lights against the sky. Neither of them looked at it.

Together, without a word, they ran away from the house into the frozen wastes of the unknown night.

MORNING TERRORS

Peter Crowther

Until he began soliciting fiction for his highly successful anthologies (Narrow Houses), we had never heard of Pete Crowther. But as soon as his stories began showing up in our mailbox, we knew his name would be forever familiar. An Englishman from North Yorkshire, Pete writes some of the cleanest, sharpest prose we've ever seen. His stories are distinctive because of their originality and their harsh vision of characters rendered utterly helpless by forces beyond their ken and control. In person, he is such a warm, friendly chap, it's hard to imagine he is the guy responsible for something as truly disturbing as the following journey beyond conventional madness.

He awoke like clockwork, jerking upright in bed, images racing through his mind in a steady stream, sweating feverishly and gripping his bottom lip with his teeth. He was already whining.

The luminous display of the clock on the mantelpiece, strangely twisted out of true and shimmering as though about to disappear, registered 3:08. To his left, the curtains were wafting gently, billowed inward by a gentle breeze which muttered around the outside of the house. He could see them out of the corner of his eye but refused to look at the window full on. Not yet. That would come soon.

He shook his head and whimpered, protesting like a cowed child. "No," he whispered faintly, as though trying not to let anyone else hear him. "No, please, no." The bed creaked and strained as the figure next to him moved slightly. He swallowed and tried to concentrate on the mantelpiece but already felt the first signs of detached curiosity that would cause him to turn around.

The wall in front of him looked wet and slimy and uneven: that had happened a week ago Tuesday. The wardrobe that should be next to the mantelpiece was not there: that had gone on the Friday. Nor was the old wicker crib and stand in front of the radiator attached to the right-hand wall: the following Sunday.

Last week it had stopped here. The week before, it had stopped at the mantelpiece. The first week, as soon as he had woken up. Last weekend he had first looked at the curtains. The weekend before, the first pains in his chest had started.

Last night he had noticed the duvet.

He lifted his hands to his face and started to sob quietly, sniveling mucous out of his nose.

Between his fingers he could still make out the orange light that shone through the curtains. He breathed in deep and wiped his eyes with his fingers, roughly. And then he turned to face the window.

It was the same again. Orange. The sky outside the window shone orange through the paisley floor-length curtains into the room. No sign of the streetlight which lit the road between his house and number 20. No vague outline of the houses across the road. No faint sound of the late-night/early-morning trucks on the motorway. Just orange, pulsating.

And hissing distantly.

Staring at the window, willing it to change, he caught sight, in the lower periphery of his vision, of the shape which was no longer his wife curled up on the other side of the bed. In front of him, wrapped tightly in what had once been a duvet, the figure moved, growing increasingly restless.

"Shhhhhh," he said softly, ignoring the tingling feeling which jabbed through his chest.

Now, he thought. *Come back now.*

This was where it had ended last night. A sound started in his throat, long and guttural, building in pitch, as he started to lower his head to look down fully at the bed.

As he lowered his eyes, he saw again that it was not a duvet which covered him and his wife but an old skin of some kind. Patches of the thick and coarse hair had worn through in some places and, in others, stains shone darkly, spotted occasionally with what looked like pieces of meat and dried grass. It smelt like the insides of the dustbins out in the yard.

The figure beneath the skin was huge. It was not — could not possibly be — Katherine. And it was misshapen, becoming larger at the feet end than at the middle, where the skin fell inward. At the top, it was enormous.

He had seen hints of all of this last night. Tonight he had seen it close up. And now he saw one more thing: the top of his wife's head protruding from the duvet.

And it was starting to move as though waking up.

"Nonononojesusjesusjesusjesusjee…"

Katherine's hands were on him suddenly, shaking him roughly.

He heard her voice and almost cried. "There, there, sweetie," it said gently. "Another dream?"

He opened his eyes and looked around, realizing vaguely that she had turned on the lamp on her side table.

He was crouched in front of her, facing the window. The curtains were still blowing and he could make out the muted white glow of the light outside. Somewhere in the distance a horn sounded, followed by the haunting lonely call of a big truck, doppering from and back to nothingness.

He looked at the clock. It registered 3:14.

Next to the mantelpiece stood the wardrobe.

In front of the radiator stood the wicker crib and stand, filled with all of Katherine's toy animals.

He looked down at the unmistakable swirls and splashes of the duvet. And then he looked up, through blurred eyes, at his wife. She stared at him wide-eyed and shook her head, settling back into bed and rubbing her hands through her long brown hair. He shuffled from his kneeling position, slipped out of the bed and padded across the carpet to the hall and the waiting toilet. His bladder felt like it was going to burst.

As he let loose a thick, strong-smelling stream into the water below, Katherine's voice called to him from the bedroom. "I don't care what you say, Terry, but it's doctor's for you in the morning."

He groaned with relief as he finished and flushed the toilet.

"You hear me?"

"Yes, I hear you," he said. He rubbed his chest. It felt strange, almost tight. And it was sticky to the touch. Must be sweat. At least the pain had gone. He rubbed his hands down the sides of his legs and ran softly back to the bedroom.

Snuggling into Katherine's back in the now restored darkness, he pulled one of his pillows so that it went down the outside of the bed behind him, protecting him from the room beyond.

He kissed the back of her head. "Love you."

"Love you too, sweetie," she said, her voice drifting back to him over her shoulder. "But you must go to the doctor's tomorrow."

"I will."

"Promise?"

"Promise."

And, his vision concentrated on the shine of the outside lamp, he slipped off into the dreamless sleep of exhaustion.

"Okay, you can put on your...er...shirt again."

Terry sat up, swung his legs over the side of the bed and reached for his shirt. "So what's the verdict, doctor?"

The other man sat down behind a wide desk and laid his stethoscope gently in an open felt-lined box. "Well, there's nothing wrong with your heart," he said, carefully avoiding looking Terry in the eye. It didn't bother Terry at all. The man was very shy and never locked eyes with anybody. There were seven doctors in the practice, not counting the endless run of trainees who spent a few months learning the ropes, and Terry rarely got to see the doctor with whom he was officially registered. He had been seen by this fellow before.

He stood up and tucked his shirt into his trousers, giving an exaggerated breath of relief. "So I'll live?"

Doctor Platt allowed himself a nervous smile and pushed his glasses farther back on the bridge of his nose. "Yes, I think it's...er...safe to say that."

Terry finished tying his necktie and folded down his shirt collar while the doctor keyed something into the computer. "So what about these dreams?"

"Well, those are probably caused by stress, tension, any

number of…er…things." He scratched absent-mindedly at his beard and made a further adjustment to his glasses. "How are things at work…er…what is it that you do again?"

"I'm in advertising," Terry said. He hated having to explain the complexities of his job with the bank, and advertising seemed to be the likeliest catchall.

"Busy?"

Does a wooden horse have a hickory dick? "Very," he replied.

"Well, it's probably just morning terrors. You probably need to…er…take a rest."

Terry nodded and sat down on the edge of the bed.

The doctor finished what he was doing at the computer screen and looked over it at the wall behind. "Everything okay at home?"

"Everything's fine at home." Terry was feeling better already. The pain in his chest — which had lingered with him for the past week, steadily growing worse — had gone completely today.

The doctor stroked his beard and then turned to face Terry, his eyes locking onto the chair back just to Terry's right. "Well, I'll give you something to help you sleep," he said, "and some cream to clear up that…er…irritation on your chest."

"Irritation on my chest?"

"Yes, just around your…er…nipples." Doctor Platt cleared his throat and reached for a pen.

"My *nipples*?" Terry was beginning to feel like a parrot.

"Mmmm, it's just a bit of soreness. Nothing to worry about. Probably been caused by rubbing, maybe a shirt or…" He let his voice trail off.

"Or?"

"Well…er…just by a shirt." He turned his attention to the little prescription pad and wrote quickly. "See if your…er…wife has recently changed washing powders.

That can often cause irritation." He finished writing and placed the top carefully back on his fountain pen. "Hadn't you noticed it?"

Terry shook his head. "No, not at all."

"Well," he held out the slip of paper to Terry while continuing to talk to the chairback. "That's...er...all right then."

"Your *nipples*?" Katherine laughed loudly as she removed her coat. "And what did he say about the dreams?"

"He said what I expected him to say, that I was just run down and that I need a rest." Terry watched her watching him. "He gave me something to put on it, anyway," he added. "A cream. And he gave me something to help me sleep better. He said it was just a case of morning terrors."

She walked over and turned on the gas beneath the kettle. "And are you satisfied with that?"

"Yes. Yes, I'm satisfied with that," he said, scratching at his left nipple without even realizing that he was doing it.

This time the clock had gone completely.

He felt groggy, doped. Must be the pills. Certainly he did not feel so concerned at waking up in what must still be the middle of the night.

The room was again bathed in an orange glow but tonight it was not silent. Tonight there was a muted sound of activity. Nothing that he could separate and identify: more a *sense* of things going on around him. And there was another sound, a low and pained moaning...several moans all joining together, drifting and wafting. He stared at the wall in front of him and suddenly realized that it looked to be farther away. He allowed his eyes to travel upward.

The wall now bore no resemblance at all to the wall of his and Katherine's bedroom. As far as he could make out in the dim orange light, it was a rock wall that went all the way up and over. Like the wall of a cave. And he could sense movements on the floor in front of him and around him.

Terry yawned and rubbed his arms around on the duvet, feeling the coarseness of the hair and picking at the occasional lumps matted within it. He turned to face the window and saw, instead of the paisley curtains, a thin veil, ripped and holey, hanging in front of a large opening. In his stomach he felt the first delicate flutterings of anxiety. There was something about the veil, something familiar....

A sound behind him, out on stairs leading up from the ground floor, disturbed his thought. He did not turn around at first but listened intently. It was a dull and rhythmic sloshy clumping, like the sound he would expect a deep-sea diver to make with his weighted boots as he moved through some kind of overgrown swampland.

Time to wake up. He looked down at Katherine's shape and saw that the bed was empty at her side.

The clumping grew louder.

He stared at the pulled back, hairy skin-duvet and then looked up again at the veil where the windows should be. The orange light showed it all exactly. It was like a patchwork quilt, only it wasn't made with material.

The clumping came nearer.

He recognized the small dark areas as hair. The lumps and holes were eye sockets and ears, boneless nose and empty fingers, limp toes and — he shook his head and felt the unmistakable warmth of urine between his legs.

His heart beating in his chest, he thrust his right hand beneath the covers.

The clumping was very near now.

His hand grabbed for his penis and...it wasn't there!

He leapt up from the bed into a standing position, ignoring the fact that the bed was surprisingly hard, like rock, and he screamed. Outside the bedroom, on the stairs, the clumping speeded up, louder and louder. He kept screaming, relishing the familiarity of his own voice, and turned to face the darkness where the bedroom door used to be. Something was moving toward him out of the gloom, getting nearer.

And now there was another sound, something calling to him, though not in any language that he knew. Nor was it a voice he recognized, if it was a voice at all.

He closed his eyes as if in prayer and pressed his hand tightly between his legs, silently mourning the loss of a close friend. There was a blinding light and then darkness.

Katherine's face shimmered above him, the familiar patterns of the bedroom wallpaper providing a comforting backdrop behind her head. He grunted and lifted himself up quickly, thrusting his hand down to his crotch to grab hold of his flaccid penis. He sighed and fell back when he felt it, turning the limp appendage around and around in his hand.

"Terry? Terry, what is *wrong* with you?"

"It was the dream again," he said simply. "But worse this time. This time I had no penis."

She rose up in front of him. "That's it," she said sharply. "That does it, Terry. I've had enough. You need help." Terry shuffled back onto the bed and winced when he sat in a cold wet patch. He clasped his hand to his chest and lifted it away immediately. It was sticky. He sniffed at his hand and almost gagged. It smelt sweet. He returned the hand to his penis and groaned. "The bed's all wet," he said.

"Yes, it's wet. It's wet because when I came in from making myself a cup of tea you were standing on the damned thing peeing all over the place."

He rolled over onto his side and curled his legs into a fetal position. "I'm tired," he said. And he went to sleep.

The following day began uneventfully with a silent breakfast, during which the usually attentive Katherine allowed him to see to himself, ensuring, with a minimum of fuss, that the two of them spent as little time as possible in the same room. As Katherine got into her car, Terry assured her that he would contact the doctor again. But this time he would insist on speaking to his own doctor. She waved a dismissive acknowledgment and drove off.

He never saw her again.

Terry rang the office and explained that he had had another bad night and that he would be in a little later than usual. It was his intention, he said, to try to catch up on a little sleep and come in around lunch time.

He cleared away the breakfast things and tidied the table. Then he went upstairs and had a long shower. The water felt good, hot and good, swilling away the memories of the previous night. He tousled his penis lovingly, soaping it until it was erect. He considered masturbating there in the shower but the thought of it made his chest hurt. Well, not his chest, actually, but rather his nipples. He looked down at them under the stream of water. Were they bigger? They felt bigger, both to the touch and also deep within him. When he had got out of his dressing gown to get into the shower, his chest hairs had all been matted and sticky, as if he had spilled something on them. But he had washed his chest well and now everything seemed as it should be.

Out of the shower, dried and shaved, Terry felt like a new man. Almost. He decided against going back to bed and instead put on the kettle for a cup of coffee while he dressed. But then it all caught up with him and he turned off the kettle and went up to bed without taking off his clothes. As he lay down, pulling the duvet around him, he failed to notice the two wet patches on his shirt front.

Sleep came immediately.

What awakened him he didn't know, but awake he was. Wide awake. And the orange light was there again.

Terry kept perfectly still and waited until his eyes adjusted to the gloom. As he lay there, now very aware of the rough and hard surface beneath him, he could hear the moans again. They were clearer now, more distinct. He was still curled up facing the bedroom door, only the bedroom door was no longer there. Now there was only blackness stretching away from him. Without moving, he lifted his eyes until he could make out the curve of the roof way overhead.

He moved his hand beneath the hairy skin which covered him and felt his trousers. His chest felt sore and heavy, but, more than that, it felt wet inside his shirt. He tried to keep his breathing slow and silent, but adrenaline was pumping around inside him so fast he fancied he could hear it swirling through his body like a swollen river. Without shifting the skin-cover, he moved his hand to the front of his trousers and felt for his penis. It wasn't there. "Oh, God," he whispered. This time was different. He knew that. This time there was nobody else in the house to break the dream. He had to escape. From what, he had no idea. He only knew that he had to escape.

But if Katherine was not in the house, then the bed should be empty. He pushed back with his left leg, feeling with his foot for some sign of another body lying next to him. There was nothing. At last, he turned over.

The room was misty.

No clock, no mantelpiece, no curtains, no wardrobe. Nothing that he could recognize as being his. Only strangeness. He looked to his side and saw that the bed was indeed empty. Over by the huge opening to the room the skin-veil shuddered and wafted softly. He sat up.

The moans seemed louder now, coming from all around him, and there was a smell of something dead or dying, like rancid meat or bad eggs. He looked around.

Shapes were moving on the floor, writhing and twisting. It was from them, he realized, that the moans emanated.

Terry pulled back the skin-cover and swung his legs out of the bed until he felt the floor. Then he stood up, maintaining a crouched position both to preserve his anonymity and also to be prepared for flight at the first sign of danger.

Each of the shapes was covered in its own hairy skin. He moved to the first one and lifted the cover gently. Beneath was what remained of a young man, a faint stubble on his chin and the light of madness shining from his eyes. The man let out a louder moan and, for a second, Terry was tempted to let the cover fall back; but he just shook his head and hissed, "Shhh!" The man's eyes focused on Terry and he stopped shaking his head. "Help me," he said.

Terry pulled the cover back fully and immediately bit hard into his bottom lip. The man's body was falling in on itself. His skin was intact but inside it there seemed to be little left of any substance. His head lay on a makeshift pillow constructed of more hairy skins. Below the head the man's neck traveled to a mound of skinfolds. He was completely naked. His arms lay outstretched beside him like empty arm-length gloves, the fingers curled and twisted and entirely incapable of any movement whatsoever.

His body, too, was devoid of filling. No ribs, no bones, no meat, no organs. Empty. From his chest extended the remains of two large breasts, spread out across his flattened stomach like cartoon condoms, their teats bitten off and ragged. And below all that carnage the *coup de grace* was a woolly patch of pubic hair, matted and slimy and smelling like an old runny cheese. There was no sign of a penis.

"Help me," the man hissed and, for a second, Terry thought he detected a slight movement in one of those flattened glove fingers. He dropped the skin back over the man, thanking whatever god was watching down on this place that it fell mercifully across his anguished face.

"Who's there?" whispered another voice.

"Help us." Another.

Yet another started to weep.

All around the floor the hairy skins were moving, though each one moved only where it might be covering a head.

Terry straightened up and stared hard into the blackness where once his landing and the sanctity of his toilet had waited. From way, way off came the sound of a bell.

At once the shapes beneath the skins began to wail, screaming pleas and curses, begging, screaming. "Quiet!" Terry hissed, but it came out more as a shout.

Ahead, in the blackness, something was moving toward him.

Terry spun around and hopped over the figures on the floor, past the foot of the bed he had just left toward the skin-veil. When he got to it, and actually started to reach out a hand, he cringed. The veil was indeed constructed from a series of human skins stitched together. Faces stared sightlessly through empty eyeholes, stitched onto a stomach or buttock. But it wasn't just the sight of the grisly curtain that made Terry's eyes water and his throat fill with bile. It was the smell. And it wasn't coming only from the skin quilt. It was coming from a large vat standing just outside the opening. Terry could see it through a ripped nipple that boasted a ragged hole so large you could have thrown a football through it. He pulled back the curtain and faced the brave new world.

It stretched into infinity, a torn and twisted orange landscape of upside down trees and smoking mountains. It was a land of nothingness.

Terry stepped fully outside and moved to the edge of the ledge he was standing upon. The ground was far, far below — too far and too steep to consider as a means of escape. He turned around and looked up. No exit there either. He took a step to the vat and peered over the rim.

Somehow he had known what would be in it. There were hundreds of them, all shapes and sizes and colors. And one of the ones on the top looked *very* familiar.

His scream was louder and more guttural than any sound issuing from a human being had any right to be. And it went on and on and on until he felt that he had completely drained himself of energy and sound and air.

Then he heard a movement from behind his back.

He spun around.

The thing stood its ground.

At first, Terry thought it was a huge balloon with two heads pasted onto the front. The faces watched him, the eyes burning into him. He broke his eyes from their stare and looked behind the thing, back into the cave. Trailing from where it now stood stretched a thick line of glistening drool. It had no feet and no other apparent means of propulsion. He looked back at it, shaking his head, and noticed that it had settled its bulk to the ground. Now it resembled a conical blimp of folds and creases, though the two heads still protruded.

And as its bulk had settled, the thing's insides had spread out so that different areas stuck out as whatever was behind pushed against the skin. Terry knew what those things were. They were bones. Nothing else mattered. Nothing else would exert any pressure.

Again Terry felt the warmth of wetness spreading down from his crotch. He lifted his hands to his shirtfront and began to undo the buttons.

Two huge breasts flopped out from within his shirt.
The thing lifted its mass to accept his offering.

He stepped slowly forward, lactating two fine mist sprays of milk into the orange air.

CIRCLE OF LIAS

Lawrence C. Connolly

Larry Connolly lives in Pennsylvania, posing as an English instructor at Sewickley Academy, a private secondary school. Actually, he is a fine writer of some of the most intensely textured psychological suspense we receive. If his first appearance in Borderlands 3 garnered him some deserved recognition, and tagged him as a writer to watch in the Nineties, then his currently offered "Circle of Lias" should solidify his status as a true craftsman. Plain and simple, this guy can write.

Sam Fric sat on the edge of a queen-size bed in the Coal Hollow Days Inn. On the bed across from him, Cloe sat tugging the tangles from Lisa's drying hair. Lisa winced at each tug of the plastic comb and her chin clenched beneath a big-toothed frown as she said, "Please, Dad — I'm *starved*!"

Cloe said, "It's not as if she's asking you for something big, Sam. Why don't you go and get the kid some honeybuns?"

Sam cradled his bristly chin in his hands. His palms felt like tanned leather. When he closed his eyes, he saw Route 80. "Listen," he said. "It's nearly midnight. The hotel kitchen is closed."

"Maybe there's a Dunkin' Donuts," said Lisa.

"Not in this town," said Sam.

"A bakery?" said Lisa

"We're in the country, honey. The middle of nowhere. I doubt there's anything open."

"There's a 7-Eleven," said Cloe.

"I don't think they'll have honeybuns," said Sam.

"You could look," said Lisa.

"Yes," echoed Cloe. "You *could* look! It's the least you could do after dragging us clear across the state for a worthless job interview."

"I didn't *drag* you," said Sam.

"No," said Cloe. "You're right. We made you take us. You never *drag* anything but your unambitious butt."

"I don't deserve that, Cloe."

"And I suppose you don't deserve being out of work." Cloe tugged the comb harder through Lisa's knotted curls while Lisa, who had grown used to the tugging, stared at Sam with imploring eyes.

Sam knew it was pointless to argue. He slid from the bed, sighing as he felt the restful support of the mattress fall away from his travel-weary butt. His car keys lay atop the TV, beside the pamphlet-size HBO program guide that he had been perusing while Cloe was helping Lisa with her shower. He had been hoping to stretch out on the bed and fall asleep while watching *Sister Act*, but now it didn't look as if he would be doing any reclining for a while. He scooped up the keys in his tired hand and headed for the door. Without looking back, he said, "Either of you want anything else?"

"No," said Cloe. "Just hurry."

"Yeah," said Lisa. "Hurry. I'm starved."

Sam left the room, pulling the door shut as he stepped into the door-lined hall. He jiggled the knob, making sure the door had locked. Then he walked on toward a middle-of-nowhere quest to satiate Lisa's honeybun jones.

As he approached the doors that led to the parking lot, he saw a large man struggling to drag a huge suitcase into the hall. The man looked up from his work as Sam neared the doors. Sam kept his face down, doing his best not to make eye contact as the man wiped his brow with the sleeve of his plaid jacket and said, "Hello, friend!"

Sam tried to keep moving, but the man side-stepped and extended a pudgy hand. Sam had no choice. He looked up.

The man's grin broadened into a smile. Thin lips rolled back to expose crowded teeth in puffy gums. "You here for the Circle, friend?"

"I'm sorry?" said Sam. He no longer said *excuse me*. For some reason, *I'm sorry* sounded much less confrontational — more sociologically correct. An out-of-work man on the interview circuit could never be too sociologically correct.

"Circle of Lias!" the man repeated. "I figured everyone in the hotel would be here for Circle of Lias."

"I don't know anything about Circle of Lias," said Sam. "I'm only here for the night."

"Still, it's good to know you."

They shook hands. Sam winced as he felt his fingers sink into the large man's doughy fist.

"My name's Parker — Parker Lewis," said the man as he pumped Sam's arm. "I'm staying in 317. That sweet lil' woman at the front desk told me 317 was the last empty room in the hotel. Guess I've got control of my reality." He winked. "How about you? How's your life loaf rising?"

Sam looked down from Parker's grinning face and found himself staring at a huge button on a wide, plaid lapel. Around the edge of the button, a circle of green letters proclaimed: I KNEAD MY LIFE LOAF AND LET IT RISE 'NEATH THE SWEET GAZE OF LIAS.

In the button's center, a swirling design formed what might've been a staring eye but which looked to Sam like the overhead view of a glazed honeybun.

"Listen," said Sam. "I don't want to be rude." He tried pulling his fingers free from Parker's doughy grip. "But I'm in a hurry. It's late, my daughter's hungry, and…"

Parker opened his hand. "Say no more, friend!" He heaved himself and his suitcase away from the door. "Got a daughter of my own, I do. Eight years old and — my, oh my! — does she love her sweets. Won't go to bed without a gooey snack. Rots her teeth but keeps her happy. Guess you know what I mean." Again, Parker winked.

"Yes," said Sam. He pushed through the door. "Nice meeting you, Parker."

"And nice meeting you, friend!"

Sam hurried through the crowded parking lot, toward the glowing 7 Eleven sign that stood at the far side of Route 322. A breeze swept between the rows of parked cars. The air smelled of approaching rain, and, as it whipped coolly about his face, Sam realized he was sweating. He wiped the sweat with his hand, and as he did his nostrils tingled with the unmistakable scent of honeybuns. The smell rose from his fingers — fingers that moments ago had struggled in the circle of Parker's grip.

Sam turned, looking back at the glass door that led from the parking lot to the rear entrance of the Days Inn. Beyond the glass, the cinderblock foyer sat empty in the flickering glow of a florescent bar. Parker and his suitcase had moved on. Just as well. Sam didn't feel up to listening to the fat man's circuitous directions to the nearest bun emporium. If the place were close by, Sam would find it on his own.

Sam's red Escort sat near the far end of the lot, a short distance from the quiet, four-lane highway that stretched between Interstate 80 and the sleepy town of Coal Hollow. Lisa's toys and books filled the Escort's back seat. An empty styrofoam cooler sat on its side beneath the glass of the hatchback door. Sam always underestimated the amount of food a family of three could consume on a weekend trip.

On the dashboard sat a map showing the way to Glennvale Country Day — a school that needed a computer teacher but wasn't interested in paying a living wage to a middle-aged man with industry expertise and three mouths to feed. If only the school's headmaster had quoted the pay scale before the Fric family had trekked across the state, the school might have saved itself and the Frics a lot of wasted time.

Sam leaned back against the Escort as he looked across the four lanes of asphalt that led to the false dawn of the cheery 7-Eleven sign. The store was too close to warrant driving, and the sweet, cool smell of the leafy, country night presented a welcome change from the stale styrofoam-and-cigarette smell of the Escort. Sam pocketed his keys and pushed on to the end of the lot. And it was then, as he approached the shoulder of 322, that Sam noticed the stickers that covered the bumpers, fenders, and rear windows of some of the cars. He read the stickers as he walked along.

I'M DRIVING 'NEATH THE SWEET
GAZE OF LIAS

FOLLOW ME TO THE CIRCLE OF LIAS TEMPLE
HOW'S YOUR LIFE LOAF RISING?

Along with the stickers, some of the cars sported license plates that read:

L EYE AS
LIAS 93
O OF LIAS

Finally, plastered to some of the rear windows were squares of clear acetate bearing the swirling eye logo that had first gazed at Sam from the button on Parker's plaid lapel.

Must be a religious thing, thought Sam as he stepped onto the smooth asphalt of the quiet, four-lane highway. A hundred feet down the far side of the road, the 7-Eleven sat like an oasis of light in the country night. He walked toward it.

Then it happened.

Blazing light raced up out of nowhere and splashed against his left shoulder. A racing engine roared into neutral. Brakes squealed on the dusty asphalt. Sam spun around as the shock of a blasting horn slammed his ears. Twenty feet away and closing, the bug-spattered grill of a small delivery van roared toward him.

Sam froze as the headlights flashed from low to high across his face. In his head, a disarmingly calm voice whispered, *You're gonna die.*

Above the headlights, Sam saw the silhouette of a driver frantically spinning the wheel. The image tilted as the van lurched to the left. Tires squealed. The van crossed the center line, missing Sam by inches while the driver screamed, *"Frickin' bastard!"*

The van swerved another hundred feet before the driver regained enough control to take a hand from the wheel and thrust it from the side window in an angry clench. Sam barely noticed the shaking fist. He did, however, notice the four letters that stretched across the van's two rear doors.

LIAS

Beneath the name, a honeybun eye stared back at him with swirling rage.

Sam hurried across the street. In the 7-Eleven lot, an old man in overalls and a striped engineer's hat stood pumping kerosene into a five-gallon drum. He turned his dried-apple face toward Sam and said, "Ought to look both ways."

But he *had* looked both ways, hadn't he? Running a trembling hand through his wind tossed hair, Sam distinctly remembered seeing that the road had been clear before he crossed…or at least he *thought* he remembered it that way. *God*, he thought to himself, *maybe I'm too tired to think*.

He walked past the fuel islands and stepped into the air-conditioned brilliance of the 7-Eleven. A burly man in bib overalls and a red vest stood by the coffee counter; he held a styrofoam cup in a gnarled hand. A young woman with big, honey-colored hair stood behind the cash register. Both people stared at Sam with eyes that said, *Ought to look both ways*.

Sam decided not to ask for help. If the place had buns, he'd find them. He started down the first aisle.

"Can I help you?" asked the woman at the register.

"Just looking," said Sam.

He found the baked goods section. Wonder Bread, Hostess cakes, Dolly Madison pies — no buns, honey or otherwise. He walked through the other aisles, making sure. He found nothing.

"Are you sure I can't help you?" said the woman at the register.

Sam looked at her as he returned to the door. "Are there any other stores around? Something like a Dunkin' Donuts or maybe an all night diner?" he asked.

"There's a diner down the road." A charm bracelet rattled on her wrist as she pointed south. "It's around the bend, maybe a quarter mile."

"Thanks," said Sam.

"Hope they got what you want," said the woman.

Sam stepped back into the breezy, country night.

The diner's flashing neon sign came into view a minute later as Sam walked quickly around the bend in 322. Beneath the sign, a half-dozen tractor trailer rigs surrounded the silver sides of a recycled train car. Behind the diner's square windows, men in baggy clothes drank coffee beneath a yellow, incandescent glow.

Since the diner stood on the far side of the road, Sam decided to cross while the asphalt was clear. He paused. He looked both ways. Then, to make sure he had looked both ways, he looked both ways again. The wide swatch of double-lined blacktop stretched clear in both directions. He set a foot upon the road...

Behind him a voice called, "Evening, friend!"

Sam turned.

The roadside scenery had changed behind his back. Where moments before there had been only a dark curtain of night, there now stood a large building fashioned from concrete slabs and plate glass. Near the building's front doors, five spotlights circled a wooden sign that rose from the center of an evergreen garden. The sign bore three words:

CIRCLE OF LIAS

Beneath the words, a swirling brown eye stared into the spotlights' glare.

Again, Sam heard the voice: "Nice night for a walk."

Sam fought back a rising sense of confusion. Like the cars that he had suddenly noticed in the Days Inn parking lot — and the racing van that had nearly killed him — the glass and concrete building had apparently materialized out of nowhere. Sam scanned the angular heap of concrete and glass, the evergreen garden, and the wide parking lot that surrounded the building. He saw no one.

Now I'm hearing voices.

No sooner had the thought formed in his mind than the building vanished back into darkness...

Then, with a flash of light, the building returned. No, *returned* was the wrong word. It hadn't *gone* anywhere. The lights surrounding the Circle of Lias sign had simply winked out, making the building seem to vanish behind a blanket of obfuscating darkness.

"Got a short somewhere," said the voice. "Can't seem to keep the lamps turned on. Pity too. The sign's a beauty, ain't she?"

Again, Sam looked around for the owner of the voice.

"You staying down at Days Inn?" asked the voice.

This time Sam saw the silhouette of a man sitting in the shadow of the garden's stone wall. The man wore a white shirt with sleeves rolled to the center of his forearms. His tie, knotted loosely about an unbuttoned collar, fluttered in the rising breeze as he stood and walked toward the road. "Guess you're here for the big doin's," said the man. "Should be a fine weekend, provided the sky gets the rain out of its system 'fore morning." He extended a pale hand. "I'm Friend Rawling. You?"

Sam shook Rawling's hand but, recalling Parker Lewis' doughy grip, quickly pulled his fingers free after a single, uneasy shake. "I'm only here for the night," said Sam.

"Just passing through."

Rawling flashed a winning smile. A gold incisor sparked in the spotlight's glow. "Now don't I feel a fool? When I seen you coming from the direction of the Days Inn, I figured you was a friend coming for a look at our new temple." He turned, looking back toward the square monstrosity of concrete and glass. "Ain't she a sweet, sweet vision?"

"Nice," said Sam.

"Had to build her," said Rawling. "We outgrew the old bakery. Got to the point where we had a fire hazard every Sunday."

"I'll bet," said Sam.

"Tell you what," said Rawling. "You got a minute, I'll give you a tour." He ran a hand along the blond fuzz on his crew cut. "You'll see it before most of the friends do. What say? You might even decide to join us for Sweet Saturday celebration tomorrow."

"Thanks," said Sam, "but I can't. I have to get back to the hotel. My wife and daughter are there. My daughter's waiting for a snack."

"I get it," said Rawling. "You was running over to the truck stop to get some buns for your honey."

"Honeybuns," said Sam. "My little girl's got a thing for honeybuns."

Rawling laughed. He turned his round face to the night sky and guffawed to the twinkling stars. "Don't we all!" he howled. He clapped his hands and wrung them together as if he were kneading dough. "Sweet, sweet vision — don't we all!" Then he reached out and clapped a hand on Sam's shoulder. "Your daughter's a friend and doesn't know it."

"I'm sorry?"

Rawling tightened his grip on Sam's shoulder. "Forget the truck stop. All they's got is day-old cinnamon swirls. If you want fresh buns," — he tugged Sam's arm, leading him back toward the concrete building — "you come to the right place."

"You have honeybuns?"

"Thousands!" said Rawling. "Sweet vision! It's Sweet Saturday Eve. Where'd we be without honeybuns on Sweet Saturday Eve?" Rawling's hand slipped beneath Sam's arm, and before Sam could protest he found himself being ushered to the back of the building where a small delivery van sat with its gated doors spread wide at the edge of a loading platform. Sam recognized the van. It was the one he had walked in front of not ten minutes ago.

The van's driver, who sat munching a roll on the edge of the platform, turned, swallowed a doughy wad, and said, "Evening, friend."

He recognizes me, thought Sam, and he stopped abruptly. He wrenched his arm free from Rawling's grip and said, "I really do have to get back to the hotel."

"I thought you wanted to see the facility," said Rawling.

"No, really," said Sam. "I have no interest at all. I'm just tired, and I want to get back..."

"A man must never get tired," said Rawling, raising an index finger toward the sky, as if the expression were a quote from somewhere. "Guard against the manipulating hands of exhaustion and hunger." He lowered his finger, waving it at Sam in admonition as he said, "Besides, you promised your daughter." He turned toward the driver. "Put some little sweets in a box for our friend."

The driver stood, popped the last chunk of bun into his mouth, and flashed Sam a sticky grin as he turned and walked into the back of the van.

Rawling looked at Sam. "It's more than coincidence, you know?"

"What is?" asked Sam.

"Your being here," said Rawling. His smile broadened as he looked into Sam's eyes. "Coincidence is a myth.

Our unconscious kneads reality; events rise to satiate secret hungers."

"I'm sorry?" said Sam.

"Only by examining the rising dough of existence can we truly understand our inner cravings."

Sam forced a smile. *Whatever you say*, he thought. He just wanted to get the buns and leave.

"Things have not been going well for you," said Rawling. "Your thoughts are troubled. Your life loaf won't rise. Events seem completely beyond your control. Am I right?"

"Things've been better," said Sam.

The driver returned from the back of the van. "Here you go, Friend Rawling." He handed down a small, white box from the loading platform. Rawling took the box.

"Your daughter will like these," said Rawling. "They're very small and soft as a wink. You want more, you come back tomorrow. Bring the family. We'll talk some more."

"Thanks," said Sam.

"No thanks needed," said Rawling.

A sudden flurry of movement from the van driver's hands caught Sam's attention. When Sam turned again toward the platform, the driver offered a lame, two-eyed wink and said, "Enjoy, *friend*."

Sam turned and hurried back to the snaking highway. The lights surrounding the Lias sign remained lighted; Sam's shadow walked before him until it faded with the bend in the road.

Anxiety and exhaustion filled Sam's mouth with a burning thirst by the time he powerwalked his way back to the glowing 7-Eleven. He decided to duck inside for a bottle of spring water — something wet and unflavored to quench his thirst.

The burly man still stood beside the steaming coffee pots; a styrofoam cup of fresh coffee steamed in his cracked and oiled hands. The honey-haired woman had the register open. She was clearing the drawer of excess tens and twenties and stuffing them into a narrow slot in the top of a night safe as Sam entered the store. She looked up as the jingling door opened and closed. "Back again?" she said.

Sam nodded and walked to the back of the store where bottles and cans stood on refrigerated racks behind thick, glass doors.

"Can I help you this time?" said the woman.

"Water," said Sam.

"There's seltzer by the milk."

"Something *without* bubbles," said Sam.

"You mean like *ordinary* water?"

"Yeah," said Sam. "Plain, ordinary water." He walked through the aisles, checking the shelves in the rest of the store.

"I got a faucet," said the woman. "Get yerself a cup by the coffee. I'll give you faucet water."

The burly man watched as Sam pulled a ten ounce cup from the dispenser.

"What's in the box?" said the man. He spoke in a strangely high falsetto and it caught Sam off guard.

"I'm sorry?" said Sam.

"The box," chirped the man. "What's in the box?"

Sam looked down at the box that he now carried tucked under his arm. "Oh," he said. "Buns…Honeybuns." He handed the cup to the woman at the register. She stepped into a back room. Sam heard water rattle into a metal sink.

"Is that what you went to the diner for?" asked the man.

"Yes," said Sam.

The woman returned with the water.

"Only problem is," said the man, "the truckstop diner down the road don't sell no honeybun."

Outside, a flashing police cruiser raced down 322.

"I didn't get them from the truck stop," said Sam. He gulped the water and set the cup down on the counter.

To the woman, the man said, "If I were you, Kate, honey, I'd have a look in that there box. I think I seen him drop something inside it when he was checking out your sodas."

"Aw *fercrysake*!" said Sam. "You saw nothing of the kind."

The woman bit the corner of her lower lip.

"I know what I saw," said the man. "You put something in there." He turned to Kate. "Have a look, honey girl. You'll see."

Kate's charm bracelet rattled as she reached across the counter. "You mind, mister?"

"Hell, no!" Sam tossed the box on the counter. "Look for yourself. It's buns, is all. I got them from that Lias place up the street."

Kate opened the lid. She looked inside. Her face blanched. She swallowed hard, looked nervously up at Sam, and then dropped the box as she whispered, "Oh, my God!"

"What?" said Sam.

"It's like I said, ain't it?" said the man. "He stole something, right?"

Kate shook her head. She wouldn't look at Sam. She wouldn't look at the box. She stared at the burly man and said, "Not from no 7-Eleven, he didn't."

That did it. Sam grabbed the box, slamming the lid back into place as he shoved it back beneath his arm. "I'm sorry!" he said. "Play your chickenshit games with someone else. I'm out of here."

He shoved his way through the door, back into the cool, country night. This time he had to wait on the edge of the road while a white van with a satellite dish on its roof and a staring Eyewitness News logo on its side panel raced by.

Evidently something big was going on in Coal Hollow.

Three more cars passed. Sam waited for the road to clear, then he hurried across. Halfway to the hotel, he heard something thump on the box beneath his arm. When he looked down he saw the gray star of a smashed raindrop on the closed lid. A second later, he felt a drop on his head. Then two more drops struck his shoulder...

He ran through the parking lot. By the time he reached the hotel, the night thundered with teeming rain. He threw himself against the hotel's rear door, grabbed the handle, pulled.

"Dammit to hell!"

It was locked.

Pasted to the glass beside the handle, a small sticker read:

USE MAIN ENTRANCE AFTER MIDNIGHT

"What luck!"

He leaned against the glass. Overhead, an eighteen inch overhang fanned the teeming rain into a cascading waterfall that sheeted down inches from his face. He pushed his rain-soaked hair back from his eyes and decided to wait for the rain to let up before heading for the main entrance.

Five minutes later, the rain showed no signs of letting up. He decided to wait a little longer. After all, it couldn't keep pouring forever. He leaned against the cold glass and stared out at the rain.

Lightning flashed overhead, slashing the night into fragments of light and dark. Thunder exploded. On 322, an ambulance screamed toward Coal Hollow; streaming water broke like surf beneath its front tires as it sped past the 7-Eleven.

Another five minutes passed. Sam decided he'd waited

long enough. He cradled his box of buns in his arms and charged into the storm.

Ages later, he reached his room.

The door stood ajar. He pushed it open.

"Okay, ladies. Dad's home. Don't all cheer at once."

Nobody cheered.

Sam walked past the dark bathroom and into the main chamber where the television played to an open flightbag, a suitcase, and a set of folded clothes. Cloe and Lisa were gone.

He set the wet box of honeybuns on the dresser and sat down to wonder what had happened. Maybe mother and daughter had gotten tired of waiting. Maybe they'd convinced the night manager to open the restaurant. Maybe....

Something on the television caught Sam's attention. A grim-faced anchorwoman with big hair and full lips was saying, "...an unidentified woman and young girl found mutilated in the shadow of the Circle of Lias Temple in Coal Hollow. Suzanne Forester is on the scene with a live report."

Sam felt slow tingles spread through his neck, shoulders, and chest.

A woman and a young girl?

Sam looked around the empty room while the scene shifted on the television screen.

Cloe? Lisa?

On the television screen, red and blue emergency lights flashed across rain-slick asphalt while policemen and paramedics crowded around the rear gates of an ambulance. In the corner of the screen, the Circle of Lias sign blazed in front of a concrete and glass building. In the foreground, a wide-eyed reporter clutched a microphone and said, "I'm here in Coal Hollow in the shadow of the Circle of Lias Temple where an unidentified woman and a child have been found brutally murdered. Their bodies were discovered a short time ago by Friend John Rawling, the pastor of the Circle of Lias Temple."

She turned. The camera panned. Beside her, Rawling's crew cut head crouched beneath a black umbrella. Speaking to Rawling, Suzanne Forester said, "Can you tell us what you found, Reverend?"

"Wasn't really me, Miss Forester. I didn't really find the bodies. The person who found them was one of our volunteers who was walking home after helping decorate our temple for Sweet Saturday. He found them lying on the shoulder about five hundred feet from the temple."

"And that's when he came and got you?"

"That's right, Miss Forester," said Rawling. "And, Miss Forester...I'd just like to say that people shouldn't associate this terrible thing with the temple here. The bodies were discovered on a state road — on route 322 — and not on Circle of Lias property."

"Tell us what you saw when you looked at the bodies, Reverend Rawling."

Rawling turned toward the camera. His deep brown eyes stared straight through the television screen — straight into the hotel room where Sam sat between the open flightbag and the pile of folded clothes. "It was a terrible thing, Suzanne. That poor, poor mother and child — they were mutilated." He winced and, as his thin lips rolled back, Sam saw a brief flash of gold. "They were lying side by side on the oily gravel. They were lying on their backs and" — he rubbed the fuzz on the top of his head — "their eyes had been gouged out. And in the holes, in the sockets where the eyes should've been, someone had dropped little, tiny honeybuns."

Cloe? Lisa? Sam's racing thoughts seemed to whisper the names to the empty room.

The camera panned back to Suzanne Forester. She

gripped the microphone, visibly shaken as she stared into the camera and said, "As of yet, the police will not say if they have a suspect or motive for this bizarre double murder. They have indicated, however, that the night manager at a nearby 7-Eleven reported seeing a suspicious individual — a person who entered her store with a box containing *four human eyes*."

Sam's gut knotted.

The reporter went on: "The individual — a haggard-looking, white male in his late thirties or early forties — was in her store less than half an hour ago. Police assure us that a full search is currently underway." She paused, drew a deep, composing breath before saying, "This is Suzanne Forester for Eyewitness News, reporting live from the Circle of Lias Temple in Coal Hollow."

Sam looked over at the dresser and the soggy box that he had carried back with him from the Circle of Lias Temple. He felt numb. Specks of light streaked like shooting stars in the corner of his vision. His fingers trembled as he reached out, took hold of the box, drew it toward him, and raised the lid.

There they were. Small and brown. *Soft as a wink*, Rawling had said. But Rawling had been talking about honeybuns, not eyes — and these things in the box were very definitely eyes: four brown eyes staring every which way from their bed of bloody tissue paper. Four eyes — two large and two small — each trailing long, gray threads of optic nerve.

A scream rocked the room. Sam snapped the lid shut and stood motionless beside the bed while the scream's echo faded into the carpeted floor and the tiled ceiling. He swallowed and felt a burning rawness in his throat, and only then did he realize that the scream had been his own.

Gotta move. Gotta do something!

He crossed the room. He slammed the door, engaged the bolt, and stumbled into the bathroom. He raised the toilet lid and dumped the eyes into the bowl. *Boink, boink, boink, boink*! Each eye rolled pupil up as it landed; they watched Sam as he wrenched the lever that flushed the commode.

Police are looking for a man with a box of eyes. Gotta get rid of the eyes. Get rid of the box.

The commode cycled. One of the eyes did a loop-the-loop in the churning water and bounced back into the refilling bowl. The eye stared at Sam as the pipes hissed with returning water. Sam shredded the blood-soaked tissue paper from the bottom of the box. He dropped the pieces into the water, letting them fall like ragged flakes of stained snow. Again he flushed the toilet. Again the eye tumbled in the slugging current at the bottom of the bowl before popping back up with the rising water. It stared at him. It was one of the smaller eyes. The child's eye.

Hurry, dad!

"Damn you," said Sam.

The eye bobbed.

Sam unbuttoned his right cuff and rolled the sleeve to his elbow. He dipped his hand into the water and shoved the eye to the bottom of the bowl. Again he flushed.

In the other room, the phone started ringing.

Water gurgled through Sam's fingers and the eye rattled against his palm before it caught the current and rode the gurgling water down into the sewery depths.

He withdrew his wet hand and crushed the box into a ball.

The phone continued ringing.

Sam pressed the smashed box between his hands, squeezing it until it resembled a battered softball. *Too big,* he thought as he turned the ball over in his dripping hand. *No way this baby's gonna flush.*

He stuffed the wadded box into the bottom of the wastebasket. He filled the basket with toilet paper. Then he stood, turned off the bathroom light, shut the bathroom door, and stepped into the bedroom.

The phone between the queen-size beds kept on ringing.

He crossed the room and grabbed the ringing phone in his damp, right hand. He raised the handset and pressed the earpiece to his ear.

A voice said, "Hello, friend."

It was the Reverend, Friend John Rawling.

Sam's knees weakened. His butt crashed down onto the folded clothes on the bed.

Sam coughed. "What the hell?"

"You see the news?" asked Rawling.

"I saw it."

"Then you know what's happened," said Rawling. "What you don't know is that the cops know who did it. They didn't want to spill everything to the folks at Eyewitness News, but they filled me in, and that's why we've got to talk."

"No," said Sam. "This is bullshit. I only know what I saw on the news. I don't know anything else, I swear!"

"Take it easy, friend. I know you're in the dark on this, but you're involved all the same. See, it was my delivery driver what murdered those two. What a sweet shame! They were his own wife and daughter?"

Sam felt the room spin about him. He swallowed and croaked, "The van driver?" he said. "*His* wife and daughter?"

"Yeah," said Rawling. "The police figure he'd been carting them around in our van for nearly an hour before he dumped their bodies on the side of the road. He must've dumped them right before he made our delivery. Darn fool drove up the road about 500 feet, pitched the bodies out the back, and then circled around to make his delivery. It's the strangest thing, ain't it? You work with a guy for months and you never suspect he's a psycho. Did you look in the box he gave you?"

"Oh, Christ!"

"I guess you did," said Rawling. "Look, friend, I'm sweetly sorry about all of this, but you got to do one thing for me."

Someone knocked on the door.

"The cops are on their way to see you," said Rawling. "They'll be knocking on your door any minute. Figuring out who you were wasn't tough. You're about the only man in that Days Inn who isn't part of our Lias block."

Again the door rattled with the thunder of an impatient fist.

"The cops," said Rawling, "they got a box of honeybuns for you and your family. All you got to do is give the cops the box with the eyes. They need it for evidence. You got that, friend? You hear me?"

The fist on the door hammered louder.

"Oh, Christ!" said Sam

"I'm sorry as all get out that you got mixed up in this, friend. I know it's small consolation, but I'd like to put you and your family on the sweet list for tomorrow's offering. All I need is names."

"Names?"

"The people in your family," said Rawling. "So I can put them on the sweet list."

"Cloe and Lisa," said Sam.

"Last name?"

"Fric," said Sam. He spelled it for Rawling while the fist on the door hammered louder.

"Well, I'll be raptured," said Rawling. "Don't this beat all!"

"What?"

"Those names — *Cloe, Lisa,* and *Fric.* You realize those names make a perfect anagram for *Circle of Lias.* Sweet vision!"

The door exploded with more knocking.

"Is that someone at your door?" said Rawling. "Better get it. Probably the police. Just give them the box of eyes. Goodbye, friend. Sweet blessings!"

The line went dead.

Sam got up and performed a weak-kneed walk to the apartment door. Maybe the cops would understand.

He threw back the bolt and opened the door.

Four angry brown eyes stared in at him.

"Jeez," said Lisa. "Don't lock us out or anything!" She wore a blue bathrobe over her nightgown. Her slippered feet stomped over the threshold as she hurried past Sam and entered the room. "Did you get my honeybunnies?" she asked.

Cloe stared at Sam. "Where the hell did you go?" she asked.

"I was looking for honeybuns."

"Where'd you go? Bangkok?" said Cloe. She pushed past Sam, following Lisa into the room. "We got tired of waiting, so we went out to look around the hotel. Some organization's having a reception in the ballroom. They have honeybuns, but Lisa didn't like them."

"Too dinky!" shouted Lisa. She formed a tight loop with her thumb and index finger to show Sam how small the honeybuns were. "Mommy said they looked like little turds and she was right." Lisa turned in place, scanning the room. "So where are they, Dad? Did you get me some buns or what?"

Sam felt something snap inside him. "Pack up!" he bellowed. "We're getting out of here."

Cloe fixed him with a wide-eyed stare. "You can't be serious."

He ignored her. He crossed the room, grabbed the handful of smashed and folded clothes that lay on the bed beside the phone, and stuffed them into the open flightbag.

Lisa looked up at him in disbelief. "Mommy," she said, "I think Dad's gone a little," — she twirled a finger beside her head — "you know?"

He zipped the flightbag. He grabbed the suitcase. "Come on," he said as he hurried past Cloe and Lisa. "We're out of here."

"What about the stuff in the bathroom?" said Cloe.

Sam's determined gait faltered as he reached the door. He turned, looking back at Cloe. "Excuse me?" he said. "What *stuff* in the bathroom? What the hell are you talking about?"

"My shampoo. My blow dryer. My curling iron, *fercrysake*!"

Oh, that stuff. A shiver of relief rushed through Sam as he regained control and barked, "Leave 'em!"

To Lisa, Cloe said, "I think you're right, honey — I think he's flipped."

The rain had stopped.

They piled into the car. Sam gunned the engine. The radio, which had been cranked up for highway driving, screamed to life in the quiet night:

"...accused in the brutal death of his wife and daughter..."

Click! Sam killed the sound with an angry flick of his wrist.

"Why would anyone kill his wife and daughter?" asked Lisa.

Sam let out the clutch. The Escort lurched from its parking space. Sam spun the wheel, steering toward the exit that led onto Route 322.

"You haven't even returned the room key," said Cloe. "They'll bill you for it, you know."

"They won't," said Sam.

"Don't sound so sure," said Cloe.

"I am sure," said Sam. Tires squealed as he weaved

between the rows of cars. "I'm in control," he said. The words Rawling had spoken less than an hour ago came back to him. "I'm kneading my reality," he said.

"You ask me," said Cloe, "you're needing a psychiatrist."

Sam glared at her. Their defiant gazes met and locked.

Lisa shoved her head between the front seats. "You guys fighting again or..." Breath hitched in her throat as she saw something move beyond the windshield. "Dad!" Her arm shot between the seats. Her finger pointed toward the road. "Dad...Dad...*you'll hit him!*"

Sam turned toward the windshield in time to see the blunt hood of his racing Escort slam into a policeman who had just stepped out from the row of parked cars. The impact resounded through the tiny Escort. The man screamed as he rolled across the hood and down the left fender. The look on his face as his cheek skidded down the corner of the windshield was one of total surprise. He simply hadn't seen the Escort coming.

"Sam, you idiot!" said Cloe. "*Your lights aren't on!*"

A white box slid from the policeman's grip. The lid flew open. Its contents pelted the windshield like tiny turds.

"Honeybuns!" shrieked Lisa.

Sam floored the gas and sped from the parking lot while Cloe glanced back through the hatchback window. "Dammit, Sam! Stop the car!"

"It's okay," said Sam. "I'm in control. I can fix it. I can make it like it never happened."

The imprints of a dozen honeybuns glazed his windshield. The swirled outlines looked like glazed eyes. Sam squeezed the lever that activated the washer fluid. Then he snapped on the wipers. The glazed eyes vanished as he spun onto Route 322. Up ahead, the highway stretched like a clean slate.

"I feel very good about this," said Sam.

"You're out of your fucking mind," said Cloe.

Sam turned on his headlights and flicked his high beams. "I feel my life loaf rising. I feel like I'm driving 'neath the sweet gaze of Lias."

MISADVENTURES IN THE SKIN TRADE

Don D'Ammassa

Being a voracious reader is one of the prerequisites for becoming a writer. If total number of volumes read means anything, then Don D'Ammassa is headed for The List. His book reviews appear in genre newsletters with great frequency. He lives in Providence, Rhode Island (home of H. P.), where he recently lost his twenty-three-year gig as a manufacturing executive. His recent success in short fiction with sales to Hottest Blood, Shock Rock, Deathport, Pulphouse, *and* The Ultimate Zombie *is no doubt highly correlated to his lack of a job. Good for you, Don.*

Someone stole my skin the other day. I know how that must sound, but it's the simple truth. They were clever though, replacing it with a substitute that was so close it fooled me for a while. But not for long. I mean, how much more intimately can you know anything than your very own skin? It's not like clothing, for Christ's sake!

Sorry. I didn't mean to lose control there, but you have to admit it's an unsettling thing to discover that your body is covered with something foreign, a synthetic of some kind, perhaps, or in this case a stranger's skin. How's that for a disgusting thought? Would you want something like that wrapped tightly around your flesh? No, I didn't think so. So maybe you can understand how I feel about it.

I have to concede I was fooled for a while, even though I noticed some inconsistencies first thing that morning. It's not the kind of conclusion you accept readily, though, and I made excuses. Perhaps I had just never noticed the small blemish on the right thigh and that fresh scratch on my side...I could have done that with a fingernail in my sleep.

There were other clues that I chose not to recognize. When Marie walked out, years ago now, she complained that I thought more of my own body than I did of hers. It did no good to point out that unless she began to take adequate care of herself, she would never regain the firm muscle tone, proper ratio of weight to height, or that wonderfully clear complexion which had attracted me to her in the first place. I myself had not varied more than a few pounds from my base weight in over a decade, and I examined my body constantly for signs of imperfection.

But on that late summer morning following the theft of my skin, there was a thin but unmistakable finger's width of loose flesh around my waist.

Still I failed to recognize the implications, assuming instead that I had been lax in my exercises or perhaps had slipped into unhealthy eating habits. This latter explanation seemed even more credible when I discovered a cluster of small dark spots on my nose, infected pores, and by the time I had thoroughly cleaned them and applied a disinfectant, my nose was as red as a drunkard's and as painful as a prizefighter's. Resolving to ruthlessly re-examine both my diet and my training routine that evening, I set off to work mildly concerned but not yet aware of the true nature of my condition.

The feeling that something was subtly wrong persisted all day. I've worked the same position on the assembly line for four years now, and I've trained my body to work as a piece of the machinery. The rhythms are a part of me as I am a part of them, and every flexing muscle, every twist of elbow and wrist, each individual stretch of skin over flesh is predictable and familiar. But not that morning.

I couldn't quite put my finger on it at first. I had fallen into the routine as always, three connections on the left, three on the right, rotate the unit, check the solder joint, rotate again, fasten the clip, arms back while the unit shifted to the next station and a new one offered itself. More than a thousand times I had merged with the operation smoothly, without a moment's hesitation. But that morning, it felt wrong, the kinesthetics were different, not enough to interfere with my performance of the work required but enough to put my nerves on edge. I've always been proud of my self-discipline, the way I've trained my body to respond instantly to everything I ask of it. If we aren't captains of our own bodies, how can we expect to control the world around us?

I was troubled throughout the day and distracted on the drive home. My work clothes went into the hamper: I never wore the same set more than once without washing them. Then my usual thorough shower, starting with my hair, which had grown to be nearly an inch long. Time for a trim. Three applications of shampoo and a rinse, then a thorough scrubbing with a stiff-spined brush followed by a final shampoo. Then my face, concentrating on my nose this time. I had installed a mirror on the shower wall years before, but it rarely proved effective, the image obscured by rising steam as quickly as I could clear it away. But I used it this time, concentrating to make certain there'd been no recurrence of the invading blackheads I'd discovered that morning.

Other than that, I kept to my routine: ears, back of the neck, then throat and chin. I scrubbed myself until the flesh was warm and glowing and the sense of wrongness started to recede. Chest and armpits and navel, shoulders and back and waist. The superfluous flesh at my midriff was still there and still worrisome, but I was confident that I could work it off in a few days.

I was tempted as always to quickly pass over my genitals, the weakest and least perfect part of the male body, but as usual I forced myself to overcompensate and lather them thoroughly, scrubbing vigorously enough that my breath became sharp and ragged. I shaved myself once a week to facilitate this process, but there were so many folds of flesh that might conceal infections or other unpleasantness, I was never completely satisfied that my efforts were complete.

Just below my left knee, I discovered a tiny, tear-shaped scar. I almost passed it by. It was faint, an absence of feature rather than a blatant disfigurement. It wasn't fresh, had in fact entirely healed. But I had never seen it before, never once in the forty years I had lived in this body.

I forced myself to eat, carefully measuring the portions, even though I had little appetite. Dressed in loose-fitting pants and sleeveless shirt, I cleared away the dishes and walked thoughtfully down to the exercise room in the basement, spent the next two hours following my established pattern, pushing each group of muscles to their limit, then slightly beyond. The routine helped to suppress the growing sense of uneasiness, shift it temporarily into some recess of my mind where I could pretend that everything was normal.

Of course you know I was fooling myself, but it's easy to judge things like this from the outside, a lot more difficult to accept that someone has violated the sanctity of your most precious possession, your body itself.

I would normally have showered again, just a warm rinse this time, but as soon as I stopped, those nagging doubts returned. So I chose instead to jog for a while, even though it was already dark outside. There's a heavily wooded area threaded with paths just a block from my house — not the safest place even in the daylight — but I wasn't afraid of being attacked. There were far easier victims available and I'd never had any trouble with the scruffy punks who frequented the area.

Moving at a carefully regulated pace, I ran north until I reached the housing project, then looped back on a narrower path, one so nearly overgrown that I was forced to use my bare arms to fend off stray branches. When the parkway lights were visible to the west, I changed routes again, angling southward, knowing I would eventually cross the paved footpath that led fairly directly back toward my house. I'd never run out here in the dark before and found it somewhat disorienting, but the forested area wasn't so extensive that there was any real chance I might lose my way.

Back home, I stripped and showered, was toweling myself dry when I found the rash. It wasn't much of one, just a thin streak of red spots along my right forearm, almost certainly an allergic reaction to something I had brushed away from my face. The only problem with that was I had never suffered from any allergies in the past. My skin was tough and resilient and resistant to irritation, just like the rest of my body.

That's when I realized I was wearing someone else's skin.

You might expect that I would have become frantic when faced with the truth, but actually I grew quite calm. Now that I had an explanation for the bizarre inconsistencies that had been showing up all day and knew that they were not signs of my own weakness — the loss of tight body control — but actually the result of a hostile act, I felt a sense of relief and prepared to deal with the situation.

Naturally my first thought was to wonder who was responsible, and why. I didn't have any real enemies, at least not since Marie walked out on me, so it wasn't malice. That left envy. Perfectly understandable, of course: everyone who knew me envied my body, the men anyway. Women admired it as well, but they just wanted to use it for their own pleasure, in ways that would weaken me. Marie had been different, at least when we first married; it was only later that she began making irrational demands, insisting that there was something wrong with using our bodies only for healthy, life-affirming purposes.

I was actually quite relieved when she finally left.

But once the motive was understood, the number of potential thieves became bewilderingly high. There was no one I knew whose body could even begin to approach my own hard-won perfection, and, frankly, I doubted that any of them would be able to substantially improve their situation just by draping themselves in my skin. But jealousy is an irrational emotion, independent of logic.

Using a yellow lined pad, I quickly made a list of every male I could think of. It had to be a man, of course. Then I put check marks next to the ones who were closest to me in size, although I made the marks darker for those who bulked a bit more than me, mindful of the misfit at my waist. There were a half-dozen prime candidates and I copied those names onto a second sheet, arranged in order of probability, based on my intuition. One of these men was almost certainly responsible, although there were a few others on my original list whom I could not completely rule out. The thought that it might be a complete stranger, someone who had watched me secretly and waited for a chance to strike, was disturbing, and I decided that if that unlikely explanation was the correct one, there was little I could do about it. It was far more likely that the man responsible was known to me, however, and I proceeded on that assumption.

Although I was impatient to act, it was impractical until the next day, a Friday. Two of my top candidates worked at Eblis, though not in my department. I would need to be circumspect. It was necessary to identify the guilty party without letting on that I knew of the switch.

I was able to eliminate Ned Sanders before the shift started, disappointing since I'd placed him at the top of my list. He was having a cigarette in the cafeteria, in violation of the posted rules, and I regretted the necessity of approaching closely enough that I would have to breathe that polluted air. Sanders was almost exactly my size, but soft, unseasoned. He was shop steward and the company always managed to find a way to assign him the less strenuous jobs: spot inspection, cycle counting, things like that. He saw me coming, turned slightly in my direction.

"Morning, Dougherty. How're they hanging?"

I was inured to Sanders' language, which was so peppered with obscenities that he has twice been reported to the shift supervisor by women working the line. Although I really hoped that he was the one I was after, I realized the impossibility of that when he raised his arm to wave at me. Sanders had a vulture tattooed on the inside of his left forearm.

Eric Nicholson was my third choice, and he worked the day shift here at Eblis, so I went looking for him at lunch time. He's kind of young, but the right size, even keeps himself in pretty good shape although his posture is bad and I've heard that he drinks. It was hot in the cafeteria and a lot of people took their lunch outside, ate it sitting on the grassy slope that faced the cemetery.

He was there all right, lying off by himself in a patch of sunlight with his shirt off. I couldn't have asked for a better chance. With one arm across his eyes to shut out the light, he didn't even see me standing there, staring down at him.

What I could see of his skin was tanned, smooth, and firm, and I experienced a sense of familiarity. There were some minor inconsistencies, but I figured whatever process had allowed him to switch his skin for mine couldn't have been absolutely perfect. Perhaps it dried out a little while in transit. The skeleton and muscles underneath had to be at least slightly different in configuration, and that would change the distribution of tautness and wrinkles, at least until the skin had a chance to adjust to its new platform. No scars, no tattoos, and the small scrape mark on his elbow was fresh, might have been done since the transfer.

I couldn't be certain, but it seemed likely Nicholson was responsible. Now all I had to do was recover my property.

Nicholson lived alone, a small rundown house in one of the older sections of Managansett. I'd driven him to work a time or two when his car was in for repairs and although I didn't remember the exact address, when I drove through the neighborhood after work that afternoon, I identified it easily. It was set all by itself at the rear of a lot cluttered with untrimmed shrubs, mock orange, rosebushes, lilacs, and forsythia. There'd be no difficulty approaching the house unseen once darkness fell.

I drove home thoughtfully, planning my attack.

For the most part, everything went quite well. I returned after midnight, parking several blocks away, then reached Nicholson's backyard by a roundabout route, easily avoiding the widely spaced streetlights that futilely attempted to bring a sense of security to the neighborhood. His doors were locked but almost all of the ground floor windows were open to the night air. I slipped inside so quietly I wondered if I had missed my calling in not taking up burglary.

The penlight in my pocket was unnecessary. A lamp was still glowing in the front room, a short neon tube buzzed over the kitchen sink. There were two bedrooms, both with their doors open, one piled high with junk, tools, furniture, boxes filled with off season clothing, even some canned goods. Nicholson was asleep in the other, sprawling naked on his stomach diagonally across the bed. Almost as if he knew I'd be coming and wanted to make it easier for me.

I regretted the necessity to damage my stolen skin but by using the wrench to crush the top of his skull, I figured most of the incidental damage would be concealed under my hair. I might have to let it grow longer in the future, but I'd just increase the number of times I shampooed it to compensate. When I was quite sure that he had stopped breathing, I turned on the bedroom lights.

Obviously Nicholson had used some more subtle technique, since he had managed his theft without assaulting me. He'd have been wiser to finish me off, but I imagine he was smugly convinced that I'd never notice the difference or, if I did, that I'd be unable to figure out the identity of the guilty party.

I went outside and retrieved the ice chest I'd left below the window. Nicholson's methods were clearly more efficient than mine, but I didn't have time to try to figure out how he'd done it. The longer my skin spent on his body, the less likely I was to retrieve it before serious damage had been done. It was a futile effort on his part, when you think about it. Sure, for the time being he'd reap the benefits of my years of discipline and conditioning, but unless he gave up his own lax ways and poor habits, deterioration would be inevitable and he'd be no better off than before. Then I realized that logically he would strike again, find a new skin to replace the old, had perhaps already gone through this same routine in the past. I had not felt any remorse when I killed him. I mean, considering the depraved nature of his crime against me, he deserved no better. But add to that the possibility...no, the probability that I was saving many others from a similar fate. Why, in a sense, I was serving the community as well as myself, destroying a monstrous wolf lurking unsuspected among the sheep.

His skin came off quite readily under the flensing knife. I took this as further proof of his guilt; the tissues had not completely reknitted themselves. After washing it off in the shower stall, I carefully folded my skin, wrapped it in cellophane, and buried it in the shaved ice, now rapidly melting into a chilly slush. It will probably involve some experimentation to put things right, so I have returned to my own place where I can work undisturbed.

I'm writing this all down in case anything goes wrong, so that there will be a record, a warning, something to alert the rest of you to the danger. I can't believe Nicholson was an isolated case; there must be others like him preying on the innocent. Those facelifts that actors and politicians have, the ones that are so unbelievably effective — at least some of those are probably excuses to cover up what has really happened.

There's no doubt in my mind that I will be able to reattach my skin. I took measurements to be certain, but there wasn't really time for it to shrink or stretch unnaturally, though I suppose it might be uncomfortable at first. Marie left behind her sewing basket, so I have needles and plenty of thread to close the seams. No, I don't expect to have any great difficulty with that part.

It's cutting Nicholson's alien skin off my body beforehand that poses the challenge.

WATCHING THE SOLDIERS

Dirk Strasser

We next offer a tale of universal truth and heartfelt emotion. It also serves very nicely as a timeless fable. Dirk Strasser is an Australian writer who has captured the ambiance of Eastern Europe in a story of extraordinary power.

They first appeared at the time of the golden skies. Mikhael saw them marching across the cloudless heavens: bright skins glinting like frosted glass, feet flashing in buoyant rhythm with each step, and hair flowing like filaments of sunlight. And by their sides marched great beasts with scales of rich leather and eyes like soft golden flames, beasts with powerfully muscled bodies and gentle faces. Although the marchers seemed as impossibly distant as stars, Mikhael felt the soft breeze of their breaths on his face, and he heard their strange, incomprehensible call filtering through the air.

"Who are they?" Mikhael cried. Adam would know. Adam was, after all, his older brother, and he had been working a man's day in the fields for as long as Mikhael could remember.

"Soldiers," said Adam, pulling back on the plough reins so that the horse would stop. "There is war and the enemy threatens our border."

"Where is the border?" asked Mikhael, shielding his eyes so that he could see the soldiers more clearly.

"I don't know," said Adam. "A long way away. Father has been there. He will tell you."

"And the enemy — who are the enemy?"

"Little brother, they are not men like us."

"But I am not a man," interrupted Mikhael.

"No," said Adam, thinking for a moment, "but you will grow into one. And when you do, you will be different to the enemy."

"How?"

"Mikhael, you ask too many questions sometimes. The soldiers are there above us, and all you can do is ask questions. Isn't it enough that they are there?"

Mikhael held his breath until he became giddy. He knew it was the only way he could stop himself from asking something else. Adam didn't like too many questions. He preferred to work quietly in the fields, to show their father at the end of a long day what he had achieved, and to sleep soundly at night. Mikhael liked to spend the early mornings in his mother's kitchen and his afternoons roaming his father's farm: the creaky old barns, the rust-colored haystacks. Most of all he liked exploring the pockets of woodland which surrounded the farm, climbing the gnarled ancient trees, and finding dark places to hide and to think about new questions. He knew he was different to his older brother. At nights, when Mikhael tossed and turned, when thoughts and unanswered questions pitched and roiled inside his head, he often wished he could sleep as peacefully as Adam.

The soldiers marched past for the rest of that golden afternoon. Adam finally tore himself away because he knew he had work to do, but Mikhael continued watching; and he could see his brother stop every now and then, look up, and cock his head as if straining to hear a whisper, only to suddenly shake his head when he realized what he was doing.

Mikhael's neck eventually became sore, and he found a soft patch of moss to lay on and stare at the sky. Tiny cloud wisps blew across the faces of some of the soldiers, and Mikhael wondered why they didn't brush them away with their hands like one did to an annoying insect. But they never flinched as the seemingly unending procession continued. It was only when dusk came that their ranks thinned and the soldiers began to fade from the sky...

"Mikhael!" His mother's voice had the shrill tone that told him she had been calling him for a long time.

He slowly got to his feet and walked toward the light of the farmhouse.

"I was watching the soldiers," he said as he stepped inside. He noticed that his mother was looking at him strangely.

"Do you see what's happening?" she asked, and Mikhael was about to answer when he realized she was talking to his father.

"Elika," said his father, "you're worrying too much."

"You're just as bad as he is, Pavl," she said. "How much work did you get done today?"

Mikhael shook his head to free himself of the burrs and seeds from his hair as he went to wash before the evening meal. It was the first time he had heard his parents use each other's first names.

Shards of pink and mauve sunlight streaked the air the day the soldiers appeared again. They were clearer this time, closer to the ground, and their call wafted to the ground like falling leaves. Mikhael could see now that what he had thought was glistening skin was in fact a bright metallic armor. There seemed to be fewer beasts than before, and their eyes were striated with red and their skins mottled. The soldiers themselves marched as before, their jaws locked in place, their eyes never turning left or right. In their hands Mikhael could see flashes of silver.

"What are they?" asked Mikhael.

"The soldiers," said Adam. "There is a war at the border. You know that." He wiped the sweat from his forehead with the back of his hand, although summer had long passed and it was no longer hot.

"No. I remember that. I mean the silver in their hands."

"Little brother, they are weapons. Soldiers always carry weapons."

Mikhael looked confused. "I don't remember the weapons from last time."

Adam grew impatient. "They carried weapons last time," he said. "You didn't see them because the soldiers were further away."

"And what are the weapons for?" asked Mikhael.

Adam threw his hoe to the ground. His face was flushed as he looked up into the sky.

"The weapons," repeated Mikhael. "Tell me what they are for."

Adam took a deep breath. "They protect us," he said. "They help us defeat the enemy."

After the meal that evening, Mikhael was sent to bed early and Adam and his parents spoke in hushed tones.

Later that night Mikhael's mind raced. The soldiers seemed to be marching just outside his room. He pushed his blanket aside and walked over to the window. He stared outside into the moonlit darkness. A wind had sprung up, and the branches of the trees creaked and groaned to a strange rhythm. The sky was flecked with stars, blotted out by fleeting shadows.

"Are they still marching?" asked Adam, who was suddenly at Mikhael's side.

"Why are you awake, Adam? You always sleep so soundly."

"That's true, little brother, but for once I cannot sleep." Adam's voice dropped to a whisper. "I can hear the soldiers."

"So can I, but I don't understand what they're saying."

"I can."

"What are...?" Mikhael felt Adam's hand squeeze his arm tightly, and he knew his brother didn't want him to finish his question. He hesitated for a moment, then said, "They didn't stop at dusk this time."

"No."

"Why not, Adam?" Mikhael turned to look at his brother. His face wore an expression he had never seen before: a hardening, a firmness of the jaw.

"Don't ask so many questions," he said. "Questions can be dangerous."

"Tell me and I will no longer ask."

Adam sighed. "The enemy that threatens our border grows. More soldiers are needed."

Mikhael looked out at the stars and something silver flashed in the sky for a moment and then was gone.

He held his breath.

After Adam left for the border, Mikhael had to work a full day in the fields even though he was not yet of age. He was no longer able to spend the mornings in the kitchen with his mother, but this suited him because she now spent too much of her time crying for there to be any real joy in their conversations.

He quickly tired of the tedium of field work, though,

and took to wandering deeper into the woods around the farm. The trees became more ancient and gnarled as every day he ventured a little further.

"Tell me how old you are," he asked of one massive oak.

A soft rustling was the only answer, but he imagined it to be an old man's whisper. "I am older than your soldiers. I am older than your soldiers."

"I don't understand you," cried Mikhael, and the leaves of the giant oak laughed at him.

But Mikhael knew one thing: He wanted to walk above the ground as he had seen the soldiers do. He started climbing up the knotted trunk of the tree. Muffled laughter fluttered around him as he scaled into the highest branches where the leaves enveloped him and brushed and tickled his face with every gust of wind.

"I want to walk in the sky like the soldiers," he said, and the leaves stopped whispering.

"Speak to me, tree," he cried. "Tell me how to march in the sky."

There was no answer.

Slowly Mikhael edged his way out along the branch until it began to bend under his weight. He looked up at the sky that peered at him from leaves above his head.

"You don't have to tell me," he said when the silence became too much. "I think I know."

Without looking down, he pushed off from the branch.

"You are a fool." It was the voice of his father. "Why can't you be more like your brother?"

"Leave him be, Pavl. He needs his rest now. He's too young to be working a full day in the fields anyway."

The first thing Mikhael saw when he managed to focus was his mother's watery, red-rimmed eyes. Then he saw his father's face, flushed and angry.

"You should be working," said Pavl, "not falling out of trees."

Mikhael could feel a pain shooting up his right hip as he shifted in the bed. "But, Father, I want to walk in the sky."

"What? What's that you say?" Pavl glared at his son.

"Let's leave him now, Pavl. He'll want to sleep."

"Wait..." cried Mikhael, "please...tell me where Adam has gone."

Pavl shook his head. "The boy's confused, but he's *still* asking questions."

"He's gone to the border," said Elika. "You know that."

"Yes," said Mikhael, "I know. But the border — where is it?"

"A long way away," said Pavl, still shaking his head, "but it's getting closer."

"Why?"

Pavl laughed a short, grim laugh. "That's what happens to borders, Mikhael. They are always moving."

"And what happens there?"

Pavl seemed to be smiling as he ushered Elika out the door. "Pretty much what happens here," he said. "There's a lot of crying and people falling out of trees."

The next time the soldiers appeared, the ash-gray winds scudded across the ground and swept the leaves up into bands of brown and amber clouds. This time they marched just overhead, barely above the treetops. Without putting on his coat, Mikhael left the warmth of his mother's firelit kitchen and raced outside.

But this time they seemed to be different men entirely. Perhaps it was only because they were so close to the ground, but he could see they were unshaven, that their hair was matted and tangled, and that their noses were large and their nostrils flared. Their armor was the same color as the gray clouds which pressed them closer to the ground, and it shared the clouds' virulent swirls and coils. The beasts that moved alongside them, he could see now, were not beasts at all but strange metallic machines which made whining noises that could be heard above the wind.

"Come inside," cried his mother, who had followed him out.

"But the soldiers," said Mikhael, "they are back."

"Don't look at them, Mikhael. I forbid you to look at the soldiers."

"Go back inside, Elika." Mikhael turned to see that his father had now joined them from the field. "Mikhael and I will watch them together."

"No!" she cried. "I won't let it happen again."

"Elika, go inside, will you? I'll look after the boy."

"But…the fields…you can't just leave…"

"Elika, I said, leave us!" Pavl's voice was hard. "The fields are almost dead. We can only hope now that the winter is not long and the soldiers will soon stop marching."

Elika tried to grab at Mikhael, but Pavl pushed her to the ground. She tried a second time and he hit her across the face. When she was about to try once more, he lifted his hand to strike her again. This time she looked up at the sky and spat in the direction of the soldiers. She let out a cry when the wind flung the spittle back into her face. Without saying another word, she turned and walked inside.

Mikhael glanced back for a moment and saw his mother's stooped figure silhouetted in the firelight, then he turned again to look at the soldiers. His father placed his hand on his shoulder and, despite the gusting wind, Mikhael could hear him breathing deeply.

"Can you hear them calling to me?" asked Pavl.

Mikhael thought he could hear a jumble of wind-driven voices, that was all.

"No," he said finally.

"I can," whispered Pavl so softly that a gust almost whisked the words away before they reached Mikhael's ears. He turned to his son and Mikhael could feel a deeper pressure from the hand on his shoulder. "I hope they stop marching before they call to you."

Mikhael looked at his father's unshaven face, at his dark, matted hair blowing in the gray wind. He shuddered for a moment because Pavl looked just like the faces in the sky, only his eyes were moist.

"Father," he said, "are you going to the border?"

"Yes," said Pavl. "Before the border comes here."

Mikhael turned to look at the soldiers again. The dark clouds seemed to be pressing them even closer to the ground. They bent their heads and stooped in an attempt to avoid them.

"These are not like the first soldiers," he said. "They are like men who…" Mikhael struggled for the words.

"I know," said Pavl, "like men who have had to *become* soldiers."

Mikhael nodded. They both watched as the soldiers and their machines were pushed lower. The marchers now barely hovered above the ground and the clouds looked like a single dark blanket which threatened to smother them.

There was a cry of pain as one of the soldiers' feet made contact with the dirt. The wind blew an acrid smell into Mikhael's nostrils.

Mikhael almost gagged. "What is it?" he asked.

Pavl shuddered too. "Sweat and confusion and…fear."

Mikhael could feel the pressure on his shoulder again. "Come on," said Pavl. "It is time we went inside."

As they turned to walk back to the farmhouse, Mikhael realized that the smell was coming from his own father.

In the first days after Pavl left for the border, Elika tried to work the fields herself. She tried to force the old horse to drag the plough through the dirt, but it was as if the earth itself was refusing to turn. Pavl had been right: the fields were dead.

Mikhael spent more time in the woodlands with the ancient trees. He found that the deeper he wandered, the more protection the giant oaks gave from the biting winds that now cut across the landscape incessantly. He could not remember a winter as bleak or as cold as this one; and since his father had left, the farmhouse never seemed quite as warm as it used to.

He climbed tree after tree but found that none of them spoke to him. He liked to close his eyes and sit in the high branches, to feel the leaves caressing his skin, and to pretend that he was in the sky, marching along with the balance and rhythm of the first soldiers he had seen on that summer's day long ago. He would almost convince himself that it was true, until a particularly sharp gust of wind would shake the tree top, and he would have to open his eyes and clutch tightly onto a branch.

After Elika gave up on the fields, she insisted that Mikhael spend his days in the kitchen with her. He would stare out of the window at the black clouds that writhed like a thousand dying serpents in the sky and at the thick mists that coated the terrain like molasses. Week after week was spent watching the landscape crack and fall apart under the strain.

Mikhael had given up asking his mother whether the soldiers would ever come again. It angered her when he spoke of them and she always sent him to bed.

"When will it end?" he would ask.

"I pray soon," Elika would answer. "It already feels like an eternity."

Then the day came when the soldiers returned.

"Mother," cried Mikhael. "The soldiers are here again."

Elika rushed to join him at the window.

Mikhael could feel his mother shiver at his side as they

watched the soldiers slowly coming into view through the mist. He shuddered; it was as if his mother's shiver had traveled into his own body.

It was wrong. It was all wrong.

The soldiers were walking on the ground, like ordinary men. And they were no longer marching. There was no rhythm. They shuffled like old men: hunched, stooped, their movements jerky and unsteady.

And they were going in the wrong direction.

"Mother, the border is the other way," said Mikhael.

Elika shook more violently. "The soldiers are coming back," she said. "They're coming back. It must be over."

"Does that mean father and Adam are coming back?"

"I hope so, Mikhael"

"But that's what it must mean. If it's over, they must be coming home."

Elika didn't answer. She was too busy straining to see through the mist-shrouded fields to make out the features of the returning soldiers.

Suddenly the mist began to lift and a brightness cut through the gray. For a moment Mikhael thought the golden skies of the first march were about to return, but then he realized that this time it was a different brightness. This time the brightness was red and chilling. As the mist cleared, he could see a river of red stretching to the horizon. He saw the soldiers through a filter of blood.

There were men with half-faces, men with scars like ploughed fields, men without arms or legs or noses or mouths, men with limbs twisted in bizarre angles, men with bodies like sacks of potatoes, men with jaws sagging and unhinged, men with insides bursting through gaping wounds, men with strips of flesh hanging from them like sodden rags; burnt men with skin like ashes, broken men with bones protruding like calcified spears, blind men with empty sockets where eyes had once been, deaf men with holes in the sides of their heads, half-men, quarter-men, and men who were barely men at all.

Mikhael screamed and turned to his mother. "They aren't soldiers," he cried. "Where are the soldiers?"

Elika stood in silence and scanned each skull-like face as they walked past. Mikhael wanted to turn away, but she grabbed him by the arm.

"Look at them," she spat. "Now look at them. That's what soldiers are." And Mikhael vomited.

Elika grew more silent with every day that passed and neither Pavl nor Adam returned. Mikhael tried to speak to her, but she rarely said more than a word or two, so he left her alone. The soldiers now passed by in intermittent intervals, always moving along the ground and in the opposite direction to the border. They no longer walked in a large procession, they crossed the fields on the edge of the farm singly or in small groups. Many of them couldn't walk at all, instead they crawled on hands and knees along the bitter, cold earth.

On several occasions Elika had raced out of the farmhouse, crying Pavl's or Adam's name when she thought she had seen one of them. But she had always been mistaken and was met only by cold, empty stares.

Eventually she gave up and didn't leave the farmhouse at all. She would sit at the table, with her back to the window, and stare at the blank wall.

Then one afternoon she heard someone calling her name. At first she thought she must have been dreaming, but then she heard it again: it was clearly her name and no one else's. And it was a man's voice.

She opened the door and raced out into the gray wind-driven mist that permanently seemed to encircle the farmhouse.

"Elika!"

The call came from one of the fields and she ran in its direction. On the ground lay a man. His fingers and knees were bleeding and he was shivering uncontrollably. She looked at the scarring on his face and saw eyes devoid of everything except a cold grayness.

"Pavl!" she cried. "You are home."

"Elika…you heard me," he said in a voice that sounded like a stranger's. "I knew I was close, but I thought I was going to die out here alone."

"You're not going to die, Pavl," she cried. "You're home." She bent down and gently placed her cheek against the side of his scarred face.

"The border," said Pavl, trembling under Elika's touch, "it's like an animal we've given life to. And now it's coming for us."

"And Adam?" she whispered, drawing away slightly.

"I'm sorry," said Pavl after a moment's silence. "I am truly sorry. But I wouldn't have been able to stop him even if I had wanted to. It was the *call*, you see…"

Pavl stiffened suddenly. "Mikhael — where is he?" An urgency had entered his voice.

"Why, he's…I…I don't know." Elika raked her fingers through her hair. "I haven't been paying him much attention…I…"

"When did you see him last?"

Elika started crying. "I…I don't know."

A look of pain crossed Pavl's face. "Find him. You must find him."

Elika's eyes darted from left to right as if she was afflicted by some strange fit. "He could be in bed…or maybe he's working in one of the far fields…or maybe…"

Pavl dug his fingers into Elika's flesh. She was surprised by the strength he still possessed. "You must find him. He has to be here." He drew his face closer to Elika's. "They're calling children now," he said.

Elika shook her head, unsure of what he was saying.

"Elika, did you hear me? I said, the children are being called now — to the border. They're the only ones left to call."

Elika shut her eyes as a wave of nausea washed through her. "No!" she screamed. "Not Mikhael as well. Not Mikhael. Not Mikhael."

Pavl tried to get to his feet, but he was too weak. "Find him," he cried. "Leave me here and find him. He might not have answered the call yet."

Elika stood up and ran back inside the farmhouse.

"Mikhael!" she shouted again and again, stopping only to listen for a reply. She raced into his bedroom, but his bed looked as if it hadn't been slept in for a long time.

"Mikhael!" she cried until the name echoed through the walls.

"Mikhael!" she cried as she raced back out into the cold, gray mist.

Only the wind gusted around her ears.

Then something spoke to her, a sound which crept in under the wind, a sound unlike anything she had heard before.

The tree.

She ran across the scarred and pitted fields until she entered the woodlands. The wind died the moment she stepped under the trees and soft whispers filtered through the leaves down toward her.

As she walked deeper into the woods, the whispers grew. She reached the ancient oak and looked up into the high branches at the figure that was perched up there. "Mikhael?" she cried.

The figure shifted slightly, then came to life. It was her son. He stretched slightly as if waking from a long sleep and then began to climb down toward her.

When his feet touched the ground, Elika threw her arms around him and pressed him close to her chest. "Mikhael," she said, "you didn't hear the call."

"I heard it," he said, "but the tree told me not to go. It's older than the soldiers, you know."

Elika stroked Mikhael's face and then ran her fingers through his mop of thick, brown hair.

"And you know what else it told me," he said.

Elika nodded slowly.

"There is no border," he said. "There is no border."

They held each other's hand tightly as they walked back out of the forest to where Pavl lay.

THE OCEAN AND ALL ITS DEVICES

William Browning Spencer

The following story from Texas writer Bill Spencer struck us both as something special the first time we read it. The author had managed to texture his story with so many diverse emotional elements that its appeal worked on multiple levels. He is the author of several novels and a highly acclaimed collection of short fiction. This is his first appearance in Borderlands, *but we expect to see him again soon.*

Left to its own enormous devices the sea
in timeless reverie conceives of life,
being itself the world in pantomime.
— Lloyd Frankenberg, *The Sea*

The hotel's owner and manager, George Hume, sat on the edge of his bed and smoked a cigarette. "The Franklins arrived today," he said.

"Regular as clockwork," his wife said.

George nodded. "Eight years now. And why? Why ever do they come?"

George Hume's wife, an ample woman with soft, motherly features, sighed. "They seem to get no pleasure from it, that's for certain. Might as well be a funeral they come for."

The Franklins always arrived in late fall, when the beaches were cold and empty and the ocean, under dark skies, reclaimed its terrible majesty. The hotel was almost deserted at this time of year, and George had suggested closing early for the winter. Mrs. Hume had said, "The Franklins will be coming, dear."

So what? George might have said. Let them find other accommodations this year. But he didn't say that. They were a sort of tradition, the Franklins, and in a world so fraught with change, one just naturally protected the rare, enduring pattern.

They were a reserved family who came to this quiet hotel in North Carolina like refugees seeking safe harbor George couldn't close early and send the Franklins off to some inferior establishment. Lord, they might wind up at The Cove with its garish lagoon pool and gaudy tropical lounge. That wouldn't suit them at all.

The Franklins (husband, younger wife, and pale, delicate-featured daughter) would dress rather formally and sit in the small opened section of the dining room — the rest of the room shrouded in dust covers — while Jack, the hotel's aging waiter and handyman, would stand off to one side with a bleak, stoic expression.

Over the years, George had come to know many of his regular guests well. But the Franklins had always remained aloof and enigmatic. Mr. Greg Franklin was a man in his mid- or late forties, a handsome man, tall — over six feet — with precise, slow gestures and an oddly uninflected voice, as though he were reading from some internal script that failed to interest him. His much younger wife was stunning, her hair massed in brown ringlets, her eyes large and luminous and containing something like fear in their depths. She spoke rarely, and then in a whisper, preferring to let her husband talk.

Their child, Melissa, was a dark-haired girl — twelve or thirteen now, George guessed — a girl as pale as the moon's reflection in a rain barrel. Always dressed impeccably, she was as quiet as her mother, and George had the distinct impression, although he could not remember being told this by anyone, that she was sickly, that some traumatic infant's illness had almost killed her and so accounted for her methodical, wounded economy of motion.

George ushered the Franklins from his mind. It was late. He extinguished his cigarette and walked over to the window. Rain blew against the glass, and lightning would occasionally illuminate the white-capped waves.

"Is Nancy still coming?" Nancy, their daughter and only child, was a senior at Duke University. She had called the week before saying she might come and hang out for a week or two.

"As far as I know," Mrs. Hume said. "You know how she is. Everything on a whim. That's your side of the family, George."

George turned away from the window and grinned. "Well, I can't accuse your family of ever acting impulsively — although it would do them a world of good. Your family packs a suitcase to go to the grocery store."

"And your side steals a car and goes to California without a toothbrush or a prayer."

This was an old, well-worked routine, of course, and

they indulged in it as they readied for bed. Then George turned off the light and the darkness brought silence.

It was still raining in the morning when George Hume woke. The violence of last night's thunderstorm had been replaced by a slow, business-like drizzle. Looking out the window, George saw the Franklins walking on the beach under black umbrellas. They were a cheerless sight. All three of them wore dark raincoats, and they might have been fugitives from some old Bergman film, inevitably tragic, moving slowly across a stark landscape.

When most families went to the beach, it was a more lively affair.

George turned away from the window and went into the bathroom to shave. As he lathered his face, he heard the boom of a radio, rock music blaring from the adjoining room, and he assumed, correctly, that his twenty-one-year-old daughter Nancy had arrived as planned.

Nancy had not come alone. "This is Steve," she said when her father sat down at the breakfast table.

Steve was a very young man — the young were getting younger — with a wide-eyed, waxy expression and a blond mustache that looked like it could be wiped off with a damp cloth.

Steve stood up and said how glad he was to meet Nancy's father. He shook George's hand enthusiastically, as though they had just struck a lucrative deal.

"Steve's in law school," Mrs. Hume said, with a proprietary delight that her husband found grating.

Nancy was complaining. She had, her father thought, always been a querulous girl, at odds with the way the world was.

"I can't believe it," she was saying. "The whole mall is closed. The only — and I mean *only* — thing around here that is open is that cheesy little drugstore and nobody actually buys anything in there. I know that, because I recognize stuff from when I was six. Is this some holiday I don't know about or what?"

"Honey, it's the off-season. You know everything closes when the tourists leave," her mother said.

"Not the for-Christ-sakes mall!" Nancy said. "I can't believe it." Nancy frowned. "This must be what Russia is like," she said, closing one eye as smoke from her cigarette slid up her cheek.

George Hume watched his daughter gulp coffee. She was not a person who needed stimulants. She wore an ancient gray sweater and sweatpants. Her blond hair was chopped short and ragged and kept in a state of disarray by the constant furrowing of nervous fingers. She was, her father thought, a pretty girl in disguise.

That night, George discovered that he could remember nothing of the spy novel he was reading, had forgotten, in fact, the hero's name. It was as though he had stumbled into a cocktail party in the wrong neighborhood, all strangers to him, the gossip meaningless.

He put the book on the night stand, leaned back on the pillow, and said, "This is her senior year. Doesn't she have classes to attend?"

His wife said nothing.

He sighed. "I suppose they are staying in the same room."

"Dear, I don't know," Mrs. Hume said. "I expect it is none of our business."

"If it is not our business who stays in our hotel, then who in the name of hell's business is it?"

Mrs. Hume rubbed her husband's neck. "Don't excite yourself, dear. You know what I mean. Nancy is a grown-up, you know."

George did not respond to this and Mrs. Hume, changing the subject, said, "I saw Mrs. Franklin and her daughter out walking on the beach again today. I don't know where Mr. Franklin was. It was pouring, and there they were, mother and daughter. You know…" Mrs. Hume paused. "It's like they were waiting for something to come out of the sea. Like a vigil they were keeping. I've thought it before, but the notion was particularly strong today. I looked out past them, and there seemed no separation between the sea and the sky, just a black wall of water." Mrs. Hume looked at herself in the dresser's mirror, as though her reflection might clarify matters. "I've lived by the ocean all my life, and I've just taken it for granted, George. Suddenly it gave me the shivers. Just for a moment. I thought, Lord, how big it is, lying there cold and black, like some creature that has slept at your feet so long you never expect it to wake; you forget that it might be brutal, even vicious."

"It's all this rain," her husband said, hugging her and drawing her to him. "It can make a person think some black thoughts."

George left off worrying about his daughter and her young man's living arrangements, and in the morning, when Nancy and Steve appeared for breakfast, George didn't broach the subject — not even to himself.

Later that morning, he watched them drive off in Steve's shiny sports car — rich parents, lawyers themselves? — bound for Wilmington and shopping malls that were open.

The rain had stopped, but dark, massed clouds over the ocean suggested that this was a momentary respite. As George studied the beach, the Franklins came into view. They marched directly toward him, up and over the dunes, moving in a soldierly, clipped fashion. Mrs. Franklin was holding her daughter's hand and moving at a brisk pace, almost a run, while her husband faltered behind, his gait hesitant, as though uncertain of the wisdom of catching up.

Mrs. Franklin reached the steps and marched up them, her child tottering in tow, her boot heels sounding hollowly on the wood planks. George nodded, and she passed without speaking, seemed not to see him. In any event, George Hume would have been unable to speak. He was accustomed to the passive, demure countenance of this self-possessed woman, and the expression on her face, a wild distorting emotion, shocked and confounded him. It was an unreadable emotion, but its intensity was extraordinary and unsettling.

George had not recovered from the almost physical assault of Mrs. Franklin's emotional state, when her husband came up the stairs, nodded curtly, muttered something, and hastened after his wife.

George Hume looked after the retreating figures. Mr. Greg Franklin's face had been a mask of cold civility, none of his wife's passion written there, but the man's appearance was disturbing in its own way. Mr. Franklin had been soaking wet, his hair plastered to his skull, his overcoat dripping, the reek of salt water enfolding him like a shroud.

George walked on down the steps and out to the beach. The ocean was always some consolation, a quieting influence, but today it seemed hostile.

The sand was still wet from the recent rains and the footprints of the Franklins were all that marred the smooth expanse. George saw that the Franklins had walked down the beach along the edge of the tide and returned at a greater distance from the water. He set out in the wake of their footprints, soon lost to his own thoughts. He thought about his daughter, his wild Nancy, who had always been boy-crazy. At least this one didn't have a safety-pin through his ear or play in a rock band. *So lighten up*, George advised himself.

He stopped. The tracks had stopped. Here is where the

Franklins turned and headed back to the hotel, walking higher up the beach, closer to the weedy, debris-laden dunes.

But it was not the ending of the trail that stopped George's own progress down the beach. In fact, he had forgotten that he was absently following the Franklin's spore.

It was the litter of dead fish that stopped him. They were scattered at his feet in the tide. Small ghost crabs had already found the corpses and were laying their claims.

There might have been a hundred bodies. It was difficult to say, for not one of the bodies was whole. They had been hacked into many pieces, diced by some impossibly sharp blade that severed a head cleanly, flicked off a tail or dorsal fin. Here a scaled torso still danced in the sand, there a pale eye regarded the sky.

Crouching in the sand, George examined the bodies. He stood up, finally, as the first large drops of rain plunged from the sky. No doubt some fishermen had called it a day, tossed their scissored bait and gone home.

That this explanation did not satisfy George Hume was the result of a general sense of unease. *Too much rain.*

It rained sullenly and steadily for two days during which time George saw little of his daughter and her boyfriend. Nancy apparently had the young man on a strict regime of shopping, tourist attractions, and movies, and she was undaunted by the weather.

The Franklins kept inside, appearing briefly in the dining room for bodily sustenance and then retreating again to their rooms. And whatever did they do there? Did they play solitaire? Did they watch old reruns on TV?

On the third day, the sun came out, brazen, acting as though it had never been gone, but the air was colder.

The Franklins, silhouetted like black crows on a barren field, resumed their shoreline treks.

Nancy and Steve rose early and were gone from the house before George arrived at the breakfast table.

George spent the day endeavoring to satisfy the IRS's notion of a small businessman's obligations, and he was in a foul mood by dinner time.

After dinner, he tried to read, this time choosing a much-touted novel that proved to be about troubled youth. He was asleep within fifteen minutes of opening the book and awoke in an overstuffed armchair. The room was chilly, and his wife had tucked a quilt around his legs before abandoning him for bed. In the morning she would, he was certain, assure him that she had tried to rouse him before retiring, but he had no recollection of such an attempt.

"Half a bottle of wine might have something to do with that," she would say.

He would deny the charge.

The advantage of being married a long time was that one could argue without the necessity of the other's actual, physical presence.

He smiled at this thought and pushed himself out of the chair, feeling groggy, head full of prickly flannel. He looked out the window. It was raining again — to the accompaniment of thunder and explosive, strobe-like lightning. The sports car was gone. The kids weren't home yet. Fine. Fine. None of my business.

Climbing the stairs, George paused. Something dark lay on the carpeted step, and as he bent over it, leaning forward, his mind sorted and discarded the possibilities: cat, wig, bird's nest, giant dust bunny. Touch and a strong olfactory cue identified the stuff: seaweed. Raising his head, he saw that two more clumps of the wet, rubbery plant lay on ascending steps, and gathering them — with no sense of revulsion for he was used to the ocean's disordered presence — he carried the seaweed up to his room and dumped it in the bathroom's wastebasket.

He scrubbed his hands in the sink, washing away the salty, stagnant reek, left the bathroom and crawled into bed beside his sleeping wife. He fell asleep immediately and was awakened later in the night with a suffocating sense of dread, a sure knowledge that an intruder had entered the room.

The intruder proved to be an odor, a powerful stench of decomposing fish, rotting vegetation, and salt water. He climbed out of bed, coughing.

The source of this odor was instantly apparent and he swept up the wastebasket, preparing to gather the seaweed and flush it down the toilet.

The seaweed had melted into a black liquid, bubbles forming on its surface, a dark, gelatinous muck, simmering like heated tar. As George stared at the mess, a bubble burst, and the noxious gas it unleashed dazed him, sent him reeling backward with an inexplicable vision of some monstrous, shadowy form, silhouetted against green, mottled water.

George pitched himself forward, gathered the wastebasket in his arms, and fled the room. In the hall he wrenched open a window and hurled the wastebasket and its contents into the rain.

He stood then, gasping, the rain savage and cold on his face, his undershirt soaked, and he stood that way, clutching the window sill, until he was sure he would not faint.

Returning to bed, he found his wife still sleeping soundly and he knew, immediately, that he would say nothing in the morning, that the sense of suffocation, of fear, would seem unreal, its source irrational. Already the moment of panic was losing its reality, fading into the realm of nightmare.

The next day the rain stopped again and this time the sun was not routed. The police arrived on the third day of clear weather.

Mrs. Hume had opened the door, and she shouted up to her husband, who stood on the landing, "It's about Mr. Franklin."

Mrs. Franklin came out of her room then, and George Hume thought he saw the child behind her, through the open door. The girl, Melissa, was lying on the bed behind her mother and just for a moment it seemed that there was a spreading shadow under her, as though the bedclothes were soaked with dark water. Then the door closed as Mrs. Franklin came into the hall and George identified the expression he had last seen in her eyes, for it was there again: fear, a racing engine of fear, gears stripped, the accelerator flat to the floor.

And Mrs. Franklin screamed, screamed and came falling to her knees and screamed again, prescient in her grief, and collapsed as George rushed toward her and two police officers and a paramedic, a woman, came bounding up the stairs.

Mr. Franklin had drowned. A fisherman had discovered the body. Mr. Franklin had been fully dressed, lying on his back with his eyes open. His wallet — and seven hundred dollars in cash and a host of credit cards — was still in his back pocket, and a business card identified him as vice-president of marketing for a software firm in Fairfax, Virginia. The police had telephoned Franklin's firm in Virginia and so learned that he was on vacation. The secretary had the hotel's number.

After the ambulance left with Mrs. Franklin, they sat in silence until the police officer cleared his throat and said, "She seemed to be expecting something like this."

The words dropped into a silence.

Nancy and Steve and Mrs. Hume were seated on one

of the lobby's sofas. George Hume came out of the office in the wake of the other policeman who paused at the door and spoke. "We'd appreciate it if you could come down and identify the body. Just a formality, but it's not a job for his wife, not in the state she's in." He coughed, shook his head. "Or the state he's in, for that matter. Body got tore up some in the water, and, well, I still find it hard to believe that he was alive just yesterday. I would have guessed he'd been in the water two weeks minimum — the deterioration, you know."

George Hume nodded his head as though he did know and agreed to accompany the officer back into town.

George took a long look, longer than he wanted to, but the body wouldn't let him go, made mute, undeniable demands.

Yes, this was Mr. Greg Franklin. Yes, this would make eight years that he and his wife and his child had come to the hotel. No, no, nothing out of the ordinary.

George interrupted himself. "The tattoos..." he said.

"Didn't know about the tattoos, I take it?" the officer said.

George shook his head. "No." The etched blue lines that laced the dead man's arms and chest were somehow more frightening than the damage the sea had done. Frightening because...because the reserved Mr. Franklin, businessman and stolid husband, did not look like someone who would illuminate his flesh with arcane symbols, pentagrams and ornate fish, their scales numbered according to some runic logic, and spidery, incomprehensible glyphs.

"Guess Franklin wasn't inclined to wear a bathing suit."

"No."

"Well, we are interested in those tattoos. I guess his wife knew about them. Hell, maybe she has some of her own."

"Have you spoken to her?"

"Not yet. Called the hospital. They say she's sleeping. It can wait till morning."

An officer drove George back to the hotel, and his wife greeted him at the door.

"She's sleeping," Mrs. Hume said.

"Who?"

"Melissa."

For a moment, George drew a blank, and then he nodded. "What are we going to do with her?"

"Why, keep her," his wife said. "Until her mother is out of the hospital."

"Maybe there are relatives," George said, but he knew, saying it, that the Franklins were self-contained, a single unit, a closed universe.

His wife confirmed this. No one could be located, in any event.

"Melissa may not be aware that her father is dead," Mrs. Hume said. "The child is, I believe, a stranger girl than we ever realized. Here we were thinking she was just a quiet thing, well-behaved. I think there is something wrong with her mind. I can't seem to talk to her, and what she says makes no sense. I've called Dr. Gowers, and he has agreed to see her. You remember Dr. Gowers, don't you? We sent Nancy to him when she was going through that bad time at thirteen."

George remembered child psychiatrist Gowers as a bearded man with a swollen nose and thousands of small wrinkles around his eyes. He had seemed a very kind but somehow sad man, a little like Santa Claus if Santa Claus had suffered some disillusioning experience, an unpleasant divorce or other personal setback, perhaps.

Nancy came into the room as her mother finished speaking. "Steve and I can take Melissa," Nancy said.

"Well, that's very good of you, dear," her mother said.

"I've already made an appointment for tomorrow morning at ten. I'm sure Dr. Gowers will be delighted to see you again."

"I'll go too," George said. He couldn't explain it but he was suddenly afraid.

The next morning when George came down to breakfast, Melissa was already seated at the table and Nancy was combing the child's hair.

"She isn't going to church," George said, surprised at the growl in his voice.

"This is what she wanted to wear," Nancy said. "And it looks very nice, I think."

Melissa was dressed in the sort of outfit a young girl might wear on Easter Sunday: a navy blue dress with white trim, white kneesocks, black, shiny shoes. She had even donned pale blue gloves. Her black hair had been brushed to a satin sheen and her pale face seemed just-scrubbed, with the scent of soap lingering over her. A shiny black purse sat next to her plate of eggs and toast.

"You look very pretty," George Hume said.

Melissa nodded, a sharp snap of the head, and said, "I am an angel."

Nancy laughed and hugged the child. George raised his eyebrows. "No false modesty here," he said. *At least she can talk*, he thought.

On the drive into town, Steve sat in the passenger seat while George drove. Nancy and Melissa sat in the back seat. Nancy spoke to the child in a slow, reassuring murmur.

Steve said nothing, sitting with his hands in his lap, looking out the window. *Might not be much in a crisis*, George thought. *A rich man's child.*

Steve stayed in the waiting room while the receptionist ushered Melissa and Nancy and George into Dr. Gowers' office. The psychiatrist seemed much as George remembered him, a silver-maned, benign old gent exuding an air of competence. He asked them to sit on the sofa.

The child perched primly on the sofa, her little black purse cradled in her lap. She was flanked by George and Nancy.

Dr. Gowers knelt down in front of her. "Well, Melissa. Is it all right if I call you Melissa?"

"Yes sir. That's what everyone calls me."

"Well, Melissa, I'm glad you could come and see me today. I'm Dr. Gowers."

"Yes, sir."

"I'm sorry about what happened to your father," he said, looking in her eyes.

"Yes, sir," Melissa said. She leaned forward and touched her shoe.

"Do you know what happened to your father?" Dr. Gowers asked.

Melissa nodded her head and continued to study her shoes.

"What happened to your father?" Dr. Gowers asked.

"The machines got him," Melissa said. She looked up at the doctor. "The real machines," she added. "The ocean ones."

"Your father drowned," Dr. Gowers said.

Melissa nodded. "Yes, sir." Slowly the little girl got up and began wandering around the room. She walked past a large saltwater aquarium next to a teak bookcase.

George thought the child must have bumped against the aquarium stand — although she hardly seemed close enough — because water spilled from the tank as she passed. She was humming. It was a bright, musical little tune, and he had heard it before, a children's song, perhaps? The words? Something like *by the sea, by the sea*.

The girl walked and gestured with a liquid motion that

was oddly sophisticated, suggesting the calculated body language of an older and sexually self-assured woman.

"Melissa, would you come and sit down again so we can talk. I want to ask you some questions, and that is hard to do if you are walking around the room."

"Yes, sir," Melissa said, returning to the sofa and resettling between George and his daughter. Melissa retrieved her purse and placed it on her lap again.

She looked down at the purse and up again. She smiled with a child's cunning. Then, very slowly, she opened the purse and showed it to Dr. Gowers.

"Yes?" he said, raising an eyebrow.

"There's nothing in it," Melissa said. "It's empty." She giggled.

"Well, yes, it is empty," Dr. Gowers said, returning the child's smile. "Why is that?"

Melissa snapped the purse closed. "Because my real purse isn't here, of course. It's in the real place, where I keep my things."

"And where is that, Melissa?"

Melissa smiled and said, "You know, silly."

When the session ended, George phoned his wife.

"I don't know," he said. "I guess it went fine. I don't know. I've had no experience of this sort of thing. What about Mrs. Franklin?"

Mrs. Franklin was still in the hospital. She wanted to leave, but the hospital was reluctant to let her. She was still in shock, very disoriented. She seemed, indeed, to think that it was her daughter who had drowned.

"Did you talk to her?" George asked.

"Well, yes, just briefly. But as I say, she made very little sense, got very excited when it became clear I wasn't going to fetch her if her doctor wanted her to remain there."

"Can you remember anything she said?"

"Well, it was very jumbled, really. Something about a bad bargain. Something about that Greek word, you know...*hubris*."

"*Hewbris*?"

"Oh, back in school, you know, George. *Hubris*. A willful sort of pride that angers the gods. I'm sure you learned it in school yourself."

"You are not making any sense," he said, suddenly exasperated — and frightened.

"Well," his wife said, "you don't have to shout. Of course I don't make any sense. I am trying to repeat what Mrs. Franklin said, and that poor woman made no sense at all. I tried to reassure her that Melissa was fine and she screamed. She said Melissa was not fine at all and that I was a fool. Now you are shouting at me, too."

George apologized, said he had to be going, and hung up.

On the drive back from Dr. Gowers' office, Nancy sat in the back seat with Melissa. The child seemed unusually excited; her pale forehead was beaded with sweat, and she watched the ocean with great intensity.

"Did you like Dr. Gowers?" Nancy asked. "He liked you. He wants to see you again, you know."

Melissa nodded. "He is a nice one." She frowned. "But he doesn't understand the real words either. No one here does."

George glanced over his shoulder at the girl. *You are an odd ducky*, he thought.

A large, midday sun brightened the air and made the ocean glitter as though scaled. They were in a stretch of sand dunes and sea oats and high, wind-driven waves. Except for an occasional lumbering trailer truck, they seemed alone in this world of sleek, eternal forms.

Then Melissa began to cough. The coughing increased in volume, developed a quick, hysterical note.

"Pull over!" Nancy shouted, clutching the child.

George swung the car off the highway and hit the brakes. Gravel pinged against metal, the car fishtailed and lurched to a stop. George was out of the car instantly, in time to catch his daughter and the child in her arms as they came hurtling from the back seat. Melissa's face was red and her small chest heaved. Nancy had her arms around the girl's chest. "Melissa!" Nancy was shouting. "Melissa!"

Nancy jerked the child upward and back. Melissa's body convulsed. Her breathing was labored, a broken whistle fluttering in her throat.

George enfolded them both in his arms, and Melissa suddenly lurched forward. She shuddered and began to vomit. A hot, green odor, the smell of stagnant tidal pools, assaulted George. Nancy knelt beside Melissa, wiping the child's wet hair from her forehead. "It's gonna be okay, honey," she said. "You got something stuck in your throat. It's all right now. You're all right."

The child jumped up and ran down the beach.

"Melissa!" Nancy screamed, scrambling to her feet and pursuing the girl. George ran after them, fear hissing in him like some power line down in a storm, writhing and spewing sparks.

In her blue dress and kneesocks — shoes left behind on the beach — Melissa splashed into the ocean, arms pumping.

Out of the corner of his eye, George saw Steve come into view. He raced past George, past Nancy, moving with a frenzied pinwheeling of arms. "I got her, I got her, I got her," he chanted.

Don't, George thought. *Please don't.*

The beach was littered with debris: old, ocean-polished bottles, driftwood, seaweed, shattered conch shells. It was a rough ocean, still reverberating to the recent storm.

Steve had almost reached Melissa. George could see him reach out to clutch her shoulder.

Then something rose up in the water. It towered over man and child, and as the ocean fell away from it, it revealed smooth surfaces that glittered and writhed. The world was bathed with light and George saw it plain. And yet, he could not later recall much detail. It was as though his mind refused entry to this monstrous thing, substituting other images — maggots winking from the eye sockets of some dead animal, flesh growing on a ruined structure of rusted metal — and while those images in memory were horrible enough and would not let him sleep, another part of his mind shrank from the knowledge that he had confronted something more hideous and ancient than his reason could acknowledge.

What happened next happened in an instant. Steve staggered backward and Melissa turned and ran sideways to the waves.

A greater wave, detached from the logic of the rolling ocean, sped over Steve, engulfing him. He was gone. Meanwhile Melissa continued to splash through the tide, now turning and running shoreward. The beast-thing was gone and the old pattern of waves reasserted itself. Then Steve resurfaced, and with a lurch of understanding, as though the unnatural wave had struck at George's mind and left him dazed, he watched the head bob in the water, roll sickeningly, bounce on the crest of a second wave, and disappear.

Melissa lay face down on the wet sand, and Nancy raced to her, grabbed her up in her arms, and turned to her father.

"Where's Steve?" she shouted over the crash of the surf.

You didn't see then, George thought. *Thank God.*

"Where's Steve?" she shouted again.

George came up to his daughter and embraced her. His touch triggered racking sobs, and he held her tighter, the child Melissa between them.

And what if the boy's head rolls to our feet on the crest of the next wave? George thought, and the thought moved him to action. "Let's get Melissa back to the car," he said, taking the child from his daughter's arms.

It was a painful march back to the car, and George was convinced that at any moment either or both of his charges would bolt. He reached the car and helped his daughter into the back seat. She was shaking violently.

"Hold Melissa," he said, passing the child to her. "Don't let her go, Nancy."

George pulled away from them and closed the car door. He turned then, refusing to look at the ocean as he did so. He looked down, stared for a moment at what was undoubtedly a wet clump of matted seaweed, and knew, with irrational certainty, that Melissa had choked on this same seaweed, had knelt here on the ground and painfully coughed it up.

He told the police that Melissa had run into the waves and that Steve had pursued her and drowned. This was all he could tell them — someday he hoped he would truly believe that it was all there was to tell. Thank God his daughter had not seen. And he realized then, with shame, that it was not even his daughter's feelings that were foremost in his mind but rather the relief, the immense relief, of knowing that what he had seen was not going to be corroborated and that, with time and effort, he might really believe it was an illusion, the moment's horror, the tricks light plays with water.

He took the police back to where it had happened. But he would not go down to the tide. He waited in the police car while they walked along the beach.

If they returned with Steve's head, what would he say? *Oh yes, a big wave decapitated Steve. Didn't I mention that? Well, I meant to.*

But they found nothing.

Back at the hotel, George sat at the kitchen table and drank a beer. He was not a drinker, but it seemed to help. "Where's Nancy?" he asked.

"Upstairs," Mrs. Hume said. "She's sleeping with the child. She wouldn't let me take Melissa. I tried to take the child and I thought...I thought my own daughter was going to attack me, hit me. Did she think I would hurt Melissa? What did she think?"

George studied his beer, shook his head sadly to indicate the absence of all conjecture.

Mrs. Hume dried her hands on the dish towel and, ducking her head, removed her apron. "Romner Psychiatric called. A Doctor Melrose."

George looked up. "Is he releasing Mrs. Franklin?" *Please come and get your daughter,* George thought. *I have a daughter of my own.* Oh, how he wanted to see the last of them.

"Not just yet. No. But he wanted to know about the family's visits every year. Doctor Melrose thought there might have been something different about that first year. He feels there is some sort of trauma associated with it."

George Hume shrugged. "Nothing out of the ordinary as I recall."

Mrs. Hume put a hand to her cheek. "Oh, but it was different. Don't you remember, George? They came earlier, with all the crowds, and they left abruptly. They had paid for two weeks, but they were gone on the third day. I remember being surprised when they returned the next year — and I thought then that it must have been the crowds they hated and that's why they came so late from then on."

"Well..." Her husband closed his eyes. "I can't say that I actually remember the first time."

His wife shook her head. "What can I expect from a man who can't remember his own wedding anniversary? That Melissa was just a tot back then, a little mite in a red bathing suit. Now that I think of it, she hasn't worn a bathing suit since."

Before going to bed, George stopped at the door to his daughter's room. He pushed the door open carefully and peered in. She slept as she always slept, sprawled on her back, mouth open. She had always fallen asleep abruptly, in disarray, gunned down by the sandman. Tonight she was aided by the doctor's sedatives. The child Melissa snuggled next to her, and for one brief moment the small form seemed sinister and parasitic, as though attached to his daughter, drawing sustenance there.

"Come to bed," his wife said, and George joined her under the covers.

"It's just that she wants to protect the girl," George said. "All she has, you know. She's just seen her boyfriend drown, and this...I think it gives her purpose perhaps."

Mrs. Hume understood that this was in answer to the earlier question and she nodded her head. "Yes, I know dear. But is it healthy? I've a bad feeling about it."

"I know," George said.

The shrill ringing of the phone woke him. "Who is it?" his wife was asking as he fumbled in the dark for the receiver.

The night ward clerk was calling from Romner Psychiatric. She apologized for calling at such a late hour, but there might be cause for concern. Better safe than sorry, etc. Mrs. Franklin had apparently — well, had definitely — left the hospital. Should she return to the hotel, the hospital should be notified immediately.

George Hume thanked her, hung up the phone, and got out of bed. He pulled on his trousers, tugged a sweatshirt over his head.

"Where are you going?" his wife called after him.

"I won't be but a minute," he said, closing the door behind him.

The floor was cold, the boards groaning under his bare feet. Slowly, with a certainty born of dread, expecting the empty bed, expecting the worst, he pushed open the door.

Nancy lay sleeping soundly.

The child was gone. Nancy lay as though still sheltering that small, mysterious form.

George pulled his head back and closed the door. He turned and hurried down the hall. He stopped on the stairs, willed his heart to silence, slowed his breathing. "Melissa," he whispered. No answer.

He ran down the stairs. The front doors were wide open. He ran out into the moonlight and down to the beach.

The beach itself was empty and chill; an unrelenting wind blew in from the ocean. The moon shone overhead as though carved from milky ice.

He saw them then, standing far out on the pier, mother and daughter, black shadows against the moon-gray clouds that bloomed on the horizon.

Dear God, George thought. *What does she intend to do?*

"Melissa!" George shouted and began to run.

He was out of breath when he reached them. Mother and daughter regarded him coolly, having turned to watch his progress down the pier.

"Melissa," George gasped. "Are you all right?"

Melissa was wearing a pink nightgown and holding her mother's hand. It was her mother who spoke: "We are beyond your concern, Mr. Hume. My husband is dead, and without him the contract cannot be renewed."

Mrs. Franklin's eyes were lit with some extraordinary emotion and the wind, rougher and threatening to unbalance them all, made her hair quiver like a dark flame.

"You have your own daughter, Mr. Hume. That is a fine and wonderful thing. You have never watched your daughter die, watched her fade to utter stillness, lying on her back in the sand, sand on her lips, her eyelids; children are so untidy, even dying. It is an unholy and terrible thing to witness."

The pier groaned and a loud crack heralded a sudden tilting of the world. George fell to his knees. A long sliver of wood entered the palm of his hand, and he tried to keep from pitching forward.

Mrs. Franklin, still standing, shouted over the wind. "We came here every year to renew the bargain. Oh, it is not a good bargain. Our daughter is never with us entirely. But you would know, any parent would know, that love will take whatever it can scavenge, any small compromise. Anything less awful than the grave."

There were tears running down Mrs. Franklin's face now, silver tracks. "This year I was greedy. I wanted Melissa back, all of her. And I thought, I am her mother. I have the first claim to her. So I demanded — *demanded* — that my husband set it all to rights. 'Tell them we have come here for the last year,' I said. And my husband allowed his love for me to override his reason. He did as I asked."

Melissa, who seemed oblivious to her mother's voice, turned away and spoke into the darkness of the waters. Her words were in no language George Hume had ever heard, and they were greeted with a loud, rasping bellow that thrummed in the wood planks of the pier.

Then came the sound of wood splintering and the pier abruptly tilted. George's hands gathered more spiky wooden needles as he slid forward. He heard himself scream, but the sound was torn away by the renewed force of the wind and a hideous roaring that accompanied the gale.

Looking up, George saw Melissa kneeling at the edge of the pier. Her mother was gone.

"Melissa!" George screamed, stumbling forward. "Don't move."

But the child was standing up, wobbling, her nightgown flapping behind her.

George leapt forward, caught the child, felt a momentary flare of hope, and then they both were hurtling forward and the pier was gone.

They plummeted toward the ocean, through a blackness defined by an inhuman sound, a sound that must have been the first sound God heard when He woke at the dawn of eternity.

And even as he fell, George felt the child wiggle in his arms. His arms encircled Melissa's waist, felt bare flesh. Had he looked skyward, he would have seen the nightgown, a pink ghost shape, sailing toward the moon.

But George Hume's eyes saw, instead, the waiting ocean and under it, a shape, a moving network of cold, uncanny machinery, and whether it was a living thing of immense size or a city, or a machine, was irrelevant. He knew only that it was ancient beyond any land-born thing.

Still clutching the child he collided with the hard, cold back of the sea.

George Hume had been raised in close proximity to the ocean. He had learned to swim almost as soon as he had learned to walk. The cold might kill him, would certainly kill him if he did not reach shore quickly — but that he did. During the swim toward shore he lost Melissa and in that moment he understood not to turn back, not to seek the child.

He could not tell anyone how he knew a change had been irretrievably wrought and that there was no returning the girl to land. It was not something you could communicate — any more than you could communicate the dreadful ancient quality of the machinery under the sea.

Nonetheless, George knew the moment Melissa was lost to him. It was a precise and memorable moment. It was the moment the child had wriggled with strange, sinewy strength, flicked her tail and slid effortlessly from his grasp.

ONE IN THE A.M.

Rachel Drummond

If the short story is the toughest piece of fiction anyone can attempt to write well, then the short-short is practically impossible. We receive literally hundreds of very short stories and most of them are disappointing. The problem is the "surprise" — in the majority of instances, the gimmick is tired and predictable, and rarely surprising. Also, we're not really looking to be surprised in Borderlands — we'd rather be impressed by good writing. Rachel Drummond probably didn't know it when she sent us "One in the A.M.," but she was bucking some very tough odds. That she scored anyway speaks very highly of the short-short you are about to read.

You're walking up those dark stairs and the house is quiet. Something doesn't feel quite right, like someone or something is watching, listening, and waiting. You don't turn on the light though, because you don't want to admit you're being paranoid. The stairs are carpeted; you realize you wouldn't hear any footsteps if they were headed your way.

You go into the baby's room, where you think you might be safe, but the room has too many shapes and shadows. Stuffed animals look like evil, glossy-eyed monsters. The crib looks like a cage with an open door, and the closet is a black cave where something clawed and fanged is hiding.

You back out of the room so the closet creature won't jump out when you turn around. Your heart is beating fast. You've got that queasy, tight feeling in your stomach, but in a strange way you're kind of enjoying being scared, really spooked out. You've always seemed to be able to scare yourself more than any film or book could.

You need to take a piss but you decide to leave the lights off in the bathroom — just to keep that feeling going. The light from a streetlight outside is enough to see your reflection in the mirror, but your face seems somehow more sinister than it usually does. It's difficult to piss while you stare into those dark eyes, but then your body finally relaxes and you feel the release and hear the stream. As you zip up and study your evil twin, you imagine it reaching out from the glass and caressing your face with one cold, gray finger. You leave the bathroom. Just in case it does.

Your stomach grumbles for a snack. The best time to eat is the middle of the night. It's easier to sleep when you have a full stomach. You go downstairs again and ram your shin into every sharp-cornered piece of furniture and trip over wheeled toys. You try to walk quickly in case a taloned hand takes a swipe at your ankle from underneath the couch or easy chair.

In the kitchen, all the glass bottles of dried beans seem like bizarre entomological samples and the hanging chili peppers is a mass of bats. Your tennis shoes squeak on the linoleum floor and you cringe at how loud the noise is. You find yourself tiptoeing to the fridge. When you open the door, the light nearly blinds you. You wonder, as you look inside, when it was last cleaned out. The white mold and green fungus on the leftovers are more frightening than any monster or animal you've dreamed up thus far. They've definitely killed your appetite.

The clock says one in the morning, your mind says it's time to see if there are any monster movies on the tube. One o'clock is when the good old black and whites are on. The slimy monsters look just rubbery enough and the zippers are visible on the ape man's back. Besides, the men are fearless heroes and the women know how to scream. You don't find that often these days.

Down to the rec-room in the basement. It isn't as creepy as a basement should be, it's been finished with wood paneling and carpet. Luckily, it's darker than the rest of the house and the air is damp and mildewy. You don't want to lose your adrenaline rush just yet.

You turn on the TV and wince as you accidentally crank up the volume and a snakelike hiss assaults your ears. Quickly, you turn it down, barely audible. You blink away the white afterimages of the static snow of the screen. A few loud kachunks of the channel changer as you search for your monster movie. There it is, an old classic, halfway finished. It doesn't matter, you've seen it at least twice before.

You sit on a threadbare basement couch, then decide to lie down as the fear wears off. The blue light of the screen and the cheesy movie make it hard to be scared anymore.

The insides of your lids feel gummy and your head suddenly very heavy. You try to watch the film, but you find yourself dozing off.

Your eyes snap open. You realize something is wrong. Not with the movie — the scientist fellow has just discovered the creature's weakness but is killed and eaten before he can tell the hero about it. Fortunately, he had written it all in his diary before the thing got him and you know the hero will find the journal entry before his girl, the scientist's daughter who was hypnotized and kidnapped by the creature, becomes the creature's bride. No, the movie is going just as it should, but did you hear a thump upstairs — like a heavy footstep or dropped object?

The fear takes hold as strong as before. You listen, is anything up there? It's too hard to tell with the heroine screaming all the time. You can't turn down the set though, because whatever might be upstairs will know that you know it's up there. Maybe you could just pretend you were asleep and it would leave you alone. Did you just hear a creak? Your heart beats faster. You can't pretend you're asleep, It will know. Besides, you want to see for yourself and you feel as insane as any movie character who ventures out to investigate a noise.

You get up from the couch, quietly and slowly. You tiptoe to the stairs. For every step you climb, there is a prayer that it won't squeak. At the top you listen again. Why didn't you pick up something heavy to hit it with? You feel defenseless. The stomach flutters are back and you know you're going to die. You begin to hyperventilate and know that whatever it is, it can hear your breathing and track you down. You swallow and try to breath slower. If it can smell you, though, what's the use? What if the nightstalker sees with infrared? What then? Yep, you are gonna die.

I have to see it, you think, I can't take the waiting. You

go into the living room and turn on the light. Nothing. Nothing under the couches or in the hall closet. Nothing in the kitchen. But whatever may be prowling around could still be on the top floor. Now, because of the light, it knows you know it's in the house. You grab an umbrella, one with a nice sharp point at the end. You don't feel much safer.

You go up the stairs with the umbrella in front of you, ready to impale anything that might launch itself at you. You turn on the hall light. Nothing moves. You almost expect to hear a growl or a hiss, but you don't hear a sound. You try to keep the two bedrooms and the bathroom in view as you turn on the lights.

Nothing in the first bedroom except innocent-looking stuffed animals and flowered, pastel wallpaper. The closet is empty except for frilly little dresses on plastic hangers.

The master bedroom. If the monster is anywhere it will be there, ready to knock your umbrella away and rip your throat out. You find yourself wondering if its breath will stink. Will it be hot and musky? Will it have matted fur? Or will it be reptilian and very cold? Can it fly or cling to the ceiling? How do you defend yourself from something that might be anything?

You turn on the last light. No monster. Boy, do you feel stupid. You go sit on the bed and let your umbrella drop to the floor. It lands next to the baby. Must not have been dead when you turned off the light up here. Probably rolled off the bed before it croaked. That explains the thump. You pick up the stiff body and lay it next to its parents.

"Sorry to bother you again, I just thought there was a monster in here," you say.

They don't respond of course. They just stare at the ceiling with glassy eyes and open mouths.

You think, maybe if you hurry, you can catch the end of that movie.

A SIDE OF THE SEA

Ramsey Campbell

*One of the most respected writers of
short dark fantasy fiction, Ramsey
Campbell continues to create stories of
profound detachment and paranoia. A past
winner of both the British Fantasy Award
and the World Fantasy Award, he is also
an accomplished novelist and anthologist.
The trademark element in a Campbell tale
is a character who gradually realizes he
has inadvertently entered a place where
things are just a bit skewed, just a little not
right. And that's when the fun begins.*

I'm among the first to use the toilet, one
of two wheeled sheds parked at the edge
of a segment of concrete, but it takes the
two coachloads of passengers so long that
I need to join the queue again. Beyond the
hedge behind the toilets, fields and a few
lonely trees turn greener as the sky fills
with black clouds. Lorries rush down the
slope into the dip in the road and out again

with a sound like waves. The plumbing too sounds like waves when at last the queue leads me back into the shed, and I'm just splashing the urinal when I seem to hear the building engulfed by the sea. People scream, but I feel safe until I venture to the exit and see it's a cloudburst so fierce that spikes of rain are leaping off the concrete. Passengers holding coats over their heads dash to the nearest vehicle, the coach I'm supposed to be on, and I can see that long before they all finish clambering up the steps I'll be drenched. I sprint to the farther coach and drag myself up the steps beside the driver's seat while trying to wipe my drowned spectacles on my jacket. "Someone took my seat," I say for the benefit of anyone who ought to be informed.

"You weren't on this coach," says a blur.

"That's what I mean. Someone from this one stole my place."

The downpour roars on the metal roof and I'm about to protest, "You wouldn't make me go out in that," when the blur retreats along the aisle and knocks on the rear window. Presumably it uses signs to tell someone on my coach that they'll exchange passengers at the next stop, because it calls to me, "Find yourself a seat."

I put on my spectacles though the lenses are still wet. Beneath the racks laden with swimming costumes wrapped in beach towels, passengers are rubbing their hair dry and turning the windows grayer with every breath. Someone near the back is trying to lead a chorus of "We're going to the sea, sea, sea" without much success. The lenses of my spectacles are blurring, transforming the passengers into statues sitting underwater, all of them gazing blankly at me. I can't see where I'm to sit until a hand begins to wave extravagantly halfway down the coach. "Here," the owner of the hand shouts. "Here, my dear."

He's wearing a flowery shirt and shorts which are even

more florid. His clothes are pasted to him by the rain so that they resemble wallpaper. He has a large round face which seems to be about to sink into its plumpness and hands so fat they have dimples for knuckles and a stomach which rests on the tops of his thighs. As I sit down he squeezes himself against the window to make room. I rub my spectacles to rid them of fog and spots of dried rain, and as I hook them over my ears my seatmate cranes his head around to me. "What's the game?" he says.

The coach lurches forward and the person who went to the rear window — a gray-suited woman with severely restrained black hair — nods curtly at me as she returns to her seat by the driver. If she's in charge of the day trip, surely she oughtn't to ignore what I've just been asked. "What do you mean?" I say loudly, hoping that will bring her.

"Name. Name of the game. Both the same. Your name, your game."

It takes me longer to understand than it takes my neighbor to say all this and longer still to decide if responding is advisable. Maybe an answer is all he requires and then he won't bother me. "Ah, you want my name. It's Henry."

"Henry." He swings his head back and forth, and I think he's contradicting me until I realize he's looking for something. He focuses on the befogged window across the aisle with an expression of relief. "Can't see the scen'ry," he crows. "Henry who? Henry what else too?"

I don't see why he should demand my surname, and so I tell him the first I can think of which might shut him up. "Hancock."

"Hancock goes to Bangkok," he cries at once.

I find his triumph so annoying that although I was planning to keep quiet in the hope that he would, I say, "No, I want to see the sea."

"See the sea," he repeats, giving me a plump nudge as

if I meant to imitate his rhyming. "Like me. You'll be like me."

"Hush for a bit now, Algernon," says my neighbor across the aisle, a woman who is knitting into a large open handbag. "We don't want you filling up Henry's head until he's got no room to think."

"Shush and hush. Don't gush. Crush your rush." My seatmate's voice dwindles with each word. "Algernon. Algy. Alg," he murmurs almost inaudibly, then he all but shouts at me, "Al's your pal."

"Of course you are," the woman soothes him, her knitting clicking quicker. "Give the glass a wipe now and see what you can see."

She gazes at him until he rubs the window with his hairy forearm, then she turns to me. Her gleaming eyes are very pale. "And what do *you* think of all this rain?"

My answer seems to be important to her. She raises her eyebrows, crinkling her papery forehead below her hair, which looks like curled shavings of tin. "It's a bit wet," I offer.

"That's how God made it. It wouldn't be rain if it was dry."

I smile and shrug in agreement, but apparently that isn't enough for her. "You can see that, can't you?" she says, halting her needles.

"I'm sure you're right."

"It isn't a question of what I am." Her eyebrows are starting to tremble from being held high. "It makes the sea, you might want to remember. Without the rain we'd all be living in the desert. We'd be eating dates for breakfast and wearing dishcloths on our heads and sitting on camels instead of riding in a coach."

"There's that," I say to placate her.

She scrutinizes my face before she lets her eyebrows down and recommences knitting. I'm watching the road beyond the wide sweeps of the windscreen wipers, though all I can see are lights like half-eaten strawberry sweets when she says, "Do you think it'll still be raining when we get to the beach?"

"I don't know."

"But is that what you *think,* what you're *thinking?*"

"I suppose I am."

"I know you are," she says in the soothing tone she used on Algernon. "Shall we see what we can do about it?"

"About my thinking?"

She drops the shapeless knitting into her handbag and wags a finger at me. "Henry," she rebukes me. "About the rain."

"Not much, I should think."

"Never let yourself despair, Henry. Just put your hands together."

I assume that's a generalized recommendation until she clasps her hands together and gazes unblinking at mine. "Henry, Henry, Henry," she says.

I'm afraid that if she keeps that up she'll provoke my seatmate into rhyming, and so I fold my hands. Raising her gaze toward the drumming on the roof, she says, "Heavenly Father…"

I glare piously at my knuckles, but that doesn't satisfy her. "Heavenly Father," she repeats slowly and firmly, raising her eyebrows at me.

"Heavenly Father," I mouth.

"Heavenly Father, we thank Thee for the sun that Thou sendest after the rain."

I'm steeling myself in case Algernon settles on a word of hers, but it's her neighbor, a bony man with a wedge-shaped face that looks as though it was lengthened by someone tugging its knob of a chin, who responds. "Heheavenly Fahatheher," he says, "wehe thahank Thehee fohor teehee suhun thahat Thououow sehehehendest ahafteherherher teehee raihaihain."

He has folded his hands on his chest and rolled his eyes up so that only the whites are visible, shivering in their sockets, and the woman seems to be as unsure as I am whether he is doing his best to pray. "If it be Thy will," she says more loudly, "let it be sunny at the beach."

"Ihif ihit behe Thyhy wihihill, lehet ihihit be, hehe, hehe, suhuhu*hun*ny ahat thehe be, hehe, heheach."

His lips are twitching. He could be struggling either to pray or not to grin. At least he has drawn the woman's attention away from me, and I no longer bother to mouth. "We ask Thee on behalf of Thy child Henry," she bellows, "that the weather forecasters may have read Thy signs aright."

Her words might let me feel protected if it weren't for the prospect of hearing her neighbor turn my name into something else. As he says "Wehe ahahask" I flex my fingers, preparing to stick them in my ears, whatever the woman will think of me for doing so. Just then, as if I've inadvertently betrayed my thoughts, someone behind me touches my shoulder.

Pain flares in my skull as I twist around. The man standing in the aisle is resting his other hand on the headrest of my seat. His fingers must have snagged my hair, though he appears not to have noticed. His ruddy big-boned mug has protruding ears for handles. "I'd like to pray if you want to change places," he says.

I shove myself to my feet as the coach speeds downhill. The seat he has vacated is four rows further back. While I stumble toward it, clutching at headrests, everyone in the intervening seats watches me. Hedges stream by like smoke beyond the obscured windows and the grayness by which the passengers are framed puts me in mind of a photograph. For some reason that idea disturbs me, but once I reach the seat I feel safer.

My new neighbor is a small neat woman with cropped red hair who is hugging a large canvas tote bag. I return her glancing smile as I sink onto the seat. Through the uproar of the downpour I hear prayers like a battle of words which the knitting woman and her new ally are winning. The sound of rain begins to fade and the praying soars triumphantly before subsiding. In the relative quiet I'm able to hear the voice of the passenger next to the window across the aisle, a moon-faced man with the left half of his scalp combed flat, the right half bristling. "Smudge Cottages," he's muttering. "Blob Hill."

His seatmate, a squat man who is either examining his own bitten fingers or counting on them, grunts and tries to squash himself smaller. "Blotch Woods," the moon-faced man declares, "Fog Field, Splosh Road," and leans forward to look at me for agreement. Just in time I realize that he's naming everything he sees through the clouded windows, and I nod and grin until he sits back. I turn away with the grin stuck to my face, and my seatmate assumes it's aimed at her, because she responds with the twin of her earlier smile. "Best to keep your mind occupied on a trip like this," she says.

"I suppose."

"Oh, I think so."

I take it she's referring to the moon-faced man until she claps her hands and says, "So what shall we do?"

I struggle to come up with a suggestion before she does, but my mind has grown as foggy as the windows. "I know," she says, "we'll show each other our things."

"Things. Ah, well, I…"

She slaps my knee playfully and gives me the smile. "Things we take with us wherever we go, silly. What did you think I meant? Here, I'll show you what I have in mind."

She lifts her bag and lowers her face and I'm reminded of a horse feeding. She twirls the bag by its handles and cocks her head, then snatches out a photograph. "Sea," she says.

It isn't the sea at all. It's a bedroom so tidy it might never have been slept in. Either a painting of blue sky or a mirror faces a window across the single bed, and a framed square of perfectly symmetrical embroidery hangs above the headboard. Of course she said, "See" — she didn't try to trick me. "Well, there you are," I say, handing back the photograph.

"Now you have to show me one or pay a forfeit."

Though she flashes the smile, a pain seems to tug at my skull. I don't like the sound of the game she has started to play; I only have one photograph. I'm suddenly too nervous to be able to resist dragging my wallet from my inside pocket and taking out the photograph.

"That's nice. Your daughter. What's her name?"

I shake my aching head. "Not my daughter."

"Your wife?"

Shaking makes the ache worse. "My mother."

"That's even nicer." The smile must have a variety of meanings, because the woman adds through it, "You should have brought her to the seaside instead of just a photograph."

"She can't get about anymore."

"So you look after her like a good boy, I can tell. And someone's taken over while you give yourself a day off."

I keep my head still in the hope that the ache will fade. "Did she use to take you to the sea?" the woman wants to know.

The questions are causing the ache; they feel like a teacher pulling my hair. "No, we never went too far," I say, though talking has begun to hurt as well. "She used to say I didn't need holidays when I had her."

"And was she right?"

When I nod as hard as I dare, the woman says, "Shall I tell you what else I think?"

"I expect so."

"I think going to the seaside will be even more of an adventure at your age."

I think so, too, and her saying, "Look, the sun's coming out for you," begins to make me feel safe. Then she says, "I'll just show you one more of my things and then I'll let you off."

She spends some time rummaging in her bag. It's this business with photographs that has made me nervous, because I'm growing surer that I've seen a picture somewhere of the people on the coach. When she hands me a photograph I'm afraid this might be the one, but it's another picture of her bedroom. Clothes — underwear and scarves and shoes — cover the bed and the floor. There's a pair of everything, arranged so that the photograph is divided into two identical halves. Down the center of the bed are six bras, their cups on either side of the dividing line; three pairs are face down, three face up. "What do you say to that?" the woman urges me.

I can't seem to grasp whether the bras with their tips pointing up or those showing their insides represent more of an absence. "Very neat," I manage to respond.

She gives me a smile as quick as the movement with which she snatches the photograph, and I don't like to wonder what the smile means, any more than I care to imagine what other photographs she may have in her bag. In a bid to avoid meeting her eyes I stare through the window across the aisle. The last of the rain is worming its way off the glass, and the people in the window-seats are erasing the communal breath.

We must be almost at the seaside. Through a patch like a gray hand squelched and dripping down the window, I see a row of tall white hotels and then two fish-and-chip shops. "Room Street," moon-face says, "Fried Bunch." Meanwhile his neighbor grabs his own right ear with his left hand and blocks his left ear with his upper arm. Are my fellow passengers a troupe of performers on their way to a seaside engagement? Is that why their faces seem familiar? If they're rehearsing, I wish they would stop. "Flag Holes," says lunar lineaments, "Stubble Humps," and I feel he is snatching reality away from me and making it his before I can perceive it. What will he do to my sea?

The coach swings into a layby alongside the golf course and halts with a gasp. "Car Clump," says selenophysiognomy, but I don't care. When the other coach draws up behind this one I'll be able to return to my own seat. The driver lets the front door puff open and tramps clanking down the steps, and I turn to watch for my vehicle. Then my neck jerks and the pain in my skull feels like a pin driven so deep into my spine that I can't move my head.

A woman is sitting in the middle of the back row with her feet propped against the seats on either side of the aisle. Her striped pink dress is raised above her waist, and I can see into her. I feel as though the bearded purplish avenue is drawing me in, as though the coach and the passengers and their hubbub have become a tunnel down which I'll go rushing helplessly unless I can look away. Just in time I glimpse the one sight which is able to distract my attention — the other coach. It races around the bend at the edge of the golf course and flashes its lights, and I succeed in swivelling my head. I grab the headrest in front of me so as to heave myself to my feet as soon as my coach stops. But the coach races past without slowing and disappears over the slope of the road.

I clench my fists and my eyes and my mouth in order not to attract attention to myself. I can't prevent my eyes from twitching open, however, because I have hardly drawn breath when the coach starts to move. Surely there hasn't been time for the driver to climb aboard — and as the coach swerves out of the layby I seem to glimpse a

figure running beside the murky windows and waving
vainly as it is left behind.

Now I know what kind of company I'm in. They aren't
actors, but I know why I would have seen photographs of
them in newspapers. Asylums have days out, even
asylums where the criminally insane are locked up, though
the public aren't supposed to know they do. It must have
been a nurse I gave my name to when I got on this coach.
Why didn't she prevent whoever's in the driver's seat
from starting the engine? She must be afraid to intervene
while the vehicle is moving, and I can't do anything, I'm
afraid to draw attention to myself. I'll be able to keep
quiet so long as we end up by the sea.

The woman next to me smiles and then she smiles and
then she smiles and I make myself smile at her and smile
and smile. What harm can there be in a smile? Moon-dial
is naming everything we pass — "Bucket Bunches,
Toddler Splash, Bloat Boats, Wheel Baldies" — but I can
cope with this, because he won't be able to bother me
once I've left the coach as soon as we get to the beach.
The man beside the knitting woman is multiplying
syllables again, and I can hear Algernon rhyming and
someone else singing "God save our gracious..." over
and over to any number of tunes as if she can't progress
to the next word until she finds the melody, but I mustn't
let all this oppress me; above all, I mustn't look back.

Through the windscreen, far away down the aisle, I see
sunlit hotels giving way to dunes ahead and then water
shines beyond the dunes. As I take a breath which I mean
to hold until my silent wish is granted, the woman beside
me smiles and says, "Do you mind if I ask you one
question?"

The road curves and I see the other coach. It's parked
at the edge of the dunes and the passengers are climbing
down the steps. "Not any more," I say.

"Who's looking after your mother while you're out for the day?"

Algernon has opened a window and I can hear the waves. They sound exactly like my mother's breathing, which I thought I'd never hear again. Once I lay my head in a hollow between two dunes I shall feel safe. I'm resisting the urge to run along the aisle so as to be first off the coach when the man in the driver's seat honks the horn and passes the parked vehicle without even slowing. "We haven't stopped," I cry. "We have to stop."

"Sand Bumps," says satellite-features. "Screech Air." The woman smiles at me and then smiles at me. The rhyming and the prayers and the syllabic babble and "God save our gracious..." and all the other tangled sounds are conspiring to steal my breath and weigh me down in my seat. "Stop!" I scream and, clawing myself out of the seat, lurch toward the front of the coach.

I've drawn attention to myself. There's no turning back now. I grab the knitting woman's needles, cracking her hands and cutting off her prayer of thanks, and poke at anyone who looks as if they might try to catch hold of me. The driver brakes and glances at me as I reach him. Now he looks like the proper driver, but how do I know that isn't a trick?

"Knit, knit," I cry — I used to shout that at my mother whenever I was afraid she was about to stop moving — and jab his face. "Snail," I announce, because that's what he looks like with the needles in his face. As he waves his hands frantically at them I heave him out of the seat and grab the wheel. The coach ploughs through the dunes, and I suffer a pang of regret until I understand that the beach and the sea are so much bigger than I am, too big for me to harm. They're waiting for me.

They will take me back where I was safe.

PAINTED FACES

Gerard Daniel Houarner

We get a lot of stories from the steaming organs school of writing, stuff that is a celebration of gore with little or no substance. If this is "splatterpunk," you will find none of it in this series. This, however, does not mean we are opposed to graphic or even overtly violent material. There really are no taboos here, as this story by New York writer Gerard Houarner will demonstrate.

At cleven in the morning, he rang a number he always called when the father in his nightmares made him scream.

"Hello," he said quietly. "This is Gene. Are you available today?"

"12:30," she answered and hung up.

He left his house at 11:30 to make sure he arrived on time. His daughter Diane ("Dad needs a shave," she says that morning) and son Art ("Dad's playing

hooky," he adds with a grin) were at school. Kim ("You'll
finish the breakfast dishes? Some of us have to go to work
this morning," his wife says as she runs out) was at the
office. She had already made her morning check in call.
He had the rest of the day free.

Her name was Evelyn, but she preferred Mistress Eve.
She opened the door to her house wearing a leather teddy
and high-heels. Her long blond hair fell past her shoulders
in what he always thought of as a shower of gold. She
appeared to be what he paid her so well to be: dangerous,
like his nightmare father. Different from the wonderful
memories of his father that needed reviving before the
nightmares destroyed them.

She motioned for him to enter with a riding crop.

He stripped in the entry hall while she strutted around
him ridiculing his flabby body, graying hair, and the
whimpering sound he made whenever she prodded him
with the crop. When he was naked she removed his glasses
and traced the wrinkles around his eyes and mouth with
a fingernail. Then she put the spiked leather dog collar
around his neck and led him down into the basement by
the leash.

They passed the hanging cage and the rack and the
suspension harness. The wooden dog house and aluminum
food dish held his glance for a moment. ("Think about
getting a dog?" his wife says as she leaves for work that
morning. "I think the kids'll get over Shamus quicker if
we get another one soon.") When he was nine years old
his father had brought home a dog, mostly collie. Gene
named him Shamus because he liked detectives. His father
always found the name very funny. The dog was gone
after a couple of years. Thirty-four years later and Gene
still couldn't hang on to an animal.

In a corner was Mistress Eve's latest toy: a coffin sitting
a foot off of the floor on concrete blocks.

Gene's heart began to race. Eve glanced over her

shoulder at him, flicking golden hair out of her eyes, and smiled. "I see we approve." She let the leash drop and pulled him by his erect penis to the foot of the coffin. She ordered him to stand on one of the blocks. After removing the leash, Evelyn took a handle with a roll of plastic shipping wrap and, starting with his ankles, bound him tightly in a cocoon of clear plastic. She asked him to beg for what she was going to give him. In a small, tremulous voice he did until she stuffed plastic in his mouth and sealed off his face, leaving only slits for his eyes and nose. When she finished he couldn't move except to sway precariously back and forth on the cinder block. She pulled his stiff penis through a hole she made in the plastic over his crotch. Her laughter punctuated his vulnerability. Sweat made his skin itch. He wondered if this was how all those bodies had felt when they were alive.

He moaned, almost lost his balance, then tried to tell her how good it felt to be with her. He tried to tell her about the dreams haunting him. Soft moans and sobs were all that emerged. He did not pay her to hear his confession.

"You're in my power, now, baby Gene," she said close to his ear. "Your life, your death, even your life after death are all mine. Yes? Squirm for me if you think I'm right."

He shook his hips and shoulders gingerly and leaned against her grip. After he steadied himself she stroked his penis for a minute, then climbed atop the block with him and squeezed his erection between her thighs while stroking his buttocks with the riding crop. He could feel the stiff leather through the plastic wrap, and he arched his back to savor and sustain the thrill of goose bumps shooting up along his spine. Her thigh muscles flexed until he was ready to come.

His gaze fixed on the dog house. Its musty, animal smell hit like an electric shock. ("Maybe Shamus'll come back," he says to his mother years ago. "With Dad." "No," his mother says. "The dog is gone." "Maybe Shamus'll come back," he says to Kim just a few hours ago. "None of the other dogs that have been disappearing around here ever come back," his wife replies.)

Suddenly Mistress Eve backed away.

"Not yet, mummy Gene." She poked him in the chest with the crop until he lost his balance. He fell backward into the cushioned coffin, hitting the back of his head against the pillowed rim. He lay stunned, pain shooting through his legs and along his back.

She climbed in after him and straddled his stomach. He gasped noisily for air as he writhed under her.

"Oh, I know you're not begging for mercy," she said, playfully holding his nose for a moment, then letting him breath. "You know I have none, and I know you don't want any. I know what you want, don't I?" She caressed and tousled his hair. Then she reached over the side of the coffin and picked up a makeup kit. She pulled her hair back and took lipstick, a deep shade of blue followed by shimmering green and the obligatory crimson, and slashed thick lines across her forehead, down her cheeks, nose and chin. With mascara she drew thick circles around her eyes that trailed off in opposing concentric circles across her face. Various hues of shading cream filled in the blank spots. Facial paint from Halloween make-up kits would have been easier and more dramatic, but that was not the way it had been done long ago.

The wrap prevented him from turning away from her. His erection throbbed and he arched his back to bring his hips closer to her.

"Getting restless, are we?" Eve shifted down and teased him with her moist sex. "Anxious for life? You know you have to die a little, first." She got out of the coffin and placed blinders with ear plugs over his eyes. Her hair brushed across his nose, then he felt the thump of the lid when it closed over him.

Blood pounded past his ear drums. Suffocating darkness closed him in.

They never come back, he thought, fighting his panic. Not the dogs, not anything else. But sometimes, if you looked deep enough you could see that the things you missed had never really left. Like corpses and treasures, they lay buried underground. The corpses came out in the dark right before sleep, or in nightmares. Whenever he saw old Shamus, his mother, his father, or all those others in the dark, his heart raced and he wept so hard Kim woke up and had to comfort him. In the nightmares, the dead acted differently. His father – he didn't want to remember the nightmares.

He had to go deeper. Beyond the day the old Shamus left, along with his father. He had to stand on death's border to find the treasures. Her painted face, like a blasting cup, uncovered the bright, shiny coins of his childhood.

Sometimes, they never left....

On the first day of school Gene is crying. He blubbers, then screams at his mother and father for throwing him out of the house, forcing him to stay with strangers. He misses his mother. His father comes to the classroom and watches over him through a window in the door. The smell of chalk and crayon makes Gene want to vomit. The other children running and screaming and pushing scare him. But he stays because his father is close by, watching over him. And later, when his mother comes to pick him up, father sends her away with the car and walks Gene home. Their first man-to-man talk is exchanged during that long walk. Gene's tears dry up and his fear evaporates when he looks up at the big man next to him, feels the big man's hand holding his, feels the strength seeping through the fingers into his small body. He wants to be just like his father.

The air in the coffin was hot and stuffy. Gene suddenly wanted someone to rescue him. He wanted to move his arms, kick his legs. He wanted to see. But Mistress Eve did not come. He had not yet given her the right signal.

His raspy breathing cut through his thoughts like a saw. He thought about the way he sometimes saw his father in the dark. In his nightmares.

(Little boy Gene watches Dad come home from his part-time banquet waiter job. The big bag carrying his uniform and other things gets tossed into the basement. Dad goes upstairs to wash his hands. Gene is in the bathroom as Dad dries his hands. He keeps rubbing them with the towel. Want to hear a story, Dad asks. Sitting on Gene's bed, Dad talks. His words become a little girl stealing a rose from a beast's garden; a boy running after someone along a road that turns into a cave that winds down into the earth; a man changing into something wild to hunt for food. Then little boy Gene's back in bed. Dad tucks in the sheets. Watches over him as he says his prayers. But then, Gene knows. He knows what's in the bag. He knows what Dad likes to do. His father's dark eyes watch him. Big, strong, gentle hands sink slowly toward the bed like pale, weighted corpses through water. His father paints a face on him. And before anything else happens, Gene wakes up screaming.)

Gene screamed. The sound squeaked past the plastic in his mouth and filled the coffin. He wept; tears pooled along creases in the plastic wrapping and spilled back into his eyes when he tried to shake his head back and forth in denial of the dream. His eyes burned.

What would his father have done if there had been an accident, if he had found Gene broken, bleeding, bone and guts showing through shredded flesh.

What if, instead of a boy, his mother had had a girl? What if a sister had come before or after Gene? What did he dream of doing to Gene's mother? To the aunts and grandmothers and cousins in the family? To the old lady living by herself in the corner house? To the teenage girl who looked after Gene when his parents went out?

Would he have asked Gene to help.

And would Gene have done it.

Bad memories. Terrible thoughts. Dead bodies mixed in with gold coins. He took deep, steady breaths and shut his eyes against the insanity. His heart slowed. He relaxed in the plastic's grip, in the power of Mistress Eve's coffin. He did not want to be gone like his father, Shamus, the bodies. No, and he did not want the nightmare father, with his bag and his hands and his long, dark gaze, to paint his face and do things to him. Or worse, ask him to do things to others. He wanted the other father, the one always home for dinner with some time to spare for his son.

He suits up for his first little league game while his father instructs him on how to hold the bat, keep his eyes on the ball, move his hips and shoulders. They play catch in the backyard, touch their toes a few times, jog between the fence and back door a few times. After the warm up, Dad drives him to the league field. They don't talk. Gene thinks about some of the other kids, even girls, who can hit and catch much better than him. He worries about disappointing his father. Maybe his father will be ashamed. Maybe he'll want to trade him for another kid. At the field Gene looks at all the parents looming over him, talking and laughing about the game being played. Gene strikes out and hits himself with the bat at his first time up, then falls on his face when he trips trying to field a ball. The ball bounces off of his head and trickles away. While other parents and kids laugh, his father watches with a quiet smile and nods his head as if to say everything is all right. He claps and yells the loudest when Gene's bat finally makes contact with the ball and when he assists in a put out.

Memories flowed, golden bright. The nightmare father receded, the bodies sank back into shadow. The father he had known in his childhood was back. Until the bodies crept out of the darkness; until his constant fear, the terrible thoughts, fed the nightmare father long enough for him to command his dreams. And then he'd have to take another day off and visit Mistress Eve again.

But now was time for Mistress Eve to scoop him out of the darkness and return him to the waking world on a magic carpet of sex.

He kicked the coffin lid with his knees. He mumbled through the gag. He rolled back and forth, knocking into the walls, bumping his butt against the floor. Twice he drove his head into the lid. She had to hear him beg with whatever means he had to catch her attention. She had to hear the signal they had agreed upon.

After a few intense moments of effort he collapsed, exhausted, desperately sucking air through his nose. His skin burned from the stifling heat of his own body. His stomach turned and he considered the possibility of choking on his own vomit.

Still, she did not come. For a dizzying moment, Gene thought he was going to cross the border. He was going to die. The golden memories would be gone, but the nightmares would also end.

(Women and girls, their torsos ripped, their faces veiled by swirling painted designs, dance around little boy Gene after Dad's tucked him in. They come closer, touch him, caress him, beg for him to be the man his father is. He looks at the door to his room. The girls are in bed with him. Footsteps boom in the hallway. The women stroke his privates with sticky hands. Lights come on. He starts to wake, he wants to wake, before his father comes. A big shadow stands in the lighted doorway. The girls shriek, the women fall over him. He screams.)

Gene screamed again. He started reaching into the golden flow of memory for a fragment of the distant past.

Then a breeze blew across his face. Strands of hair tickled his nose. Something pressed against his cheek, his forehead. He felt wet lips kiss the tip of his nose.

He groaned with relief, and with disappointment.

The plastic wrap came apart around his legs. The cold metal of a knife slid over his arms, freeing them. Fresh moisture beaded on his skin where the knife had passed.

A casual brush knocked the blinders askew. A distant voice giggled. The sound of running steps faded away.

Slowly, Gene freed himself and sat up in the open coffin. In the darkness, he rubbed life back into his sweat-slick, trembling limbs and breathed in the basement's cool air. The entrance to the dimly lit stairwell at the other end of the room was empty. He called for Mistress Eve, but she did not answer.

He shivered. He listened for her in the room but heard only his breathing. The ritual had broken down.

With elaborate care, Gene crawled out of the coffin, wincing at the flashes of pain calling attention to his body's fresh bruises. He put his foot down on the floor, discovered a slick spot and slid before he could pull back his weight.

He fell and cried out as much from fear as pain. The dampness from the floor, warm, thick, sticky, covered his hands. The taste was coppery, the smell sickening.

Gene loped toward the stairwell, shoulders hunched against an unexpected blow. His head bumped against the hanging cage. A knee brushed against the gear wheel at the end of the rack. Gene reached the bottom of the stairs and looked back. The basement's darkness rushed toward him, propelled by the blackness at the furthest corner where the coffin lay.

Gene backed up the stairs toward the closed door at the top.

Daylight streamed in from the living room and kitchen windows when he opened the door. The hinge squeaked. A clock ticked steadily in another room. Otherwise, the house was quiet. Gene tiptoed to the entrance where he found his clothes. He reached for his underwear, then hesitated. His hands were covered with blood, and drops of blood crept down his forearms and thighs.

Animal blood, he thought quickly. But Evelyn never involved animals in her fantasy enactments. Human blood. An even more ridiculous possibility.

Stage blood. She was luring him on, digging deeply into his mind to find the triggers to his secret pleasures.

His penis jumped, stiffened into an erection.

He called for her again, held his hands against his chest so the blood would not drip over the carpet and tiles as he searched for her on the first floor, then went upstairs. A thick trail of blood on the carpet led to the bedroom.

He found Evelyn naked, tied spread-eagled to her brass bed, gutted. A pink, flowery design lanced with jagged lines in yellows and black covered her face. Her mouth was open, as were her eyes. She stared at the doorway, at Gene, with a frozen expression of terror.

Gene felt only numbness as he stared at the scene. Horror came when he realized he had not lost his erection.

He stares at the pieces of the airplane model spread out before him and wonders with a growing sense of helplessness how he will ever put it together. He glances at the picture on the box cover. The old World War II bomber flies effortlessly through Nazi flak, turret guns blazing and distant Luftwaffe fighters falling away in trails of fire and smoke. On the table, the pale plastic pieces mock him from their grids. The instructions on the sheet read like the Egyptian hieroglyphics from the Mummy's tomb. He feels like throwing up from the smell of the open tube of rubber cement. Then his father's hand settles on his shoulder. The solid weight anchors him. His

*father's towering presence at his back fills him with
confidence. Together they sit at the little desk in his room
and begin to build the airplane. The picture on the box
cover starts to look like something he can make.*

He backed out of the room, but her stare still burned in
his thoughts as he leaned against the hallway wall. He
looked at his bloody hands and suddenly saw his name in
headlines. He remembered a newspaper his mother had
snatched out of his hands long ago. ("He's gone. Your
father's gone," she cries. "Stop looking for him.") Then
he remembered the kiss on his nose, the brush of hair
across his skin, the faint giggling. Gene lost his erection.
The killer had set him free. The killer might still be in
the house.

Breathing deeply, he went to the bathroom. Listening
for the faint whisper of footsteps on carpeting, he washed
the blood from his hands. After he put his clothes on, he
looked at the front door while listening to the silence.
The murderer could be watching him now from a closet,
from behind a sofa, he thought. But when the police
arrived they would find the wrappings downstairs with
his hair. They would find his fingerprints, the book he
knew Evelyn kept with information about her johns. There
might be videotapes, tape recordings, photographs.

He decided he'd rather die than live with Kim, Art and
Diane believing the news reports and fearing him.

It took three hours to search the ground and upstairs
floors. He tapped for false bottoms, hollow walls; he
searched through every box, every bag and pocket. He
found her phone book, the notes she had taken when
discussing the fantasy he had wanted to enact, a book of
photographs (taken secretly) featuring all her johns in
various restraints and humiliating postures. The tape he
removed from her answering machine had captured his
last call. He stowed them all in a knapsack.

The anticipation of hearing the police sirens or the doorbell ringing, of being attacked by a knife-wielding madman never left him.

He left by a side door, sneaked through a neighbor's lawn and walked briskly to his car parked several blocks away. He drove slowly to a Burger King where he tried to settle his stomach with a soda. When the cup was empty he slipped dropped the unwound tape cassette into it, then stuffed the cup into a paper bag and the bag into the trash bin. The phone book, notes, and pictures of himself in bondage he tore methodically into small pieces which he mixed together and then dumped in various trash bins at two different nearby malls. He tossed the bag with the photo album into a dumpster at a road-extension construction site.

Kim's car was in the driveway by the time Gene came home. He put his car in the garage while rehearsing the litany of excuses he had decided to use to explain his absence and the lack of dinner: restlessness, an attack of claustrophobia, traffic, shopping. Kim would be irritated and might even ignore him. He'd retreat to his study, help the kids with their homework, stay home tomorrow again and try to figure out what had happened.

And what, with a killer imitating his nightmare father stalking him, might yet happen.

"Kim?" Gene called out as he walked in through the front door. "Kids? Sorry I'm late." He went through the living room into the empty kitchen. There was nothing on the stove, in the microwave, or in the sink. The morning dishes remained where he had left them in the plastic drip stand. The silence in the house collapsed over him like a suffocating blanket.

"Kim?"

Somebody from the family came by and took them all out to dinner, Gene thought as he left the kitchen and headed upstairs. Kim should have left a note, but she must have been mad at him.

Halfway up the stairs, his fingertips brushed against something cold and sticky on the banister. He jerked his hand back and hastily wiped it against his shirt. When he looked down at himself, a reddish-brown streak marked his chest.

At the top of the stairs, partially covering a fresh stain on the carpet, Gene found several sheets of yellowed, crinkled paper on the floor. Across the top of one sheet capital letters had been clipped from magazines and newspapers to form a title:

THE BLANK GENERATION

Below the title, in the uneven and faded lettering of an old manual typewriter, Gene read phrases he had not seen since his childhood:

America, its genius, assimilation of everything that is capable of being assimilated, sucking everything in, but nothing underneath, just hunger, hunger, deep and ugly, the blank generation with their painted faces, watching TV, listening to music, slaves to fashion, to whatever the glowing screen tells them they should do, what is normal, going to the colleges like breeding coops, breeding the next generation of dead thinkers and consumers, full of hunger and devoid of wisdom, tell them what is and they laugh, speak to them in the night language and they don't know, they've never heard, ignorant, don't see the corners with history, accumulated blood, frustrations, hate all around them, festering disease, pain, too busy with careers and paychecks and all masks of normality, it's the women, don't they see, mothers to us all, they bring it all upon us, breeding the blank generation, raising the blank generation, have to teach them what is underneath it all, what is real, what is the nature of their hunger and

*the craving of their children, show them all what they
have assimilated, what it means, how they can use...*

He remembered reading the same kind of chaotic
rambling in a newspaper as a child. The story had been
about his father, accompanied by a picture of him in front
of the house. After what happened to Shamus. His mother
had torn the paper from his hands. ("He's gone. Daddy's
gone.") His father was gone. His mother was gone,
withered away, haunted and eventually consumed by the
fear of what she had lived with for all those years. All
those bodies, gone. Gene shut his eyes.

A voice whispered in his head like it sometimes did
late at night when he was tired and angry at all the
advertising and vacuous programs clogging the television
and restless because things weren't going well at the office
and afraid to fall asleep because the whispering voice
would only get louder and angrier as the hands came down
on him and painted his face. And the whispering voice
rambled and talked nonsense, like in the newspaper
article, and after awhile the voice became his own and he
was speaking and he was painting his father's face and
he was carrying the heavy bag home and he was going
after Shamus as the cars pulled up —

He opened his eyes and steadied himself with a hand
on the banister. His hoarse, rapid breathing filled the air.
He looked up, away from the pile of papers on the floor.

He thought of Art and Diane and Kim. He became cold,
bloodless.

He checked his son's bedroom. The smell assaulted him
first: rancid, like meat left in the sun to rot for days, and
pungent like the stench of Evelyn's insides spilled across
the bed. His hand instinctively found the light switch,
and he was startled when the overhead lamp came on.
What lay on the bed was unrecognizable.

On the headboard, a painted face design leered at him.
He found another rent carcass and painted face in

Diane's room. He lingered for a moment, staring at the scattered dolls and stuffed animals all stained with blood. He tried to vomit, but only a searing, bitter stream of bile spilled from his mouth.

He was ready for his wife's corpse in their bedroom. When he opened the door and found the remains, he went to the bed and sat on the edge. He studied their wedding pictures on the dresser, the family portrait on the wall, the painted face — in blue and violet, with glitter highlighting the eyes — on the headboard. Then he slipped to the floor and put his hands to his face to try and shut out the world. Cool, thick blood soaked the back of his shirt and the seat of his pants.

His fingers began to tingle, then his hands, arms and legs. Numbness crawled in from his extremities, along his spine, toward his heart. He sat for a while hoping for a heart attack or a stroke. Then something brushed against his hair. Gene looked up, startled, blood suddenly rushing to his head. His eyes refused to focus for a moment. Then he fixed his gaze on a figure in front of him.

"Hi, Daddy," Diane said as she backed away. Her hair was tucked back into a pony tail, and her round face was flushed as if she had been outside running and playing.

"You okay, Dad?" asked Arthur. His son wore old jeans and sneakers, and his Guns 'N Roses T-shirt was spotted with brown stains.

At the company barbecue, while his father is talking to the boss, little Gene spills mustard on his shirt. He takes a napkin and tries to wipe himself, but as he rubs he knocks over the boss' beer on the picnic table. Someone cries out. Mother's face turns red and her lips disappear. The boss looks down with his mouth open and turns his big eyes on Gene. People stop talking. Father chuckles and scoops Gene up. "Now, now, son, there's plenty of time yet before you start drinking." The boss laughs. His face bounces up and down. His mother's smile is thin, and her eyes give a spanking warning to Gene. But the people around them start laughing too and little baby Gene buries his hot face in his father's neck and lets his father's big hand pat him on the back.

(He opens his mouth to scream, but nothing comes out. The big figure in the doorway moves into the room. The girls covering Gene stop shrieking. He doesn't feel their weight on him anymore. He pulls the sheet over him and peeks out. The big figure stands in the middle of a circle of women. He reaches out and rips the face from a woman. He puts the painted face on his chest. He rips another face off and puts it on his shoulder. The figure goes around the circle. Then he turns to face Gene's bed.)

Kim slid quietly past the door frame, her gaze flitting between the kids and Gene. She gave him a smile, came up behind her children, and drew them behind her. Then she went down on one knee halfway between the door and the bed.

"Gene?" she said huskily. "Baby? Can you talk?"

Her beat up sneakers were muddy, and there were holes in her jeans and sweat shirt. She passed a hand over the kerchief covering her head.

"I have to ask you, were you careful at Evelyn's house? Like your father would've been?"

The urgency in Kim's voice forced him to consider what he had done that afternoon. "Yes," he answered at last.

Kim's tense expression relaxed and she sat down on the carpet, hugging her knees against her chest. Diane lay down on her side while Art put his hands on his hips and began to shift from one foot to the other.

"Be still," Kim said without turning around. "Your father has a lot to think about."

"Hope he straightens out soon," Art mumbled as he sat down on the floor and began to study a blood stain on the carpet.

"We're covered," Kim said, tapping a finger rapidly against her knee cap. "I left work and took the kids out of school at eleven. I told people we were supposed to meet you at the doctor's because you weren't feeling well and I was afraid the kids might have caught something. If anybody asks, we can always say you felt better by the time we got there and instead we went together to the malls." She paused, studying Gene's face. "Don't worry, me and the kids came at Evelyn's house from different directions, and not all at the same time. Diane went in through a ground floor window and opened the door for us. Your father would've been proud of the plan."

Gene pictured Evelyn spread-eagled on the bed. He blinked away the image and stared at his family. "Wha — what?" he stuttered, struggling to find a question to ask.

"We killed her, Daddy," Diane said as she played with a lock of her hair. "Just like Mommy showed us. Like Grandpa used to do."

A family picnic day, bright sun shining in a pristine blue sky, light bathing over a green meadow bordered by trees. His father and mother on the grass, in each other's arms, wine on their breath. Gene tries to look away, tries to disappear into the earth. But his father invites him into the circle of his parents' embrace. Gene feels as if he's melting into the press of bodies.

(The figure is standing next to Gene's bed. The painted faces on his body stick their tongues out, roll their eyes, bare pointed teeth. The figure reaches down. A big, dark hand closes over his face. Gene has a hard time breathing for a moment. Then he sees the hand lift something up. The figure slaps the limp thing in its hand against its head. Gene looks down at himself and starts to paint a face on the little boy on the bed.)

"We had to kill Shamus, too" said Diane. She looked down at the rug and her pink face paled slightly.

Art laughed. "Yeah, and every other mutt in the neighborhood. For the practice and the guts." An expression of comic disgust passed over his face as he thrust his chin at the bed, then wriggled his fingers over his stomach.

Father sitting next to him, putting his fingers in the paint and joining Gene in the fingerpainting —

(Black sedans pulling up to the house, no sirens but flashing lights on their dashboards. Mother screaming at the door to the house. "Gene, for God's sake, come inside. Please, dear God." Dad looks around, smiles at Gene. Shamus runs out of the dog house, barking.)

"It's not a dream," Gene said, his voice a croak.

Kim slid closer to Gene and put a hand on his knee. His legs began to tremble.

"No, baby, it's for real," she said. "Your father, he saw things so clearly. I was sure you'd be so much more like him. For years, I waited for you to understand. Your nightmares, Evelyn and the ones before her, I knew they were all signs. But you just got stuck right on the edge. All you needed was a little push."

Father pushing little boy Gene on a swing —

(Dad calls Shamus to him, holds him by the collar. Gene starts to walk to Dad. Car doors slam. Men in suits and in uniforms stand on the curb and driveway. They have guns in their hands. Gene starts walking toward his father. Dad looks at him, smiles. The smile stops Gene.)

Kim turned to Art. "Why don't you and Diane go to your rooms and start cleaning up like I showed you?"

"Aw, ma," Art complained, but Diane led him away by the hand.

Father raking the leaves from the lawn while little Gene held the bag —

(Men in uniform swarm around the house, flash a piece of paper in front of mother and then pull her into the house. Dad calls Shamus to him, holds him by the collar.

A man in a suit comes toward Gene. Gene backs away, turns and heads toward the house, stops as an officer comes out for him. Gene runs to the dog house. He crawls in, turns around and looks out through the opening. Dog hairs tickle his nose. Dog smell curls in his stomach and makes him want to throw up.)

"How…how…" How could you? he wanted to ask.

"Did I know what you really are?" Kim shifted, straightened her legs, leaned forward. "I read every word written about your father. I fucked the investigating detective on your father's murders when I was old enough. I got him to talk about the case and show me the files. Then I stole them. You should see the pictures. I have them in albums downstairs. That's where I got those pages from your father's diaries."

Gene shook his head back and forth. He closed his eyes and tried to cover his ears with his palms.

Father with little boy Gene on his lap, turning the pages to the family photo album —

(The men in suits close in on Dad. A uniformed man bursts out of the house. "We found it. The knives, the make-up. He's the one. Take him, take him." The men in suits rush Dad. Dad kneels, rubs Shamus' head. Then he pulls the dog's jaw up and bites him on the neck. The dog jumps, kicks his legs out, howls. The men try to pull him away. Blood is everywhere. On Dad's face. On the suits. On the men's faces. The men drag Dad away. He still tries to finger the blood on his face, on the faces of the men taking him away. He still tries to paint faces.)

Kim took his hands and drew them down into her lap. She massaged heat back into his flesh. "I knew you were the one for me. Even as a little kid, you were always the one I wanted. The little boy in the dog house. I knew somewhere deep inside you shared the truth with your father, the truth I wanted to share. I understand, you see? Under the painted face of normality there's a secret. The truth. The hunger that nobody wants to look at. Mothers, most of all, have to recognize it. Its the only way to stop the selfishness, the materialism. Together we can teach them. Just like your father, Gene. Just like your father."

Art and Diane came back complaining about the clean up. Large white circles traced in red surrounded Art's eyes, and triangular yellow teeth ringed his lips. Diane's nose was blackened and served as the anchor for web-like traceries covering her face. They sat next to Gene as Kim continued to talk in a low, husky voice, telling him things about her family he had never heard before. She spoke of the lovers her mother and father brought home when the other was out, the fights, the shopping sprees that were supposed to make everything all right.

As she spoke, Art and Diane took out eyeliner pencils and began to draw on Gene's face. Their exhalations filled his lungs, their hands pressed his skin against bone. As they drew, he felt himself falling away from the world, plunging into a dark grave already crowded with his father's corpse and the bodies of the women he had murdered. There were no more golden memories to grasp.

Rage burst in him and took hold like fire to dry wood, feeding on lies spread by television and advertising; hypocrisies politicians mouthed; hunger for things and positions and power that seethed in his co-workers and in himself.

"I know your father's special way of looking at things didn't skip a generation, Gene," Kim said. "I know you've only been trapped behind a painted face all these years. Let it go, baby. Set yourself free. Come join us."

An erection grew in his lap. The fire took hold there, as well.

His father came out of shadows in a corner of the room. He still wore the grin that had stopped Gene from going to him the day he left. Behind him, his mother appeared, emaciated, eaten by cancer, a shell of flesh. From between her feet crawled the first Shamus, his head lolling slightly. And behind her stirred the bodies. They had all come to stay.

Somewhere in his mind his father tucked him in.

Gene crossed the border.

"The dog, he never left," he said.

Kim came close, studied his eyes. Then she smiled and nodded her head.

He took an eyeliner pencil from Diane and began tracing the pattern for a painted face on his wife. "Neither did Dad," he said at last.

MONOTONE

Lawrence Greenberg

We always try to make room for stories that need to stretch and play and perhaps break a rule or two. They are a vital component of any creative genre. New Yorker Lawrence Greenberg tells us he has a "useless" Masters degree in Telecommunications from NYU, but we have a feeling he prefers it to being an uneducated pinhead. His articles, poetry, reviews, and short fiction have appeared in places as diverse as The Washington Post, The Complete Vampire Companion, *and* Peter Straub's Ghosts.

Morning. Fog. Thick. Hiding everything. Making everything the same. She liked it. Like this. Settled. Calm. Soothing. An atmosphere of comfort. Knock on the door. Was it? Yes. She came downstairs. Opened the door. No one. Looked around outside. Couldn't see. Fog too thick. Everything the same. Everywhere the same. Fog. Covering, surrounding everything. She remembered when she was a girl. Wanting to melt into it. Blend with it. Merge. Long ago. She remembered.

Package at her feet. Rectangular. Not large. Not that small. No address. No return address. Picked it up. Heavy. Took it inside. Black paper. Unwrapped. Red paper. Unwrapped. White box. Opened it. Packaging material. Removed it. Something amorphous. Pinkish. No. Flesh-colored. She touched it. Smooth. Soft. A trace of dampness.

Call Jim? No. Don't disturb him at the office. Should she? Maybe. Maybe not. Too busy. Involved with clients. Busy with all his things. No. The phone rang. She went into the kitchen. Lifted the wall receiver. "Hello?" "Use it well." Soft voice. Deep. Hung up after the three words.

What was it? Unknown. Nothing like it. Who called? Unknown. She went back to the foyer. To the package. Looked down into the box. A lump. What was it for? What did it do? Who was it from? Why'd they send it? Unknown. All unknown.

It couldn't just sit in the box. Could it? She touched it again. Almost warm. Was it? Soft. Like baby skin. No. Where would she put it? What would she use it for? Decoration? Conversation piece? Who knew? Throw it out? Maybe not. Too strange. Table center piece? Too big. Paperweight? No. Doorstop? Of course not. Bookend? Stop. Getting carried away. Getting silly.

The phone rang again. Back to the kitchen. Picked up the wall receiver again. "Hello?"

"Hey, babe."

"Jim."

"Who else? Had to run this morning. All this stuff to do. All these things. You know. Always got a lot to do.

All the time. Missed you. Right? Slept okay, huh? How's things?"

"Jim, we, ah…"

"What?"

"We got a package."

"Oh, yeah? From who? Something you ordered?"

"No, I, ah…"

"Something wrong, babe?"

"No. No, nothing. Just…"

"Just what? C'mon, babe. All these things to do. You know?"

"Just come home."

"Home? Oh, yeah. I knew I called for some reason. Listen, sorry I forgot to tell you. Having dinner with the marketing VP from Pepsi I've been working with. Dinner and a show. Going to see *Will Rogers*. Yee hah and all that. All-American, right? Hey, just like Pepsi. So listen, I won't be home until 11:30, okay?"

"11:30? Are you…?"

"Am I what? Look, babe. Gotta go, okay? Hey, I'll make it up to you. Really. Good stuff tonight. Right?"

"Tonight. Oh, yes. Tonight."

"Yeah?"

"I want you to come home. I want you to see this, ah, package. It's different. Strange."

"Strange? You all right? Oh, yeah. I asked you that. Okay. Great. No sweat. Don't worry, I'll be home. Later. See it and you later. Hey, sorry, but you know this is important. All this stuff's important. All these things I gotta do. Okay?"

"Okay? I don't know. No. I mean no. Not okay. No."

"No? What're you talking about? What no? What's wrong, babe? Huh?"

"No. No 'babe.' It's me. I'm Linda. Remember? Do you remember?"

"What? What's wrong with you? What're you talking

about, 'remember'? What, like I don't know you? Is that what you're saying?"

"Jim, no, you don't. You don't remember. You forget. You forget. All your things. All the things you have to do. People you have to see. All for you. Always for you. Only you."

"Hey, what do you want, babe? I got work to do. Things. Yeah, that's right. All the things I have to do. People? That's right. People I have to see. Yeah."

"Like that woman tonight? You forget. You forget me. You forget everything. Don't you?"

"What? Okay. Now I know there's something wrong. Isn't there? Look, forget it. That's right. I'm saying forget it. I have to go now."

"Then go. Just go. Do whatever you have to do. And then..."

"Then what? Don't come back? Is that what you're going to say? Is it? Okay. I won't. How's that?"

He hung up. She hung up. That was it then. And there was a sound. A hum? Something like. Where was it? The back door? She walked there from the kitchen. No. The sound was no louder. No softer. The same. From the dining room?

Walked over. No. The box. From the box. Went back to the foyer. Yes? Yes. From the box. From the lump. The thing. It was humming. Making a sound. Not exactly a hum. A sound. The same sound. Continuous. Constant. What was this?

The sound. The same sound. She could feel it. The sound resonated. The sound. The same. Constant. Continuous. Low. High. Deep. Soft. Loud. She covered her ears. Still there. The same. Constant. Looked at her watch. 9:30 a.m.

She picked up the box. Not heavy now. Warm. Was it? It sang to her. For her. Did it? She felt it. The sound. She would get rid of it. Yes. Would she? The sound continued.

In the air. Everywhere. Inside her. She carried it. Toward the back door. Stopped. The sound. Constant. Continuous. It sang to her. Inside her. What was it? Deep. Soft. High. Loud. Low. Not human. Angel? No. Who knew? Put it down on the kitchen table. Couldn't get rid of it. Too…too different. Too warm. To her. Too much. Too friendly. Was it? Touched it again. Friendly. The song. The sound. Kept her hand on it. In it. Soft. Smooth. A trace of dampness. She felt it. The sound. In the air. Within her. From long ago. Her hand felt good. Held. Like it was held. Being held. Warm. She remembered.

It calmed her. Soothed her. Made her feel good. Nice. Secure. Comforted. Like she remembered. The way she'd felt. Used to feel. Before. The sound. The song. The hum. Not exactly a hum. Constant. Continuous. Her hand. Warm. She wanted it. Wanted it to be there. For her. Constant. She wanted warmth. Comfort. Security. Her memory. Wanted what it had. What she used to have. Long ago. What it was giving her. What it could give. What could Jim give? What? A house. Car. Furniture. Things. All his things. All the time. His affair. Was there one? Too flip. Facetious. Love. Love? She wanted it. Wanted love. So much. He fucked her. A lot. Liked to fuck. Was it love?

She cried.

The lump. The thing. Her tears fell on it. In it. Absorbed. Drawn in. Like a sponge. She cried. More tears. Her tears made it glisten. Shine. Was it love? It sang. It made its sound. Comforting. Her hand felt warm. Secure. Against the smoothness. The softness. She cried. Warmth. Within her. Her need. Her memory. Felt nice. Felt good. Her hand in it felt soft. Smooth. The sound. Constant. Continuous. Her breasts. So nice. Soft. And hard. The sound within her. Flowing. Singing. Resonating. Sighing. Vibrating. She remembered. Long ago. She cried. Her tears. Flowing.

Her hand. Love. Warmth. She came. So nice. So loving. Soft. Smooth. The sound. Constant. Continuous. For her. With her. To her. Inside her. Within her. The sound. She came with it. The sound of her desire. Returning. To return.

The doorbell rang. The door. Someone there. Should she answer it? Wanted to stay. Where she was. So nice. Comforting. The door. She turned. Walked to the door. A man. In uniform. She opened the door.

"Uh, excuse me, ma'am. This the Linzer residence?"

"Ah...yes."

"Yeah. Great. I believe a package was delivered here?"

"A...package? Ah...no. No, I don't think so."

"Sorry to bother you, ma'am, but I believe we show on our records that you received a package this morning. We're pretty sure — I mean, I think the package was s'posed to have gone to a different address. I guess we made a mistake. I'm sorry, but I guess I'll have to take the package with me." He looked apologetic.

She didn't. "We...didn't get a package this morning. I got up just a little while ago. No package. The mail hasn't even come yet. You must have made a different kind of mistake than the one you thought. Sorry. No package." She smiled. Tried to look convincing.

"Jeez, I could've sworn...Uh, what's that sound?"

"Sound? What sound?"

"I hear something. Kind of like a hum. Not quite. Like a woman. An older woman, I think. Singing. Kind of. You don't hear it, ma'am?"

"No. Sorry. I don't hear anything."

"Huh. Okay. I'll let them know the package didn't get here. Thanks for your help. Sorry to trouble you. Have a good day now." He left.

She went back to the kitchen. The box. The thing was still in the box.

She looked inside. Her hand. Left its imprint. In the thing. Soft outline. She looked at it. It smoothed over as she watched. Imprint gone. But she was there. Her need.

Memory. In the thing. Within it. She knew it. Felt it. Remembered. She was part of it.

Its one need.

She would remove it. Take it out of the box. She reached in with both hands for its underside. Felt her fingers slide under it. Like they were made to be there. She cupped it. Like a huge child. Like the body of a loving man. Lifted it out. It warmed to her touch. Did it? Placed it on the table. Beside the box. The sound.

Always there. Always with her. Inside her. Like the sound of her heart. Pulsing of her blood. Like her need. Returning. Remembering. Knowing her.

She looked at it. So simple. Warm. Friendly. It knew her. Was her. Part of her. She placed her hand on it again. Both hands. They fit its softness. Its smoothness. Its trace of dampness. It felt so good. So kind. So warm. She wanted it.

Wanted to know it. Be it. Feel it. It wanted her. Wanted to give to her. She knew it did. Wanted her to return. Wanted her return. Her hands were so smooth. Soft. Her hands. Blending into the thing. The lump. Like clay. Like she was molding clay. Like the clay was molding her. Living clay. The thing breathed. Loving the thing that sang. That made its own constant sound. The need to return. Merge. She remembered. Long ago.

She pushed. Pushed against it. Tried to shape it. Give it her own shape. The shape she wanted it to be. The lump moved between her hands.

Changed. Singing as it changed shape. Making its constant sound. To her. For her. Its warm sound. She molded it. Gave it features. Nose. Mouth. Eyes. A face. The mouth smiling. The eyes open. Awake. A man's face?

A kind face. A warm face? The smiling mouth sang its constant sound. Was it her face?

She felt the sound within her begin to move. Inside her. Wanting to come out. Wanting to feel the air. Wanting her return. Her need. Memory. The sound came from her. She began to hum. Not exactly a hum. Continuous. Resonating. With the sound of the thing. Long ago. Her hands were warm. Soft. Smooth. Slightly damp. The sound. Resonating. Constant. Her hands. Moving into the face-thing.

One on each cheek. In each cheek. Inside it. Up to her wrists. So nice. Warm. Secure. Comforting. Giving. Giving itself. Its one need. Past her wrists. So good. So warm. It wanted her. She wanted its warmth. Felt her own need. To return. So friendly. Its comfort. She felt so nice. So comforted. Up to her elbows. She loved it.

Its one need. Her desire. Remembering.

She glanced over her shoulder. The kitchen clock. 2:30 p.m. The time. It had gone by so fast. She knew what it was. Love. The comfort. The warmth. So nice. So deep. Her need. Past her elbows. Returning. Long ago. Her face. Against the face-thing. Her breath. Breathing her life into it.

The pulse of her life. Into its mouth. Its mouth so full of sound. Warmth. She breathed her sound into it. Sang her breath. Moved herself. Her need. Up to her shoulders.

She kissed it. Felt its warmth. With her mouth. Her tongue. Warm. Soft. Smooth. Slightly damp. Like she was. Like she had always been. From long ago. Like she would always be. Just like this. It felt like her. Tasted like she would taste. She remembered. Remembered.

They sang. With each other. Into each other. It was warmth. Complete security. She loved it. Complete. She wanted so much. Its one need. Her desire. Her return. She pushed within it for leverage. Climbed up on a kitchen chair. Needing it. Wanting herself. Her memory. Wanting her return. Her one desire. And entered it.

Head first. So warm. All the way inside. So deep. All of her. So loving. Her return. At last.

It was her. Pure sound. Constant. Continuous. Pure warmth. Comfort.

She was where she wanted to be. Within herself. She sang the sound. Her song. The same. Constant. Everywhere the same. This was her. What she was. This constant warmth. Continuous sound. Pure comfort. This was her. She would stay. Here.

Wthin. Always. Inside. From long ago. Long ago.

DEAD LEAVES

James C. Dobbs

James C. Dobbs was born in 1937 in a log cabin in Kentucky with no electricity or plumbing. His first eight years of education were at a one-room mountain school. He's worked as a social worker, long-haul trucker, and professional gambler. He's written a book on gambling strategy and several articles for Win *magazine. He now lives in Baltimore with his wife, Dusty, and assorted animals. He likes bluegrass music, nude beaches, and red wine.*

Curious as to what brought the buzzard so close to the ground, the two boys detoured from the path to the pond and waded through a field of weeds to the fence row at the edge of the pasture. They soon smelled and then saw close up what had attracted the buzzard: a week-dead opossum, stiff and grinning, laying near the base of a large white oak. The older boy poked the carcass with a stick. This alarmed a host of maggots and several crawled out a hole in the opossum's side and others crawled out its mouth. Several large green flies reluctantly gave up their feeding and buzzed about. He almost threw up but got control.

"Let's get goin'," he said, "this thing stinks."

But the memory of the opossum stayed with him for days...how the side next to the ground had stiffened, gravity pulling it to fit the contour of the ground on which it lay, blending back into the earth. How dead it had been.

PRE-EMBALMING PROCEDURES
(From *The Embalmer's Handbook*)

A. Protective Gear/Clothing for the
   Embalmer
B. Preliminary Procedures
   1. Remove articles of clothing.
   2. Position body squarely on the
      table.
   3. Elevate head by placing it on a
      head rest. Make sure the head
      rest will not interfere with
      fluid distribution or blood
      drainage.
   4. Spray body and external orifices
      with a reliable disinfectant
      (e.g., Phenol or fumeless
      cavity fluid).
         * mouth
         * nose
         * pubic areas
   5. Nose and mouth
         * wash with soap and water
         * insert hose into nostrils
           and mouth and flush and
           rinse with running water
   6. Clean fingernails.

John Meaks followed the contour line of the hill, shaded from the fall sun by the canopy of oak and ash and poplar, the brown carpet of dry, dead leaves making the way slippery on the steep parts of the hill. He steadied himself with the dead branch he was using for a walking stick. *Dead leaves*, he thought, smiling inwardly at the irony as he slipped again and almost fell, his foot plowing a two-foot long furrow down the steep slope, the unexpected movement sending pain shooting through his body. It was the memory of these leaves that had brought him here. He sat down beside the furrow to allow the pain to subside, picking up a few dry and brittle leaves from the top layer. Digging down further, he noticed how they started to lose their individuality, to become moist as they continued the metamorphosis from leaf to earth.

Higher up the hill he heard the bark of a gray squirrel and through the high canopy of hardwoods he caught a glimpse of the dipping flight of a wood hen, its cackle trailing it from one hill across the hollow to an adjacent hill. A pileated woodpecker to the ornithologist, but in these Kentucky hills it was known only as a wood hen.

The raucousness of crows in the distance, the buzz of the early fall insects, the angle of the sun's rays through the trees, the earthy smell of the woods…hundreds of sights and smells and sounds triggered memories from the time when these hills had been his daily playground. A great sadness welled up and for a few minutes he sat motionless, his brain numbed by the overload of memories.

```
Putrefaction at 70° F
(if body exposed to air for 1-3 days):
      * Eyeballs are flattened
      * Greenish discoloration over
        abdominal area
      * Postmortem stain
      * Dehydrated lips and eyelids
```

But all the experiences that had created those memories
led inexorably to the awful finality of his now. This was
the last day of his life. The snub-nose .38 in his pocket
would see to that. *Death is my servant*, he thought. *He
must always come when I call.* His servant would deliver
him from the pain and sickness of cancer and the
chemicals and radiation that were its feeble enemies. Soon
he would meld with the leaves and the earth. But he still
had to get to the spot and his strength was fading fast. If
he lost consciousness or simply got too weak to go any
farther, his body would be filled with embalming fluid
instead of being allowed to gently reunite with Mother
Earth.

The turkey vulture (*catures aura*) is common from
Canada to South America. It feeds almost exclusively on
carrion. It has excellent eyesight and a highly developed
sense of smell.

The words of an old song came to him...

> The shells in the ocean / will be my death bed;
> The fish in deep water / swim over my head.

Additional Preliminary Procedures for
Head Post

(Skull has been opened and
examined by medical examiner)

1. Clean forehead.
2. Open cranial incision (remove
   sutures made by medical
   examiner's office).
3. Remove calvarium.
4. Remove brain and place in
   visceral bucket.

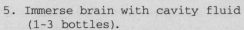
5. Immerse brain with cavity fluid
   (1-3 bottles).
6. Cover visceral bucket.
7. Ligate/clamp any vessels that
   were cut by the ME during
   arterial injection of the head.
8. Clamp off:
    *2 vertebrals
    *2 internal carotids (found
       in the *sella turcica* at
       the base of the cranium)
9. Force 2 closed hemostats into the
   external carotids.

The black vulture (*coragyps atratus*) is found from Canada to South America and feeds mostly on carrion. It has been known to kill weak and dying prey and will also consume the feces of dead animals. It has no highly developed sense of smell but uses its excellent eyesight to locate carrion lying in the open or by observing the behavior of other scavengers.

He had considered the ocean as the final resting place for his sick body. When she got the note, that's where she would think he had gone. But the ocean wasn't his first choice. Although he loved the ocean and had spent many happy days sailing its surface and strolling its shores, the deep recesses where his body might end up were foreign to him. He preferred to know at least the common names of the creatures his death would nourish.

The opossum is the only North American marsupial. It is a nocturnal scavenger and will eat almost anything. It is particularly fond of persimmons, grubworms, and carrion.

Anytime a body has been laying in the woods for over twenty-four hours, you

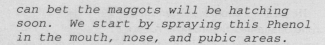

can bet the maggots will be hatching
soon. We start by spraying this Phenol
in the mouth, nose, and pubic areas.

He held a single dry oak leaf, feeling how the smoothness of the top contrasted with the slight roughness of the bottom. He turned it over. The bottom looked like the earth's terrain carved by a river and its tributaries as seen from 35,000 feet.

Next we wash the body with this
disinfectant soap. Stick the hose in
each nostril and flush it thoroughly.
Now the mouth.

This fellow, he said to himself, probably fell in October. Last spring and summer were its halcyon days…a small bud materializing on a high branch, growing each day, weeks of sunshine and rain and wind and darkness…doing its part to absorb the sun, to energize the tree, to shade the earth and to join forces with the branches and trunk and roots and other leaves to help cleanse the atmosphere. And now to have its death nourish the earth. Soon he would join forces with the leaves. Together they would feed the earth and the earth's creatures.

A number of insects, primarily beetles and flies, have a life cycle that includes the laying of eggs on dead or dying animals. The larva hatch and burrow into the body and feed there as what we commonly call maggots until the next stage of their metamorphosis.

Gunshot wounds to the head are a
challenge to our profession. We want
this guy to lay in his open coffin and
look like he died in his sleep.

He picked a damp leaf from further down the strata. A relic of summer before last. What part of my strut-and-fret act was I doing while this fellow was doing its thing? He replayed mental tapes of that summer…finally making a success of the business he had struggled with for five years, finally rid of that gut-gnawing feeling of not quite being able to afford the lifestyle he was living, of feeling dependent on his wife's income for vacations and cars.

The black vulture is more aggressive than the turkey vulture and will usually drive the turkey vulture away from the feast. The turkey vulture, thanks to its highly developed sense of smell, usually arrives first, however, managing to get in a meal before the black vulture arrives.

It had been a wonderful, heady summer. He worked long hours, but evenings and weekends they spent together, dining at their favorite restaurants and taking trips to New York and Montreal and the beaches. In late September, when this now dull fellow was donning its fiery coat, they spent two wonderful weeks in Paris and the French Riviera.

They had retraced the steps of Hemingway and partook of the movable feast. They visited the graves of Piaf and Morrison and sat for hours at the outdoor cafés. He had thought, as they strolled the beach at St. Tropez, that he would live out the remainder of his years like that.

Both the turkey vulture and black vulture are bald about the head and neck. This allows them to stick their head deep inside decaying carcasses without becoming infected, even when the animal died of disease or is highly decomposed. What germs attach themselves to the bare head and neck are soon killed as the head and neck dry out during flight and by exposure to sunlight.

Over the Atlantic, on their way home, she brought up the subject of children. Some survival-of-the-species urges buried deep in her female brain began to manifest themselves. She had no children. His were grown and he wanted no more. Overpopulation, he said, was the root of all the environmental problems. Keep adding a million people to the face of the earth every five days like we're doing now and eventually the earth must scream out in pain.

But he didn't refuse to consider it. He wanted her to be happy, but deep down he felt that children meant the end of his happy times with her. They discussed adoption. He stated bluntly that he felt they had the perfect life, and hoping to improve it by introducing a child was like shooting a bullet into an alarm clock, hoping it would improve the mechanism. She let the matter drop, but he sensed resentment.

Anger and resentment lingered on both sides. The matter of moving to a nicer house was debated…she wanted to, he didn't. That winter he wanted to take a week's vacation in the Caribbean. She wanted to go to Hawaii for two weeks. They each got on a position and he finally booked a trip to the Caribbean for himself and spent a lonely five days gambling and reading.

They stopped talking about the business. He hired an assistant who gradually assumed her former duties. He immersed himself in the work and it became more prosperous. They got annoyed with each other over small things. He missed the old days and he hoped she did too, but missing them was to admit they were gone.

They were civil and occasionally they had sex, but the romance was gone. The more and more infrequent good times and sex seemed to be something they did, not for their own sake…but something each knew they had to have at least a minimum of to justify staying together.

They were both at that stage where neither had the energy for any major change like divorce. They joined a few million other couples by staying together for convenience but looking outside the relationship for whatever satisfaction could be found. It was to this unhappy home that cancer came.

Vultures, like many birds, are equipped with a crop, an expandable pouch in the chest, which allows them to store food once they have eaten their fill. Later, when food becomes scarce, they can regurgitate from the crop and eat. They also feed nesting young in this manner.

The prognosis was bad. He had refused to admit it was worth seeing a doctor until the cancer had metastasized throughout his body. Once he understood the situation, he resigned himself to a fairly imminent death. He never planned to live forever and started thinking about how to make his final few months as painless as possible.

He busied himself getting his affairs in order. He put the business up for sale. He checked on his life insurance policies and updated his will and tried to look at the situation with the rationality he had always prided himself on. But his impending death clouded his days and encroached often into his dreams.

Where would he be when he breathed his last? In a hospital bed, comatose with pain-killing drugs? Would his relatives be gathered around? Where would he be buried — at the family cemetery in Kentucky with his parents and cousins and grandparents? None of these options seemed very acceptable. He had been in charge of his own life, he wanted to stay in charge until the end. He began giving a lot of thought to the orchestration of his death.

She did not accept the inevitability as easily. The love

buried by resentment and disappointment quickly resurfaced. She read everything available on the nature of his sickness and the current theories on treatment. He went to two specialists at her insistence. He began radiation and chemotherapy. Buying time to hope for a miracle.

Soon, however, he knew the fight was not for him. He could endure the inpatient and outpatient treatments and the loss of his hair and the nausea, but for what? Another year or so of treatments? No, thank you, he said. He would finish the series of treatments but that would be it. She said she understood. He didn't notice the strange way she looked at him.

A few days later she came to him and asked if they could talk. Her face showed worry and fear and determination and something else he couldn't quite grasp. They sat on the couch and she took his hand. His eyes searched her face for some clue as to what she was going to say, but she stared at the floor as she spoke. The words came very hard, forced out by her resolve, "I want you to have your vasectomy reversed. I want to get pregnant."

He stared at her, stunned, as his mind fought to put things into perspective. Her eyes slowly left the floor and met his. He saw the hurt and the embarrassment, as if she felt she had asked a drowning man for a drink of water. He saw the pain and knew she still loved him and that his pain was her pain. But beyond all these things he saw something else, something very large and demanding, something he knew he could never understand.

His impending death had made him more aware of the finiteness of life and how rudimentary birth and death were to all species, but he had been thinking mostly about the death side of it. Suddenly, he was slapped with the realization that she was looking beyond his death. She needed something from him now, something physical, something primal. What he thought of as himself, his body, his intellect, his personality, would soon be gone. She wanted him right now for none of these things. She wanted his sperm to fertilize her eggs. She didn't give a shit about his personality.

He got up from the couch, walked across the room, and turned and looked at her. With a poker player's instinct, he wanted to be able to read her body language as well as her eyes.

Her body communicated such a singlemindness of purpose that he almost felt he could see a monstrous aura hovering around her, a shimmering green being with arms held up prayerlike in a posturing position, dictating the course of action that she must take. "He is a source of the sperm that you must have," it was telling her, "you must get it at any cost."

A chill went through him and, as it subsided, he was overcome with a terrible loneliness. Suddenly he felt no closeness to Laura...she was a beast as he a beast. They had met randomly in the jungle and temporarily used each other for self-preservation motives. The feeling stayed with him and intensified until not even the beasts described the feeling. It was colder than that: beasts breathed out warm vapors and blood ran through their veins. He and Laura were not two beasts, not reptiles or strange slippery creatures from the ocean's depths, not even slimy mud-dwellers. For a moment he saw only electrical charges and force fields and the cold physics of the universe. He and Laura were nothing but two charges with an attraction for each another, an attraction whose roots went to the essence of the survival of their carbon-based life form. The aura was some manifestation of the forces that orchestrated the attraction.

He had the sudden sensation of faintness, of falling into a terrible abyss and a horrible sense of isolation. He held his head and staggered to keep his balance.

Laura was quickly beside him, holding his arm, helping

him to the couch. Overcome with emotion, she started crying, putting her arms around him, holding him tightly.

"I'm so sorry, John, I really am. I don't want to put you through any more pain. But I could accept your death better if I had your child. After you're gone I'm going to be alone."

He still didn't know how he felt. The aura he had seen frightened him. He had sensed it before in Laura and in other women, but never so vividly. But now it was gone and only her warm femininity remained. He held her, stroking her hair as she sobbed. The sense of belonging to the flesh-and-blood world, of having a relationship with Laura, slowly came back. The stark world he had visualized briefly was too painful and frightful to allow into his consciousness. They sat on the couch and she gradually stopped crying.

"I don't know how I feel about it," he began. "You know the percentages aren't particularity good, even if I agree to try."

"I've talked with three specialists."

"What did they say about getting pregnant by someone dying of cancer?"

"It's not in your reproductive system. There's no reason to think the baby is at any more risk than normal."

"I asked the doctor who did the vasectomy about the possibility of reversal. He said it is very painful, about a 50% success rate."

She started crying again. "With new techniques, it's probably a little better. I know it's a very painful recovery period and I don't want to put you through any more pain, it's just that…" She looked at him, pleading with him to understand. He didn't.

"You know how I feel about the population problem," he said.

"I know," she said.

"It's not something I want to do at any level.

Intellectually and emotionally, I'm opposed to it. I'm not egotistical enough to think that my offspring are going to save the world, and I can reasonably assume they will be the same sort of habitual consumers that we are: parasites on the ecosystems of the earth. And, at this stage of my life, I'm not crazy about some doctor yanking my balls and my prick around so he can tie them back together."

"So you won't consider it?" Only a glimmer of the aura was still present.

"When's the last time I refused to consider anything you wanted me to do?"

The aura disappeared completely. She laid her head on his chest and cried softly.

That night as he lay in bed reading and listening to a blues show on the radio, she walked into the room to get ready for bed herself. She spontaneously started doing a strip to an old version of "Tin Roof Blues." He had always found the song erotic anyway, as it had been very popular when he was going through puberty.

She started swaying her hips to the music, unbuttoning her cotton shirt from the top down. She let the shirt slide off her shoulders and then turned her back to him, swaying as she unbuttoned and unzipped her jeans. Pulling them slowly over her hips, she kicked them into a corner. She turned to face him, wearing her bikini panties and flimsy bra. He put down his book and turned up the volume a little.

She did a few seductive moves and reached behind her back to unsnap the bra. This particular maneuver had always been very erotic for him and he now had a tremendous erection. She tossed the bra in his face with an impish smile and put both hands behind her head and did some bumps and grinds that reminded him of the old-time strippers from his college days. She turned her back to him and slowly worked her panties down over her hips.

Keeping her legs straight, she lowered them to her ankles and stepped out of them. As the song wound down, she turned to face him, totally naked, improvising an incredibly erotic dance.

As the song ended, she slipped under the cover, taking his erection in her left hand, running her other hand through his chest hair up to his neck, across his ear, and through his hair. She gently pushed his head to the pillow, as he started to move she held him down.

Before he could say anything, she had the head of his penis in her mouth, slowly moving it in and out. She gently rubbed the fingertips of her left hand over his balls, continuing the delightful oral stimulation. All the while her right fingertips kept moving from his pubic hair across his navel, up to his chest hair, his nipples and back again.

A few minutes was all it took before he was consumed by orgasm. He was surprised that she was swallowing as he ejaculated; she had never done this before. Usually her fellatio was foreplay to intercourse, but now she literally drank him in.

As his final spasms subsided, he opened his eyes. In the subdued light he saw it again, more plainly this time, the female aura hovered around her, arms and hands raised in a peculiar prayerlike position. It was looking down upon them with a faint, approving smile.

His head was swimming with thoughts and images. He had a knot in his stomach, but the rest of his body was glowing from the extraordinary erotic experience he had just experienced.

She kissed him deeply, her tongue caressing his as he tasted his own cum. He had never known her to be so sensuous. She snuggled against him, almost snakelike. Her fingers stroked his hair and caressed his ears. Her head lay on his chest. She was no longer the sensuous temptress, she seemed more like a vulnerable child.

"Will you go with me tomorrow to talk with Dr. Moore?" she asked.

He didn't have to ask who Dr. Moore was.

"Sure, it won't hurt to talk with him."

He squinted through barely open eyelids. As he expected, the green aura hovered above them, smiling gently, approvingly.

In the fall the abdomen of the female praying mantis is swollen with eggs that must be fertilized. The male approaches her carefully from behind, clasps her body and transfers a capsule containing the spermatozoa that will fertilize her eggs. When finished, he disengages the embrace and flees as quickly as possible. Many are unable to escape the female after mating and are decapitated and eaten. Some are decapitated during the mating process.

The next morning when he woke, she lay sleeping beside him. All night, he remembered, she snuggled against him, occasionally lovingly stroking his shoulder or chest. But he also remembered the green female aura and the stark vision of himself and Laura being nothing but energy forces. He closed his eyes again to try and sort things out.

For the next few days he relaxed in the back yard, enjoying the late summer days. He spent a lot of time playing with Rex, their golden retriever. He allowed himself to accept the world of energy forces as natural. That must really be all there is, he told himself. These horribly complicated situations we build out of emotions and matter must just be another version of the iron filings reacting to the magnet's forces. Finally he decided that, if he remained a bit of energy after his death, he could be quite happy.

The praying mantis lives for a single season. It breaks out of the egg mass on a warm June day and feasts on bugs and worms. The victim is eaten alive, held like an ear of corn. After eating the mantis goes through a cat-like ritual of cleaning itself. In the late fall, after mating, its movements grow slow. By November, it is dead.

The doctor leveled with them. He could try to reverse the vasectomy. There was a fifty or sixty percent probability of success. John was due more radiology treatments. They agreed it was better to wait until they were finished. But John had another agenda.

He had made his peace with the situation. His will was drawn up. Insurance policies guaranteed she would be comfortable, wealthy by some standards. His children were grown and successful. She would have the dog and cats and her friends to comfort her. And she would have other options. He had consulted another doctor without telling her. His time was drawing near. He didn't tell her how near.

```
Pose features
  1. Shave men.
     (Do not remove beards or mustaches.)
  2. Prepare face with massage cream, oil,
     etc.
  3. Apply massage cream, petroleum
     jelly, etc., to dehydrated areas.
```

The more he thought about his death the more important it became to be a part of the cycle. Living, dying, and rebirth...the essence of nature. He didn't want his body posed in a casket, his friends and relatives forced to come admire the mortician's art. He wanted to die quietly, without fanfare, to have his death be as meaningless or as meaningful as that of a bug in a swimming pool.

He planned his escape with considerable detail. He didn't want her or his children burdened with details of the funeral, disposal, where to bury him, etc. But not leaving a body caused its own problems. There were all sorts of legalities, he discovered, concerning when a person who has disappeared can be considered dead.

Finally, he decided it was worth it. Any doctor would surely testify he couldn't have lived more than a year...and he was leaving suicide notes. Besides, he would make sure that not all that much was tied up in the estate.

He sold the business for half a million, less than what it was worth, but he was in a hurry. He deposited the proceeds in their joint savings account. He put cash in two envelopes for his children. Enough to let them know he was thinking about them until he was declared legally dead and they got their share of his estate.

Both the red fox and the gray fox are primarily hunters. They will occasionally eat carrion and carry bones of the larger animals back to their den to gnaw.

All of this took a couple of months. Time was running out. He had considerable pain at times, but he could still walk and drive. He had one more thing left to do.

He entered Johns Hopkins for some additional tests, but this time there would be something additional. He was there for ten days. Laura visited every day. The doctors told him everything had gone fine.

He planned it for the following weekend. She was in charge of a charity fundraiser and would be very busy. He told her he was going to Kentucky for the weekend. They had an A-frame on the farm in the foothills of the Cumberlands where he had grown up. He would take Rex even though the dog would present a logistics problem for him. But he knew that she would be suspicious if he didn't take him. Also, he wanted a companion on his final voyage.

```
Close the Mouth
        1. Relax face and relieve rigor
           mortis.
        2. Observe the normal bite and
           points of natural expression in
           closing the mouth.
        3. Secure the mandible.
           a. Normal methods
                * Run suture from the
                  mantalis muscle of the
                  chin through the septum of
                  the nose and then tie the
                  remaining suture in a bow
                  or
                * Use a needle gun
           b. Gun Shot Wounds
                * Use a hand/manual drill.
                * Bore a small hole through
                  the mandible and  through
                  the maxilla at the root of
                  the teeth.
                * Pass a wire through the
                  holes.
                * Position the mandible.
                * Twist the ends of the wire
                  together.
```

He spent several days composing his final letters. Are letters this long still called suicide notes? he wondered.

The common crow and its cousins the rook and raven are found throughout most of the world. The common crow is gregarious, boisterous, and very intelligent. It eats corn sprouts, mice, insects, and carrion. Its main source of food in the United States is road kill.

He kissed her goodbye on Friday morning. It wasn't as difficult as he had feared. He still had a couple of days and he would call her that night to tell her he had arrived safely. He told her he had made an appointment to have his vasectomy reversed. It was something of a lie, but when she got the letter she would understand.

```
Pose Lips
        1. Raise corners of the mouth
           slightly.
        2. Fill out the cheek slightly with
           cotton.
        3. Apply stay cream to cotton.
        4. Use aneurysm hook and forceps to
           insert cotton in the mouth to
           keep lips together.
        5. Place wet cotton strips above the
           upper lip and under the lower
           lip.
        6. Exert pressure downward and
           upward to keep lips closed.
```

The drive from Baltimore was emotional for him. Like the last day of a summer romance, but with a heavy finality looming on the horizon. He exited the Baltimore beltway and headed west on I-70, a maneuver he always enjoyed. The idea that beyond the western horizon lay the cornbelt, the plains, the Rockies and the Pacific always stimulated interesting thoughts about the early settlers or plans for future vacations. But this time the memories of a thousand or so like maneuvers bombarded him. Every exit he passed brought back memories of times he had taken the exit and what direction his life was taking then. The memories were vivid, high-density videos with surround-emotion. He knew he was passing each exit for the last time. Mentally he followed several byways from the interstate exit, visualizing what lay around each bend, remembering the reasons he had followed them in the past.

Rex kept looking at him quizzically, a smile on his face but with worry in his eyes. The dog usually loved riding in the van, in the front seat looking for horses, cows, or other dogs. But Rex sensed something was wrong. This should be a happy time, but Rex could sense the sadness. He patted the dog's head and forced himself into a happier state of mind. He wanted Rex to be happy on their last trip together.

A host of insects, primarily ants and beetles, survive by living off death. Every dead bug, mouse, bird, snake, rabbit, squirrel, opossum, deer — or any other organism composed of flesh, blood, bones, or cartilage — means days or weeks of sustenance for the tribe. They come to the wake as individuals, as groups, or as highly organized societies to pick the bones...to cleanse the earth as they nourish their own bodies.

He arrived in Summerville a little after dark. Jimmie and his family were expecting him and had prepared supper. He played the father and grandfather roles for the last time. They ate and talked for a couple of hours. He called Laura to tell her they had arrived safely. About 10:30 p.m. he left his son's hometown and drove the ten miles out to the farm.

He loved driving the dark country roads, with no street lights and most of the homes along the way dimly lit. He turned off the main road and took the one-lane gravel road up the hollow to the A-frame. A motion detector activated the floodlights as he entered the driveway. Rex got excited when he recognized the place of former good times.

He was weary from the long drive, the pain, and the drugs but the night sounds brought back fifty-year-old

memories. He carried in his backpack, gave Rex some
food and water, and got out a bottle of Maker's Mark.
Sitting on the porch, he let the bourbon and the pleasant
ambience of the Kentucky night sooth his soul.

The last of the katydids were going strong, proclaiming
that frost wasn't many weeks away. A host of other bugs
joined the chorus.

```
Eye Closure
        1. Lift eyelid with aneurism hood.
        2. Use flat forceps to insert eye
            caps.
        3. Apply stay cream.
                * under the lids and
                * on top of the eye caps
        4. Close eyes at the inferior 1/3 of
            the eye socket.

    Position Elbows (close to sides of
    the body)

    Position Hands (leisurely position)

    Position Legs (straight and close
    together)
```

He sipped the whiskey slowly. Rex lay beside him on
the porch, his ears twitching at unfamiliar sounds as
nightbirds and insects filled the hollow with a primeval
symphony. A fox barked on the opposite hill and the sound
echoed down the hollow. Rex leaped to his feet, his back
hair forming a mohawk, a primitive growl welling up from
within him. "It's okay," he told the dog, "it's just one of
your distant cousins." Rex searched his face to be sure
there was no cause for alarm and lay back down, resting
his chin on his front paws. His ears stayed cocked to the
degree gravity would allow, however. His being was not

far removed from that of his ancestors who had guarded
the mouth of the cave.

Pre-embalming analysis will determine
what type of solution to use and what
arteries and veins to use for injection.
Usually for a head post you inject the
femoral artery and drain from the
femoral vein. In cases of generalized
decomposition, a 6-point injection may be
required.

Incision
   1. Make incision 3 inches deep (go
      through skin and superficial
      fascia).
   2. Use aneurysm hook to separate
      artery from vein, nerves, and
      fascia.
   3. Ligate artery/vein with 6 inches
      of suture.
   4. Make a transverse incision in the
      artery/vein.
   5. Insert cannula tube and tighten
      ligature.
   6. Determine locations for the
      drainage points.
   7. Insert drain tubes into drainage
      points far enough to pass all
      valves.

In spite of his circumstances, being able to orchestrate
his final exit gave him a feeling of control. The sense of
being one with the earth, the universe, was becoming more
powerful. Sounds from the trees and ponds and grasses
merged with the buzzing within his own head, and they
harmonized into a comforting mantra. He took another
sip of whiskey and planned his final day. On the hill

behind him a whippoorwill gave its last plaintive call of the night.

Vultures have an "industrial strength" digestive system that lets them filter out even the most pernicious bacteria. They have no trouble digesting the putrefied result of the most vicious plagues or infections. They literally eat disease and turn it into nutrient for the earth.

He arose at daylight with only a slight headache from the whiskey, but the pills would take care of that along with any serious pain. He felt some numbness in his right leg and knew the cancer was starting to attack his spinal cord. He only needed another twelve hours. God forbid that, after fifty years of service, his central nervous system would succumb at the eleventh hour.

```
Embalming Machine
     1. Pour embalming fluid into
        machine.
     2. Add cold water to make
        approximately three (3) gallons
        of solution.
     3. Set rate of flow (moderate flow
        for generalized decomposition).
     4. Set pressure control (low
        pressure for generalized
        decomposition).
```

He called Rex and they walked together through the barnyard. His neighbor boarded two horses and a mule there, and the horses strolled over for a closer look at Rex. Rex only barked a couple of times and tentatively approached the nearest horse. They sniffed noses.

He climbed the hill above the barn, the morning dew

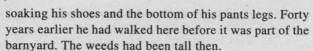

soaking his shoes and the bottom of his pants legs. Forty years earlier he had walked here before it was part of the barnyard. The weeds had been tall then.

The white oak still stood, serving as a post for the barbed wire now enclosing the barnyard. He remembered the exact spot where the opossum had lain. Now there was nothing to distinguish it. Small sandrocks that had washed down from higher up the hill lay on an outcropping of limestone. An ant struggled backward, dragging a cricket leg. He stood looking at the spot for several minutes. From the field and trees below the barn came the din of grasshoppers and jarflies. He walked back to the barn.

One of the barn stalls had been screened in at one time to house a goat. This was where he planned to leave Rex. A round tub used as a watering trough was already in the stall. He carried it outside, hosed it out, put it back in the stall and filled it with the hose. Enough water to last Rex a month and he should only be there a couple of days max. He went into the house and got a large bag of dry dog food and dumped it in the feed trough. Rex wasn't one to overeat, particularly with dry dog food. He would be okay.

He climbed into the barn loft and threw down a pitchfork of hay and put it in the stall. He took off the St. Martin Beach Paradise T-shirt he was wearing beneath his flannel shirt and laid it over the hay. His scent would comfort Rex even after he was no longer alive.

```
Arterial Embalming
        1. Clamp off corresponding vein to
           create back pressure and prevent
           short circuits (back pressure
           needed to overcome vascular
           resistance and loosen clots).
        2. Inject downward into the artery
           (torso first then appendages).
```

3. Inject approximately one (1)
   quart of embalming solution.
4. Vigorously massage body, arms,
   and legs toward the heart.
5. Stop machine when vein begins to
   distend.
6. Open drain tube pump.
7. Pump out blood until drainage
   stops.
8. Repeat steps.

He still had to drive ninety miles to Lexington, sell the van, mail some letters, and then somehow get back to the farm and into the woods without anyone recognizing him.

He packed his backpack, the same one that had ridden his back across a hundred miles of Appalachian Trail with Laura and Rex and the length of Isle Royale with his first wife.

He had planned to leave Rex in the barn while he went to Lexington, but at the last minute he decided to take him along. It would rule out a bus back to Summerville, but that would have left the problem of getting from the bus station to the farm. Also, if his neighbor came by to feed the horses, he might discover Rex in the stall.

He loaded the few things he had brought into the van and locked up the A-Frame. They drove into Summerville where he stopped at a phone booth and called Jimmie to tell him he had business in Lexington and would be back late that night. He also invited them out to the farm the following day for a barbecue. Of course, they would only find his note instructing them to look in the barn where they would find Rex and the other things he was leaving.

About the size of a cat but with only 1/5 the mass of its brain, the opossum makes up in appetite what it lacks in intelligence. Opossum have been discovered inside the carcasses of large animals such as deer, so ravenous is their appetite.

It went quicker in Lexington than he thought it would. He drove into the used car lot of the Toyota dealer and quickly sold the van for several hundred less than what it was worth. He had them make the check out to Laura and he signed over the title. He asked the salesman to call a cab for him, saying he had a plane to catch. "The dog going on the plane too?" the salesman asked.

"Yeah, they furnish crates for them," he replied.

At first the cabbie didn't want to take Rex, but the promise of an extra large tip changed his mind. He directed the driver to a familiar downtown intersection. He then walked to a small park and finished his letter to Laura.

Dearest Laura,

By the time you read this, my pain will have ended. I'm taking what I think is the easiest way out for both of us. I'm sorry that not having a body to prove I'm dead will cause some legal headaches, but I'm sure you understand.

It's very important to me that I go quietly, without forcing you and others who love me to watch me slowly die.

I know you will wonder about my final days. After leaving Rex at the farm this morning, I drove to Lexington and sold the van. The check is enclosed. I had them make it payable to you. Call and cancel the insurance.

I mailed this letter and took a plane south under a different name. Please don't bother trying to trace my path from Lexington. I have a plan to die at sea. But if you take a trip to the Caribbean with your next husband and see a sea gull with binoculars looking at the topless girls, you'll know there may be such a thing as reincarnation.

In spite of our problems the last couple of years, I want you to know our years together were the happiest of my life. If sometimes we didn't see things the same way, that's just how life is when you share it with someone. Your love and kindness the past few months have made the pain much easier to bear.

More than anything, I want the rest of your life to be happy; but there are no words I can say that will guarantee that. You are a wonderful person and you deserve much happiness. Do whatever it takes to achieve it.

Although legally and physically I will be dead by tomorrow night, I visualize myself as existing on another plane or in another dimension. I hope you are able to think of me in the same way.

I am aware of your maternal instincts; I've seen some of the forces involved. If you still want to bear my child, you have my blessings. Call Doctor Godfrey at the Johns Hopkins sperm bank. I've been working with him. Using some experimental techniques, he was able to get an adequate supply of my sperm without exactly reversing the vasectomy. If for some reason it doesn't work, he has a bunch of interns willing to donate.

If you do have my child, please save all my books and CDs and things I have written. When he or she is old enough, make sure they know they were things that were important to me. That's all I can offer to give them a clue to their roots.

I've had a wonderful life and you were one of the things that made it so wonderful. I'm glad I had the opportunity to tell you these things.

It's been real. Je ne regrette rien.

Love you,

John

He put the check for the van and the letter into a stamped envelope and walked with Rex to a mailbox and mailed it.

He walked another two blocks to a gas station and asked the attendant if he knew anyone who would like to make $100 plus gas to drive him to Summerville.

Sure enough, one of the mechanics had a brother-in-law out of work, and, after a couple of phone calls and a thirty minute wait, they were headed south on Route 27 in an '85 Chevy van.

```
Aspiration
     1. Use a trocar with clear rigid
        plastic tubing.
     2. Insert the trocar 2 inches above
        and 2 inches to the left of the
        umbilicus.
     3. Aspirate from high to low areas
        until all liquids are  removed
        from the viscera.
     4. Puncture and aspirate in this
        order:
              * lungs
              * heart
              * nine (9) regions of the
                abdomen
```

The van stopped where a logging road exited the woods on the ridge road above the farm. It would have been two miles to the A-Frame by the road, but by walking through the woods and down the hill it was less than a mile. He told the driver he had a cabin back on the lake. He gave him the $100 and a $20 tip. The heartfelt thanks cheered him on the hike down to the farm.

The route took him through the area he had decided would be where this life ended. He had thought about it carefully. It was imperative that it be somewhere he would not be discovered. A spot so remote that not even his bones would be discovered until they decayed.

The vulture population of southeastern Kentucky is enormous. On any day suitable for flying, it is almost impossible to go outside and look up without seeing at least one buzzard circling overhead.

They followed another abandoned logging road down from the ridge. The timber hadn't been cut in twenty years and the overhead canopy of hardwoods kept sunlight out so the underbrush was sparse. *Nice for squirrels but not likely to attract many deer*, he thought. About halfway down he stopped and walked along the contour line perpendicular to the logging road. There was a sprinkling of redbud and dogwood. The brown carpet of dead leaves was everywhere. They were dry, at least on top, and crunched with each step. Even Rex's paws made a *pdit pdit pdit* sound as he trotted ahead, fell behind, and then ran to catch up.

He noted with pleasure that the canopy was starting to turn. Leaves that were green a week or two ago were now getting rusty and a few had already changed color and were dipping and stalling as they fell.

It was getting difficult for him to walk. There was numbness in his right hip and he had a problem controlling his leg. It was still almost a mile back to the barn to leave Rex and a half a mile back to the spot. He had to push on.

He remembered a spot where there were fewer oak and hickory and the underbrush had more of a chance to thrive. A little farther around the hill and he saw the woods brighten up. It was as he remembered. Oak, poplar, and ash grew sparse enough that a grove of sourwood and ironwood grew thick. On the fringes of the grove was a tangle of briers and weeds. If a hunter were walking through here, he would give it a detour. There were easier routes to follow. Yes, this was the spot.

Later, he would make his way into that thicket. He hoped it would be a long time before anyone else did. In that friendly thicket, he would let go of his ego and become part of the whole. If he still remained as a charged ion or magnetic force, so be it. Natural forces, honed by millions of years of evolution, would dispose of his body. He would feed the ants and the vultures and benevolently act as host for the maggots. The leaves would cover him and his flesh would nourish the fauna.

```
Cavity Embalming

(to disinfect contents of the hollow
   organs)

      1. Use gravity bottle holder.
      2. Insert trocar high to allow fluid
         gravitation.
      3. Inject cavity fluid into:
            * lungs
            * heart
            * nine (9) regions of the
              abdomen
```

He called to Rex, who had found an animal den in a limestone ledge and had his whole head inside trying to get every smell. Rex came reluctantly.

They got to the bottom of the hill and he paused to listen before exiting the woods to cross the road which led to another small farm farther up the hollow. Hearing nothing, he crossed the road and was quickly into the woods on the next hill. They climbed part way up and then followed the contour line around until they were above the A-Frame.

He called Rex to him and sat for a while at the edge of the woods, watching. There was a fresh load of hay in the hay rack and the horses were eating, so his neighbor had already been there to feed them and probably would not return until tomorrow. The sun was approaching the hill to the west. He still had an hour or more of daylight. The day had been an eternity. The pain was considerable; he had not wanted to be slowed down by the pills. He wanted to rest, but now he could not...not yet.

```
Hypodermic Embalming

Use trocar to inject cavity fluid into
areas embalmed during the arterial
embalming process (e.g., shoulder,
buttocks, etc.).

Surface Embalming

Use preservative jelly or cavity packs on
surface areas that did not receive
embalming solution during arterial
embalming process.
```

He walked quickly to the barn, passing again the spot where the opossum had lain. He called Rex into the goat stall, locking the door behind them. He still had to write a note to Jimmie and put it on the door of the A-frame. He didn't want any passing cars to catch sight of Rex. He settled down on the hay, on his Island Paradise T-shirt, and wrote

Dear Jimmie,
    Look in the goat stall in the barn. You'll find Rex and my backpack containing several letters (including one to you) that will explain everything. Please call Laura after you have read your letter. I will mail a letter to her from Lexington, but she probably won't get it until Tuesday.
        Love you,
          Dad

Treatment for the Head Post
1. Clean and dry interior of cranium.
2. Dip batting cotton in preservative jelly.
3. Pack the foramen magnum.
4. Apply incision sealer down *foramen magnum.*
5. Force cotton into spine for tight seal.
6. Cover skull base with quick-drying incision sealer.
7. Apply hardening compound and cotton in cranial cavity.
8. Put brain in a plastic bag.
9. Saturate with one bottle of cavity fluid.
10. Knot the bag.
11. Place bag containing brain in skull.
12. Saturate calvarium with hardening compound.
13. Attach calvarium and anchor the ligature behind each ear and at the center of posterior flaps.
14. Cover calvarium with a prep towel.
15. Apply preservative jelly.
16. Return skin flaps to normal position.
17. Pull scalp back into position.
18. Arrange features.
19. Prepare half a moon-needle with a thin double strand of ligature cord and sew skin flaps from right ear to left ear.

He left Rex in the stall and walked to the A-frame. He opened the storm door and stuck the note by the knob. As he started back to the barn, he heard tires crunching gravel. He crouched behind the bannister. The car went by without slowing. He peered over the bannister: it was the game warden's green Bronco. *Glad I'm not shooting anything out of season*, he thought sardonically.

He went back to the barn. Rex was puzzled and a little agitated at being locked in. He sat down on the T-shirt again and Rex licked his face.

He made sure all the letters were under the main flap of his backpack and leaned it against the wall. He figured the T-shirt and the backpack would keep Rex from being too upset and he would mostly sleep until Jimmie came tomorrow.

He put his arms around Rex and cried. Rex licked at the tears. "This is it, pal. You take care of Laura. You'll be back with her before you know it." He started for the door; Rex moved with him. "Stay," he said, giving the open palm sign. "Stay." Rex sat down and looked at him. He closed and locked the stall door. He left quickly without looking back.

He climbed the hill above the barn, passing the opossum place again, giving it another glance. Just before he entered the woods, he looked skyward. The sun was almost touching the hill now and high up he spotted two buzzards, not circling but flying in a straight line back to their roosts. Up the hollow, a half mile away or so, he heard the boom of a 12-gauge. It was squirrel season. He knew that the blatt of his .38 snub-nose would be mistaken for a .410 if anyone heard it at all.

The dead leaves rustled under his feet. He was limping badly now. He picked up a dead but still sturdy branch to use for a walking cane.

Casketing
1. Position chin.
2. Tilt head *15°* to the right.
3. Shoulders level with the top body
   flange of the casket.
4. Aim tip of the nose on the same
   planeas the big toe of the right
   foot.

The red fox froze like a bird dog on point, one front paw in the air. It smelled something that was similar to man but different. It cautiously sat to watch and listen. The sun was just rising and, as it brightened the woods, the fox saw a shape in the thicket. Not liking the daylight, it finally trotted off toward its den, its paws making *pdit pdit* sounds on the dead leaves. It would come this way again tonight and tomorrow night until it understood what was in the thicket. A green fly buzzed past, heading into the thicket.

A mile away a turkey vulture hopped to the end of a dead limb. It tilted its head and lifted its wings slightly, feeling for the currents that would soon be rising.

Above the thicket a morning breeze stirred and a number of leaves came down from the forest canopy. Some spiraled, some dived and stalled, a couple had the aerodynamics to glide like airplanes. All eventually landed, forming a new crisp carpet, covering up last year's blanket.

A female praying mantis, her abdomen so heavy with eggs that she had to climb on only the more sturdy weeds, slowly crept onto a small locust tree. A much smaller male, already in the tree, watched her carefully and, when she stopped, cautiously approached her from behind.

A half a mile away, near the head of the George Rob Hollow, sixteen-year-old Joe Fred Hargis sat in the kitchen of the small frame house and sipped coffee as he loaded Federal .22 long-rifle hollow-points into the magazine of his Savage semi-automatic with the 4X Weaver scope. His mother scooped two fried eggs out of a black skillet and they joined three squirrel's hind legs, two biscuits, and a helping of thick milk gravy on the plate. It was almost daybreak.

"Where ye a goin' a squirrel huntin' this mornin'?" she asked as she set the plate in front of him.

"I ain't right decided. I reckon I'll walk around the ridge and I might head down toward the lake er I might foller them loggin' roads down t'other side on John Meaks' place."

"Well, I shore hope ye get a few, with the price uv meat in town a bein' what it is."

Joe Fred finished his breakfast, walked outside, pumped a shell in the cylinder, and clicked on the safety. He walked leisurely to the top of the ridge and then slowed to a few steps a minute as he followed the backbone of the hill, his eyes scanning the trees for movement and his ears listening for the sounds of gnawing, or falling nuts, or moving tree branches.

FROM THE MOUTHS OF BABES

Bentley Little

*Only one writer has appeared in all four
volumes of this anthology — Bentley Little.
There are two reasons for this: he is prolific
(he sends us at least four or five stories per
mailing) and he is simply a wonderful writer.
He won a Bram Stoker Award for Superior
Achievement for a first novel and has
published his short fiction in just about every
magazine and anthology in existence. He
writes from a place that is unknown to the
rest of us, a place where everything seems
normal but nothing is. (We know that sounds
like England, but it is actually the real
Borderlands....)*

Selena looked from the red line of the
thermometer to the pale skin of her son's face.
A hundred and one. She set the thermometer

down on the dresser and put one hand on Bobby's forehead, one hand on her own. There was a marked difference between the two. She looked at him sympathetically. "How do you feel?"

He leaned back on the bed and pulled the covers up to his chin. "Cold," he said. His voice was shaky, weak.

"What else is wrong? Do you have a headache? A stomachache? Feel like throwing up?"

"My stomach hurts a little."

"Well, you're not going to school today. I want you to stay home. I'll call the office and tell them you're sick." She took the thermometer off the dresser and placed it in the small plastic carrying case, snapping the case shut. "Do you want anything to eat? Toast? Juice? Tea and honey?"

He shook his head.

"You get some rest then. I'll be in the kitchen." She tucked in the sides of his blanket and kissed his warm cheek. "Call me if you need anything."

He cleared his throat. "Mom?"

She turned around. "What?"

"Can I watch TV?"

She smiled at him, shaking her head in mock-disapproval. "Television in the daytime," she said, "what's this world coming to?"

Bobby was about to say something in reply when his eyes suddenly widened and he clapped a hand over his mouth, jumping out of bed. He ran down the short hall to the bathroom, and Selena, following immediately after, heard him vomiting loudly into the toilet. She rushed into the tiny bathroom, an expression of worried concern etched on her features. Bobby was still vomiting heavily, and she put a reassuring hand on his back. The stench was powerful and almost overwhelming within this confined space, and she took a deep breath before peeking over his shoulder into the toilet.

She screamed.

Floating amidst the orangish-brown mixture of half-digested bits of food and thick gloppy liquid was the severed head of a rat. He heaved again, and she saw in the vomit several black beetles and what looked like a furry, gray cat's paw. Breathing heavily, his eyes closed, he spit into the bowl several times and wiped his mouth with the back of his hand.

Selena grabbed his shoulders and jerked him to his feet. "What is that?" she screamed, pointing into the toilet. "What have you been eating?"

"Nothing," Bobby said, holding onto his still aching stomach.

"That's not nothing!" She shook him hard.

"I don't know!" he cried. Tears streamed down his cheeks, washing clean his face.

"What the hell have you been eating?"

He said nothing, staring down at the ground, and she angrily wiped his mouth with a towel before taking him back to bed. She did not flush the toilet. She would wait until Wade came home and then have him look at it. He could decide what to do.

Bobby crawled back into bed and, shivering, pulled the covers up to his chin. She looked down at him, saying nothing. She was angry with him, but she was concerned for him as well. She would call a doctor and find out if he needed to get any shots or take any medicine, if it was likely that he'd contract any diseases.

What had he been doing?

Bobby's eyes were now closed, and he appeared to have already fallen asleep. He looked so clean, so wholesome, so innocent. It was hard to believe that those disgusting insects and animal parts had come spewing forth from his mouth.

School, Selena thought. It had to be school. He had

spent all day Sunday home with them, and on Monday he had gone only to school.

She walked down the hallway to call Wade, to tell him to come home immediately.

She purposely looked away from the open doorway of the bathroom as she passed by.

With Wade sitting home with Bobby, Selena drove to the elementary school. The checkup had gone well, and the doctor had given the boy only a general antibiotic to combat possible infection. Now he was home, resting, and Wade was watching over him.

Selena pulled into the narrow parking lot of the school and stopped in front of the office. It was late afternoon, and two older students were solemnly taking down the flag from the pole. She got out of the car, locking the door, and strode purposefully up to the office.

The secretary looked up from her typewriter as Selena pushed open the door. "Hello, may I help you?"

"I'm Mrs. Donaldson. I'm here to see the principal and Miss Banks."

The secretary's face reddened, and she grew suddenly flustered. "Uh, right away, Mrs. Donaldson. They're already waiting for you in the principal's office." She almost tripped over the typewriter cord as she led the way past a row of desks to the principal's door. She knocked timidly. "Mrs. Donaldson's here," she said.

Selena was escorted into a rather small office where the principal, a short bald man, and Bobby's teacher were seated on comfortable chairs. Both of them looked nervous and ill at ease. The principal stood up and gestured for her to take a seat. "Hello, Mrs. Donaldson," he said. "Nice to see you."

"Well, it's not nice to see you. I never in my wildest dreams thought I'd ever be here for this reason."

The principal smiled uncomfortably. "I must assure you, Mrs. Donaldson..."

"My son puked up a dead rat, a cat's paw and several beetles," she said. Her hard, angry gaze swept from the principal to Miss Banks. "I know damn well that he didn't eat those things at my house. What I want to know is where and how he did eat them."

"Maybe something happened on the way home from school," the principal suggested.

"I pick him up every day," she said shortly.

"The children here are always strictly supervised," Miss Banks offered. "Bobby is in my class at all times, and during lunch and recess there are monitors who..."

The principal stood up once again. "Perhaps we should take a tour of the classroom and playground area."

"I think that would be a good idea," Selena said coldly.

There had been nothing unusual or out of the ordinary in either Bobby's classroom or the playground. The janitors questioned had not seen any children eating bugs or animals or anything strange, and one of the lunch monitors, coming back to pick up her check, claimed to have seen Bobby playing tetherball with two of his friends on Monday.

Selena left the school feeling both angry and ineffectual. She drove home quickly, taking her frustrations out on the road. She believed Miss Banks when she said that nothing peculiar had happened in her class recently, and she believed the janitors and the lunch monitor.

So what had happened?

She pulled into the driveway and put the car into park, switching off the ignition. She thought of Bobby, bending over the toilet, throwing up the cat's paw and the beetles, and she shivered. She had been thinking of her son as a victim, as the butt end of some perverse conspiracy, but in the dim light of dusk he seemed far more culpable. She saw in her mind his innocent eyes, his angelic mouth, and she was suddenly afraid of him.

What is wrong with my son?

She glanced at the clock on the dashboard and was shocked to see that it was already a quarter to seven. She shook her head. That wasn't possible. She had gone to the school just before three, had spent little more than an hour there, and had driven straight home.

But the clock said she had been gone over three hours.

She got out of the car, feeling slightly disoriented. She walked up the front steps, opened the door, and stepped into the living room. Immediately, her stomach revolted, and she felt a powerful nausea well up within her. She dashed down the hall to the bathroom and barely had time to drop to her knees and pull up the toilet seat before she vomited.

Wade, behind her, watched as a dog's tongue and several worms were ejected from her mouth into the water of the bowl.

Selena awoke with a splitting headache and a painfully upset stomach. The drapes were drawn, but bright morning light spilled through a crack in the curtains. She sat up slowly, leaning against the headboard. Wade was conked out in a chair he had pulled next to the bed, his head resting at an uncomfortable angle on his shoulder. "Wade?" she said softly. "Dear?"

He jerked instantly awake. His eyes quickly scanned the room. "What?"

She smiled at him, and her head throbbed. "Nothing. It's just me."

He leaned forward, grasping her hand in his. "How are you? How do you feel?"

"I'm fine." She pressed a hand to her abdomen. "My

stomach still hurts a little, and I have a headache, but other than that…nothing."

His eyes held hers. "What happened? What did you do yesterday? How did you…"

"I don't know."

"Do you realize what you ate?"

She squeezed his hand reassuringly. "I'm fine. How's Bobby?"

He closed his eyes for a second and, when he opened them again, she saw the red lines. He was tired, she realized, and he had probably slept only an hour or so last night. "Bobby seems okay. He still won't tell me anything, though. He says he can't remember."

"He probably can't," she said. "I can't."

Wade ran a hand through her hair, letting his fingers gently trace the outline of her face. "What are we going to do?" he asked.

"We're going to let him go to school," she said.

"What?" He stared at her, shocked.

"We're going to let him go to school and spy on him."

They sat in the car for the better part of the morning, across the street from the school. They had a good view of both Bobby's classroom and the playground. No matter where he went, they would be able to see him.

Nothing happened during the first recess, and, afterward, Wade went to McDonald's to grab some food for an early lunch. Selena stayed across the street from the school, watching carefully from behind a large oak tree. Wade returned and they ate their fries and hamburgers silently. At precisely eleven-thirty, a bell rang loudly, and the kids came out for lunch. They ate on the rows of wooden tables and benches adjacent to the classrooms, then moved to the playground.

Nothing happened.

Bobby ate quickly, then joined his friends in a game of

kickball. The bell rang again and the students filed into their classrooms.

"What are we going to do?" Wade asked after Bobby had gone into his class.

Selena closed her eyes. Her stomach hurt. She shouldn't have eaten that hamburger. "I don't know," she said.

The bell rang for afternoon recess at 1:45.

The students did not head for the playground.

They marched, single file, into the auditorium.

Wade woke up Selena, who had been dozing. "Come on," he said excitedly. "We've caught em!"

They got out of the car and walked across the street, not bothering to remain concealed. They hurried across the playground and reached the auditorium just as the last student shuffled inside. Selena, her heart pounding in her chest, looked at Wade, then threw open the door.

The walls of the auditorium were white and padded, made from some ballooning, cushiony material. The floor was yellow tile, unbroken by either chairs or tables. The 350 students, unnaturally silent for elementary school children, were lined up in six parallel rows, facing the side wall, where hundreds of dogs, cats, and other small animals were crammed into a wire-mesh enclosure.

In the front of the auditorium, on a raised stage, was a quivering mass of shapeless translucent flesh the size of a small car.

Beneath the stage, in the tile, was an open pit in which a greenish fire blazed smokelessly.

Selena felt a hand touch her back and she jumped. She whirled around to see the principal smiling at her. "I'm glad you came back," he said. "Every little bit helps."

Selena grabbed Wade's hand and held tight as the principal made his way toward the front of the auditorium. He climbed onto the stage, grabbed a microphone, and tapped it to make sure it was working. "Listen up," he said, and his voice echoed from several hidden speakers.

All eyes turned toward the principal.

"I know we've been asking a lot of you lately," he said. "But this school needs your help." He gestured toward the mass of gelatinous flesh behind him. "We need more school spirit. So come on, all of you, I want you to do your best for your school."

He put the microphone down and jumped off the stage. Ten or fifteen students had lined up in front of the fire, each holding an animal. Selena watched in horror as the first child, a young girl, held forth an orange cat. The principal looked at the animal, said something to the girl, and she bit off the cat's tail, swallowing the tail whole.

She then dropped the screeching cat into the fire, which flared brightly.

The boy behind her bit off his dog's nose before sacrificing it to the fire, and the boy behind him ate a gerbil's body, dropping its head into the flames.

Selena, watching this spectacle in shocked paralysis, holding Wade's hand in a vise-like grip, noticed that the quivering form on the stage grew more substantial, less translucent, as the sacrifices increased. It also seemed to expand slightly in size.

Bobby stepped forward, chomped the head of a sparrow, and dropped the bird's body into the fire.

"We need all the help we can get," Miss Banks said from behind them. She handed Wade a puppy and Selena a small monkey, pushing them toward the front of the auditorium. "Come on. You'll set a bad example for the children. That's why we have such a hard time drumming up school spirit. People are too apathetic these days."

"School spirit," Wade repeated. He glanced up at the mass of flesh on the stage. Its quivering had slowed to a gentle pulse. It looked fuller, less shapeless.

"Come on." The teacher led them to the front of the hall.

"Mrs. Donaldson," the principal said, nodding at her.

He looked at the monkey. "The right front paw," he said. "Our school can't use the paw."

Aware of what she was doing but unable to stop herself, powerless to resist, she raised the animal to her lips and bit hard. The dry, hairy paw and a flood of warm blood spilled into her mouth. She swallowed and dropped the screaming creature into the fire.

Wade ate the puppy's ears and dropped the squealing animal into the flames.

Most of the children were gone now, and both Selena and Wade allowed themselves to be taken to a side door. Three large barrels flanked the open doorway, and Miss Banks said they had a choice. Wade took several butterflies and put them in his mouth, chewing them before swallowing. Selena chose a handful of crunchy beetles.

Outside, they blinked in the harsh afternoon sunlight. Selena turned to her husband, confused. "Where's Bobby?"

He shook his head. "In class, I guess." He looked around, puzzled. "Come on," he said. "Let's get back to the car before anyone sees us. I want to get to the bottom of this."

She followed him across the playground. "Maybe it happened on Saturday," she said. "He was over at Carl's house on Saturday. He might have eaten something there."

"But what about you? You certainly didn't go to Carl's."

"That's true," she said. "I forgot."

They waited in the car until the final bell rang at three o'clock. Bobby saw their car immediately and ran across the street, getting in the back seat. He handed his mother a sheet of paper. "We're having spirit week next week," he said. "Everyone's supposed to wear a costume."

Selena looked at him. "We'll see." She put one hand

on his forehead, one hand on her own. There was no difference. "How do you feel?" she asked.

He shrugged. "My stomach hurts a little."

Wade started the car. "We'd better get you home."

That night, Selena vomited up a monkey's paw and several beetles. Wade threw up puppy ears and butterflies. Bobby regurgitated a sparrow's head and some worms.

None of them knew why.

The next day, the principal called Selena to thank her for all she and her family had done to strengthen school spirit. The school spirit was strong this year, and he hoped it would be equally strong next year, when Bobby was in fourth grade.

Selena began to sew Bobby a costume for spirit day.

THE LONG HOLIDAY

William Ellis

*Sometimes we get stories that are so strange
they are simply unforgettable and practically
demand to be included in an anthology such
as this. The byline for the following weird
fantasy is a pseudonym for a professor
working the fields of Academe at a southern
university. He admits to not writing this kind
of fiction very often, but perhaps he should
reconsider.*

We're trapped here, bugs beneath a bell jar,
floundering in thick air. Like wet wool, the
gloom in the cavern dampens sound. Time
hangs motionless, the catch between the beat
of a heart: we work on and on.

The wall in front of me is ice, thick and
gray and wet. It meets the cavern's roof above
my head and forms large, hanging pools. The
gray pools thin continually and drop cold
tendrils of stinking water. I count the drops
of water to mark time passing, but they fall
unevenly, without rhythm. Each time I feel

the freezing rain strike me I scream, vowing that it will be the last. It never is. I am constantly damp. I rub myself briskly to try to avoid what has happened to some of the others, yet I still find small patches of mold here and there.

There must be hundreds of us here, perhaps thousands. I can't be certain. I can only see one end of the conveyor belt as it emerges from the distant maw of stone and flames. The flames leap darkly, flaringflaringflaring in the gloom, throwing forth only a meager light, and creating monstrous shadows. The belt travels onward, disappearing into the darkness. I don't know where it ends. All I know is that we make things. That is our labor. I don't know how I came to be here, or even where here is. I do know that I will leave, that I will escape. I must. No one can stand this forever.

We are all chained by thick links of rotting metal, bolted to large rusting eyebolts set firmly into the stone floor. We are given enough chain to stand and strain completely across the four-foot-wide belt. The chain is bound to a heavy iron band set deeply into the flesh of our lower thighs. The skin is tight and swollen around the metal, but there is no pain. Neither I nor any of the workers I can see clearly have shirts, although some of the workers closer to the flames seem to have a dark, loose material flapping from their arms and shoulders. None of us have hair, and the light reflects from gleaming skin in dark hues of orange and red. I am the only one who looks around or even raises their head. All of the others do their work grimly, silently, over and over again. I have screamed, kicked, spit and whimpered at the others, but they take no notice of me. The silence is only broken by the distant roar of the furnace and the steady drip of water. Here, the mindless are the fortunate. I believe I've become insane.

I see the shapes form in the shadows. They are always preceded by the high, light tinkling of bells. The sound turns the marrow of my bones to ice. They snatch the slower workers from the assembly line, carry them quickly off into the darkness, and replace them with others. They seem to have no dearth of replacements. I also see the creatures passing behind the thick sheet of ice: small dark shapes, vaguely human in form — but miniature, with the long, loose arms of apes. They scuttle back and forth, hunched over like wizened old men, then disappear in the wink of an eye. Only the airy sound of bells linger. I keep an eye on the darkness surrounding me. I would sooner work, I believe, than have them come from behind and touch me with their thin jointed fingers.

I'll tell you what I do. The conveyor moves at a steady pace and brings down all manner of strange and peculiar things. Each of us has different tasks. For instance, the worker to my left picks up small pieces of green board and, with a hot gun, melts wire onto it in three certain places. I have a short, blunt screwdriver. I tighten screws, but only in a red, rectangular metal frame with wheels. It is the size of a large loaf of bread and, obviously, incomplete. I don't know what it's used for. The conveyor belt itself is made of long sections of some sort of hide, held together by crude stitching. It is torn in places and, whatever kind of rancid hide it is, it was improperly cured. It smells and is greasy to the touch. The belt is carried along by large, ancient cogs, clotted and black with grease.

Then I was moving, under the belt, through the dirt and debris, and out the other side. I didn't stop. I dove at the ice wall's weak spot and began chopping with my stub of a screwdriver. I dug furiously, maniacally. The light shone on the ice spray as I worked, transforming the crystals into a shower of red and gold, like sparks from an anvil. I felt I was being burnt alive. As the shadows danced I dug harder, my wide eyes transfixed upon the thinning wall, terrified of what might be approaching from behind me.

The ice fell apart in ludicrously large chunks, and in seconds I was scraping through the ragged hole, the ice cutting into my shoulders and belly like glass. I leapt to my feet in a horizonless mist of ice and snow. Then I ran.

I was beyond the sensation of what must have been sub-zero temperature as I stumbled through the drifts, half-clothed and shoeless. My thoughts were still dim, lost somewhere in the back of my mind, trying to keep up with my body's actions. My eyes tried to focus on the measureless gray distance as I ran on and on. What was left of the chain slapped across my legs, and several times I became entangled, burying myself face first in the harsh ice. The drifts were thick and crusted, and as I ran I broke through them with angry, shattering sounds. The weight of fear and exhilarating panic kept me moving. I never looked back, not once. I couldn't have even if I'd wanted. They might have been back there coming for me, gaining on me.

At last I could run no farther. The landscape had changed: the hard dunes of packed ice had become billowing white drifts of thick, moist snow. The ground rose and fell in rolling waves, and I slid down a gully headfirst and lay quietly at the bottom. The snow piled around me as my vision became blurred in the swiftly falling flakes. The ice crystals fell faster, whirling around my face like diving insects, stinging my eyes and nose. I could smell the cold. It was a sharp, silver smell, a taste in the back of my mouth. But I still couldn't feel it.

Laying there in the vast silence with the snow falling, I felt peace at last. My hard lips struggled across my teeth as I tried to pray and failed. Then, upon the wind, I heard the sounds that extinguished any spark of hope that had burned in my chest: the bells.

Softly at first, only hallucinatory whispers carried by
the crying wind, they crept inexorably closer, until they
left no doubt that they were coming for me. The chiming
rose and fell in the Arctic night as I fought to move my
frozen limbs. Kicking and flailing, I burrowed backward
into the white bank, under the growing wave. I drove
myself deeper and deeper into its depths, a lost swimmer
in a frozen sea. I lay still at last, resting and hidden in the
insulating security of the snow. The outer world was gone,
lost in a world of utter silence and dark gray vision. The
hunter's bells had finally ceased. They had grown dim
and muffled, and then disappeared altogether. I listened,
straining to hear anything in the crystalline silence. There
was nothing: no heaving of breath, no pounding heart in
my chest, no rush of blood in my ears. Nothing. Then the
cold engulfed me, hidden there in my brittle womb of
ice.

I screamed with my frozen voice as the rough, gnarled
hands tore me from my burrow. The scream echoed only
through my mind, soundless across the frozen waste. The
squat figures picked me up in their bone-ridged arms as
easily as one would a child, and I found myself face up
upon a wide, muscled back. The sky faded from gray to
black as the troop began loping across the snow, bells
tinkling from their jerkins of skin and fur. All light faded
from my eyes as we rushed along the tundra, frozen
laughter and silver notes hanging in the air behind us.

The fire danced close before my eyes, too close. I threw
myself backward, slinging the highback chair in which I
had been sitting to the floor. I had successfully freed
myself from the chair and had been navigating faster than
a crab across the floor when I rammed into the wall
headfirst. My vision blurred and my ears rang. As my
eyes cleared, I found myself staring at the ceiling, where
a repeating pattern of skulls and snowflakes was stamped

onto squares of antique metal. Then I became aware of the laughter.

Deep and rich bellows of mirth filled the small room. The room was wood-paneled, dark, and quite warm. I clutched at the sparse hairs on my scalp and at the arm of the chair. I stood slowly, the pain still deep in my head, overcome with weariness but filled with an odd, uncomfortable warmth. The laughter continued and became even gustier. Finally, struggling to gain control between rolling bursts of mirth, a voice as warm as the room spoke from behind an even taller chair and wide desk.

"Sit, sit...the chair."

The first thing I noticed, after maneuvering the tall wingback into its previous position, was the firelight glistening from the plump man's shining bald head. He had swung the chair around abruptly and now sat staring at me, smiling. Tufts of snow-white hair stood out beyond two large red ears. His jowls echoed with smaller and smaller shockwaves as his humor slowly faded. Small, porcine eyes glistened above ruddy cheeks and a broad, scarlet nose. As I sat back on the dry leather of the chair, my legs twitching, he unfolded his fingers from atop his stout belly and slammed his dimpled hands down upon the desk in front of him.

"By Jove, you ran, didn't you? Ran and ran and ran!" His voice shook with renewed laughter, and I could see the sweat beading upon his forehead. The warmth had become suffocating. I could smell the fat man in the close room. The air was thick with the odor of sour grease.

His laughter ceased abruptly as one sausage finger plucked a bit of twitching debris from his furred vest. He held it up and stared at it contemptuously before crushing it and flicking it toward me. I jumped. It landed on my forearm, and I could see that what remained resembled a thin shard of white bone. I looked up into a wide, toothsome smile.

"Well, we admire you…yes, we do," he said. "You must be admired! Only a rare few achieve what you have." His smile loosened, hanging upon his mouth like an artificial decoration. "You had hope, didn't you? No matter how brief a space of time, your mind was allowed relief. You thought you had a chance and your soul found peace for an instant, did it not? Remarkable. And totally against policy."

The light in his eyes faded to a dull, flat black. His mouth became a pit framed by bearded lips. "The last to accomplish what you have done was over six hundred years ago!" he continued. "I suppose it's inevitable. Complacency is mathematically certain in an eternity. I try to keep my little fellows on their toes, but nothing works permanently." He lapsed into silence, his hands absently scratching his protruding stomach. I leaned forward slightly, my legs throbbing.

"Sit down!" he shrieked, his eyes glowing with hate. "We're not finished!"

My body shook in terror as he lowered his bulk back into his chair and the echoes of his roaring faded. After several minutes of silence, I couldn't bear his gaze any longer. His infinite eyes bored into me with a bloody, unblinking stare.

"Who…who are you?" I asked softly. "Why am I here…in this place…the cavern?"

His face lit up with a gentle smile. "Because you have been naughty," he said, "and because you have work to do. At last, from your sin comes joy. It's an endless penance. You were given a chance, you threw it away, and it's been decreed.

"For close to two thousand years now, He and I have had this arrangement, and it works quite well. I get my work completed and you receive your punishment. It's a wondrous, magical world we live in, don't you think? It's absolutely beautiful!" He stood.

"But of course you don't see things that way, do you?" He walked to the corner of the room closest to the fireplace, his tail dragging along behind him. "It was a very good try, by the way; but futile and doomed of course. Where did you think you were going, surrounded by countless miles of polar ice? That miserable shell your soul resides in was lucky to make it as far as it did." He clapped his huge, meaty hands together. "Enough chitchat. It's time to return. Back to work now, eh?"

Huge leathery wings spread majestically from beneath the man's red suit as the sound of bells filled the room. The elves appeared, growing into substance from the shadows pooled in the corners and beneath the furniture. They were dressed in green and red, holiday colors, with small glittering eyes like glass. Their ears were long and pointed, and their hands were covered with coarse, spine-like hair. Behind the desk a door swung open and I could see a line of elves dragging the damned that were beyond work, dragging them like cords of wood down a sloping stone corridor. The light was a hellish, bloody orange, flaringflaringflaring. My eyes watered from the suffocating heat rushing in through the open door. I tried to shield my eyes from the blistering wave, but with the missing fingers it did little good. As I watched, more and more creatures grew from the floor's shadows. Then they came for me. The fat man's laughter became a bell-filled shriek. And when the elves smiled, their teeth flashed like knives.

THE LATE MR. HAVEL'S APARTMENT

David Herter

Well-drawn characters and the ability to evoke a sincere emotional response are two qualities we always look for in a story for this anthology series. The following story is reminiscent of Rod Serling at the top of his game. David Herter lives in Washington State, where he runs the computers for a wholesale book distributor. "The Late Mr. Havel's Apartment" was written at the 1990 Clarion West workshop.

Robin Myers was twenty-nine, employed as a secretary at a roofing firm, and single. These were the general facts, available to anyone.

She wanted a child, and a husband, but her relationships never lasted longer than a few months. She was behind on her car payment and usually missed the rent deadline by a day or two. She was a hypochondriac: every stomach pain was sinister, every chestache put thoughts of death into her head. She collected china figurines of horses; she didn't know how to swim. These facts were more particular. Some were secret, some were never spoken aloud.

And the old man upstairs had known none of this, she was sure. Until the night he died, she'd only seen him once, in the lobby. He stood outside, struggling to hold onto a huge grocery bag and pull keys out of his pocket. He was stooped and feeble, so she walked over, turned the door's handle and let him in. "I'm Havel," he said, "Mr. Havel from 214."

"I'm Robin from 114," she replied as he squeezed through the door. He nodded and walked slowly past.

From then on she'd only heard his footsteps through the ceiling, muffled as if he were trying to control the noise. She was never bothered by a television too loud, which pleased her. She liked living quietly. She liked being able to go to bed at 9:00 p.m. and drift to sleep with only an occasional sound from Havel: his footsteps padding across the floor, the creak of his bed (which must have been directly over hers, she decided) as he lowered himself onto the mattress. Sometimes in the early hours of the morning she would wake to hear a sound like ball-bearings rolling inside a box, but that was rare.

On Friday evening the ambulance had come screaming up front. She'd rushed to the window to see them pulling out a stretcher, and Mrs. Bulmer, the landlady, scurrying out to grab a medic by the sleeve. She walked back to the stove to turn down the heat, so the chicken wouldn't burn, then stepped quietly toward her door. She could hear the medics hustle the stretcher into the elevator and she could hear the elevator open onto the second floor, and she followed the footsteps over her own room. She heard anxious voices and the creak of the bed, then the sounds had diminished.

A half hour later they loaded Havel into the ambulance. Gazing down at the humped sheet, she thought *poor man*. The ambulance door shut, and that was that. She went back to her chicken. Police drifted in and out for the rest of the evening, and by 11:00 p.m. the apartment was once again quiet.

She didn't think about Havel until the next afternoon. A knock interrupted a phone call from her latest boyfriend. "There's someone at the door, John. I'll see you next week, okay? I'm worn out. I don't even want to get up and answer the door. Give me a call. Goodbye." She replaced the receiver and walked to the door.

Mrs. Bulmer stood outside. "Robin, I was just upstairs..." She paused, mouth open. Her teeth were narrow and yellow and reminded Robin of soft wood. "I was just upstairs straightening the late Mr. Havel's apartment and I came upon a few of your things. Did you want them back?"

Robin raised an eyebrow. "Things?"

"I'm not suppose to disturb the room since they're still trying to locate his family," said Mrs. Bulmer, "but I thought I'd let you sneak in there and grab your stuff if you want to?"

Robin bit her lower lip, thinking about Havel's footsteps and the mattress creaking as he settled into bed. "Sure," she said. "Wait just a minute." She pulled on some wool socks, grabbed her keys, and locked the door behind her.

"What are these things, Mrs. Bulmer?" They stepped into the cramped elevator and Robin pulled shut the gate. With a lurch, it began to climb.

"Just a few knickknacks. You don't remember giving them to him?"

"Uh uh." The car jolted to a stop and, after a long moment, the doors parted.

"It shook me," said Mrs. Bulmer as she selected a dull gold key from her key ring. "Finding him like that." As she struggled to get the key into the lock, Robin wanted to ask, "Like what?"

"Don't forget the rent, dear." Mrs. Bulmer pulled out the key and selected another one. "It's ten dollars a day overdue."

"Remind me to give you a check. I was finally paid yesterday."

The lock sprang this time. "You should tell your employer to pay you on time. There's laws in this state, you know."

"Yeah," said Robin as the landlady pushed open the door.

Havel's apartment was cold. White sheets were draped over a long couch and an easy chair. The carpet was older than hers, faded into a light gray.

"Poor Mr. Havel never married. Many times I tried to introduce him to my single friends, but he always declined."

Robin noticed a stack of cardboard boxes beside the sofa. "Where are these items, Mrs. Bulmer?"

"Back here," said the landlady, and Robin followed her across the living room, through the open bedroom door.

The curtains were pulled wide and sunlight revealed stained diamond-print wallpaper and a frayed rug. A king-size bed occupied the corner directly above her own. The closet door was open and she saw slacks and shirts, a collection of wingtip shoes, and a lone golf club. The room smelled of disinfectant.

Mrs. Bulmer walked to the foot of the bed. "Here," she said, pointing to a box. Black socks spilled over the sides, but Mrs. Bulmer was pointing to something gold and glittering. Robin waited for her to lift it up.

"It's yours," Mrs. Bulmer said, trying to sound uninterested. "It has your name on it."

The gold and glittering item was a bracelet and, after close scrutiny, she recognized it: something her parents had bought her when she went to summer camp in the seventh grade. An identity bracelet, usually worn to label yourself a diabetic or allergic to penicillin. *Robin Myers/ 411 South Templeton Street, Seattle/ We LOVE you, darling* was engraved on the metal. She'd been embarrassed by it. She recalled how she had cast it into Lake Sealth her first day at camp.

"Yes," said Robin. "It belonged to me."

She thought of what she would eat for lunch; she recalled snatches of her argument with John; all the while holding the bracelet between two fingers without listening to Mrs. Bulmer.

"...and I know it isn't proper," the landlady said, "but if you want, I'll let you rummage around in here, to see if there's anything else of yours."

"No." She had dropped the bracelet on the floor. "I lost that in the lobby a few months back. He must have found it and not bothered to return it."

"Oh."

"If that's everything, I should get back to my apartment." She looked in the direction of the front door. She knew the route but expected the sheeted furniture to rise in her path. "I'll write you that rent check."

"So you don't want the bracelet?" Mrs. Bulmer held it out.

She smiled. "Of course," she said and took it.

"And you'll want the other thing as well, won't you?"

"What other thing?"

"The photograph." Mrs. Bulmer fished it out of the box. "I could tell it was you immediately. Your eyes haven't changed." She held it up to Robin and, though her landlady held it in a steady hand, Robin felt the photograph move away — as if she were looking through the wrong end of a telescope.

"Thanks," she said, realizing there was nothing else to say that would wipe the smile from Mrs. Bulmer's face.

Later, she sat cross-legged on her bed, the photograph in front of her, a wine cooler clutched in her hand.

She closed her eyes. The details of the photograph were burned in her memory: the square border with *June 1973* written along the lower right-hand side; the little girl standing at the edge of the dock, the green waters of Lake Sealth lurking indistinctly behind her. The little girl held an oar in both hands, and the photo captured her smiling as she struggled to stay balanced. The smile was enough to remind her of that day, her second day at camp, her first time in a canoe; but she didn't remember posing for the picture.

She opened her eyes.

No, she was positive. There had been a group of kids on the dock, not just her alone. They had been so unruly that the counselors threatened to veto the canoe trip if they didn't calm down. "Safety first," the counselors said, showing the group the proper way to put on a life jacket.

They had loaded four children and a counselor into each canoe, and there'd been no time to stand, no time to pose. Indeed, she remembered the entire summer as a flurry of group activity.

Finishing the cooler, she picked up the bracelet and examined the words. They were exactly as she remembered them, every embarrassing syllable. Also, stretching from one side to the other, barely discernible, was a scratch in the metal. She'd slashed at it with a utility knife before leaving for camp and tossed it into the lake that first day....

She brought the photo close to her eyes and examined the bracelet on the little girl's wrist. The image stayed with her for the rest of the day, haunted her dreams that night. She got up early the next morning, thankful it was

Sunday, and tried to explain everything away over a bowl of granola.

"Hello, Mrs. Bulmer. Sorry to bother you, but I've changed my mind. I'd like to go into Mr. Havel's apartment and see if I've left anything else. Am I too early?"

"No, no, no, let me find my housecoat."

Mrs. Bulmer appeared in the hall ten minutes later, dressed in a canary-yellow robe, and led Robin into the elevator.

The apartment looked dreary this morning. The sheets seemed to grow out of the gray carpet and the light had a diffused, dusty quality.

"I can't leave the keys," Mrs. Bulmer said from the hallway, "so just come get me when you're done."

Mrs. Bulmer gently shut the door and all was silent. Robin walked across the living room and stopped next to the covered couch. She imagined the old man's body beneath the sheet, equally gray and dry, his sightless eyes watching her through the fabric, and she forced herself to lift the edge of the sheet. The material refused to yield, then billowed from green velour upholstery. She let the sheet fall.

Glancing at the taped boxes beside the couch, she decided to postpone those. First, the bedroom.

As she walked toward it she conjured up Havel: his wide face and narrow, sleepy eyes, his receding white hair, his jowls. How much could he have changed in thirteen years? She was sure she'd never seen him at summer camp; she'd never seen him before the time in the lobby.

Swallowing hard, she approached the box at the end of the bed where Mrs. Bulmer had found the bracelet. She crouched in front of it and reached inside. Her right hand moved through underclothes. Just underclothes. She overturned it, spilling boxer shorts and black socks onto the carpet.

As she straightened, she noticed something in the corner of her vision. Something on the bed, amid the sheet, almost lost in a fold. The figure of a woman standing on a pedestal. Robin picked it up, weighed it in her palm, and studied its sleek black polish. At first she thought it was a chess piece, but this woman wore no robes, no crown. She was nude. One slender arm was lifted in greeting, and Robin noticed a smile on her tiny face.

As she set it back on the bed, leaving it to slumber in the folds of the sheet, she was reminded of Havel.

How did he die? She would have to ask Mrs. Bulmer for the details.

She walked through the living room and checked the kitchen. In the refrigerator she found a bottle of olives, a few celery stalks, and an open box of baking soda. She found dry cereal and two cans of tuna in the cupboards. Nothing exciting. Which left her with the sealed boxes next to the couch.

Mrs. Bulmer would undoubtedly notice if the tape was cut, but she decided to open this first box, then stack the second on top.

Kneeling beside them, she pulled out her apartment key and ran the jagged teeth along the tape. She grasped the flaps and yanked them free, revealing a loose collection of photographs: polaroids of Robin as a teen; an eight by ten of Robin caught unaware as she sat on a bench downtown, her skin pale, her arms almost skeletal, her eyes gazing down at nothing; another eight by ten of a heavier Robin, her face aglow, holding an infant to her breast; still another depicting a backyard party in a backyard she'd never seen, a handsome man lifting Robin's bridal veil and leaning in for a kiss.

Beneath the layer of photographs she found a small pair of shorts, a T-shirt and a pair of tennis shoes, all dirt-encrusted, stiff and smelling of mildew. Tendrils of dry weed tangled in the shoe laces. She lifted out the T-shirt and shook it, releasing a cloud of dust, and read the words Camp Sealth printed across the front.

She pushed the box away and stood, almost falling over.

She left the room. She shut the door without locking it and walked slowly down the stairs, thinking of Havel's footsteps, of his bed creaking, of the strange sounds in the early morning. Once inside her apartment, she could only find the phone and dial John's number.

He answered on the twelfth ring. "Yeah, Robin. What now?"

"I've been thinking," she said, biting her lower lip again. "How about going out tonight? Please?"

"What's up?"

"I'd just like to see you."

John sighed. "We were going to go out last night," he said. "Instead, I ended up with nothing to do, all my plans shot to hell."

"We don't need to go anywhere. Just come over, okay?"

"I'm afraid I have other duties today, Robin. Let's make a tentative date for next Saturday, huh?"

She sat on her sofa through the afternoon, until Mrs. Bulmer knocked on the door.

"Are you done upstairs?"

Robin thought for a moment.

"No, but please come in."

Mrs. Bulmer stepped inside. She clutched a dust rag in both hands. "What is it, dear?"

Robin shook her head. "Please do me a favor, would you? Tell me what you found Friday evening."

The old woman sat down beside her. She cleared her throat and squinted at the ceiling. "I was going up there to get the rent. It was his habit to stay in his room a lot, so I would visit on the first and fifteenth and he would always have the cash on hand."

"He never went out?"

"For grocery shopping, sure. And he went out once a week, on Friday afternoon, to play his game. He would walk out with a board under his arm and tell me he was meeting some friends. 'Going out for a game of possibilities, Mrs. Bulmer,' he would say. So he did go out at least once a week. I was glad he had friends.

"That evening I knocked on the door and I received no answer. I became worried, because he was always home from his game before nightfall and he was an old man. I tried the door and it was unlocked. I pushed it open and found all the furniture covered, all the boxes stacked by the sofa."

"Like he was packing to move out?"

"Not to move out," said Mrs. Bulmer. "He hadn't packed up his furniture, only covered it, remember? Like he was going on a long trip.

She cleared her throat. "I found him on the bed. His eyes were closed and he was smiling. All dressed up in his nice black suit. He looked like my Roger looked during the funeral ceremony." Mrs. Bulmer blinked slowly.

Robin nodded.

"The medics said it was old age." Mrs. Bulmer shook her head. "I've seen my share of deaths, Robin, but I've never seen one so peaceful, so…unusually laid out. They told me that every so often a person just knows they're going to die and they dress up all fine; they choose the time and place to go. It's sort of like winning a game." Mrs. Bulmer smiled. "He was a gamesman till the end," she said and stood.

"I got a call from the social service, and you'll be happy to know they found some of Mr. Havel's relatives. Two of his brothers. They've arranged to ship his body to the family plot in Bucharest, and they're coming tomorrow to claim his belongings. Thank God. I wasn't looking forward to clearing it out myself."

"The white lady," Robin said, "what did you do with it?"

"I tucked it into his breast pocket before they carried him out. I felt that he wanted it with him."

That evening, she became sick. She threw up her stir-fried vegetables and tried to settle her stomach with lime soda. She sat on the edge of her tub and gently touched her abdomen, trying to recall the symptoms for stomach cancer.

At 8:00 p.m. a headache appeared and sank needles into her right eye. She swallowed two aspirin and a few Rolaids and walked upstairs to Havel's apartment. She was wearing a sweater and wool socks, but she was cold. Her teeth chattered; her fingers shook. Cold air seemed to come in waves off the furniture, from beneath the sheets.

Sitting down on the living room rug, she proceeded to open the other two boxes with the jagged edge of the key. The first contained more photos of lives she'd never led. They showed an exuberant young Robin and her child. The handsome husband. The life she had once planned until reality or something drained her of the will.

The box also contained seven notebooks filled with cramped handwriting, each labeled with her name. The first page of the first book was dated June, 1973. The seventh notebook ended halfway through, with Friday's date. Columns of figures and bizarre equations crowded each page:

$$Q^\wedge 1 * X2, \; Q\backslash 2 = Q^\wedge 1! X2.$$

In the second box she found her death certificate. *Snohomish County Coroner's Office*, it read. The date was

June 3, 1973. Cause of death: drowning. And beneath the certificate, she found a game board.

It was made of heavy wood, with a raised edge about an inch high. An uneven division of small squares covered it, with three interlocking circles transposed.

She lifted it out and found three metal balls. She dropped them onto the board and listened to the slick, low sound of the balls moving across the wood, encountering an edge and darting back, finally resting atop a particular square and circle.

She sat with the board on her lap, idly tilting it left and right, watching the zigzagging paths. Then she was a young girl again, standing on a dock in the summer sun. She held a huge oar and smiled for the nice man and his camera. She held the pose for a long moment, almost losing her balance, and then she heard the click and he lowered the camera. He smiled. He said, "That's it, I've got you."

UNION DUES

Gary A. Braunbeck

Some stories just plain hit you right where you live. By odd coincidence, our fathers were machinists, both working in monstrously large, hellishly loud factories. We saw the toll this kind of work can take on a person, and when Gary Braunbeck's story of the life and death of a factory man arrived, we were touched by the achingly accurate portrait of pain and desperation he had captured. Braunbeck is one of the brightest young talents working this field. We think you'll agree that his time to be recognized is at hand because he's more than paid his own union dues...

It is one of the great tragedies
of this age that as soon as man
invented a machine he began to starve.
— Oscar Wilde
The Soul of Man Under Socialism

**(here is my son
does he have the makings of a factory man?
does he have the mark of a worker?
Will he do me proud?)**

A man works his whole life away, and what does it mean?

Please don't ask me that question, Dad.

On the line your hands grow aching and callused, your body grows sore and crooked, and your spirit fades like sparks between the gears. The roar of machinery chisels its way into your brain and spreads until it is the only thing that's real. The work goes on, you die a little more with each whistle, and the next paycheck is tucked inside the rusty metal lunch pail that really ought to be replaced but you can't afford to right now.

A man works his whole life away. For twenty-three years he reports to work on time, punches the clock, takes his place on the line and allows his body to become one half of a tool. He works without complaint and never calls in sick no matter how bad he feels, and for this he gets to come home once a week and present his wife and two kids with a paycheck for one hundred and eighty-seven dollars and sixteen cents. Dirt money. Chump change. Money gone before it's got. Then one day he notices the way his kids look at him, he sees their disappointment, and he wants to scream but settles for a few cold beers instead.

And what does it mean? It means a man becomes embarrassed by what he is, humiliated by his lack of education, ashamed that he can only give his family the things they need and not the things they want.

So a man grows angry —
— because even in his dreams —

(...doors open and the Old Worker is cast away...)

— the work goes on —

— and the machines wait for him to return and make them whole again.

Don't say these things, Dad.

I can't help it, boy.

Sometimes it gets to be too much.

2

Sheriff Ted Jackson held a handkerchief over his nose and mouth as he surveyed the wreckage of the riot.

(...as the production line begins again...)

A cloud of tear gas was dissipating at neck level in the parking lot of the factory, reflecting lights from the two dozen police cars encircling the area. Newspaper reporters and television news crews were assembling outside the barricades along with people from the neighborhood and relatives of the involved workers. Silhouetted against the rapidly setting cold November sun, the crowd looked like one massive cluster of cells, a shadow on a lung x-ray. Sorry, bud, this looks bad.

Men lay scattered, some on their sides, others on their backs, still more squatting and coughing and vomiting, all wiping blood from their faces and hands.

A half-foot of old crusty snow had covered the ground since the first week of the month, followed by days and nights of dry cold, so that the snow had merely aged and turned the color of damp ash, mottled by candy wrappers, empty cigarette packs, losing lottery tickets, beer cans, and now bodies. The layer of snow whispering from the sky was a fresh coat of paint, a whitewash that hid the ugliness and despair of the tainted world underneath.

A pain-filled voice called out from somewhere.

Fire blew out the windshield of an overturned semi: it

jerked sideways, slammed into a guardrail, and puked glass.

The crowd pushed forward, knocking over several of the barriers. Officers in full riot gear held everyone back.

The snow grew dense as more sirens approached.

The searchlight from a police helicopter swept the area.

A woman in the crowd began weeping loudly.

You couldn't have asked for an uglier mess.

Jackson pulled the handkerchief away and took an icy breath; the wind was trying to move the gas away but the snow held it against the ground. He turned up the collar of his jacket and pulled a twenty-gauge pump-action shotgun from the cruiser's rack.

"Sheriff?"

Dan Robinson, one of his deputies, offered him a gas mask.

"Little late for that."

"I know, but the fire department brought along extras and I thought…"

"Piss on that." Jackson stared through the snow at the crowd of shadows. The revolving cruiser lights perpetually changed the shape of the pack: red — *blink* — a smoke crowd; blue — *blink* — a snow-ash crowd; white — *blink* — a shadow crowd.

"You okay, Sheriff?"

"Let's go see if they cleared everyone away from the east side."

The two men trudged through the heaps of snow, working their way around the broken glass, twisted metal, blood, grease, and bodies. Paramedics scurried in all directions; gurneys were collapsed, loaded, then lifted and rolled toward waiting ambulances. Volunteers from the local Red Cross were administering aid to those with less serious wounds.

"Any idea how this started, sir?"

"The scabs came out for food. Strikers cut off all deliveries three days ago."

"Terrible thing."

"You got that right."

They rounded the corner and took several deep breaths to clear their lungs.

(...the shift whistle blows like a birth scream and the factory worker springs forth, with shoulders and arms made powerful for the working of apron handwheels...)

Jackson remembered the afternoon he'd had to come down and assist with bringing in the scabs...the strikers behind barricades on one side of the parking lot while the scabs rode in on flatbed trucks like livestock to an auction. Until that afternoon he'd never believed that rage was something that could live outside the physical confines of a man's own heart, but, as those scabs climbed down and began walking toward the main production floor entrance, he'd felt the presence of cumulative anger becoming something more fierce, something hulking and twisted and hideous. To this day he couldn't say how or why, but he could swear that the atmosphere between the strikers and scabs had rippled and even torn in places. It still gave him the willies.

He blinked against the falling snow and felt his heart skip a beat.

Twenty yards away, near a smoldering overturned flatbed at the edge of the east parking lot, a man lay on the ground, his limbs twisted at impossible angles. A long, thick smear of hot machine oil pooled behind him, hissing in the snow.

Maneuvering through the snowdrifts, Jackson raced over, slid to a halt, chambered a shell, and dropped to one knee, gesturing for Robinson to do the same.

Jackson looked down at the body and felt something lodge in his throat. "Damn. Herb Kaylor."

"You know him?"

Jackson tried to swallow but couldn't. The image of the man's face blurred; he wiped his eyes and realized that he was crying. "Yeah. Him and me served together in Vietnam. I just played cards with him and his wife a couple nights ago. *Goddammit!*" He clenched his teeth. "He wasn't supposed to be workin' the picket line today. Christ! Poor Herb…"

He turned away, shook himself, and looked back at the man whose company he'd known and treasured, and cursed himself for never letting Herb Kaylor know just how much his friendship had meant.

Kaylor's neck was broken so badly that his head was turned almost fully around. Jackson reached out to close his friend's dead eyes —

— his fingers brushed the skin —

— *I barely touched him* —

— and the eyes fell through the sockets into the skull. There was no blood.

"Jesus!" shouted Robinson.

"I hardly…" Jackson never completed the sentence.

With a series of soft, dry sounds, Herb Kaylor's skull collapsed inward; the flesh crumbled and flaked away as his face sank back, split in half, and dissolved.

Robinson was so shaken by the sight that he lost his balance and pushed a hand through Kaylor's hollowed chest. He tried to pull himself from the shell of desiccated skin and brittle bone but only managed to sink his arm in up to the elbow. Jackson pulled him out; Robinson's arm was covered in large clumps of decayed, withered flesh. Bits and pieces of Herb Kaylor blew away like so much soot.

Jackson stared into the empty chest cavity.

Robinson backed away, dry retching.

A strong gust of wind whistled by, leveling to a chronic breeze.

(...the factory man turns his gaze toward the plant's ceiling...)

Unable to look at Herb's body any longer, Jackson rose to his feet and turned toward the sliding iron doors that served as the entrance to the basement production cells.

He could feel the power of the machines inside; at first it was little more than a low, constant thrum beneath his feet, but as he began to walk toward the doors the vibrations became stronger, louder; snaking up out of the asphalt and coiling around his legs, soaking through his skin and latching onto his bones like the lower feedfingers of a metal press, shuddering, clanking, hissing and screeching into his system, fusing with his bloodstream as carbon fused with silicon and lead with bismuth, riding the flow up to his brain and spreading across his mind: it became a deep, rolling hum in his ears, then an enveloping pressure, and, at last, a whisper.

Welcome, my son —

— a powerful gust of wind shrieked around him, kicking against his legs —

— welcome to the Machine.

It came from the opening between the doors, and as Jackson moved toward them something long and metallic slipped out, flexed, then vanished back into the darkness of the plant before he could get to it. Jackson blinked against the snow and shook his head. Every so often he'd see something like that in his dreams, a prosthetic hand, its metal fingers closing around his throat, and the thing he'd glimpsed had been like the hand in his dreams, only much, much larger —

— Jesus, I gotta start sleeping better, can't start seein' shit like that while I'm awake or —

"Christ Almighty!" shouted Robinson.

Jackson whirled around and instinctively leveled the shotgun but the wind was so strong he lost his grip and the weapon flew out of his hands, slamming against a far wall and discharging into a four foot snowdrift.

He stared at the body of Herb Kaylor.

No way, no goddamn way he can still be alive —

— moving, no mistaking that, Herb was moving; one arm, then another, then both legs —

— Jackson reached out and grabbed the iron handrail leading down the stairs; it was the only way he could keep his balance against the wind —

— that seemed to be concentrated on what was left of Herb's body, lifting it from the ground like a marionette at the end of tangled strings, its limbs twisted akimbo, shaking and flailing in violent seizure-like spasms, flaking apart and scattering into the wind, churning into dust and dirtying the funneling snow; even the clothes were shredded and cast away.

It was over in less than a minute.

Jackson slowly climbed the steps and rejoined Robinson. They stood in silence, staring at the spot where Kaylor's body had been —

— the steps into the basement —

(*It sure as hell* looked *like a hand of some sort.*)

— but the pressure returned to his ears, three times as painful —

— *what are these marks, Daddy? They're just like the ones on your back only mine don't bleed* —

— he shook his head and pressed his hands against his ears as he spiraled back to that morning so many years ago, during a strike not unlike this one; his own father, so desperate because the strike fund had gone dry and he'd been denied both welfare and unemployment benefits, had decided to cross the picket line. He remembered the way his mother had cried and held Dad's hand and begged him not to go, saying that she could get a job somewhere, maybe doing people's laundry or something —

— and the look on her face later, when the police came to tell her about the Accident, that Dad had somehow ("We're not sure how it happened, ma'am, no one wants to talk about it.") been crushed by his press, and Jackson remembered, then, the last thing Dad had said to him before leaving that morning, something about being welcome to come and see his machine —

— Jackson took a deep breath and stood straight, clearing his head of the pain and pressure.

"What the hell happened, Sheriff?" asked Robinson, handing back Jackson's shotgun.

"I never saw anything like it," whispered Jackson. "How do you suppose a man could get crushed in a press like that and no one saw it happen?"

"What are you talking about, Sheriff?"

Jackson blinked, cleared his throat, and faced his deputy. "I mean...Jesus...how could a body just...dry up like that? You had your arm in there, Dan. The man had no internal organs. When his head collapsed there was no brain inside the skull." He fished around inside his pocket, found his cigarettes, and lit one for himself, one for Robinson.

They smoked in silence for a moment.

Around the corner, the sounds of the crowd grew angrier, louder. The chopper made another sweep of the area. Sirens shrieked as ambulances sped from the scene with their broken and bleeding cargos.

Jackson crushed out his cigarette, turned to Robinson, and said, "Listen to me. I don't want you *ever* to tell anyone what happened out here, understand me? Not the other guys, your girlfriend, your parents, *nobody*. This stays between us, all right?"

"You got my word, Sheriff."

A gunshot cracked through the dusk and the crowd erupted into panic. Jackson and Robinson grabbed their weapons and ran to lend what assistance they could.

(...the iron support beams in the factory's ceiling ripple and coil around one another, becoming sinewy muscle tissue that surges down and combines with the cranks...

...which become lungs...

...that attach themselves to the press foundation...

...which evolves into a spinal column...

...that supports the control panel as it shudders...

...and spreads...

...and becomes the gray matter of a brain signaling everything to converge...

...pulsing steelbeat pounding faster and faster...

...moist pink muscle tissue, tendons, bones, sparks, tubes, metal shavings, flesh, iron, organs, and alloys coalescing...

...and the being that is the Machine stands before the factory man, its shimmering electric gaze drilling into them as it reaches down and lifts them to its bosom, feeding, draining them of all essence until they are little more than a clockwork doll whose every component has been removed...

...doors open and the Old Worker is cast away...

...a hiss...

...a clank...

...the next shift arrives...

...as the production line begins again...)

The east parking lot was now empty. No one was there to hear the sounds from behind the iron doors.

Squeaking, screeching, loud clanking: heavy equipment dragging across a cement floor.

Something long, metallic, and triple-jointed pushed through the doors, folding around the edge. Another glint as more metal thrust out and folded back.

Throwing sparks, the mechanical hand raked down, gripped the handle, and pulled the doors closed.

The violence in the parking lot started anew.

The structure of the factory trembled.

The breeze picked up, swirling snow down the steps and up against the doors with a low whistle, a groan in the back of a tired man's throat.

A man works his whole life away, and what does it mean?

The wind stilled.

It means he has the makings of a factory man.

Shadows bled over the walls.

He has the mark of a worker.

A small shredded section of Herb Kaylor's shirt drifted to the ground, floating back and forth with the ease of a feather. It hit the dirty snow and was covered by a rolling drift of chill, dead white.

3

Hearing the noise is nothing at times. No, the worst part is that, after a while, you start to wear it. All over your face, in your eyes, on your clothes.

Stop it, Dad, just knock it the hell off!

It's a mark, this sound, that people can see and recognize. You might be at the grocery store or just walking outside to get the mail and people will look at you and see what you are, what you can only be, and that's a factory worker, a laborer all your life, and they know this by looking at you because you wear the noise.

I never asked you to give up any of your hopes or dreams to go work there, you gave those up on your own!

A man works his whole life away and he grows angry because he can't make anyone understand how it feels to scrub your hands so hard after a day's work that the palms start to bleed.

Goddammit, Dad, shut up! I know it's crummy, but it's not my fault!

I remember my Daddy's hands, the machine stink on them. The day he had my dog put down he tried to apologize to me, told me about how sick old Ralph was, but I was too hurt to listen. He just stood there and touched my cheek. I opened my eyes and looked at his hand and saw it was stained with machine grease. It was the hand that fed me but it was also the hand that killed my dog. He did it. Because he had to. Had to and hated it. He knew he'd never have to tell me he was sorry because his hand against my face, trying to wipe away my tears, said it all. His cruel dog-killing hand with its grease and machine stink so lightly against my face.

Take a good look at my hands, boy. A man's flesh was never meant to be like this, the lines so dark from oil stains they might as well be cracks in plaster. Sometimes I hate the idea of touching your mother with these hands, having her feel the calluses and cuts, the roughness on her cheek. She deserves tenderness, boy, the soft, easy touch of a lover, and she ain't never gonna feel it from these hands.

But she loves you, we all do, you should know that.

I know you do, boy. And I wish it helped more than it does, but sometimes it don't and that just makes me sick right down to the ground.

4

Jackson climbed the front steps of Herb Kaylor's house and knocked on the door. Darlene answered, nodded, and invited him inside.

The house smelled like coffee, uneaten dinner, and grief.

"I made meatloaf tonight," whispered Herb Kaylor's widow. "It was always his favorite. Don't know what I'm gonna do with it now…" She bit her lower lip and closed her eyes, locking her body rigid against Jackson's embrace. Pulling away, she ran a hand through her thinning gray hair and coughed. "I have to…apologize for how the place looks. I, uh…I…"

"Place looks fine," whispered Jackson as she led him toward the kitchen.

"Nice of you to say so." Her eyes were puffy and red-rimmed, making the lines on her face harsher.

Her son, Will, was making coffee; the teenager exchanged terse greetings with the sheriff and took his coffee into another room.

"Would you like a cup?" asked Darlene. "I grind the beans myself. Herb says…*said* that it made all the difference in the world from the store-bought kind."

"Yes, thank you."

As she handed him the cup and saucer, her hand began to shake and she almost spilled the coffee in his lap. She apologized, tried to smile, then sat at the table and wept quietly. After a moment she held out her hand and Jackson took it.

"Darlene," he said softly, "I hate to ask you about this, but I gotta know. Why was Herb working the picket today? He wasn't supposed to be there again until Friday."

"I swear to you I don't know. I asked him this morning right before he left. He just kind of laughed — you know how he always does when he don't want to bother you with a problem? Then he kissed me and said he was sorry he'd got Will into this and he was gonna try to fix things.

"He got Will on at the plant. Was even gonna train him." She shook her head and sipped at her coffee. "You know Herb's father did the same for him? Got him a job workin' the same shift in the same cell. I guess a lot of workers get in that way. Didn't your father work there, too?"

Jackson looked away and whispered, "Yeah."

"Place is like a fuckin' family heirloom." Will stood in the doorway.

Jackson turned to look at him as Darlene said, "What did I tell you about using that kind of language in the house? Your Daddy..."

"— was stupid! Admit it. It was stupid of him to go down there today."

Darlene stared at him with barely contained fury worsened by weariness and grief. "I won't have you bad-mouthing your father, Will. He ain't" — her voice cracked — "here to defend himself. He worked hard for his family and deserved a hell of a lot more respect and thanks than he ever got."

"*Thanks?*" shouted Will. "For what? For reminding me that he put his obligations over his own happiness, or for getting me on at the plant so I could become another goddamn factory stooge like him? Which wonderful gift should I have thanked him for?"

"You sure couldn't find a decent job on your own. Somebody had to do something."

"Listen," said Jackson, "maybe I should come back..."

"I think you'd better go to your room."

"No," said Will, storming into the kitchen and slamming down his coffee cup. "I'm eighteen years old and not once have I ever been allowed to disagree with anything you or Dad wanted. You weren't the one who had to sit down here and listen to him ramble on at three in the morning after he got tanked. To hear him tell it, working the plant was just short of Hell, yet he was more than happy to hand my ass over..."

"He was only trying to help you get some money so you could finally get your own place, get on your own. He was a very giving, great man."

"A *great* man? How the hell can you say that? You're wearing clothes that are ten years old and sitting at a table we bought for nine dollars at Goodwill! Maybe Dad had some great notions, but he wasn't great. He was a bitter, used up, little bit of a man who could only go to sleep after work if he downed enough booze, and I'll be damned if I'm gonna end up like…"

Darlene shot up from her chair and slapped Will across the face with such force he fell against the counter. When he regained his balance and turned back to face her, a thin trickle of blood oozed slowly from the corner of his mouth. His eyes widened in fear, shock, and countless levels of confusion and pain.

"You listen to me," said Darlene. "I was married to your father for almost twenty-five years, and in that time I saw him do things you aren't half man enough to do. I've seen him run into the middle of worse riots than the one today and pull old men out of trouble. I've seen him give his last dime to friends who didn't have enough for groceries and then borrow money from your uncle to pay our own bills. I've seen him be more gentle than you can ever imagine and I've been there when he's felt low because he thought you were embarrassed by him. Maybe he was just a factory worker, but he was a damn decent man who gave me love and a good home. You never saw it, maybe you didn't want to, but your father was a great man who did great things. Maybe they weren't huge things, things that get written about in the paper, but that shouldn't matter. It's not his fault that you never saw any of his greatness, that you only saw him when he was tired and used up. And maybe he did drink, but, goddammit, for almost twenty-five years he never once thought about just giving up. I loved that…*factory stooge* more than any man in my life, and I could've had plenty. He was the best of them all."

"Mom, please, I..."

"— You never did nothing except make him feel like a failure because he couldn't buy you all the things your friends have. I wasn't down here listening to him ramble at three in the morning? *You* weren't there on those nights before we had kids, listening to him whisper how scared he was he wouldn't be able to give us a decent life. You weren't there to hold him and kiss him and feel so much tenderness between your bodies that it was like you were one person. And twenty-five years of that, of loving a man like your father, that gives you something no one can ruin or take away, and I won't listen to you talk against him! He was my husband and your father and he's dead and it hurts so much I want to scream."

Will's eyes welled with tears. "Oh god, Mom, I miss him. I'm so...sorry I said those things. I was just so angry." His chest began to hitch with the abrupt force of his sorrow. "I know that I...I hurt his feelings, that I made him feel like everything he did was for nothing. Can't I be mad that I'll never get the chance to make it up to him? Can't I?" He leaned into his mother's arms and wept. "He always said that you gotta...gotta look out for your obligations before you can start thinking about your own happiness. I know that now. And I'll...I'll try to...oh, Christ, Mom. I want the chance to make it all up to him..." Darlene held him and stroked the back of his head, whispering, "It's all right, go on...go on...he knows now, he always did, you have to believe that..."

Ted Jackson turned away from them and swallowed his coffee in three large gulps, winced as it hit his stomach, and was overpowered by the loss that soaked the room. He'd never felt more isolated or useless in his life.

Someone knocked loudly on the front door. Darlene turned toward Jackson. "Would you...would you mind answering the door, Ted? I don't think I'm...up to it just now."

Jackson said of course and went into the front room, quickly wiped his eyes and blew his nose, then turned on the porch light and opened the door.

5

Even if you manage to scrub off all the dirt and grease and metal shavings, you've still got the smell on you. Cheap aftershave, machine oil, sweat, the stink of hot metal. No matter how many showers you take, the smell stays on you. It's a stench that factory workers carry to their graves, a stink that's on them all the days of their life, squatting by them at the end like some loyal hound dog that sits by its master's grave until it starves to death, reminding you that all you leave behind is a mortgage, a pile of unpaid bills, children who are ashamed of you, and a spouse who will grow old and bitter and miserable and empty and will never be able to rid the house of that smell.

Stop.

That smell is your heritage, boy, don't deny it. You were born to be part of the line, part of the Machine, and it will mark you just like it marked me.

I won't listen to this.

Breathe it in deep.

SHUT THE FUCK UP!

That's a good boy.

6

Seven men stood on the porch, each with some sort of bandage covering a wound. Though Jackson recognized all of them as strikers, he only knew a few by name.

A barrel-chested man in old jeans and a grimy sweatshirt stepped forward and offered a firm handshake. "Evenin', Sheriff. We come to…to pay our respects to the family. Herb was one of the good guys and we're sorry as hell that he died because of this."

"Darlene's not feeling up to a bunch of company," said Jackson. "I shouldn't even be here myself but…"

"Nonsense," said Darlene from behind him. "Herb would never turn away a fellow union man, and neither will I."

Jackson stepped back as the men entered and stood in a semicircle, each looking sad, awkward, lost, and angry.

The barrel-chested man (Darlene called him "Rusty") offered the group's sympathy — each man muttering agreement and nodding his head — and said that if there was anything they could do she was to give the word and they'd be right on it.

Darlene thanked them and offered them some coffee. The men seemed to relax a little as each found a place to sit.

Then Will came into the room.

Once, when Jackson had still been a deputy, he'd arrested a man suspected of child molestation. When he'd opened the door to the holding cell every prisoner there had looked at the man with such cold loathing it made Jackson's blood almost stop in his veins. The guy hadn't lasted the night; Jackson found him the next morning beaten to a pulp. He'd choked on his own vomit with three socks rammed in his mouth.

The workers in the room were looking at Will Kaylor exactly the same way. Jackson felt the nerves in the back of his neck start tingling. He released a slow, quiet breath and surreptitiously unbuttoned the holster strap over his revolver.

"Hello," said Will flatly.

The men made no reply. Eyes looked back and forth from Will to Jackson.

"Well," said Darlene with false brightness, "would one of you like to give me a hand in the kitchen?"

Rusty and another man said they'd love to and followed her in, but not before giving Will one last angry glance.

As the remaining men started to whisper among themselves, Will touched Jackson's elbow and asked the sheriff to follow him upstairs.

Jackson excused himself and went after Will. They walked quickly up to Will's room at the end of the hall and closed the door.

Will turned on a small bedside lamp. "You know they really came here to see me, don't you?"

"I figured it was something like that."

"I was supposed to work the picket line today. My first day at work was the morning the strike started. Dad barely had a chance to show me the press before the walkout. He figured being part of the strike would be a nice way to start paying my real union dues." His eyes filled with pleading. "Please believe I loved my dad and I appreciated what he tried to do for me, but I...didn't want to end up like him. He was so goddamn tired and unhappy all the time. I just...didn't want to let that happen to me."

Jackson put his hand on Will's shoulder. "Your dad told me once that he hoped you'd do better than he had. I really don't think he'd blame you, so don't go blaming yourself."

"But those guys downstairs blame me. As far as they're concerned, I should have been the one who died today." He crossed to the window and pulled back the curtain. The factory in the distance shimmered with an eerie phosphorescence that seemed both peaceful and mocking.

"Have you ever been in the lobby of the bank downtown?" asked Will. "All those windows facing every direction? Have you noticed that you can't see any part of the factory from there, not even the smokestacks? I worked for a while last summer as a caddy at the Moundbuilder's Country Club. They used to give us a free lunch. The factory's only five miles away and you can't see it from anywhere on the club grounds, even using binoculars."

"You're not making any sense."

"It's almost as if the people who don't want to know about it can't see it." He turned around and pulled the curtain farther back. "Can you see the factory, Sheriff?"

"Yeah."

"My room faces north, all right?"

"Okay…?"

Will dropped the curtain and crossed to open the door, gesturing for Jackson to follow him to the other end of the hall. They entered Herb and Darlene's room. Will pointed at the curtains.

"Their window faces the exact opposite direction of mine. Pull back the curtain."

Confused, Jackson did as Will asked —

— and found himself facing a view of the factory. The angle was slightly different, but it was undeniably the factory.

"That's impossible," he whispered. "The damn thing's north and this window…"

"Dad showed it to me the night before I started at the plant. If you go downstairs and look out the back door, you'll still be able to see it. Look out any door or window facing any direction in this house and you'll see the plant."

Jackson let the curtain fall back.

Will shrugged his shoulders in defeat. "I don't know why I'm showing you this, telling you these things. I doubt you even understand."

Jackson faced him. "I know exactly how you feel, Will. My dad was killed in an industrial accident at the plant when I was seventeen. Up until the day he died he'd been priming me to go work the line. I didn't want to, God knows, I saw what it did to him, how it sucked his life away. He was dead long before the accident. I watched it happen bit by bit, the way his spirit just ground to a halt in a series of sputtering little agonies. I hated that place, even used to have these dreams where the machines came alive and chased me. The morning he was killed my mom started in on me to go get a job there. I didn't know what to do. But I got lucky and was drafted. Even Vietnam was preferable to that place. Mom died while I was over there.

"As terrible as it sounds, for as much as I loved her I was almost relieved that she was dead because it meant she wouldn't hound me about taking my father's place at the plant."

"Why did you stay here?"

"I wish I knew." Jackson absentmindedly scratched at an area near the center of his back, thinking about the marks he'd found there when he was a child, and pulled his hand away. "Maybe it was my way of defying that place. I kept remembering the passage from Revelations that the priest read at Dad's funeral: 'Yea, sayeth the spirit, that they may rest from their labours, and their works do follow them.' Well, I wasn't going to follow and I was damned if that place was gonna drill into my conscience and follow me. For so many years I'd listened to Dad talk about it like it was an actual living thing that I came to think of it that way, so I guess part of me decided to stay here just to spite it, to drive past it every day and think, 'You didn't get me, fucker!' At least that way I can...I dunno, make my Dad's death count for something." He exhaled, smiled, and put his hand on Will's shoulder. "Those men can't force you to do anything you don't want, not while I'm wearing a badge, anyway."

"Thanks, Sheriff. Dad always said you were one of the good guys."

"So was he. So're all the workers."

Will stared down at his trembling hands. "You know the funny thing? I keep thinking about being...a virgin. I've never even *kissed* a girl. I've been trapped here all my life, waiting to follow in my dad's footsteps, watching him and Mom waste away, not able to do a goddamn thing about it. I spend half my time feeling like shit and the other half mad that I feel that way. I look in mirrors and think I'm seeing a picture of my dad. I think of everything he and Mom have missed out on and I just...surrender, y'know? Because I love them. And I don't know if I'm my own man or just the sum of my family's parts."

Jackson started out of the room. "You stay here. I'm gonna go send those men on their way."

Will rose from the bed. "Sheriff?"

"Yeah?"

"Thanks for telling me about your dad. It helped me to decide. I'm gonna go with them."

"Jesus, Will, you just said that..."

"— I said that I *didn't* want to go, but I've been thinking about what Dad said, about looking out for obligations before thinking about your own happiness, and he was right. And just like you, I gotta make my dad's death count for something."

Jackson stared at him. "You sure about this?"

"Yes. It's the first thing I have been sure of. It's about time."

The boy was now resigned.

The son would become the father.

"All right," said Jackson, swallowing back his rage and disgust.

"I'd...I'd really appreciate it if you'd come along, Sheriff."

"Why's that?"

"I think you and I have something in common. I think we both never understood what our fathers went through, and I think we've both always wanted to know."

Jackson glanced out the window, at the factory. "I could never imagine what he must've...felt like, day after day. I could never..." He blinked, looked away. "Yeah. I'd like to come along."

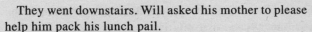

They went downstairs. Will asked his mother to please help him pack his lunch pail.

The other men seemed pleased.

Jackson shook his head, offered his sympathy to Darlene once again, and left with Will and the others.

7

— someday you'll understand, boy, that a man becomes something more than part of his machine and his machine becomes something more than just the other half of a tool. They marry in a way no two people could ever know. They become each other's God. They become a greater Machine. And the Machine makes all things possible. It feeds you, clothes you, puts the roof over your head, and shows you all the mercy that the world never will.

The Machine is family.

It is purpose.

It is love.

So take its lever and feel the devotion.

There you go, just like that.

8

The parking lot was deserted, save for cars driven by the midnight shift workers.

They milled about outside the doors to the basement production cell, waiting for Jackson and Will.

As they approached the group, Will gently took Jackson by the arm and said, "I think it'd be nice if you didn't stop coming around for cards Saturday nights."

"Wouldn't miss it for the world."

They stood among the other workers. Barrel-chested Rusty smiled at Will, nodded at Jackson, and said, "We got to make sure."

"I figured," said Jackson.

"Sure of what?" asked Will.

And Rusty replied: "You never actually started working with the press, did you?"

Will sighed and shook his head. "No. The strike was called right after I clocked in." Without another word, he took off his jacket, then unbuttoned and removed his shirt, turning around.

Rusty pulled a flashlight from his back pocket and shone the beam on Will's back.

Several round scarlike marks speckled the young man's back, starting between his shoulder blades and continuing toward the base of his spine. Some were less than an eighth of an inch in diameter, but others looked to be three times that size, pushing inward like the pink indentations left in the skin after a scab has been peeled off.

"Damn," said Rusty. "Shift's gotta start on time."

"Don't you think I know that?" snapped Will. "Dad used to talk about how…oh, hell." He took a deep breath. "Better get on with it."

Rusty pulled a small black handbook from his pocket, then turned toward the other men. "We're here tonight to welcome a new brother into our union — Will Kaylor, son of Herb. Herb was a decent man, a good friend, and one of the finest machinists it's ever been my privilege to work beside. I hope that all of us will treat his son with the same respect we gave to his father."

The workers nodded in approval.

Rusty flipped through the pages of his tattered union handbook until he found what he was looking for. "Sheriff," he said, offering the book to Jackson, "would you do us the honor of reading the union prayer here in the front where I marked it?"

"It would be…a privilege," replied Jackson, taking the book.

Will was marched to a nearby wall, then had his face and chest pressed against it, his bare back exposed to the night.

"Just clench your teeth together," whispered Rusty to Will. "Close your eyes and hold your breath. It don't hurt as much as you think."

The other shift workers were opening their lunch pails and toolboxes, removing Philips-head screwdrivers.

Jackson would not allow himself to turn away. His father had gone through this, as had his father before him. Jackson had been spared, but that did not ease his conscience. He wanted to know.

He *had* to know.

Rusty looked toward Jackson and gave a short, sharp nod of his head, and Jackson began to read: "'Almighty God, we, your workers, beseech Thee to guide us, that we may do the work which Thou givest us to do, in truth, and beauty, and righteousness, with singleness of heart as Thy servants, and to the benefit of our fellow men.'"

The workers gathered around Will, each choosing a scar and then, one by one, in succession, plunging their screwdrivers into it.

"'Though we are not poets, Lord, or visionaries, or prophets, or great-minded leaders of men, we ask that you accept the humble labor of our hands as proof of our love for You, and for our families.'"

Blood spurted from each wound and ran down Will's back, spattering against the asphalt.

His scream began somewhere in the center of the earth, forcing its way up through layers of molten rock and centuries of pain, shuddering through his legs and groin, then lodging in his throat for only a moment before erupting from his throat as the howl of the shift whistle growing in volume to deafen the very ears of God.

Jackson had to shout to be heard over the din. "'We thank Thee for Thy blessing as we, your humble workers, welcome a new brother into our ranks. May You watch over and protect him as You have always watched over and protected us. Who can be our adversary, if You are on our side? You did not even spare Your own Son, but gave Him up for the sake of us all.'"

"'And must not that gift be accompanied by the gift of all else?'" responded the workers in unison.

"'So we offer our gift of all else, Lord, we offer our labours for the glory of Thy name, Amen.'"

"Amen," echoed the workers, backing away.

"Amen," said Will, dropping to his knees, then vomiting and whimpering.

Jackson closed the union handbook and came forward, tears in his eyes, and began to cradle Will in his arms; the boy shook his head and rose unsteadily to his feet, then began staggering toward the slowly opening basement doors —

**(here is my son
does he have the makings of a factory man?)**

— squeaking, screeching, loud clanking: heavy machinery dragging across a cement floor —

— the doors opened farther: something long, metallic, and triple-jointed pushed through, folding around the edge. A glint as more metal thrust out and folded, seizing the door —

— throwing sparks, the mechanical hand raked down, gripped the handle, and pulled the door wide open.

...doors open and the Old Worker is cast away...

Something crumpled and manlike was tossed out over their heads and landed with a soft *whump*! in the snow.

Will turned toward Jackson. "A man works his whole life away, and what does it mean?"

Jackson and the workers stared into the shimmering electric gaze beyond the iron doors.

"Welcome, my son," whispered Jackson —

— in a voice very much like his own father's —

— "Welcome to the Machine."

...as the production line begins again...

9

You'll be a worker just like me, that's the way of it.

Work the line, wear the smell; the son following in his father's footsteps.

Something like this, well...it makes a man's life seem worthwhile.

I always knew you'd do me proud.

I love you, Dad. I hope this makes up for a lot of things.

I love you too, son.

Best get to work.

That's a good boy....

This one is for my father

EARSHOT

Glenn Isaacson

Here is another short-short that hits the mark from a writer in Baltimore (a writer whom, by the way, we've never met — in case you're wondering if he was running on an inside track). Glenn Isaacson works for the behemoth government industry known as the Social Security Administration and has spent many years trying to break into the song-writing business. His first published story, which recalls the subtle yet caustic style of John Collier, follows henceforth.

"How can she be real? She's too perfect, too beautiful. She can't even be of the same species I am. How can she be real?" he said to the rabbit, and its long gray ears perked forward a little and its pink nose quivered.

But the rabbit never talked.

It never talked.

It never, ever, ever talked.

"How can she be human? How can she have thoughts in that beautiful head? How can she have hopes and desires and dreams and goals and preferences and prejudices? She can't. And if she does, I don't want to know. All she has to be is gorgeous. That's all she ever has to do." He gently stroked the rabbit's head and looked imploringly at its luminous black eyes.

But the rabbit never talked.

It never talked.

It never, ever, ever talked.

"Her body is perfection. The most beautifully sleek and lusciously rounded body to ever walk the earth. She smells good. I'll bet she tastes good, too. I know she must. Delicious. And to touch her? Sheer heaven. But she wouldn't feel anything if I touched her. She couldn't. Because there's nothing inside there. She's not a person. She's not even an animal. She's a thing." He picked up the rabbit, cradled it in his arms, and began walking around the room in a circle. It snuggled comfortably against his chest.

But the rabbit never talked. It never talked.

It never, ever, ever talked.

"She has a name. Can you believe it? A name. As if she needs one. As if it matters. Linda Greaves! What a laugh! Who could've given her a name? She had no parents, no childhood, no past, no experiences, no friends. Nothing at all." He stopped walking, staring at a knot in the paneling.

"I could do her, you know. Fuck her. Like she was a warm pillow or a hole in the wall. And it would be the best sex I ever had. The best. A feast for my mouth and my nose and my eyes and my hands and the nerve endings all over my body." He began pacing back and forth in a straight line, holding the rabbit tighter.

"And when I was done with her, I could throw her out

like a piece of garbage. Garbage with a name, yet! Linda Greaves, garbage."

"Or better yet…better yet, I could eat her for dinner. I could cut her up into pieces and roast her over an open fire and she would be delicious, just the right amount of fat and meat. Her skin would turn the prettiest red." He paused, thinking.

"Or…I could strangle her." He grabbed the rabbit under its forelegs and let the rest of its chubby gray and white body dangle down. He held it up and stared into its face. "Just like this." His hands tightened. "I could ask her if she wanted to die and her answer wouldn't matter at all. I could squeeze the life out of her in less than one minute. Just like this." His hands tightened more. "Do you want to die?" he asked. "Do you? Do you want to be dead?"

But the rabbit never talked.

It never talked.

It never, ever, ever talked.

He slowly relaxed his grip and set the rabbit down gently on the polished mahogany desk. It backed away from him a little nervously then seemed to relax and began leisurely exploring the desktop, sniffing at pens and folders and paper clips.

There was a knock on the door.

"Yes?" he called.

The door opened slightly and his secretary leaned in. "Your two o'clock is here, Dr. Grossman."

"Oh, okay," he said.

"She asked if she could have an hour today instead of her usual forty-five minutes. She seems pretty upset."

He glanced at his schedule. "Tell her that's fine." He began to pick up the rabbit to put it back into its cage, but remembered that this patient was one who liked to hold the rabbit in her lap and pet it. It helped relax her when she talked about her difficult childhood and her generally catastrophic, miserable life. "Why don't you just send her in. I'll tell her."

His secretary turned from the door and said, "You can come in, Ms. Greaves."

Grossman waited expectantly. The vision appeared at his door. A halo of fluffy, honey-blond hair. Sparkling blue-gray eyes. Golden skin. Tight blue jeans. A little gold cross that nestled above her sweetly rounded chest. A delicate scent of exotic flowers and spices and warm flesh.

Her nose was red from crying and was dripping onto her upper lip.

Grossman took a tissue from a box on his desk and handed it to her. "Sit down, Linda," he said. "The extra time today will be no problem at all."

She sat down, wiping her nose with the tissue.

"Here," he said, "I have a friend that'll be glad to see you." He handed her the rabbit and she smiled, probably for the first time today, Grossman thought.

She put the rabbit on her lap and looked at it fondly. "Only you and Dr. Grossman know all my problems, Mr. Bunny," she said to the rabbit. She lightly stroked its long ears.

Grossman sat down on his thickly padded leather chair and leaned back. "So, tell me what's been happening since I last saw you," he said.

Peter Straub

When we finished the following story, we had undergone as heartfelt an emotional experience as literature can ever hope to bring. Writing with subtle power in a style that is both elegant and precise, Peter Straub drops us into the center of a small boy's terrifying world. As we traverse the landscape of childhood, Straub reminds us about where all the monsters really come. The award-winning author of Ghost Story, Koko, Houses Without Doors *and* The Throat *makes his first appearance in* Borderlands *with a novella you will not forget.*

Part One

1

Fee's first memory was of a vision of fire, not an actual fire but an imagined fire, leaping upward at an enormous grate upon which lay a naked man. Attached to this image was the accompanying memory of his father gripping the telephone. For a moment his father, Bob Bandolier, the one and only king of this realm, seemed rubbery, almost boneless with shock. He repeated the word, and a second time five-year-old Fielding Bandolier, little blond Fee, saw the flames jumping at the blackening figure on the grate. "I'm fired? This has got to be a joke."

The flames engulfed the tiny man on the slanting grate. The man opened his mouth to screech. This was hell, it was interesting. Fee was scorched, too, by those flames. His father saw the child looking up at him, and the child saw his father take in his presence. A fire of pain and anger flashed out of his father's face and Fee's insides froze. His father waved him away with a curious back-paddling gesture of his left hand. In the murk of their apartment, Bob Bandolier's crisp white shirt gleamed like an apparition. The creases from the laundry jutted up from the shirt's starched surface.

"You *know* why I haven't been coming in," he said. "This is not a matter where I have a choice. You will never, ever, find a man who is as devoted…"

He listened, bowing over as if crushing down a spring in his chest. Fee crept backward across the room, hoping to make no noise at all. When he backed into the chaise against the far wall, he instinctively dropped to his knees and crawled beneath it, still looking at the way his father was bending over the telephone. Fee bumped into a dark furry lump, Jude the cat, and clamped it to his chest until it stopped struggling.

"No, sir," his father said. "If you think about the way I work, you will have to…"

He blew air out of his mouth, still pushing down that coiled spring in his chest. Fee knew that his father hated to be interrupted.

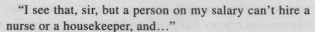

"I see that, sir, but a person on my salary can't hire a nurse or a housekeeper, and…"

Another loud exhalation.

"Do I have to tell you what goes on in hospitals? The infections, the sheer sloppiness, the…I have to keep her at home. I don't know if you're aware of this, sir, but there have been very few nights when I have not been able to spend most of my time at the hotel."

Slowly, as if he had become aware of the oddness of his posture, Fee's father began straightening up. He pressed his hand into the small of his back. "Sometimes we pray."

Fee saw the air around his father darken and fill with little white sparkling swirling things that winked and dazzled before they disappeared. Jude saw them too, and moved backwards, deeper beneath the chaise.

"Well, I suppose you are entitled to your own opinion about that," said his father, "but you are very much mistaken if you feel that my religious beliefs did in any way…"

"I dispute that absolutely," his father said.

"I have already explained that," his father said. "Almost every night since my wife fell ill, I managed to get to the hotel. I bring an attitude to work with me, sir, of absolute dedication…"

"I'm sorry you feel that way, sir," his father said, "but you are making a very great mistake."

"I mean, you are making a *mistake,*" his father said. The little white dancing lines spun and winked out in the air like fireworks.

Both Fee and Jude stared raptly from beneath the chaise.

His father gently replaced the receiver, and then set the telephone down on the table. His face was set in the cement of prayer.

Fee looked at the black telephone on its little table

between the big chair and the streaky window: the headset like a pair of droopy ears, the round dial. On the matching table, a porcelain fawn nuzzled a porcelain doe.

Heavy footsteps strode toward him. Jude searched warmth against his side. His father came striding in his gleaming shirt with the boxy lines from the dry cleaners, his dark trousers, his tacked down necktie, his shiny shoes. His mustache, two fat commas, seemed like another detachable ornament.

Bob Bandolier bent down, settled his thick white hands beneath Fee's arms, and pulled him up like a toy. He set him on his feet and frowned down at the child.

Then his father slapped his face and sent him backward against the chaise. Fee was too stunned to cry. When his father struck the other side of his face, his knees went away and he began to slip toward the rug. His cheeks burned. Bob Bandolier leaned down again. Silver light from the window painted a glowing white line on his dark hair. Fee's breath burned its way past the hot ball in his throat, and he closed his eyes and wailed.

"Do you know why I did that?"

His father's voice was still as low and reasonable as it had been when he was on the telephone.

Fee shook his head.

"Two reasons. Listen to me, son. Reason number one." He raised his index finger. "You disobeyed me, and I will always punish disobedience."

"No," Fee said.

"I sent you from the room, didn't I? Did you go out?"

Fee shook his head again, and his father gripped him tightly between his two hands and waited for him to stop sobbing. "I will not be contradicted, is that clear?"

Fee nodded miserably. His father gave a cool kiss to his burning cheek.

"I said there were two reasons, remember?"

Fee nodded.

"Sin is the second reason." Bob Bandolier's face moved hugely through the space between them, and his eyes, deep brown with luminous eggshell whites, searched Fee and found his crime. Fee began to cry again. His father held him upright. "The Lord Jesus is very, very angry today, Fielding. He will demand payment, and we must pay."

When his father talked like this, Fee saw a page from *Life* magazine, a torn battlefield covered with shell craters, trees burned to charred stumps, and huddled corpses.

"We will pray together," his father said, and hitched up the legs of his trousers and went down on his knees. "Then we will go in to see your mother." His father touched one of his shoulders with an index finger and pressed down, trying to push Fee all the way through the floor to the regions of eternal flame. Fee finally realized that his father was telling him to kneel, and he too went to his knees.

His father had closed his eyes, and his forehead was full of vertical lines. "Are you going to talk?" Fee said.

"Pray *silently,* Fee, say the words to yourself."

He put his hands together before his face and began moving his lips. Fee closed his own eyes and heard Jude dragging her tongue over and over the same spot of fur.

His father said, "Well, let's get in there. She's our job, you know."

Inside the bedroom, he opened the clothing press and took his suit jacket from a hanger, replaced the hanger and closed the door of the press. He shoved his arms into the jacket's sleeves and transformed himself into the more formal and forbidding man Fee knew best. He dipped his knees in front of the bedroom mirror to check the knot in his tie. He swept his hands over the smooth hair at the sides of his head. His eyes in the mirror found Fee's. "Go to your mother, Fee."

Until two weeks ago, the double bed had stood on the far end of the rag rug, his mother's perfume and lotion bottles had stood on the left side of what she called her "vanity table," her blond wooden chair in front of it. His father now stood there, watching him in the mirror. Up until two weeks ago, the curtains had been open all day, and the bedroom had always seemed full of a warm magic. Fat, black Jude spent all day lying in the pool of sunlight that collected in the middle of the rug. Now the curtains stayed shut and the room smelled of sickness...it reminded Fee of the time his father had brought him to work with him and, giddy with moral outrage, thrust him into a ruined, stinking room. *You want to see what people are really like?* Slivers of broken glass had covered the floor, and the stuffing foamed out of the slashed sofa, but the worst part had been the smell of the lumps and puddles on the floor. The walls had been streaked with brown. *This is their idea of fun*, his father had said. *Of a good time.* Now the rag rug was covered by the old mattress his father had placed on the floor beside the bed. The blond chair in front of the vanity had disappeared, as had the row of little bottles his mother had cherished. Two weeks ago, when everything had changed, Fee had heard his father smashing these bottles, roaring, smashing the chair against the wall. It was as if a monster had burst from his father's skin to rage back and forth in the bedroom. The next morning, his father said that Mom was sick. Pieces of the chair lay all over the room and the walls were covered with explosions. The whole room smelled overpoweringly sweet, like heaven with its flowers. *Your mother needs to rest. She needs to get better.* Fee had dared one glance at her tumbled hair and open mouth. A tiny curl of blood crept from her nose. *She's sick, but we'll take care of her.*

But she had not gotten any better. As the perfume explosions had dried on the wall, his father's shirts and socks and underwear had gradually covered the floor between the old mattress and the bare vanity table, and Fee now walked over the litter of clothing to step on the mattress and approach the bed. The sickroom smell intensified as he came closer to his mother. He was not sure that he could look at his mother's face...the bruised, puffy mask he had seen the last time his father had let him into the bedroom. He stood on the thin mattress beside the bed, looking at the wisps of brown hair that hung down over the side of the bed. They reached all the way to the black letters stamped on the sheet that read ST. ALWYN HOTEL. Maybe her hair was still growing. Maybe she was waiting for him to look at her. Maybe she was better...the way she used to be. Fee touched the letters and let his fingers drift upward so that his mother's hair brushed his hand. He could hear her breath moving almost soundlessly in his mother's throat.

"See how good she looks now? She's looking real good, aren't you, honey?"

Fee moved his eyes upward. It felt as though his chest and his stomach, everything inside him, swung out of his body and swayed in the air a moment before coming back inside him. Except for a fading yellow bruise that extended from her eye to her hairline, she looked like his mother again. Flecks of dried oatmeal clung to her chin and the sides of her mouth. The fine lines in her cheeks looked like pencil marks. Her mouth hung a little bit open, as if to sip the air, or to beg for more oatmeal.

Fee is five, and he is looking at his mother for the first time since he saw her covered with bruises. His conscious life — the extraordinary life of Fee's consciousness — has just begun.

He thought for a second that his mother was going to answer. Then he realized that his father had spoken to her as he would speak to Jude, or to a dog on the street. He let his fingertips touch her skin. Unlike her face, his mother's hands were rough, with enlarged knuckles like knots and calloused fingertips that widened out at their ends. The skin on the back of her hand felt cool and peculiarly coarse.

"Sure you are, honey," said his father behind him. "You're looking better every day."

Fee clutched her hand and tried to squeeze some of his own life into her. His mother lay on her bed like a princess frozen by a curse in a fairy tale. A blue vein pulsed in her eyelid. All she could see was black night.

For a second Fee saw night too, a deep swooning blackness that called to him.

Yes, he thought. *Okay. That's okay.*

"We're here, honey," his father said.

Fee wondered if he had ever before heard his father call his mother *honey*.

"That's your little Fee holding your hand, honey, can't you feel his love?"

A startling sense of total negation of revulsion caused Fee to pull back his hands. If his father saw, he did not mind, for he said nothing. Fee saw his mother floating away into the immense sea of blackness inside her.

For a second he forgot to breathe through his mouth, and the stench that rose from the bed assaulted him.

"Didn't have time to clean her up yet today. I'll get to it before long…but, you know, she could be lying on a bed of silk, it'd be all the same to her."

Fee wanted to lean forward and put his arms around his mother, but he had to step back.

"We're none of us doctors and nurses here, Fee."

For a moment Fee thought there must be more people

in the room. Then he realized that his father meant the two of them, and that put into his head an idea of great simplicity and truth.

"Mommy ought to have a doctor," he said, and risked looking up at his father.

His father leaned over and pulled him by the shoulders, making him move awkwardly backwards over the mattress on the floor. Fee braced himself to be struck again, but his father turned him around and faced him with neither the deepening of feeling nor the sparkling of violence that usually preceded a blow.

"If I was three nurses instead of just one man, I could give her a change of sheets twice a day...hell, I could probably wash her hair and brush her teeth for her. But, Fee..." His father's grip tightened, and the heavy wedges of his fingers drove painfully into Fee's skin. "Do you think your mother would be happy, away from us?"

The person lying on the bed no longer had anything to do with happiness and unhappiness.

"She could only be happy being here with us, that's right, Fee, you're *right*. She knew you were holding her hand...that's why she's going to get better." He looked up. "Pretty soon, you're going to be sitting up and sassing back, isn't that right?"

He wouldn't allow anybody to sass him back, not ever.

"Let's pray for her now." His father pushed him down to his knees again, then joined him on the blanket. "Our Father who art in heaven," he said. "Your servant, Anna Bandolier, my wife and this boy's mother, needs your help. And so do we. Help us to care for her in her weakness, and we ask You to help her to overcome this weakness. Not a single person on earth is perfect, this poor sick woman included, and maybe we all have strayed in thought and deed from Your ways. Mercy is the best we can hope for, and we sinners know we do not deserve it, amen."

He lowered his hands and got to his feet. "Now leave the room, Fee." He removed his jacket and hung it on one of the bedposts and rolled up his sleeves. He tucked his necktie into his shirt. He stopped to give his son a disturbingly concentrated look. "We're going to take care of her by ourselves, and we don't want anybody else knowing our business."

"Yes, sir," Fee said.

His father jerked his head toward the bedroom door. "You remember what I said."

2

His father never asked if he wanted to kiss his Mom, and he never thought to ask if he could...the pale woman lying on the bed with her eyes closed was not someone you could kiss. She was sailing out into the vast darkness within her a little more every day. She was like a radio station growing fainter and fainter as you drove into the country.

The yellow bruise grew fainter and fainter over the days, until one morning Fee realized that it had faded altogether. Her cheeks sank inward toward her teeth, drawing a new set of faint pencil lines across her face. One day, five or six days after the bruise had disappeared, Fee saw that the round blue shadows of her temples had collapsed some fraction of an inch inward, like soft ground sinking after a rain.

Fee's father kept saying that she was getting better, and Fee knew that this was true in a way that his father could not understand and he himself could only barely see. She was getting better because her little boat had sailed a long way into the darkness.

Sometimes Fee held a half-filled glass of water to her lips and let teaspoon-sized sips slide, one after another, into the dry cavern of her mouth. His mother never seemed to swallow these tiny drinks, for the moisture slipped down her throat by itself. He could see it move, quick as a living thing, shining and shivering as it darted into her throat.

Sometimes when his father prayed, Fee found himself examining the nails on his mother's hand, which grew longer by themselves. At first her fingernails were pink, but in a week they turned an odd yellowish-white. The moons disappeared. Oddest of all, her long fingernails grew a yellow-brown rind of dirt.

He watched the colors alter in her face. Her lips darkened to brown, and a white fur appeared in the corner of her mouth.

Lord, this woman needs Your mercy. We're counting on You here, Lord.

When Fee left the bedroom each evening, he could hear his father go about the business of cleaning her up. When his father came out of the room, he carried the reeking ball of dirty sheets downstairs into the basement, his face frozen with distaste.

Mrs. Sunchana from the upstairs apartment washed her family's things twice a week, on Monday and Wednesday mornings, and never came downstairs at night. Fee's father put the clean sheets through the wringer and then took the heavy sheets outside to hang them on the two washing lines that were the Bandoliers'.

One night, his father slapped him awake and leaned over him in the dark. Fee, too startled to cry, saw his father's enormous eyes and the glossy commas of the mustache glaring down at him. His teeth shone. Heat and the odor of alcohol poured from him.

You think I was put on earth to be your servant. I was not put on earth to be your servant. I could close the door and walk out of here tomorrow and never look back. Don't kid yourself...I'd be a lot happier if I did.

3

One day Bob Bandolier got a temporary job as desk man at the Hotel Hepton. Fee buffed his father's black shoes and got the onyx cufflinks from the top of the dresser. He pulled on his own clothes and watched his father pop the dry cleaner's band from around a beautiful stiff white shirt, settle the shirt like armor around his body and squeeze the buttons through the holes, coax the cufflinks into place, tug his sleeves, knot a lustrous and silvery tie, button his dark suit. His father dipped his knees before the bedroom mirror, brushed back the smooth hair at the sides of his head, used his little finger to rub wax into his perfect mustache, a comb no larger than a thumbnail to coax it through the whiskers.

His father pulled his neat dark topcoat on over the suit, patted his pockets, and gave Fee a dollar. He was to sit on the steps until noon, when he could walk to the Beldame Oriental Theater. A quarter bought him admission, and fifty cents would get him a hot dog, popcorn, and a soft drink; he could see *From Dangerous Depths*, starring Robert Ryan and Ida Lupino, along with a second feature, the travelogue, previews, and a cartoon; and then he was to walk back down Livermore without talking to anybody and wait on the steps until his father came back home to let him in. The movies ended at twenty-five minutes past five, and his father said he would be home before six, so it would not be a long wait.

"Now, we have to make it snappy," his father said. "You can't be late for the Hepton, you know."

Fee went dutifully to the closet just inside the front door, where his jacket and his winter coat hung from hooks screwed in halfway down the door. He reached up dreamily, and his father ripped the jacket off the hook and pushed it into his chest.

Before Fee could figure out the jacket, his father had opened the front door and pushed him out onto the landing. Fee got an arm into a sleeve while his father locked the door. Then he pulled at the jacket, but his other arm would not go into its sleeve.

"Fee, you're deliberately trying to louse me up," his father said. He ripped the jacket off his arm, turned it around and jammed his arms into the sleeves. Then he fought the zipper for a couple of seconds. "You zip it. I have to go. You got your money?"

He was going down the steps and past the rose bushes to the path that went to the sidewalk.

Fee nodded.

Bob Bandolier walked quickly down the path without looking back. He was tall and almost slim in his tight black coat. Nobody else on the street looked like him — all the other men wore plaid caps and old army jackets.

In a little while smiling Mrs. Sunchana came up the walk carrying a bag of groceries. "Fee, you are enjoying the sunshine? You don't feel the cold today?" Her slight foreign accent made her speech sound musical, and her creamy round face, with its dark eyes and black eyebrows beneath her black bangs, could seem either witch-like or guilelessly pretty. Mrs. Sunchana looked nothing at all like Fee's mother...short, compact, and energetic where his mother was tall, thin, and weary; dark and cheerful where she was sorrowing and fair.

"I'm not cold," he said, though the chill licked in under the collar of his jacket, and his ears had begun to tingle. Mrs. Sunchana smiled at him again, said, "Hold this for me, Fee," and thrust the grocery bag onto his lap. He gripped the heavy bag as she opened her purse and searched for her key. There were no lines in her face at all. Both her cheeks and her lips were plump with health and life...for a second, bending over her black plastic purse and frowning with concentration, she seemed almost volcanic to Fee, and he wondered what it would be like to have this woman for his mother. He thought of her plump strong arms closing around him. Her face expanded above him. A rapture that was half terror filled his body.

For a second he was her child.

Mrs. Sunchana unlocked the door and held it open with one hip while she bent to take the groceries from Fee's lap. Fee looked down into the bag and saw a cardboard carton of brown eggs and a box of sugar-covered doughnuts. Mrs. Sunchana's live black hair brushed his forehead. The world wavered before him, and a trembling electricity filled his head. She drew the bag out of his arms, then quizzed him with a look.

"Coming in?"

"I'm going to the movies in a little while."

"You don't want to wait inside, where it is warm?"

He shook his head. Mrs. Sunchana tightened her grip on the grocery bag. The expression on her face frightened him, and he turned away to look at the empty sidewalk.

"Is your mother all right, Fee?"

"She's sleeping."

"Oh." Mrs. Sunchana nodded.

"We're letting her sleep until my dad gets home."

Mrs. Sunchana kept nodding as she backed through the door. Fee remembered the milk and the sugary doughnuts, and turned around again before she could see how hungry he was. "Do you know what time it is?"

She leaned over the bag to look at her watch. "Just about ten-thirty. Why, Fee?"

He turned around again quickly to face the street. A black car moved down the street, its tires swishing through the fallen elm leaves. The front door clicked shut behind him.

A minute later, a window slid upward in its frame. A painful self-consciousness slowly brought him to his feet. He put his hands in his pockets.

Fee walked stiffly and slowly down the path to the sidewalk and turned left toward Livermore Avenue. He remembered the moment when Mrs. Sunchana's electrically alive hair had moved against his forehead, and an extraordinary internal pain lifted him off his feet and sent him gliding over the pavement.

The elms of Livermore Avenue interlocked their branches far overhead. Preoccupied men and women in coats moved up and down past the shop fronts. Fee was away from his block, and no one was going to ask him questions about his mother and father. Fee glanced to his right and experienced a sharp flame of anger and disgrace that somehow seemed connected to Mrs. Sunchana's questions about his mother.

But of course what was across the street had nothing to do with his mother. Between the slowly moving vehicles, the high boxy automobiles and the slat-sided trucks, was a dark arched passage that led into a long narrow alley. In front of the brick passage was a tall gray building with what to Fee looked like a hundred windows, and behind it was the blank facade of a smaller, brown brick building. The gray building was the St. Alwyn Hotel, the smaller building its annex. Fee felt that he was no longer supposed to really look at the St. Alwyn. The St. Alwyn had done something bad, grievously bad…it had opened a most terrible hole in the world, and from that hole had issued hellish screams and groans.

A pure, terrible ache occurred in the middle of his body. From across the street, the St. Alwyn leered at him, and cold gray air sifted through his clothing. Brilliant leaves packed the gutters; water more transparent than the air streamed over and through the leaves. The ache within Fee threatened to blow him apart. He wanted to lower his face into the water…to dissolve into the transparent stream.

A man in a dark coat had appeared at the end of the tunnel behind the St. Alwyn, and Fee's heart moved with an involuntary constriction of pain and love before he consciously took in that the man was his father.

His father staring at a spot on the tunnel wall.

Why was his father behind the hated St. Alwyn, when he was supposed to be working at the Hotel Hepton?

His father looked from side to side, then moved into the darkness of the tunnel.

Bob Bandolier began fleeing down the alley. A confusion of feelings like voices raised in Fee's chest.

Now the alley was empty. Fee walked a few yards along the sidewalk, looking down at the beautiful clear water moving through the brilliant leaves. The sorrow and misery within him threatened to overflow. Without thinking, Fee dropped to his knees and thrust both of his hands into the clear rushing water. A shock of cold bit into him. His small white hands sank further than he had expected into the transparent water, and the ribbed cuffs of his jacket got soaked. Handcuffs made of burning ice formed around his wrists. The leaves drifted apart when he touched them. A brown stain oozed out and drifted widely out, obscuring the leaves. Gasping, Fee pulled his burning hands from the water and wiped them on his jacket. He leaned over the gutter to watch the brown stain pour from the hole he had made in the leaves. Whatever it was, he had turned it loose, set it free.

4

The box of popcorn warmed Fee's hands. The Beldame Oriental Theater's huge, luxurious space, with its floating cherubs and robed women raising lamps, its gilded arabesques and swooping curves of plaster, lay all about him. Empty rows of seats extended forward and back, and high up in the darkness behind him hung the huge rafter of the balcony. One old woman in a flowerpot hat

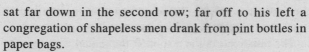

sat far down in the second row; far off to his left a congregation of shapeless men drank from pint bottles in paper bags.

This happened every day, Fee realized.

MOVIETONE NEWS blared from the screen, and a voice like a descending fist spoke incomprehensible but thrilling things over film of soldiers pointing rifles into dark skies, of a black boxer with a knotted forehead knocking down a white boxer in a brilliant spray of sweat and saliva. Women in bathing suits and sashes stood in a long row and smiled at the camera; one woman in a long gown raised a crown from her head and placed it on the glowing black hair of a woman who looked like Mrs. Sunchana. It *was* Mrs. Sunchana, Fee thought, but then saw that her face was thinner than Mrs. Sunchana's, and the panic calmed in him.

The grinning heads of a gray cat and a small brown mouse popped onto the screen. He laughed in delight. In cartoons the music was loud and relentless, and the animals behaved like bad children. Characters were turned to smoking ruins, pressed flat, dismembered, broken like twigs, consumed by fires, and in seconds were whole again. Cartoons were about not being hurt.

Abruptly, he was running alongside a cartoon mouse in a cartoon house. The mouse ran upright on his legs, like a human being. Behind him, also on whirling back legs, ran the cat. The mouse scorched a track through the carpet and zoomed into a neat mouse hole seconds before the cat's huge paw filled the hole. Fee brought salty popcorn to his mouth. Jerry Mouse sat at a little table and ate a mouse-sized steak with a knife and a fork. Fee drank in the enormity of his pleasure, the self-delight and swagger of the mouse; and the jealous rage of Tom Cat, rolling his huge bloodshot eye at the mouse hole.

After the cartoon, Fee walked up the aisle to buy a hot dog. Two or three people had taken seats in the vast space

behind him. An old woman wrapped in a hairy brown
coat mumbled to herself; a teenage boy cutting school
cocked his feet on the seat in front of him. Fee saw the
outline of a big man's head and shoulders on the other
side of the theater, looked away, felt an odd sense of
recognition, and looked back at an empty seat. He had
been seen, but who had seen him?

Fee pushed through the wide doors into the bright lobby.
A skinny man in a red jacket stood behind the candy
counter, and an usher exhaled smoke from a velvet bench.
The door to the men's room was just now swinging shut.

Fee bought a steaming hot dog and squirted ketchup
onto it, wrapped it in a flimsy paper napkin, and hurried
back into the theater. He heard the door of the men's room
sliding across the lobby carpet. He rushed down the aisle
and took his seat just as the titles came up on the screen.

The stars of *From Dangerous Depths* were Robert Ryan
and Ida Lupino. It was directed by Robert Siodmak. Fee
had never heard of any of these people, nor of any of the
supporting actors, and he was disappointed that the movie
was not in color.

Charlie Carpenter (Robert Ryan) was a tall, well-
dressed accountant who lived alone in a hotel room
exactly like those at the St. Alwyn. Charlie Carpenter put
a wide-brimmed hat on the floor and flipped cards into
it. He wore a necktie at home and, like Bob Bandolier, he
peered into the mirror to scowl at his handsome,
embittered face. At work he snubbed his office mates,
and after work he drank in a bar. On Sundays he attended
Mass. One day, Charlie Carpenter noticed a discrepancy
in the accounts, but when he asked about it, his angry
supervisor (William Bendix) said that he had come upon
traces of the Elijah Fund...this fund was used for certain
investments, it was none of Charlie's business, he should
never have discovered it in the first place, a junior clerk
made a mistake, Charlie must forget he ever heard of it.

When Charlie pressed for the names of the corporate officers in control of the fund, his supervisor reluctantly gave him two names, Fenton Welles and Lily Sheehan, but warned him to leave the matter alone.

Fenton Welles (Ralph Meeker) and Lily Sheehan (Ida Lupino) owned big comfortable houses in the wealthy part of town. Charlie Carpenter scanned their lawn parties through field glasses, he followed them to their country houses on opposite sides of Random Lake, fifty miles north of the city. Lily Sheehan summoned Charlie to her office. He feared that she knew he had been following her, but Lily was almost flirtatious. She gave Charlie a cigarette and sat on the edge of her desk and said that she had noticed that his reports were unusually perceptive. Charlie was a smart loner, just the sort of man whose help she needed.

Lily had suspicions about Fenton Welles. Charlie didn't have to know more than he should know, but Lily thought that Welles had been stealing from the company by manipulating a confidential fund. Was Charlie willing to work for her?

Charlie broke the lock on Fenton Welles' back door and groped through the dark house. Using a little flashlight, he found the staircase and worked his way upstairs. He found the master bedroom and went to the desk. Just as he opened the center drawer and found a folder marked ELIJAH, the front door opened downstairs. Holding his breath, he looked in the file and saw photographs of various men, alone and in groups, in military uniform. He put the file back in the drawer, climbed out the window, and scrambled down the roof until he could jump onto the lawn. A dog charged him out of the darkness, and Charlie picked up a heavy stick beneath a tree and battered the dog to death.

Lily Sheehan told Charlie to take a room at the Random Lake Motel, rent a motor boat, and break into Welles' house when he was at a country club dance. Charlie and Lily were both smoking, and Lily prowled around him. She sat on the arm of his chair. Her dress suddenly seemed tighter.

In the dark behind him, somebody whistled.

Charlie and Lily kissed.

The music behind Charlie Carpenter announced *doom, ruin, death*, and he pulled a carton from a closet in Fenton Welles' lake house and dumped its contents onto the floor. Stacks of bills held together with rubber bands, thousands of dollars, fell out of the carton, along with a big envelope marked ELIJAH. Charlie opened the envelope and pulled out photographs of Fenton Welles and Lily Sheehan shot through the window of a restaurant, Fenton Welles and Lily walking down a street arm in arm, Fenton Welles and Lily in the back seat of a taxi, driving away.

"Aha," said a voice from the back of the theater.

An angry, betrayed Charlie shouted at Lily Sheehan, waved a big solid fist in the air, kicked at furniture. These sounds, Fee knew, were those that came before the screams and the sobs.

But the beatings did not come. Lily Sheehan began to cry, and Charlie took her in his arms.

He's evil, Lily said.

A stunned look bloomed in Charlie's dark eyes.

It's the only way I'll ever be free.

"Watch out," the man called, and Fee turned around and squinted into the back of the theater.

In the second row from the back, far under the beam of light from the projectionist's booth, a big man with light hair leaned forward with his hands held to his eyes like binoculars. "Peekaboo," he said. Fee whirled around in his seat, his face burning.

"I know who you are," the man said.

I'm all the soul you need, Lily said from the screen.

Fenton Welles walked in from a round of golf at the

Random Lake Country Club, and Charlie Carpenter came sneering out from behind the staircase with a fireplace poker raised in his right hand. He smashed it down onto Welles' head.

Lily wiped the last trace of blood from Charlie's face with a tiny handkerchief, and for a second Fee *had* it, he knew the name of the man behind him, but this knowledge disappeared into the dread taking place on the screen, where Lily and Charlie lay in a shadowy bed talking about the next thing Charlie must do.

Death death death sings the sound track.

Charlie hid in the shadowy corner of William Bendix's office. Slanting shadows of the blinds fell across his suit, his face, his broad-brimmed hat.

A sweet pressure built in Fee's chest.

William Bendix walked into his office, and suddenly Fee knew the identity of the man behind him. Charlie Carpenter stepped out of the shadow-stripes with a long knife in his hands. William Bendix smiled and waggled his fat hands, what's going on here, Miss Sheehan told him there wouldn't be any trouble — Charlie rammed the knife into his chest.

Fee remembered the odor of raw meat, the heavy smell of blood in Mr. Stenmitz's shop.

Charlie Carpenter scrubbed his hands and face in the company bathroom until the basin was black with blood. Charlie ripped towel after towel from the dispenser, blotted his face and threw the damp towels on the floor. Impatient, Charlie Carpenter rode a train out of the city, and two girls across the aisle peeked at him, wondering *Who's that handsome guy?* and *Why is he so nervous?* The train pulled past the front of an immense Catholic church with stained glass windows blazing and streaming with light.

Fee turned around to see the big head and wide shoulders of Heinz Stenmitz. In the darkness, he could just make out white teeth shining in a smile. Joking, Mr. Stenmitz put his hands to his eyes again and pretended to peer at Fee through binoculars.

Fee giggled.

Mr. Stenmitz motioned for Fee to join him, and Fee got out of his seat and walked up the long aisle toward the back of the theater. Mr. Stenmitz wound his hand in the air, reeling him in. He patted the seat beside him and leaned over and whispered, "Now you sit here next to your old friend Heinz." Fee sat down, and Mr. Stenmitz's hand swallowed his. "I'm very, very glad you're here," he whispered. "This movie is too scary for me to see alone."

Charlie Carpenter piloted a motorboat across Random Lake. It was early morning. Drops of foam spattered across his lapels. Charlie was smiling a dark funny smile.

"Do you know what?" Mr. Stenmitz asked.

"What?"

"Do you know what?"

Fee giggled. "No, what?"

"You have to guess."

There was blood everywhere on the screen, but it was invisible blood; it was the blood scrubbed up from the office floor and washed away in the sink.

The boat slid into the reeds, and Charlie jumped out onto marshy ground — the boat will drift away, Charlie doesn't care about the boat, he stole it, it's nothing but a stolen boat, let it go, let it be gone....

An unimaginable time later Fee found himself standing in the dark outside the Beldame Oriental Theater. The last thing he could remember was Lily Sheehan turning from her stove and saying, *Decided to stop off on your way to work, Charlie?* She wore a long white robe, and her hair looked loose and full. *You're full of surprises. I thought you'd be here last night.* His face burned, and his heart was pounding. Smoke and oil filled his stomach.

He felt appallingly, astoundingly dirty.

The world turned spangly and gray around him. The headlights on Livermore Avenue swung toward him. The smoke in his stomach spilled upward into his throat.

Fee moved a step deeper into the comparative darkness of the street and bent over the curb. Something that looked and tasted like smoke drifted from his mouth. He gagged and wiped his mouth and his eyes. It seemed to him that an enormous arm lay across his shoulders, that a deep low voice was saying…was saying…

No.

Fee fled down Livermore Avenue.

PART TWO

1

He turned into his street and saw the neat row of cement blocks bisecting the dead lawn and the two concrete steps leading up to the rose bushes and the front door.

Nothing around him was real. The moon had been painted, and the houses had no backs and everything he saw was a fraction of an inch thick, like paint.

He watched himself sit down on the front steps. The night darkened. Footsteps came down the stairs from the Sunchana's apartment, and the relief of dread focused his attention. The lock turned and the door opened.

"Fee, poor child," said Mrs. Sunchana. "I thought I heard you crying."

"I wasn't crying," Fee said in a wobbly voice, but he felt cold tears on his cheeks.

"Won't your mother let you in?" Mrs. Sunchana stepped around him, and he scooted to one side to let her pass.

He wiped his face on his sleeve. She was still waiting for an answer. "My mother's sick," he said. "I'm waiting for my daddy to come back."

Pretty, dark-haired Mrs. Sunchana wrapped her arms about herself. "It's almost seven," she said. "Why don't you come upstairs? Have some hot chocolate. Maybe you want a bowl of soup? Vegetables, chicken, good thick soup for you. Delicious. I know, I made it myself."

Fee's reason began to slip away beneath the barrage of these seductive words. He saw himself at the Sunchana's table, raising a spoon of intoxicating soup to his mouth. Saliva poured into his mouth and his stomach growled.

By itself, a sob flexed wide black wings in his throat and flew from his mouth.

And then, like salvation, came his father's voice. "Leave my son alone! Get away from him!" He opened his eyes.

Mrs. Sunchana pressed her hands together so tightly her fingers looked flat. Fee saw that she was frightened, and understood that he was safe again...back in the movie of his life.

And here came Bob Bandolier up the walk, his face glowing, his eyes glowing, his mustache riding confidently above his ready mouth, his coat billowing out behind him.

"Fee was sitting here alone in the cold," Mrs. Sunchana said.

"You will go upstairs, please, Mrs. Sunchana."

"I was just trying to help," persisted Mrs. Sunchana. Only her flattened out hands betrayed her.

"Well, we don't need your help," bellowed Fee's glorious Dad. "Go away and leave us alone."

"There is no need to give me orders."

"SHUT UP!"

"Or to yell at me."

"LEAVE MY SON ALONE!" Bob Bandolier raised his

arms like a madman and stamped his foot. "Go!" He
rushed toward the front steps, and Mrs. Sunchana went
quickly past Fee into the building.

Bob Bandolier grasped Fee's hand and yanked him
upright and pulled him through the front door. Fee cried
out in pain. Mrs. Sunchana had retreated halfway up the
stairs, and her husband's face hung like a balloon in the
cracked-open door to their apartment. In front of their
own door, Bob Bandolier let go of Fee's hand to reach
for his key.

"I think you must be crazy," said Mrs. Sunchana. "I
was being nice to your little boy. He was locked out of
the house in the cold."

Bob Bandolier unlocked the door, pushed it open, and
turned sideways toward her.

"We live right above you, you know," said Mrs.
Sunchana. "We hear you. We know what you do."

Fee's father pushed him into their apartment, and the
smell from the bedroom announced itself like the boom
of a bass drum. Fee thought that Mrs. Sunchana must have
been able to smell it, too.

"And what do I do?" his father asked. His voice was
dangerously calm. "What do you know?"

Fee knew that his father was smiling.

He heard Mrs. Sunchana move one step up.

"You know what you do. It is not right."

Her husband whispered her name from their door at
the top of the stairs.

"On the contrary," his father said. "Everything I do,
Mrs. Sunchana, is precisely right. Everything I do I do
for a reason." He moved away from the door, and Mrs.
Sunchana went two steps up.

Fee watched his father with absolute admiration. He
had won. He had said the brave right things, and the
enemy had fled.

Bob Bandolier came scowling toward him. "Get inside," he said.

Fee backed into the living room. His father strode through the doorway and pushed the door shut. He gave Fee one flat, black-eyed glare, removed his topcoat, and hung it carefully in the closet without seeming to notice the smell from the bedroom. He unbuttoned his suit jacket and the top of his shirt and pulled his necktie down a precise half-inch.

"I'm going to tell you something very important. You are never to talk to them again, do you hear me? They might try to get information out of you, but if you say one word to those snoops, I'll wail the stuffing out of you." He patted Fee's cheek. "You won't say anything to them, I know." Fee shook his head.

"They think they know things...ten generations of keyhole listeners."

His father gave his cheek another astounding pat. He snapped his fingers. At the code for catfood, Jude stalked out from beneath the chaise. Fee followed both of them into the kitchen. His father spooned half a can of catfood into Jude's dish and put the remainder of the can into the refrigerator.

Bob Bandolier was an amazing man, for now he went whirling and dancing across the kitchen floor, startling even Jude. Amazing Bob spun through the living room, not forgetting to smile up at the ceiling and toss a cheery wave to the Sunchanas, clicked open the bedroom door with his hip, and called *Hello, honeybunch* to his wife. Fee followed, wondering at him. His father supped from the brown bottle of Pforzheimer's beer, Millhaven's own, winked at Sleeping Beauty, and said, *Darling, don't give up yet*.

"Here she is, Fee," his father said. "She knows, she knows, you know she knows."

Fee nodded: that was right. His mother knew exactly what it was that he himself had forgotten.

"This lady right here, she never doubted." He kissed her yellow cheek. "Now let's rustle up some grub, what do you say?"

Fee was in the presence of a miracle.

2

After dinner his father washed the dishes, now and then taking a soapy hand from the foam to pick up his beer bottle. Fee marveled at the speed with which his father drank…three long swallows and the bottle was empty, like a magic trick.

Then Bob Bandolier filled a plastic bucket with warm tap water, put some dishwashing powder in the bucket, swirled it around with his hand, and dropped in a sponge.

"Well, here goes." He winked at Fee. "The dirty part of the day. Your mother is one of the decent people in this world, and that's why we take care of her." He was swirling the water around in the bucket again, raising a white lather. "Let me tell you something. There's a guy who is not one of the decent people of the world who thinks all he has to do is sit behind a desk all day and count his money. He even thinks he knows the hotel business." Bob Bandolier laughed out loud. "Well, I have a little plan, and we'll see how fine and dandy Mr. Fine and Dandy really is, when he starts to sweat." His face was red as an apple.

Fee understood…his father was talking about the St. Alwyn.

He squeezed the sponge twice and water drizzled into the bucket. "Tonight I'm going to tell you about the blue rose of Dachau. Which was the bottom of the world. That was where you saw the things that are real in this world. You come along while I wash your mother."

"Not all the way in," his father said. "You don't have to see the whole thing, just stay in the door. I just want you to be able to hear me."

Bob Bandolier put a hand on Fee's shoulder and showed him where to stand.

"This one's going to be messy," he said.

The smell in the bedroom took root in Fee's nose and invaded the back of his throat. Bob Bandolier set down the bucket, grasped the blanket near his wife's chin, and flipped it down to the end of the bed.

As the blanket moved, his mother's arms jerked up and snapped back into place, elbows bent and the hands curled toward the wrists. Beneath the blanket lay a sheet molded around his mother's body. Watery brown stains covered the parts of the sheet clinging to her waist and hips.

"Anyway," Bob said as he grabbed the sheet with one hand and walked down the length of the bed, pulling it way from his wife's body. At the bottom of the bed, he yanked the end of the sheet from under the mattress and carefully wadded it up.

From his place in the doorway, Fee saw the yellow soles of his mother's feet, from which six-inch toenails twisted away; the starved undersides of her legs, peaking at her slightly raised knees; her bony thighs, which disappeared like sticks into the big St. Alwyn towel his father had folded around her groin. Once white, this towel was now stained the same watery brown that had leaked through to the sheet. Above the towel was her small swollen belly; two distinct, high-arched rows of ribs; her small flat breasts and brown nipples; shoulders with sunken flesh from which thin straight bones seemed to want to escape; a lined, deeply hollowed neck; and above all these, propped on a pillow in the limp nest of her hair, his mother's familiar and untroubled face.

"How does stuff still come out, hey, when so damn little goes in? Hold on, honey, we gotta get this thing off of you."

Dedicated Bob Bandolier tugged at the folds of the wet towel, managing with the use of only two fingers to pull it free, exposing Anna Bandolier's knife-like hipbones and her astonishingly thick pubic bush…astonishingly, that is, to Fee, who had expected only a smooth pink passage of flesh, like the region between the legs of a doll. Where all the rest of his mother's skin was the color of yellowing milk, the area uncovered by the towel was a riot of color: milk-chocolate flecks and smears distributed over the blazing red of the thighs, and the actual crumbling or shredding of blue and green flesh disappearing into the terrible wounds where her buttocks should have been. From this wound surrounded by evaporating flesh came the smell that flooded their apartment.

Fee's heart froze, and the breath in his lungs turned to ice. He watched the movie.

Deep within the hole of ragged flesh that was his mother's bottom was a stripe of white bone.

His father slid the dripping sponge beneath her arms, over the pubic tangle and the reddish-gray drooping flesh between her legs. After every few passes he squeezed the sponge out into the bucket. He dabbed at the enormous bedsores. "This started happening about a while ago…figured it would take care of itself long as I kept her clean, but…well, I just do what I can do." He touched the oddly stiff bottom sheet. "See this? Rubber. You just sponge it off, it's good as new. Weren't for this baby, we'd have gone through a lot of mattresses by now. Right, honey?"

His father knew he was in a movie.

"Get me another sheet and towel from the linen cabinet."

His father was wiping the rubber sheet with a clean section of the old towel when Fee came back into the bedroom. He dropped the towel on top of the wadded sheet and took the new linen out of Fee's arms.

"Teamwork, that's what we got."

He set the linen on the end of the bed and bent to squeeze out the sponge before lightly, quickly passing it over the rubber sheet.

"I don't know if I ever told you much about my war," he said. "You're old enough now to begin to understand things."

It seemed to Fee that he had no heartbeat all. His mouth was a desert. Everything around him, even the dust in the air, saw what he himself was seeing.

"This war was no damn picnic." Bob Bandolier tilted his wife's body up to wipe beneath her, and Fee raised his eyes to the top of the bedstead.

Bob wiped the fresh towel over the damp sheet, straightened it out, and turned his wife over onto the towel. Her toenails clicked together.

"But I want to tell you about this one thing I did, and it has to do with roses." He gave Fee a humorous look. "You know how I feel about roses."

Fee knew how he felt about roses.

From the bottom of the bed, his father snapped open the clean sheet and sent it sailing over Anna Bandolier's body. "I was crazy about roses even way back then. But the kind of guy I am, I didn't just grow them, I got interested in them. I did research." He tucked the sheet beneath the mattress.

Bob Bandolier smoothed the sheet over his wife's body, and Fee saw him taking a mental picture of the tunnel behind the St. Alwyn hotel.

"There's one kind, one color, of rose no one has ever managed to grow. There has never been a true blue rose. You could call it a Holy Grail."

He lifted first one arm, then the other, to slide the sheet beneath them.

He moved back to appraise the sheet. He gave it a sharp tug, snapping it into alignment. Then he stepped back again, with the air of a painter stepping back from a finished canvas.

"What it is is an enzyme. An enzyme controls the color of a rose. Over the years, I've managed to teach myself a little bit about enzymes. Basically, an enzyme is a biological catalyst. It speeds up chemical changes without going through any changes itself. Believe it or not, Millhaven, this city right here, is one of the enzyme centers of the world — because of the breweries. You need enzymes to get fermentation, and without fermentation you don't get beer. When they managed to crystallize an enzyme, they discovered that it was protein." He pointed at Fee. "Okay so far, but here's your big problem. Enzymes are picky. They react with only a tiny little group of molecules. Some of them only work with one molecule!"

He pointed the forefinger at the ceiling. "Now, what does that say about roses? It says that you have be a pretty damn good chemist to create your blue rose. Which is the reason that no one has ever done it." He paused for effect.

"Except for one man. I met him in Germany in 1945, and I saw his rose garden. He had four blue rose bushes in that garden. The ones on the first bush were deep, dark blue, the color of the ink in fountain pens. On the second bush the roses grew a rich navy blue; on the third bush, they were the most beautiful pale blue...the color of a nigger's Cadillac. All of these roses were beautiful, but the most beautiful roses grew on the fourth bush. They were all the other shades in stripes and feathers, dark blue against that heaven-blue sky, little brush strokes of heaven-sky blue against that velvety black-blue. The man who grew them was the greatest gardener in the history of rose cultivation. And there are two other things you should know about him. He grew these great roses in ten square empty feet of ground in Dachau, a place that was a concentration camp during the war. He was a guard there. And the second thing is, I shot him dead. I killed him."

He put his hands on his hips. "Let's go get this lady her dinner, okay? Now that she had her bath, my baby's hungry."

3

Fee's father busied himself measuring out dry oatmeal into a saucepan, poured in milk, lit a match and snapped the gas flame into life. He stood beside the stove, holding a long wooden spoon and another bottle of beer, looking as though a spotlight was trained on him.

"We get this job," he said, giving the oatmeal another twirl of the spoon. "It could have been any company, any unit. It didn't have to be mine, but it was mine. We were going to be the first people into what they called the death camp. I didn't even know what it meant, 'death camp.' I didn't know what it was.

"There were some English soldiers that met us there, sort of share the glory, Allied Effort. Let the English grab their share. The officers of the camp will surrender to a joint Anglo-American force, and the prisoners will be assisted in their eventual relocation to destinations of their choice. Meaning, we'll ship them someplace after somebody else decides what to do with them. We liberate them. That's about it. We're the liberators. What does that mean? Women, music, champagne, right?"

He stirred the oatmeal again, looking down into the saucepan and frowning as if in regret for what he had seen.

"So we get lined up on the road to the camp. We're just outside this little town on some river. From where we're standing, I can see a castle, a real castle on a hill over the river, like something out of a movie. There's us, and there's the British. There's photographers, too, from the newsreels and the papers. This is a big deal, because nobody really knows what we're going to find once we get in. The brass is in front. We start moving in columns toward the camp, and all of a sudden everything looks ugly…even the ground looks ugly. We're going toward barbed wire and guard houses, and you know it's some kind of prison.

"I was wrong about everything, I see that right away. The place is like a factory. Once we go through the gates, we're on a long straight road, everything right angles, with little wooden buildings in rows. Okay, we're ready."

He upturned the pot and spooned oatmeal into a bowl. He added butter, brown sugar, and a splash of milk. "Perfect. Let's feed your mother, Fee."

In radiant humor, he stood beside the bed and raised a spoonful of oatmeal to his wife's lips. "You have to help me out now, honey, I know you have to be hungry. Here comes some delicious oatmeal…open your mouth." He pushed the spoon into her mouth and slid it back and forth to dislodge the oatmeal. "Attaway. Getting a little better every day, aren't we? Pretty soon we're going to be up on our feet."

Fee remembered what his mother's feet looked like. It was as though a vast dark light surrounded them, a light full of darkness with a greater, deeper darkness all around it, the three of them all alone at its center.

His father slid the spoon from his mother's mouth. A trace of oatmeal remained in the bottom of the spoon. He filled it again and pushed it between her lips. Fee had not seen his mother swallow. He wondered if she could swallow. His father withdrew the spoon again, and a wad of oatmeal the size of a housefly stuck to his mother's top lip.

"Right away I noticed this terrible smell. You couldn't imagine working in a place that smelled that bad. Like a fire in a garbage dump.

"Anyhow, we go marching up this street without seeing anybody, and when we pass this courtyard I see something in there I can't figure out at all. At first, I don't even know what it is. You know what it was? A giant pile of glasses. Eyeglasses! Must be a thousand of them. Creepy. I mean, that's when I begin to get the idea. They were saving the metal, you did that during the war, but there used to be people that went with those glasses.

"We can see those smokestacks up ahead, big smokestacks on top of the furnaces. We go past buildings that seem like they're full of old clothes, piles and piles of shirts and jackets...."

The spoon went in full and came out half-full. Flecks of oatmeal coated his mother's lips.

"And then we get to the main part of the camp, the barracks, and we see what the people are like. We're not even marching in step any more, we're not marching at all, we're just moving along, because these are people out in front of these barracks, but you never saw people like this in your life. They were walking skeletons. They are bones and eyes, like monkeys or something. Big heads and these tiny little bodies. You wonder how smart is it to liberate these zombies in the first place. The ones that can talk are whining and crying, they're like worms that just crawled out of a cave...man! You could put your hand around their waists. You can't tell the men from the women. These people are scary. They are watching every move we make, and what you think is: these animals want to eat us alive.

"So I'm walking along with my company. Half of us want to throw up. These things, zombies, are watching us go by, most of them too weak and stupid to do anything but prop themselves up, and I actually realize what is going on. This is the earth we live on, I say to myself. This is what we call earth. There was no *pretending* about what was going on in this place. This was it. This was the last stop."

Bob Bandolier absentmindedly ate a spoonful of oatmeal. His eyes shone. He licked the spoon.

"They'd been working overtime, but even those efficient Nazis, the most organized people on earth, couldn't move all these people through the gas chambers and into the ovens. So besides the zombies, they had all these dead bodies left over. This place where I was, this most horrible place the world has ever seen — it was holy."

Bob Bandolier noticed he was still holding a spoon and a bowl of oatmeal. He smiled at himself, and began again to feed his wife. Oatmeal bubbled out past her lips.

"Finished, honey? Looks like you had enough for today. Good baby."

He ran the edges of the spoon over her mouth and scraped off most of the visible oatmeal. Then he set the bowl down on the bed and turned to Fee. He was still smiling.

"And then I knew I was exactly right, because we turned into this square where the Germans were waiting for us, and here was this ordinary little house, a fence, a walk to the front door, and in this little lot beside it was the rose garden. With those four bushes full of blue roses.

"I stepped right out of the column and went up to the garden. Nobody said anything. We were past that. I sort of heard what was going on…the Captain was taking over from the Commandant, and the two of them and some other brass went to the back of the square and into the Commandant's office. What did I care? I was looking at a miracle. In this miserable hell, someone had managed to grow blue roses. It was a sign. I knew one thing, Fee. I was in the only place on earth where a blue rose could grow.

"So I turned around and went into the square. Our guys were just standing around gaping. They didn't get it. Nobody but me had even seen those roses. I wanted to grab people and say, For God's sake, look at that garden over there! But why waste my time? They were just staring at the zombies or the guards.

"But everybody felt *something*, Fee. You couldn't be immune.

"I looked each one of those guards in the face. And they'd just look straight ahead, no expression, nothing in their eyes, no fear, not even contempt...For these guys, it was just business, they were just doing their jobs like good little cops, they had no more imagination than they were allowed. Except for one man, the one I wanted to find.

"And of course it was easy. He was the only one who actually looked back at me. He had the moral courage of knowing who he was. He had seen me standing in front of his roses. Maybe the Commandant thought they were *his* roses, maybe some of the zombies even thought they were *their* roses, but they really belonged to one man, their gardener. That goddamned genius who was the right man in the right place at the right time. He knew what he had done, and he knew that I knew too. He looked straight into my eyes when I stood in front of him.

"You'd never pick him out of a crowd. He was a big bullet-headed guy with a wide nose and little eyes with thin eyelashes. Shoulders that sloped. Big, fat hands and a huge chest. Sort of...sort of like an overgrown dwarf. I would have gone right past him, I almost did go right past him, but then I caught his eye and he caught mine, and I saw that *light*...he was the one. He didn't give a damn about anything else on earth.

"I stood right in front of him and I said, *How did you do it?* The guys who heard me thought I was asking how he could have treated people the way they had, but he knew what I meant.

"Our Captain and the Commandant come out of the office and the Captain gets everybody back into formation and tells my platoon to keep watch on the guards for a few hours. The Captain goes away to take care of business. The guys are loading prisoners on trucks, they're setting up desks and taking down names, I don't know, my job is to keep an eye on the guards until someone else shows up to take them away.

"Pretty soon it's just us and the guards in the square. Ten of us — about fifteen to twenty of them. There are Americans running all over the camp by now, the place is organized chaos. I decide to try again since we're just waiting and I go up to the guy, the gardener, and, boy oh boy, I know I'm right all over again because his eyes light up as soon as I come up to him. I have eyes, I can see.

"I ask him again, *How did you do it?* This time he almost smiles. He shakes his head.

"*I want to know about the roses*, I say. I point at them, as if he didn't know what I was talking about.

"*Do any of you people speak English?*

"A guy off to the left, a tall gray-haired character with a scar on his forehead, sort of looks at me, and I tell him to come up and help me or I'll blow his head off. He comes up. I say, *I want to know about the roses*. He can hardly believe that this is what I'm interested in, but he gets the idea, and I hear him say something about *blaue rose*.

"My guard, the genius, the one man on earth who ever managed to create a blue rose, finally starts talking. He's bored...he knows this stuff backwards and forwards, he worked it all out by himself and I'm some American private, I don't deserve to know it. But he's under arrest, he'll tell me, all right? He starts spouting this scientific gobbledegook German full of chemical formulas, and not only do I not have any chance of understanding it, neither does the *other* guy, the other Nazi. The gardener knows we don't get it.

"When he's done talking, he shuts up; he came to the end and he stopped, like he read the whole thing off a card. Nobody has the faintest idea what he said. Some of the other guys are giving me funny looks, because the zombies get all worked up, they can't hear what the guard is saying but they're excited anyhow.

"Picture this. There's us and them, and then there's the screaming freak show behind us. On the other side of the guards are the camp offices, two wooden buildings about ten feet apart. Between the offices, you can see walls of barbed wire and an empty guardhouse, maybe fifty yards away. Way off to the left are those chimneys. There's just a muddy field between the offices and the fence.

"So the gardener spits on the ground and starts walking away. He just walks right through the other guards. Now the zombies are going crazy. The guard is going toward the space between the two office buildings. The other guards sort of watch him out of the corner of their eyes. I figure he's going to take a leak, come back.

"One of our guys says, *Hey, that Kraut's getting away.*

"I tell him to shut up.

"But he doesn't stop when he gets to the offices, he just keeps walking on through.

"The rabble is screaming the place down. Some guy says, *What do we do? What are we supposed to do?*

"The gardener just keeps on walking until he's in the field. Then he turns around and looks at me. He's one ugly fucker. He doesn't smile, he doesn't blink, he just gives me a look. Then he starts running for the fence.

"You know what he thinks? He thinks I'll just let him get away, on account of I know how great he is. This is what I know…this guy is taking advantage of me, and I do know how great he is, but nobody takes advantage of me, Fee.

"Our guys all start yelling, too. I raise my rifle and aim at the bastard. I pull the trigger, and I shoot him right in the back. Down he goes, boom. One shot. That's all she wrote. We just left him there. None of the rest of those assholes made a move until the truck came for them, you can bet on that."

His father picked up the bowl of oatmeal and smiled. "I never even knew his name. For two weeks, me and my platoon, all we did was identify corpses. I mean, that's what we tried to do. The survivors who could still get around made the identifications and we wrote them down. In the end, the Corps of Engineers dug these big trenches and we just plowed 'em in there. Men, women, and children. Poured lime over them and covered them up with dirt. When I went back to see those roses again, the bushes were all pulled up and chopped to pieces. The Colonel came in, and he thought they were the ugliest things he'd ever seen in his life. The Colonel said: *Rip these ugly goddamned blue nightmares out of the ground and chop 'em up pronto.* The guy who cut them down told me that. You know what else he said? He said they gave him the creeps, too. We're in a concentration camp and some *roses* gave him the creeps."

Bob Bandolier shook his head. He leaned over and lightly kissed his wife's waxy forehead.

"We'll let her get some rest."

They returned the bowl and spoon to the kitchen. "I have to go back to the Hepton tomorrow. So you'll get another day at the movies." He was mellow and slow, tonight Bob Bandolier was a satisfied man.

Fee could not remember having been to a movie.

"You know what you are? You're a little blue rose, that's what you are."

Fee brushed his teeth and put himself to bed while his father leaned against the wall with an impatient hand on the light switch. Fee's breathing lengthened; his body seemed to grow mysteriously heavy. The noises of the house, the creaking of boards, the wind moving past his window, the slow chugging of the washing machine, carried him to a boat with a prow like an eagle's head before the similarly proud and upright head of his mother, whose silken hair stirred in the sea air. They sailed far and away for many a day, and then he found himself bobbing and blooming in a garden. Bob Bandolier moved his hand toward the bulging pocket of his beautiful gray suit and took out a pair of shears. He grinned and raised the shears, and Fee woke up screaming and sobbing.

4

Fee came awake with no memory of what had happened in the night. His father was leaning against the wall, flipping the light on and off and saying, "Come on, come on." His face was blotchy and white. "If you make me one minute late for work at the Hepton, you are going to be one sorry little boy; is that understood?"

He walked out of the room. Fee's body seemed to be made of ice, of lead, of a cold heavy substance impossible to move.

"Don't you understand?" His father leaned back into the room. "This is the Hepton. You get out of bed, little boy."

His father's breath still smelled like beer. Fee pushed back his covers and swung his legs over the side of the bed.

"You want oatmeal?"

He nearly threw up on Bob Bandolier's perfect black shoes.

"No? Then that's it, I'm not your personal short-order

cook. You can go hungry until you get to the show."

Fee struggled into underpants, socks, yesterday's shirt and pants. His father stood over him, snapping his fingers like a metronome.

"Get in the bathroom and wash up, for God's sake."

Fee scampered down the hall.

"You made a lot of noise last night. What the hell was the matter?"

He looked up from the sink and saw, behind his own dripping face, his father's powerful, scowling face. Pouches of dark flesh hung beneath his eyes.

Into his yellow towel, Fee mumbled that he did not remember. His father batted the side of his head.

"What the hell was wrong with you?"

"I don't know," Fee cried. "I don't *remember*."

"There will be no more screaming and shouting in the middle of the night. You will make no noise at all from the time you enter your bedroom until the time you leave it in the morning. Is that understood?" His father was pointing at him. "Or else there will be punishment."

"Yes, sir."

His father straightened up. "Okay, we understand each other. Get set to go and I'll get you a glass of milk or something. You have to have something in your stomach."

When Fee had dried his face and pulled on his coat and zipped it up, when he went down the hall and into the kitchen with Jude winding in and out of his feet, his father, also enclosed in his coat, held out a tall white glass of milk.

"Drink up, drink up, we only got a minute or two."

Fee took the glass from his hand.

"I'll just go in and say goodbye to your mother."

His father hurried out of the kitchen, and Fee looked at the glass in his hand. He raised it to his mouth. An image blazed in his mind and was banished before he had even a glimpse of it. His hand started shaking. In order to keep from spilling the milk, Fee swung the glass toward the counter with both hands and set it down. He moaned to see a pattern of little white drops on the counter.

"God damn, GOD DAMN, GOD DAMN," his father shouted.

Fee wiped the dots of milk with his hand. They turned to white streaks, then smears, then nothing. He was panting, and his face was hot.

Bob Bandolier raged into the kitchen and Fee quailed back against the cabinets. His father seemed hardly to notice him as he turned on the water and passed a dishtowel back and forth beneath the stream. His face was tight with impatience and disgust.

"Go on, get outside and wait for me."

He ran back towards the bedroom. Fee poured the milk into the sink, his heart beating as if he had committed a crime.

Jude followed him to the front door, crying for food. He bent over to stroke the cat, and Jude arched his back and made a noise like fat sizzling in a pan. Still hissing, he moved back several steps. His huge eyes gleamed, but not at Fee.

Fee groped for the doorknob. Through the open bedroom door, which stood in a straight line with the front door, he saw his father's back, bent over the bed. His hand found the knob. He turned around and pulled the door open.

Standing before him were the Sunchanas, he in a suit, she two steps behind him in a long, checked robe. Both of them looked startled.

"Oh!" said Mr. Sunchana. His wife clasped both hands in front of her chest. "Fee," she said and then she looked past her husband into the apartment. The cat sizzled and spat.

"David," said Mrs. Sunchana.

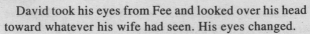

David took his eyes from Fee and looked over his head toward whatever his wife had seen. His eyes changed.

Slowly, Fee turned around.

Bob Bandolier was stepping away from the bed, holding stretched out between his hands a dishtowel blotched with brilliant red. The usual odor floated from the bedroom. Fee heard the Sunchanas reacting as the stench reached them.

Something black and wet covered his mother's chin.

Bob Bandolier glared at them. He dropped one end of the cloth and began moving toward the bedroom door. He did not shout, although he looked as though he wanted to yell the house down. He closed the door.

"Last night..." said Mr. Sunchana.

"We heard you last night," said Mrs. Sunchana.

"You were making a lot of noise."

"And we were worried for you. Are you all right, Fee?"

Fee swallowed and nodded.

"Really?"

"Yes," he said. "Really."

The bedroom door burst open, and Bob Bandolier stepped out and immediately closed the door behind him. He was not holding the dishtowel. "Haven't we had enough violations of our privacy from you two? Get away from our apartment or I'll throw you out of this house. I mean it."

Mr. Sunchana backed away and bumped into his wife.

"Out, out, out."

"What is wrong with your wife?" asked Mrs. Sunchana.

Fee's father stopped moving a few feet from the door. "My wife had a nosebleed. She has been unwell. I am in danger of being late for work, and I cannot allow you to delay me any longer."

"You call that a nosebleed?" Mrs. Sunchana's wide face had grown pale. Her hands were shaking.

"There is nothing else to call it." Bob Bandolier slammed the door in their faces.

Outside, white breath steamed from his father's mouth. "You'll need money." He gave him a dollar bill. "This is for today and tomorrow. I hope I don't have to tell you not to talk to the Sunchanas. If they won't leave you alone, just tell them to go away."

Fee put the bill in his jacket pocket.

His father patted his head before striding down South Seventh Street to Livermore Avenue and the bus to the Hotel Hepton.

5

Fee paused again on his way to the Beldame Oriental, feeling dazed, as if caught between two worlds, and stared down into the moving water.

A huge man with warm hands was waiting to pull him into a movie.

6

Most of the seats are empty. The big man with kind eyes and a flaring mustache looms beside you. He puts his arm around your shoulder. A Negro boxer knits his forehead and batters another man. Mrs. Sunchana accepts her crown. She looks at him and he whispers, *nosebleed.* God's arm tightens around his shoulders and God whispers *nice boy.* The cat chased the mouse on whirling legs. I know you're glad to see me. God's hand is huge and hot, and the gray slab of his face weighs a thousand pounds. You came back to see me. With Robert Ryan, Ida Lupino, and William Bendix. You could hear Jerry's ghost sobbing in the black and white shadows. Charlie Carpenter sat in a long quiet church and turned his

attention to God, who chuckled and took your hand.
Candles flared and sputtered. Mrs. Sunchana bowed her
head at the edge of the frame. You don't remember what
we did? You liked it and I liked it. Why did God make
lonely people? Answer: He was lonely, too. Some of my
special friends come to visit and we go into my basement.
You're the special friend I go to visit, so you're the most
special of all the special friends. There is a toy you have
to play with now. Lily Sheehan takes Charlie Carpenter's
hand. Here it is, here's the toy. Lily smiles and places
Charlie's hand on her toy. Unzip it, God says. Come on.
Lucky Strike Means Fine Tobacco. I'd Walk a Mile for a
Camel. You see it, here it is, it's all yours. You know what
to do with it. Little dear one. God is so stern and tender.
Our good ship is called the Elijah Fund. Have a cigarette,
Charlie. It likes you, can't you see how much it likes you?
Random Lake is a pretty good lake. I need you to help
me. Here we are, on Fenton Welles' long lawn. If you
stop now, I'll kill you. Hah hah. That's a joke. I'll cut
you up and turn you into lamb chops, lambie pie, I know
how to do that. But here is the envelope marked ELIJAH,
here are the photographs. Every one of those soldiers has
one like mine, a big thick one that likes to come out and
play. The dog jumps up from Fenton Welles' lawn and
you smash its head in with a stick. You are kissing a long
kiss. Smoke from his mouth fills the air. God placed both
hands on the sides of your head and pushed your head
down toward the other little mouth. Hello, Duffy's Tavern,
Duffy speaking. Jack Armstrong, the All-American boy.
Welcome to the Adventures Of. The roaring in his ears.
He pushed the big thing into his cheek so he would not
gag, but God's hands raised his head and lowered it again.
Charlie and Lily kissed and Lily's huge penis threshed
out like a snake. A woman should put your mouth on her
breast and milk should flow. I'm all the soul you need.

The second you take it in your mouth, it moves…it twitches and shoves itself upward. God's pleasure makes him sigh. His hand around yours. Now kiss. It finally fills all the space inside your mouth. They are burning photographs, the smell is harsh. The taste is sour burning. Wait for it, the music says, it's coming. Mrs. Sunchana covers her face. The world bursts into flame. From up out of that long thing, all the way up from its bottom, from the deep bottom of the well, rushes the sea-milk. God presses His hands against your head. You open your mouth and smoke and drool leak out. If he wanted, God could drown the world. Maxwell House Coffee Is Good To The Very Last Drop. The tiny Arab man on the lip of the huge tilted cup. What is in your mouth is the taste of bread. The taste of bread is warm and silky. To be loved. Charlie in his good suit rides the train, and the girls stare. Bunny is good bread. A normal girl is attracted by a handsome man. Invisible blood, God's white blood, washes through the world. Charlie Carpenter rides across the lake and water mists his lapels. Now he can lean back against God's giant chest. His hand strokes your cheek. Jack Armstrong eats Wheaties every day. The boat slides into the reeds. Water-music, death-music. God rubs your chest and His hand is rough. Make big money selling Christmas cards to all your neighbors. The hotel business is America's business. Don't you think that they all take towels, the big guys? The best hamburgers come with the works. Charlie shoved the boat into the reeds, and now he strides across the lawn to Lily's house. Oh, the face of Charlie Carpenter. Oh, the anger in his stride. You could be crushed to death. This man is holding on. The little Arab clings to his giant cup. What grows out of him is not human, that thing is not human. His arms surrounding you blue rose, little blue rose.

7

The Story of The Leaves

His mother had a nosebleed from her mouth. The boy put his hand in the water to stop her from going, and a great cloud swarmed out of the leaves and darkened all the water like a stain.

The Story of the Movie

Charlie Carpenter and Lily Sheehan held hands and looked out of the screen. Kiss me, Lily said, and the dead boy leaned over and kissed it by taking it into his mouth. Every day the same thing happened in the seats of the Beldame Oriental. The end of the movie was so terrible that you could never remember it, not even if you tried.

The Story of the Nosebleed

When Mrs. Sunchana saw it, she said, "Do you call that a nosebleed?" His father said, "What else could you call it?"

The Story of the Movie

Lily Sheehan wrapped her arms around Charlie Carpenter the way Someone wrapped his arms around the dead boy. Something grew up between her legs and from that Something Charlie Carpenter did take suck. We remember folds of gray flesh. Charlie Carpenter swallowed, and whenever the warm silky fluid shuddered out, it tasted like bread.

The Story of the Blue Rose

Charlie Carpenter rang Lily Sheehan's bell and, when she opened the door, he gave her a blue rose. This stands for dying, for death. My daddy met the man who grew them; and when the man tried to run away, my daddy shot him in the back.

The Story of the Movie

After a long time, the movie ended. Robert Ryan lay in a pool of blood, and a rank, feral odor filled the air. Lily Sheehan closed her front door and a little boat drifted away across Random Lake. A few people left their seats and walked up the aisle and swung open the doors to the lobby. My entire body is buzzing, with what feelings I do not know. In my hands I can feel the soft weight of two plums in their coarse sack, my fingers retain the heat of…my hands tingle. No other world exists but this, with its empty seats and the enormous body beside mine. I am doubly dead, I am buried beneath the carpet, strewn with white flecks of popcorn, of the Beldame Oriental. My heart buzzes when the enormous man pulls me tight into his chest. The story of the movie was too terrible to remember. He asks and I say, yes, I will be back tomorrow. I have forgotten everything that happened. Words from the radio gong through my mind. Jack Armstrong, Lucky Strikes, the Irish songs on St. Patrick's Day when I was sick and stayed in bed all day and heard my mother humming and talking to herself while she cleaned the rooms we lived in.

The Story of My First Victim

The first person I ever killed was a six-year-old boy named Lance Torkelson. I was thirteen. We were in a quarry in Tangent, Ohio, and I made Lance hold my erection in his hand and put the tip against his face. Amazed by sensation, I cried out, and the semen shot out like ropes and clung to his face. If I had kept my mouth shut he would have been all right, but my yelling frightened him and he began to wail. I was still shooting and pumping...some of it hit Lance's throat and slid down inside his collar. He screamed. I picked up a rock and hit Lance as hard as I could on the side of his head. He fell right down. Then I hit him with the rock until something broke and his head felt soft and squashy. My cock was still hard, but there was nothing left inside me. I tossed aside the rock and watched myself stay so stiff and alive, so ready. I could hardly believe what had happened. I never knew that was how it worked.

8

A sudden change in air pressure brought him groaning out of the movie. His entire body felt taut with misery. *She's dead*, he thought, *she just died*. Into his bedroom floated the odors of beer and garbage. The darkness above his bed whirled itself into a pattern as meaningless as an oil slick. He tossed back his covers and swung his feet over the edge of the bed. The shape in the darkness above him shifted and rolled.

Everything in his room, his bed and dresser, the toys and clothes on the floor, had been thrown into unfamiliarity by the white light that filtered in through the gauze curtains. His room seemed larger than in the daytime. A deep sound had been reaching him since he had thrown off his blankets, a deep mechanical rasp that poured up from the floor and through the walls. This sound flowed up from the earth…it was the earth itself at work, the great machine at the heart of the earth.

He came into the living room. Pale moonlight covered the carpet and chaise. Sleeping Jude had curled into a dark knot from which only the points of his ears protruded. All the furniture looked as if it would float away if he touched it. The bedroom door had been closed. The earth's great chugging machine-like noise went on.

The sound grew louder as he approached the bedroom door. A great confusion went through him like a fog.

He stood in the moonlight-flooded room with his hand frozen to the knob and gulped down fire. A certain terrible knowledge had come to him: the rasping sound which had awakened him was the sound of his mother's breathing, a relentless struggle to draw in air and then force it out again. Fee nearly passed out on the spot…the cloud of confusion had left him so swiftly that it was as if he had been stripped. He had thought his mother was dead, but now she was going to have to die all over again.

He turned the knob and pulled the door toward him, and the rattling sounds not only became louder but *increased in size and mass.* Inside the Beldame Oriental, you paused while your eyes adjusted to the darkness. Then the first uncertain steps. Lightly counterpointing the noises of his mother's body attempting to keep itself alive came the milder sounds of his father's snores.

He stepped into the bedroom without closing the door behind him, and the shapes before him gradually coalesced and solidified. His mother lay with her hands on her chest, her face pointed to the ceiling. It sounded as if, length by length, something long and rough and reluctantly surrendered were being torn out of her. Face up on the mattress to the right of the bed, clad only in white boxer shorts, lay his father's pale, muscular body, an arm curved over the top of his head, a leg bent at the

knee. A constellation of beer bottles fanned out beside
his mattress.

Fee wiped his hands over his eyes and finally saw that
his mother's hands shook up and down with a rapid
regular quiver like a small animal's heartbeat. He reached
out and lay his fingers on her forearm. It moved with the
same quick pulse as her hands. Another ragged inhalation
negotiated air into his mother, and when he tightened his
hold on her arm, invisible hands tore the breath out of
her. The little boat his mother rowed was now only the
tiniest speck on the black water. Machinery had taken
over, and the machine was breaking down.

His mother's body seemed as long as a city block. How
could he do anything to affect what was happening to
that body? The hands curling into her chest were as big
as his head. The nails that sprouted from those hands were
longer than his fingers. Her chin separated volumes of
darkness. His mother's face was as wide as a map. All of
this size and power shrank him…her struggle erased him,
breath by breath.

The enormous hands on her breasts jittered on. The
sounds of taking in and releasing air no longer seemed to
have anything to do with breathing. They were the sounds
of combat, of scores of men dying at either hand, of heavy
feet thudding into the earth, of shells destroying ancient
trees, land mines blowing off a leg in an explosion of dirt
and blood, of enormous aircraft moving through the air.
Men screamed and groaned on a battlefield. The sky was
pink with shellburst. Garish yellow tracers ripped across
it.

Fee opened his eyes. His mother's body was a
battlefield. This was warfare. Her feet trembled and shook
beneath the sheet, at first moving together, in seconds
jittering into an irregular alternating pattern. Her
breathing settled into a raspy, inhuman chug. He reached

out to touch her arm again, and the arm danced away from his fingers. He wailed in loneliness and terror, but the harsh sounds coming from her mouth obliterated his cry. Her arms shot up three or four inches and slammed down onto her body. Two fingernails cracked off with sharp popping sounds like the snapping of chicken bones. The long yellow fingernails rolled down the sheet and clicked together at the side of the bed. His mother's hips shook. Fee felt that whatever was happening inside his mother was happening also to him. He could feel the great hands reaching down inside him, grasping his essence and tearing it out.

Then for an instant she stopped moving. Her hands hung in the air with their fingernails intertwined; her feet were planted flat on the mattress; her hips floated up. Her feet skidded out, and her hips collapsed back to the bed. The sheet drifted down to her waist. The smell of blood suddenly filled the room. His mother's hands fell back on her breasts, and the rumpled sheet turned a deep red which quickly soaked down to her knees. At her waist the blood darkened and rose through the gathered sheet. The wrinkles and folds glistened.

Something inside his mother made a soft ripping sound.

Her breathing began again in mid-beat, softer than before. Fee could feel the enormous hands within him pulling harder at some limp, exhausted thing. Groans and screams rose up from the ruined earth. The ground bounced beneath him, and some of the dead shifted as if they were still alive. Her breathing moved in and out like a freight train. His own breath pounded in and out with hers.

One long rattling breath after another burned her throat. Her hands settled into the sides of her chest. The long nails clicked. He looked for, but did not see, the broken fingernails that had rolled toward him...he was afraid to look down and see them curling beside his naked feet. If he had stepped on them, he would have screeched like an owl.

He pulled in a long, searing rush of air and felt he was drinking down blood and death. Blood and death dragged themselves far into his body and snagged on his flesh so that they stayed behind when he exhaled in time with his mother. Somehow blood had coated his hands, and he left dark prints on the bed.

The rhythm of their breathing halted, and his heart halted too. The giant hands clamped down inside his mother's body. A breath caught in her throat and pushed itself out with a sharp exclamation. He and his mother drew in a long, ragged lungful of blood and death and released a mouthful of steam.

The little rower on the black lake trembled on the horizon.

Now the softer breathing melted into the battlefield groans. Sips of air entered her mouth, paused, and got lost. She took in two, waited, waited some more, and released one. A long time passed. The world itself was dying, himself with it. Blood dripped onto the floor. Amazed, he noticed feeble daylight leaking into the room. Her mouth was furry with labor and dehydration. His mother took another sip of air and lost it inside herself. She did not take another.

Fee observed that he had left his body and could see himself standing by the bed.

He waited, not breathing, for what would happen next. He saw that he was smaller than he had imagined, and that beneath the streaks of blood on his face he looked blank with fear. Bruises covered his chest, arms, and back. He saw himself gripping his mother's arm…he had not known he was doing that.

A ripple moved through his mother's body, beginning near her ankles and passing up her legs and into her hips.

It rolled through her belly and entered her chest. Those powerful hands had found what they wanted, and now they would never let go of it.

Her face tightened as if around a bad taste. Both of them, his body and himself standing beside his body, leaned over the bed. The movement made its way from her chest into her throat, then moved like a current up into her head. Something inside him grabbed his essential substance and squeezed hard. His feet left the ground. A tremendous and silent explosion transformed the shape and pressure of the air, transformed color, transformed everything. A final twitch cleared her forehead of lines, her head came to rest on the pillow, and it was over. For a moment he saw or thought he saw some small white thing move rapidly toward the ceiling. Fee was back in his body. He cried out in a mixture of emotions that threatened to blow him apart while they left him standing. He reeled back from the bed.

His father said, "Hey? Huh?"

Fee screamed...he had forgotten that his father was on the other side of the bed.

Bob Bandolier's lined, puffy face appeared above the midpoint of the body on the bed. He rubbed his eyes, then took in the bloody sheet. He staggered to his feet. "Get out of here, Fee. This is no place for you."

"Mom is dead," Fee said.

His father moved around the bed so quickly that Fee did not see him move at all...he simply appeared beside him and slapped his face. He pushed him toward the door. "Do what I say, right now."

Fee looked back at his parents and walked out of the bedroom.

His father yelled, "She's going to be okay!"

Fee moved on damp, cold feet to the chaise and lay down on his side.

"Close your eyes," his father said.

Obediently, Fee closed his eyes. When he heard the bedroom door close, he opened them again. The sheet made a wet, sloppy sound when it hit the floor. His face burned — he could feel a stripe from each individual finger. These sensations held him within his body.

Fee let himself revisit what had happened. He heard the inhuman, chugging noise come out of his throat. He drummed his feet against the back of the chaise. Something in his stomach flipped into the back of his throat and filled his mouth with the taste of vomit. In his mind, he leaned over and smoothed the wrinkles from his mother's forehead.

The bedroom door banged open, and he closed his eyes.

Bob Bandolier came walking fast through the living room. "You ought to be in bed," he said, but without heat. Fee kept his eyes shut. His father went into the kitchen. Water gushed from a tap, a drawer opened, an object rustled against other objects, the drawer closed. All this had happened before, therefore it was comforting. In his mind Charlie Carpenter stood at the wheel of his motorboat and sped across the glossy lake. A bearded man in Arab dress lifted his head and took into his mouth the last drop from an enormous cup. The warm liquid fell on his tongue like bread, but burned as he swallowed it. His father carried a sloshing pail past him, and the pail exuded the surpassing sweetness and cleanliness of the dishwashing soap. The bedroom door slammed shut, and Fee opened his eyes again.

They were still open when Bob Bandolier walked out with the bucket and sponge in one hand, a huge red wad wrapped in the dripping rubber sheet under the other arm. "I have to talk to you," he said to Fee. "After I get this stuff downstairs." He kicked the door shut behind him. "Stay in here."

Fee nodded. His father walked straight past him toward the kitchen and the basement stairs.

Downstairs, the washing machine gurgled and hummed. Footsteps came up the stairs, the door closed. There came the sound of cupboard doors opening and closing. Liquid gurgled from a bottle. Bob Bandolier came back into the living room. He was wearing a stretched out T-shirt and striped boxer shorts, and he was carrying a water glass half-full of whiskey. His hair stood up on the crown of his head, and his face was still puffy.

"This isn't easy, kid." He looked around for somewhere to sit and moved backward three or four feet to lower himself into a chair. He swung his eyes up at Fee and sipped from the glass. "We did our best, we did everything we could, but it just didn't pan out. This is going to be hard on both of us, but we can help each other out. We can be buddies." He drank without taking his eyes from Fee.

"Okay?"

"Okay."

"All that help and love we gave your mother...it just didn't do the job." He took a big swallow of his drink, and this time lowered his eyes before raising them again to Fee's. "She passed away last night. It was very peaceful. She did not suffer, Fee."

"Oh," Fee said.

"When you were trying to get her attention in there, before I chased you out, she was already gone. She was already in heaven."

"Uh huh," Fee said.

Bob Bandolier dropped his head and looked down for a little time. He scratched his head. Then he swallowed more whiskey. "It's hard to believe." He shook his head. "That it could end like this. That woman." He looked away, then turned back to Fee with tears in his eyes. "That woman, she loved me. She was the best. Lots of people think they know me, but your mother knew what I was really capable of...for good and bad." Another shake of the head. He wiped his eyes. "Anna, Anna was what a wife should be. She was what people should be. She was *obedient*. She knew the meaning of *duty*. She didn't question my decisions more than three or four times in all the years we spent together, she was *clean*, she could *cook*..." He raised his wet eyes. "And she was one hell of a mother to you, Fee. Never forget that. There was never a dirty floor in this house."

He put down his glass and covered his face with his hands. Suffocated sobs leaked through his fingers.

"This isn't over," his father said. "This isn't over by a long shot."

Fee sighed.

"I know who's to blame," his father said to the floor. Then he raised his head. "How do you think this all started?"

Fee said nothing.

"A hot shot at the St. Alwyn Hotel decided that he didn't need me any more. *That* is when the trouble started. And why did I miss some time at the job? Because I had to take care of my wife."

He grinned at nothing. "They didn't have the simple decency to understand that a man has to take care of his wife." He gave Fee a ghastly smile like a facial convulsion. "But my campaign has started, sonny boy. I have fired the first shot. Let them pay heed." He leaned forward. "And the next time *I won't be interrupted*."

"She didn't only die," Bob Bandolier said. "The St. Alwyn killed her." He finished his whiskey and his face convulsed again. "They didn't get it. In sickness as in health, you know? And they think someone else can do Bob Bandolier's job. You think they asked the guests? They did not. They could have asked that nigger saxophone player...even *him*. Glenroy Breakstone. Every night that man said, "Good evening, Mister Bandolier," when he wouldn't waste two words on anyone else...thought he was too important. But he paid his respects to me, he did. Did they want to know? Well, now they're going to find out. Things are going to happen. Mr. Ransom is going to have a thing or two to worry about." He composed his face. "It's my whole life...like that woman in there."

He stood up. "Now there's things to do. Your mom is dead, but the world goes on."

All of a sudden the truth came to Fee. He was one-half dead himself; half of him belonged to his dead mother. His father went to the telephone. "We're going to be all right. Everybody else, watch out." He peered at the telephone for a second, trying to remember a number, then dialed.

The Sunchanas got up and began walking around their bedroom.

"Doctor Hudson, this is Bob Bandolier." His imitation of a smile appeared and disappeared. "I know it's early, Hudson. I'm not calling to pass the time of day. Do you know where I live? Because...Yes, I'm serious. You better believe I'm serious."

Fee got off the chaise. He bent down and picked up fat, black Jude, who began purring. His hands and arms were still covered with drying blood, and his fingers showed red against the black fur.

"Because I need you here right now, old pal. My wife died during the night, and I need a death certificate so I can take care of her."

Long individual cat hairs adhered to the backs of Fee's fingers.

"Hudson."

Overhead, a toilet flushed.

Fee carried Jude to the window.

"Hudson, listen to me. Remember how I covered your ass? I was the *night manager*, I know what goes on."

Fee wiped his eyes and looked out the window. Some invisible person was out there, looking in.

"I'd say you were a busy boy, that's what was going on."

"Call it heart disease," his father said. "Call it cancer."

Jude could see the invsible person. Jude had always seen the invisible people...they were nothing new to her. The Sunchanas moved around in their bedroom, getting dressed.

"We'll cremate," his father said.

For some reason, Fee blushed.

"Hello, give me Mister Ledwell," his father said. "I'm Bob Bandolier. Mr. Ledwell? Bob Bandolier. I'm sorry to have to say that my wife passed away during the night and unless I am *absolutely* required, I'd like to stay home today. There are many arrangements to make, and I have a young son....She'd been ill, yes, sir, gravely ill, but it's still a great tragedy for the two of us...."

Fee's eyes filled, and a tear slipped down his cheek. Held too tightly, Jude uttered a high-pitched cry of irritation and sank a claw into Fee's forearm.

"That is much appreciated, sir," said Bob Bandolier. He put down the phone and in a different voice said, "That old lush of a doctor will be here as soon as he can find a whole suit from the clothes on the floor. We have work to do, so stop crying and get dressed. Hear me?"

9

Bob Bandolier opened the door as Mr. Sunchana was leaving for work, and Fee saw their upstairs neighbors take in their undistinguished-looking visitor: the black bag, the wrinkled suit, the cigarette burned down to his lips. Doctor Hudson was shown to the bedroom and escorted in. Fee had a brief glimpse of a long white body left lying on its side, exposing a deep black hole glistening on its hip.

When Doctor Hudson came back out of the bedroom, he looked at his watch and began filling out a printed form at the dining room table. Bob Bandolier supplied his wife's maiden name (Dymczeck), date of birth (August 16, 1928), place of birth (Azure, Ohio). The cause of death was respiratory failure.

Half an hour after the doctor left, two men in dark suits arrived to wrap Fee's mother in the sheet that covered her and carry her away on a stretcher.

Bob Bandolier shaved twice, giving his face a red military glaze. He dressed in a dark blue suit. He took a shot of whisky while he looked through the knife drawer. Finally he slipped a black-handled paring knife into the pocket of his suit jacket. He put on his splendid dark overcoat and told Fee that he should be home soon. He let himself out of the apartment and locked the door behind him.

An hour later he returned in a mood so foul that when he struck Fee, his son could tell that he was being beaten simply because he was within reach. It had nothing to do with him. To keep the Sunchanas from hearing, he tried to keep silent. Anger made Bob Bandolier so clumsy that he cut himself taking the paring knife out of his pocket. Bob Bandolier raged and stamped his feet and wrapped his finger in tissue paper — another outburst when he could not find bandages, I can't find any bandages, don't we even have any goddamned *bandages*? He opened a fresh bottle and poured drink after drink after drink.

In the morning, Bob Bandolier dressed in the same blue suit and returned to the Hotel Hepton. Fee, who had said he was too sick to go to the movies, spent the day waiting to see the invisible people.

Some nights later, Bob remembered to cook dinner, and

long after the moon had risen and his son lay in a semi-conscious stupor on the living room rug, sucking on his own pain as if a bitter piece of candy, he returned to the knife drawer in ruminating, well-fed, well-exercised fashion, and selected a six-inch blade with a carved wooden handle. Many hours later, Fee came awake long enough to register that his father was actually carrying him to bed, and knew at once from the exultant triumph he saw in his father's handsome face that late at night, when no one had seen him, Bob Bandolier had gone back to the St. Alwyn Hotel.

Their life became regular again. Bob Bandolier left sandwiches on the table and locked the door behind him...he seemed to have forgotten about the Beldame Oriental or to have decided that going to and from the theater exposed his son to unwelcome attention from the neighbors: better to lock him up and leave him alone.

One night Fee awakened when his father picked him up from the chaise, and when he saw the gleeful face burning over his, he knew again that his father had been to the hotel he hated: that his father hated the St. Alwyn because he loved it, and that this time at least he had managed to get inside it.

Sometimes it was as if Fee had never had a mother at all. Now and then he saw the cat staring at empty air, and knew that Jude could see one of the people from the invisible world. *From Dangerous Depths* returned to him, and alone in the empty room he played at being Charlie Carpenter...Charlie killing the big dog, Charlie stepping away from the wall to batter William Bendix to death, Charlie dying while Lily Sheehan smiled.

One night his father gave him a box of crayons and a pad of outsized paper left behind by a guest at the Hepton, and Fee spent days drawing pictures of enormous feet smashing houses, feet crushing men and women, crushing whole cities, of people sprawled dead in bomb craters and encampments as a pair of giant feet walked away. He hid these exciting drawings beneath his bed. Once he lowered a drawing of a naked foot onto his exposed penis and nearly fainted from a combination of bliss and terror. He was Charlie Carpenter, living out Charlie Carpenter's secret history.

Whenever he saw the Sunchanas, either alone or with his father, they fled behind their front door. Bob Bandolier sniffed: "Never said a word about your mother, never dropped a card or paid her the honor of making a telephone call. People who behave like that are no better than animals."

On the night of October twenty-fifth, Bob Bandolier came home from work restless and impatient, despite the two steaks and the bottle of whisky he had in a big brown bag, and he slapped his son almost as soon as he took off his coat. He fried the steaks and drank the whisky from the bottle. Every ten minutes he left the table to check on the state of his collar, the perfection of the knot in his necktie, the gloss of his mustache. The Hotel Hepton, once second only to the Pforzheimer, was a "sewer," a "sty." He could see it now. They thought they knew what it was all about, but the penny-pinching assholes didn't have the first idea. They get a first-class hotel man, and what do they do to him? Give him lectures. Suggest he say less to the guests. Even the St. Alwyn, even the *St. Alwyn,* the hotel that had done the greatest damage to him, the hotel that had *insulted and injured* him, had *actually managed to kill his wife,* hadn't been as stupid. Maybe he ought to "switch operations," "change the battlefield," "carry the fight into another theater." You give and give, and *this* — this humiliation — was how they repaid you.

Staring through the window the next morning, Fee finally glimpsed one of the invisible people. He nearly fainted. She was a pale, unhappy-looking blond woman, a woman who had seemed ghostly even when she had been alive. She had come to see him, Fee knew. She was looking for him — as if his lost mother were trying to find him. The second that the tears came into his eyes, the woman on the sidewalk vanished. Hurriedly, almost guiltily, he wiped the tears off his face. If he could, he would have gone through the door and followed her — straight to the St. Alwyn Hotel, for that was where she was going.

The next great change in Fee's life began after his father discovered his stack of drawings. In the midst of the whirlwind caused by this next change, for the second time an inhabitant of the invisible world appeared before Fee, in a form and manner suggesting that he had caused a death.

It began as a calm dinner. There was the "hypocritical lowlife" who gave orders to Bob Bandolier, there was an "untrustworthy and corrupt" colleague, there were mentions of the fine Christian woman Anna Bandolier had been — Fee warmed his hands at the fire of his father's loves and hates. In the midst of the pleasure he took from this warmth, he realized that his father had asked him a question. He asked to hear it again.

"Whatever happened to the drawing paper and those crayons I gave you? That stuff costs money, you know."

It had not cost Bob Bandolier any money, but that was secondary: the loss or waste of the precious materials would be a crime. You did not have to want to be bad to succeed in being as bad as possible.

"I don't know," Fee said, but his eyes shifted sideways.

"Oh, you don't know," said Bob Bandolier, his manner transformed in an instant. Fee was very close now to being beaten, but a beating was preferable to having his father see his drawings.

"You expect me to believe that?"

Again Fee glanced toward the hallway and his bedroom.

His father jumped out of his chair, leaned across the table, and pushed him over in his chair.

Bob Bandolier rushed around the table and pulled him up by his collar. "Are you so goddamned stupid you think you can get away with lying to me?"

Fee blubbered and whined, and his father pulled him into the hallway.

"You could have made it easy for yourself, but you made it hard. What did you do? Break the crayons? Tear up the paper?"

Fee shook his head, trying to work out how much truth he could give his father without showing him the drawings.

"Then show me." His father pulled him into his room and pushed him toward the bed. "Where are they?"

Again Fee could not avoid self-betrayal: he looked beneath his bed.

"I see."

Fee wailed *nooo* and scrambled under the bed in a crazy attempt to protect the drawings with his own body.

Swearing, his father got down on the floor, reached beneath the bed, grabbed Fee's arm, and pulled him out. Sweating, struggling, Fee threw his armful of drawings into the room and feebly struck his father. He tried to charge out of his arms to destroy the drawings — he wanted to cram them into his mouth, rip them to confetti, escape through the front door and run down the block.

For a time they were both roaring and screaming. Fee ran out of breath, but he continued to writhe.

His father hit him on the ear and said, "I should rip your heart out."

Fee suddenly went limp — the drawings lay all about them, looking up to be seen. Bob Bandolier's attention went out to the images on the big pieces of paper. Then he put Fee down and bent to pick up the two drawings closest to him.

Fee put his face in his arms.

"Feet," his father said. "What the hell? I don't get it?"

He moved around the room, turning over the pictures. He flipped one over and displayed it to Fee: the giant's feet striding away from the broken people in a flattened movie theater.

"You are going to tell me what this is about, right now."

An absolutely unprecedented thing happened to Fee Bandolier: he opened his mouth and spoke words over which he had no control at all. Someone else inside him spoke these words. Fee heard them as they proceeded from his mouth, but forgot them as soon as they were uttered.

Finally he had said it all, though he could not have repeated a single word if he had been held over a fire. His father's face had turned red. Troubled in some absolutely new way, Bob Bandolier seemed uncertain whether to comfort Fee or to beat him up. He could no longer meet Fee's eyes. He wandered around the room, picking up scattered drawings. After a few seconds he dropped them back onto the floor.

"Pick these up. Then get rid of them. I never want to see any of this ever again."

The first sign of the change was in Bob Bandolier's new attitude toward his son. For Fee, the new attitude suggested that he had simultaneously become both much better and much worse. His father never struck him any more, but sometimes Fee felt that his father did not want to touch him in any way. Days and nights passed almost wordlessly. Fee began to feel that he too had become invisible, at least to his father. Bob Bandolier drank, but instead of talking he read and reread that morning's copy of *The Ledger*.

On the night of November seventh, the closing of the front door awakened Fee. From the perfect quiet in the apartment, he knew his father had just gone out. He was sleeping again when his father returned.

The following morning, Fee turned toward his bedroom window as he zipped up his pants, and all the breath seemed to leave his body. A dark-haired boy roughly his own age stood looking in from the little front lawn. He had been waiting for Fee to notice him, but made no effort to communicate. He did not have to. The boy's plaid shirt was too large for him, as if he had stolen or scrounged it, and his dirty tan trousers ended above his ankles. On a cold November morning in Millhaven, his feet were bare. The boy did not seem languid or passive. The dark eyes beneath the scrappy black hair burned angrily, and the sallow face was frozen with rage. He seemed to quiver with feeling, but Fee had the oddest conviction that all this feeling was not about him — it concerned someone else. The boy had come because of a complicity, an understanding, between them. The dirty, battered-looking boy stared in to find his emotions matched by Fielding Bandolier. But Fielding Bandolier could not match the feelings that came streaming in from the boy: he could only remember the sensation of speaking without willing to speak. Something inside him was weeping and gnashing its teeth, but Fee could scarcely hear it.

If you forgot you were in a movie, your own feelings would tear you into bloody rags.

Fee looked down to fasten the button on his waistband. When he looked back through the window, he saw the boy growing fainter and fainter, like a drawing being erased. Traces of the lawn and sidewalk shone through him. All at once it seemed to Fee that something vastly important, an absolutely precious quantity, was fading from his world. Once this quantity was lost, it was lost forever. Fee moved toward the window, but by now he could not see the blazing dark eyes, and when he touched the cold pane of glass the boy was gone.

That was all right, he told himself: really, he had lost nothing.

Bob Bandolier spent another evening poring over *The Ledger*, which had a large photograph of Heinz Stenmitz on its front page. He ordered Fee to bed early, and Fee felt that he was being dismissed because his father did not want to have a witness to his anxiety.

For he was anxious — he was nervous. His knee jumped when he sat at the table, and he jumped whenever the telephone rang. The calls that came were never the call that his father feared, but their innocence did not quiet his anxiety. For something like a week, Fee's few attempts to talk to his father met either angry silence or a command to shut up, and Fee knew that only his father's reluctance to touch him saved him from a blow.

Over the following days, Bob Bandolier relaxed. He would forget who was in the room with him, and lapse back into the old talk of the "hypocritical lowlife" and the "corrupt gang" that worked with him. Then he would look up from his plate or his newspaper, see his son, and blush with a feeling for which he refused to find words. Fee witnessed the old anger only once, when he walked into Bob Bandolier's bedroom and found him sitting on the bed, leafing through a small stack of papers from the shoebox beside him. His father's face darkened, and his eyes darkened, and for a second Fee knew the sick familiar thrill of knowing he was to be beaten. The beating did not happen. His father slipped the papers into the shoebox and told him to find something to do in the other room, fast.

Bob Bandolier came home with the news that the Hepton had let him go — the hypocritical lowlife had finally managed to catch him in the meat locker, and the bastard would not listen to any explanations. It was okay, though. The St. Alwyn was taking him back. After everything he had been through, he wouldn't mind going back to the old St. Alwyn. He had settled his score, and now they could go forward.

He and Fee could not go forward together, however, at least not for a while. It wasn't working. He needed quiet, he had to work things out. Fee needed to have a woman around, he needed to play with other kids. Anna's sister Judy in Azure had written, saying that she and her husband Arnold would be willing to take the boy in if Bob was finding it difficult to raise the boy by himself.

His father stared at his hands as he said all this to Fee, and looked up only when he had reached this point.

"It's all arranged."

Bob Bandolier turned his head to look at the window, the porcelain figures, the sleeping cat, anything but his son. Bob Bandolier detested Judy and Arnold, exactly as he detested Anna's brother Hank and his wife Wilda. Until this time, he had refused any contact with his wife's family. Fee understood that his father detested him, too.

The next day Bob Bandolier took Fee to the train station in downtown Millhaven, and in a confusion of bright colors and loud noises passed him and his board suitcase, along with a five-dollar bill, into the hands of a conductor. Fee rode all the way from Millhaven to Chicago by himself, and in Chicago the pitying conductor made sure he boarded the train to Cleveland. He followed his father's orders and spoke to no one during the long journey through Illinois and Ohio, though several people, chiefly elderly women, spoke to him. At Cleveland, Judy and Arnold Leatherwood were waiting for him, and drove the sleeping boy the remaining two hundred miles to Azure.

10

The rest can be said quickly. Though nothing frightening or truly upsetting ever happened — nothing *overt* — the Leatherwoods, who had expected to love their nephew unreservedly and had been overjoyed to claim

him from the peculiar and unpleasant man who had
married Judy Leatherwood's sister, found that Fee
Bandolier made them more uncomfortable with every
month he lived in their house. He screamed himself awake
two or three nights a week, but could not speak about
what frightened him. The boy refused to talk about his
mother. Not long after Christmas, Judy Leatherwood
found a pile of disturbing drawings beneath Fee's bed,
but the boy denied having drawn them. He insisted that
someone had sneaked them into his room, and became so
wild-eyed and terrified that Judy dropped the subject. In
February, a neighbor's dog was found stabbed to death in
an empty lot down the street. A month later, a
neighborhood cat was discovered with its throat slashed
open in a ditch two blocks away. Fee spent most of his
time sitting quietly in a chair in a corner of the living
room, looking into space. At night, sometimes the
Leatherwoods could hear him breathing in a loud,
desperate way that made them want to put the pillows
over their heads. When Judy discovered that she was
pregnant that April, she and Arnold came to a silent
agreement and asked Hank and Wilda in Tangent if they
could take Fee in for a while.

Fee moved to Tangent and lived in Hank and Wilda
Dymczeck's drafty old house with their fifteen-year-old
son, Hank Junior, who regularly beat him up but otherwise
paid little attention to him. Hank was the vice-principal
of Tangent's Lawrence B. Freeman high school and Wilda
was a nurse, so they spent less time with Fee than the
Leatherwoods had. If he was a little quiet and a little
strange, he was still "getting over" his mother's death.
Because he had nowhere else to go, Fee made a greater
effort to behave in ways other people expected and
understood. In time his nightmares went away. He found
a safe secret place for the things he wrote and drew.
Whenever anyone asked him what he wanted to be when

he grew up, he answered that he wanted to be a policeman.

Fee passed through grade school and his uncle's high school with average grades. A few animals were found killed (and a few more were not), but Fee Bandolier was so inconspicuous that no one imagined that he might be responsible for their deaths. Lance Torkelson's murder horrified the community, but Tangent eventually decided that an outsider had killed the boy. At the end of Fee's senior year, a young woman named Margaret Loewy disappeared after dropping her two children off at a public swimming pool. Six months later, her mutilated body was discovered buried in the woods beside a remote section of farmland, and by that time Fielding Bandolier had enlisted in the army under another name. Margaret Loewy's breasts, vagina, and cheeks had been sliced off, along with sections of her thighs and buttocks; her womb and ovaries had been removed; and traces of semen could still be found in her throat and anus, and in the abdominal wounds.

Far more successful in basic training than he had ever been in high school, Fee applied for Special Forces training. He called his father's telephone number when he learned of his acceptance, and when Bob Bandolier answered by saying, "Yes?," Fee held onto the telephone without speaking, without even breathing, until his father swore at him and hung up.

This is for Stephen King

About the Editors

ELIZABETH E. MONTELEONE worked in advertising and radio in Baltimore for seven years before becoming President of Borderlands Press. Recently, she has worked as a layout and page designer in addition to her duties as a proofreader and electronic typesetter. She likes art galleries, museums, traveling to far off lands, reading, culinary experimentation, history, and Broadway show tunes. She's not really all that crazy about contemporary music or actors with blue eyes and blonde hair.

THOMAS F. MONTELEONE has been a professional writer since 1972. He has published more than 80 short stories as well as his notorious column of opinion and entertainment, THE MOTHERS AND FATHERS ITALIAN ASSOCIATION, which appears in *Cemetery Dance* magazine. He is the editor of six anthologies, the most recent of which is the highly acclaimed *Borderlands 3*.

Of his eighteen novels, his most recent, *The Blood of the Lamb*, received the 1993 Bram Stoker Award for Superior Achievement. His two collections of short fiction are *Dark Stars and Other Illuminations* and the forthcoming *Fearful Symmetries*.

He has also written for *Tales From the Darkside* and PBS Television. His script *Mister Magister* won the Bronze Award for Best Drama at the 1984 International Film and TV Festival of New York. *U.F.O.!* was produced at the first Baltimore Playwrights Festival and won the award for Best Play. He has written four feature-length screenplays, the most recent of which received an awards grant from the Maryland State Arts Council.

He likes baseball, computers, British ales and stouts, comic books, tons of magazines, all kinds of music, Ginsu knife commercials, getting lots of mail everyday, and playing with his children.

Tom and Elizabeth live in Baltimore, Maryland, with son Brandon and daughter Olivia. They have no dogs, cats, or any other animals in their midst.

In the wake of an eco-catastrophe, civilization has risen again in a form at once familiar and horrific...

The Psalms of Herod

It is an age that has elevated Herod's Slaughter of the Innocents into a sacrament, justifying hideous deeds with the blessings of a twisted faith. All life is sacred — until it is born.

A woman's place is to submit; to obey. A woman's place is to give over her newborn for exposure on a hillside if the child is flawed in any way, even if it is born the wrong sex. A woman's place is not to decide these things.

One woman, Becca of Wiserways Stead, will not accept her place. Becca's desire for change forces her to ultimately confront her vision of herself as she was raised. But though she is named a vessel of miracles by Gilber Livvy of the hidden tribes, will the secret she carries be miracle enough to redeem a world?

Psalms of Herod is the first release in White Wolf Publishing's continuous series of original novels. A Nebula finalist for her story "All Vows," award-winning science fiction and fantasy author Esther M. Friesner has published over twenty novels to date.

Available November, 1995

Stock# 12025
ISBN 1-56504-916-0
Retail price: $5.99 US/$7.99 CAN

The following is a short excerpt from *Psalms of Herod*.

When the men came to bring her to Adonijah's bed, Becca was ready. Her heart thudded against her breastbone like a fist. She made an effort to bridle her every movement and seeming.

I am Becca of Wiserways, she told herself. *I know a woman's proper place and all the ways to pleasure a man. I am going to serve my lawful master in thanks and humility, the way I've been brought up to do. I am. There is no taint of anything wild or unwomanly to me. I am Becca, Hattie's child, Paul's get, of Wiserways Stead.*

So she told herself, over and over, using words to form the bonds that must hold the crumbling shell of appearances together, words that must prevent her true self from bursting through too soon.

Through the mask of her face she cast sly eyes from one to the other of her escorts. Did they suspect? Didn't it show? Couldn't they guess what manner of creature they were bringing to the bed of their new master? Their faces were slack, as empty gunnysacks, bored with a chore like fetching water or drawing firewood. One of them was an older male, Wiserways bred and maybe born, the other a youngling from Adonijah's invading pack. He caught a glimpse of her quick, studying glance and winked, mistaking it for what he wished to see in a woman's face.

Let him think what he likes. Becca let the corner of her lips tease him with a hinted smile. *Let him think anything at all. But if he tries to put some bone behind his wishings, I've got the power by me now to blast him clean to hell.*

The gun was slung in a pocket she'd made by tucking up the front part of her underskirt and pinning it secure. A small, wolfish grin licked her mouth when she thought of which pins they were that had served her so neatly. Only two, but two were plenty strong enough to hold; strong with her sire's death, strong with her ravished maidenhead.

The weapon's swinging weight was a pendulum that sometimes bounced against one leg, now the other as the men marched her up the stairs. Any bruises she got would be lost among the rest that Adonijah had already gifted her. They dappled her skin, angry marks darkening on breast and arm and hip. The place where she'd bitten her lip open was swelling, giving her mouth a ripe, pouting look. She thought of Del, practicing such vixenish airs in a basin of water when she thought no one was watching, all to lure a man to her come harvest-home.

I could lesson you some now, Del love. I could show you how to come by the look that brings you a man. I learn fast—ask any who've lessoned me: Miss Lynn, Katy, Selena, Gram Phila's Martha. Yes, I learn fast, and I lesson faster, and there's that I'd teach you, Adonijah, that you won't soon forget.

After all the hard lessons of her life, learning the gun had come almost too easy. Aside from not knowing how much time she'd have alone in that room with the dead— the jump-stomach way she had to hunch over the piece, ready to thrust it beneath her skirts every time she dreamed she heard a sound at the locked door—it had been simple. The weight surprised her some, but the talebooks Katy loaned her made some mention of men managing such weapons two-handed as well as one. The trickiest part was making the bullets go in, and that all came right when her thumb found the little latch. The spinning chamber fell open like a welcome.

Bullets were round and the chamber holes were round and the pointier end had to point the way the bullet must go once launched—it would take an idiot to foul up something so obvious, so plain to any sighted person. She filled each hole just as slick as sticking seed-corn into the earth and clapped the chamber back so it stayed. The trigger too was an invitation, its shape just calling for a finger to crook 'round it and pull. In the stories they always *squeezed* the trigger when they shot, gentle. She'd remember that. It was going to be easy as pie.

Shifra. . . The weight of steel pulled at her skirt no heavier than her sister's name pulled at her heart. *Hold on, baby, I'm coming for you. You hold on, and Becca's going to bring you something better than that old raggy sop.* Her heartbeats measured out too much time since she'd tucked up the child the safest place she knew and prayed sweet Mary Mother to keep her safe from harm. Every pulse of Becca's blood stood alone, another slab to mark the paces time was taking, putting more and more distance between the babe and any chance of life.

Soon, Shifra. It's going to be soon. It must.

They stood before the bedroom door once more. The younger man knocked, grinned like a cat at Becca when Adonijah bellowed for them to bring her in. He was waiting for her by the window, wearing just his robe. The bed was new-made, the sheets crisp and white, all properly turned back over a quilt Becca recognized as the work of Thalie's hands.

She dropped her head as if it were a sickle-ready head of barley, heavy with seed. His chuckle of satisfaction rasped her skin, made her clench her legs tight together beneath her skirts when he strode by her to send his men about their other business. She folded her hands before her, pressing them down against the comforting shape of the gun.

"Come willingly, I see," he said, flicking the iron bolt into its hold high on the doorframe. "Changed your way of seeing it, then?"

She said nothing. With her eyes downcast she could only hear the brush of his bare feet over the floorcloth, the creaking protest of old boards in a house he had conquered by deceit.

"Well?" His voice rose a little with irritation; the knowledge left her strangely warm. This was a game to play, a pleasure knowing she could still provoke him so, without saying a word. Then he was suddenly before her, her jaw vised between his fingers, old hurts blazing back from dull aches to searing life. "You'll answer me." She felt the hot pollution of his spittle on her chin. "Yes you will, or it will be *this* again for you—" a splinter of grey metal hovered at the border of her sight "—and then I'll give you over to the rest of them."

Her gasp was not calculated nor her fear feigned. All that he had done to her in the little room below came back, torn from the cold safety of memory by that tiny pin. Her tongue was papery as she faltered, "No. . .please."

Then the shame of her own fear rose out of her belly in a spate of acid. What he had to hand to use against her was nothing, *nothing!* Her demurely folded hands darted back, jammed into the hidden pocket, clasped the smooth handle of the gun and jabbed it hard into Adonijah's belly.

She could have laughed out loud at how his face went all fishy white, bugeyed with startlement. *Dear Lord, what's he think I've got under here?* Just so he'd know, just so he'd mind close when she gave him his long-coming lessoning, Becca said woman-soft and gentle, "I've a gun, Adonijah; that's what you feel. I haven't been wonder-touched to grow an Adam's mark, so clean your mind of miracle tales. This gun's miracle enough for me. You know what guns can do? You have that much learning at Makepeace Stead?'

"Where did you get—?" His voice was parched with terror. *He* knew about guns, that much was plain.

"Shut up." Again she jabbed it into him. He staggered back and she jerked the weapon from concealment, let him feast whitening eyes on its sleekness and its silent message of power. "You listen."

"You can't shoot that, Becca." Oh, how the words shivered with sick laughter! He was trying to put a bold face between himself and his fright. "One shot would be loud enough to bring down the roof on you and me both, like Samson in the Philistines' temple. Those things bang so loud, it'd bring everyone on the stead running."

"I'll risk it. Will you? Your head would be split right

open, Adonijah, your facebones smashed bloody right back through your brain." She told him that in the same way she'd always recited her lessons for Katy when she was dead sure of the answers. Her certainty left him no margin to doubt her, to save himself with hope. "They'd come running and they'd find you dead, crushed worse'n if any temple building fell in on you. Half your skull lifted off, and all your face torn away so raw they'd have to remember real hard what you ever looked like. You want that, Adonijah?" Coaxing sweet she spoke to him, rasing the barrel so that she could aim her sight right down to the little niblet of metal perched on the end. "'Cause if that's what you want, I can give it to you any time."

Adonijah said nothing. His mouth opened once, but no words came out and he lost the will to close his lips again. He blinked and gulped, his hands making little flapping motions at his sides.

Trying to shoo me off, trying to blink himself awake from a nightmare. If Becca smiled any broader her cheeks would split like overripe fruit. Her front teeth were dry from the deep gusts of air she sucked in through them, cold as the weapon in her hands.

Adonijah wasn't talking any more. He wasn't moving, or blinking, or taking breaths deep enough to move his ribs so she could see it. Stillness had settled over him like a soft blanket drifted down over a cradle, a witchery of her weaving.

"All right." Her own words were cotton-light. She didn't wnat to risk loud speech that might fray the spell. "Now you'll just listen. Listen close, and do as I say, and then I'm going to let you live." She saw doubt spark up in his eyes and it made her face ache with wanting to laugh. Instead she just nodded. "I said that, Adonijah; you heard right. I'll swear it to you by the Lord's own Name, and by sweet Mary Mother, if you want; it's so. If you do what I tell you, it'll be so. I promise. I swear. I'm leaving Wiserways and I don't care who's alph here after I'm gone. I don't want another winnowing if it doesn't need to be. When I've got what I want off this place, you can have the rest."

His mouth wobbled, like he was struggling between wanting to ask her something and fearing what would befall him if asking wasn't allowed. Becca nodded curtly so he'd know she'd tolerate maybe one question.

"Where—?" It sounded like a sifting down of sand in the watch-glass. "Where will you go?"

He could ask, but he couldn't force any more answers. Just knowing that was like a tonic to her heart, a strong heat in her that fast kindled to a clean white light. *He can't force me to anything anymore!* It burned away all the pain he'd forced on her, lifted her spirit high as any littlesinger's soaring flight. Part of her joyed from soles to crown. Gratefulness brimmed up in her, all of it for the long-gone coop man who'd taken such a shine to Eleazar and left this gun with her pa. He'd given more than he knew, whoever he'd been. If there was any way to learn his name once she brought Shifra into the gates of the city, she'd offer him the Kiss and the Sign freeheart, in thankfulness of soul for this, her freedom.

But part of her still bled. Part was hurt deep, too deep to the bone for any fire of joy to ever fully burn it out. She forced the pain away, focusing all her being on the task ahead.

"The first place I want to go, Adonijah, you'll take me."